SPLIT

BOOKS BY S.E. LYNES

THE
SPLIT

S. E. LYNES

bookouture

Published by Bookouture in 2024

An imprint of Storyfire Ltd.
Carmelite House
50 Victoria Embankment
London EC4Y 0DZ

www.bookouture.com

ISBN: 978-1-83525-315-1
eBook ISBN: 978-1-83525-314-4

For Penny. Without you, I would not be me.

The presents of the wicked are pure poison.

MEDEA, BY EURIPIDES

A well done is better than a well said sort of thing.

BENJAMIN FRANKLIN, PARAPHRASED BY
IAN ROBBINS

PROLOGUE

It's not completely dark in Jessica's room. The light from the street comes in through the gap in the curtains. There's always light leaking in from somewhere or other in this house. That's what Dad says.

A giggle comes from downstairs. That's what's woken her, she's pretty sure, that giggle. There it comes again, high and tinkly. It's coming from a woman, but she doesn't sound like Mum.

Jessica's digital clock says 02:04. The green glowing seconds fold over: 27, 28, 29. The woman's sing-song voice. Dad's deep rumble answer. His chuckle. A pit forms in Jessica's stomach.

42, 43, 44.

Another giggle. A *shh*. The scrape of one of the kitchen chairs across the floor. A burning feeling sparks in Jessica's chest, like she's in trouble at school. She's heard these noises before, but only in dreams; they are the sounds of things she knows but doesn't know she knows. She closes her eyes tight, hopes the noises will go back into her dreams, where they are not real.

'Eric,' the woman says. '*Stop* it.' She doesn't sound cross. She sounds like she's laughing and talking at the same time.

Jessica's eyes pop open. The flowers on her Laura Ashley lampshade are fuzzy.

02:05. The seconds are 14, 15, 16.

'Stop it, will you?'

A cry that sounds like a little scream you're trying to hold in. It's definitely not Mum, because Mum is on night shift and won't be home until Jessica wakes up, and then they'll have breakfast together, Mum in her blue uniform with the white piping and her NHS lanyard round her neck, her eyes purple underneath from tiredness. Mum will sit with her and tell her stories from the hospital. She will ask her: *What're you up to today, love?*

When Mum's on nights, Jessica has to be quiet when she gets in from school. She has to be a big girl because Dad's at work then, but she has Cynthia next door and of course Mum is only upstairs in case of emergencies. Sometimes Jessica makes the tea for a surprise. She can do tinned chicken curry with rice, and baked beans on toast with grated cheese. Once she made the sauce for spaghetti bolognese, but Mum was there that time to help if she got stuck. Mum tells her other girls can't do half the things she does.

'Eric Jackson.'

The strange woman giggles through her dad's name, like it's funny. She still doesn't sound cross, even though she used his full name. When Dad uses Jessica's full name – Jessica Annabel Jackson! – it means she's *for it*.

02:08. 53, 54, 55.

Jessica's chest is tight. When she breathes, the air doesn't go all the way in. She throws back the covers and puts her feet into her slippers. Maybe Dad could give her a glass of milk to help her sleep. Across her room she creeps, then out onto the landing. From the top stair she hears an out-of-breath gasp like one you do after a race.

She takes the stairs one at a time. She's careful not to make a noise, but her heart sounds like horses' hooves. Downstairs, the hall is a bit light because of the front door having a bobbly window. The light in the kitchen is borrowed too – that's how Mum says it, like it's a pen or a stapler. It's borrowed from Barry-on-the-other-side's strip light, which Dad says could divert planes from Speke Airport, that's how bright it is. Barry keeps that light on all blooming night. Dad would hate to see Barry's electricity bill.

There is bobbly glass in the kitchen door as well. Behind it, a grey shape moves. Like the noises that woke her, she has a feeling about the shape, something that hovers just out of sight, daring her to look round and face it head on.

Her fingers close around the metal door handle. Her heart is so loud now she is scared they will hear, but above it she can make out that weird breathless breathing, little murmurs. The feeling she is doing something wrong fills her. The thing she can't see edges closer. If she could only turn her head and see. She is desperate to see; doesn't dare look. She pushes the handle down but doesn't let go. Her dad showed her how to spray the hinges with WD-40 last week. He said it's important to keep the doors lubricated, what with Mum being on nights.

'Listen to that,' he said, moving the door back and forth. 'Not a squeak.'

Jessica lets go of the handle. The door swings open without a sound. Her dad's trousers and underpants are pooled round his ankles. His tan leather belt lolls out. Heat flames in her face, flushes through the length of her. Dad is bent over the kitchen table, a woman's leg hooked around him, bluish in the borrowed light – thin, like a chicken wing, knee bony like an elbow. Not Mum's leg, not like Mum's legs at all. Not Mum's shoe either. Mum hasn't got high-heeled shoes like that. The thing Jessica knows and doesn't know is coming into view. The thing that has to do with half-asleep dreams and hovering shadows and doors oiled to make no sound.

Over Dad's shoulder, through smudgy black eye make-up, the woman is staring right at her.

'Eric,' she says. This time, she is not laughing.

Dad turns, croaks *Jessie*. Then he says: 'Fuck.'

Jessica runs back down the hall. She's burning, burning all over. Dad has never said that word, never. She flies up the stairs. Dad calls her name again and again: 'Jessica. Jessica, love? Jess!'

On the landing, she crouches, staring through the banister rails at the bald pink circle in her dad's brown hair. He is halfway up the stairs now, but he can't see her, isn't looking in her direction.

'Jess,' he says quietly to the place she is not. 'Love? Whatever you saw, it's not... it's not what you think.'

It's never completely dark in this house. Always light leaking in from somewhere or other. The thing is clear to her now. It is what she knows. It is exactly what she knows.

CHAPTER 1

JESSICA

When they get back from the restaurant, Jessica takes Will by the hand and leads him upstairs. Shushing each other, they are giddy after the fizz, the red, the complimentary limoncello given to them by the manager of Gino's, their local Italian.

On opposite sides of the bed, they take off their clothes with the excessive focus of the little bit tipsy. Once undressed, she slithers into the new silk slip she bought last week especially for tonight and turns to see Will standing up to take off his sock, the only remaining item he is wearing. He is hopping about now, trying to hold on to one foot. The sock is stripy. There is a hole in the big toe. He loses the battle to stay upright and falls over with a thud.

Jessica claps her hand over her mouth, suppressing a burst of laughter. A snort escapes, making her laugh even more.

From the floor, Will grins up at her, one eye closed. He swirls the lone sock in the air before tossing it aside with comic nonchalance.

'Still refining my routine,' he says, then jumps up and dives to join her under the covers. His hands slide underneath the silk, warm on her skin.

'You. Smell. Amazing.' He mutters the words between the baby kisses he's planting on her belly. 'You. Smell. So. Good.' He slides his nose up to her neck, causing her to shiver.

Tingling with anticipation, she raises her arms, lets him pull the slip over her head. He hasn't even noticed it's new, but at this point it doesn't matter. Nothing matters save for his lips on her shoulder, his hand running down over her breasts to her waist. Lightly he pinches her there, making her squeal.

'Shh,' she whispers, slapping him on the shoulder. 'We'll wake the kids.'

He pulls back a little and stares into her eyes. In daylight, his are green with flecks of yellow and brown. Sometimes, when the sun is bright, they are almost blue. Right now, in the dimness, they are a solid, velvety teal.

'Seven years,' she says softly, grabbing a handful of his hair, peppering now at the hairline.

'Fifteen if you count from when we got together.'

'A long time.'

'It is. Thank you. For all of it.' He kisses her deeply. It has been weeks, maybe months since he's kissed her like that, and she feels the familiar pulse of tiny electrical currents shooting through her. The rest follows naturally – quietly – in the way they have got used to since the kids were born. They know each other's bodies; what works, what doesn't. There is beauty in this, she thinks. Beauty and a kind of relief.

Afterwards, they lie back, her left leg over his right, her heart slowing. The street lamp leaks amber through the curtains. They should have blinds fitted, she thinks vaguely, before her mind turns to all that she has, all that she never expected to have, not in a million years. To Cassie and Charlie, asleep along the landing, surrounded by their precious things: for Cassie, her football trophies, her swimming medals and school certificates; for Charlie, his hamster, Bud, and some strange Jurassic prawn-type creatures that Will helped him to grow from a kit and which now live in a two-foot-long rectangular fish tank. Without Will, she would never have had children. He gave her the courage, the faith.

Her eyes fill.

'Happy anniversary,' he whispers hazily.

'You too, baby.' But the last word is half stolen by sleep. She has been working such long hours lately. Tonight, over dinner, she really had to dig deep, regaling Will with the funniest stories from her recent business trip to New York, the humour mainly centring on her colleague, Doug, who is, as their American counterparts put it, a real *asshole*. She hasn't had time to tell Will anything about the trip before tonight. They haven't really talked, evenings fit only for cuddling up in front of an hour's television before, groaning like pensioners with exhaustion, they collapse into bed. In the restaurant this evening, Jessica held up a pasta butterfly on the end of her fork and, in a sniffy imitation of her pompous workmate, proclaimed, 'This is all right, I suppose, but it isn't a patch on the spaghetti alle vongole I had in Umbria.'

Will laughed. After all these years, she still loves to make him laugh.

'I love you,' she hears him whisper now, his hand coming to rest lazily on her hip.

'Love you too.'

The claw of sleep pulls her under. Blissfully, she surrenders, safe in the knowledge that she can let herself be taken, that Will is there beside her, that he will be there when she wakes up.

Will.

The slow-rising tones of Radio 4 announce the 6.30 alarm. The war in Ukraine. A car has driven into a hotel in Eastbourne. A woman has been charged with the murder of her stepson. Grim, all grim.

Jessica mutes it, throws her legs out of the bed before she can succumb to the false comfort of the snooze button. Being in the shower before you've fully woken up; that's the trick. The water soaks her hair, runs over her shoulders. Last night echoes in her body. She smiles a private smile to herself.

Back in the bedroom, Will is snoring softly. She slips on the silk blouse and the suit she left ready before they went out last night. Will teases her, but every act of planning the night before equals an extra minute in bed the morning after. Unlike him, she can't just throw on any old thing.

She creeps downstairs, makes coffee and brings it back up. Will is still dozing, but she can tell from the set of his head that he is half awake. His thick brown hair has been squashed flat on both sides, the top standing on end so that he looks like a snoozing rockabilly. She leaves his cup on the bedside table next to the wedding photo she keeps meaning to move. She's getting less keen on the comparison between herself then and now, with forty rushing towards her at the speed of a train.

Ruffling Will's hair with one hand, she reaches for her coffee with the other. A sip, two, then she places her cup on her bedside table, picks up her iPhone and turns it on.

There are two WhatsApp messages. One from Lena: *Hey babes, u OK? Haven't seen you for ages*, which gives her a pit of guilt in her stomach – she hasn't checked in with Lena for a couple of weeks, will remedy that today; and one from an unknown number: *Thought you should see these. From a friend.*

Frowning, she opens what turns out to be a photograph of Will entering a posh hotel – wide stone steps, lollipop shrubs in sleek black planters. A second photo shows a pin-thin woman going into the same hotel. She has black hair in a classic short bob. Chic black capri pants hover over bony tanned ankles, black pumps. Her white jacket... wait, is that *Chanel*?

Jessica's frown deepens. The message tells her there are +25 photos. She pushes her thumb to the screen and the rest of the images unfold in a long concertina, like one of those cheap plastic photo wallets.

The third photograph is of Will and this same woman. They are holding hands on what looks like a street in Central London. The follicles of Jessica's hair lift. Her eyes cannot leave their interlocking fingers. Why is her husband holding hands with a woman she doesn't recognise?

The fourth shows the two of them entering another elegant five-star place: smoked-glass revolving doors, a uniformed white-gloved doorman. Will's arm hovers protectively at the woman's waist. Is he touching her?

A queasy feeling rolls in Jessica's gut. Her hand flies to her throat, catching her in a soft stranglehold. Breath quickening, she scrolls through the remaining photos: Will and the same woman embracing on the street, that Chanel jacket again; Will and this woman, impeccably dressed once more, bent close in conversation in an urban park – is that Embankment Gardens? Will and this woman—

'Oh my God,' she whispers, hand closing over her mouth.

A lovers' clinch behind the sheer muslin curtain of a hotel window.

Jessica's insides are collapsing. She can't breathe. She can't...

Steadying herself against the windowsill, she scrolls through the rest, not wanting to look but unable to stop herself.

'No.' The word is no more than a whimper. 'No, no, no, no, no.'

She turns to her husband, her gentle, unassuming husband, the man who last night told her he loved her, showed her he loved her with a hundred kisses. The only man she could ever have imagined marrying. His eyes are still closed. A bitter taste pools on her tongue. She takes a breath and—

CHAPTER 2

WILL

'Bastard!'

Yellow daylight leaks through the dusty brush of his eyelashes.

'You absolute *bastard.*'

'What? *What?*' He shields his eyes with his hand.

Jessica is standing above him, dark against the bright bedroom window. His vision adjusts, focuses. He scrabbles for his glasses and puts them on. Her outline sharpens. She is dressed in her black suit, white shirt, her hair combed back, still wet. The scent of her Jo Malone shower gel fills the air.

'Jess? What's the matter? What's happened?'

But Jessica appears unable to speak. Her mouth is open, but nothing is coming out. She is gripping her head with her hands. Her freckles are flushed with pink, her mouth is contorted. A moment later, a great gasping sob breaks from her. She dips her head. A lock of wet hair falls across her face.

Jessica is crying. His wife is crying, tears fat and round rolling down her face. She hardly ever cries. When she does, she hides it.

Tenderly he says her name again, forms a question with it –

Jessica? Sitting up now, propping himself against the head-board, a fist of unease clenches in his gut. To his left, a fresh cup of coffee. Jessica always brings them both coffee in the morning. He loves the ritual of it, the calm before the storm of the day. But this is a different kind of storm.

'I... can't... believe...' Her voice is thin and high, each word punctuated with a tearful intake of breath. She bends forward, one arm across her waist. Straightens up, the flat of her hand covering her mouth, dropping away, rising again, as if she has no idea where to put it, what to do with herself. Both hands now rise, press themselves over her face.

'Jessie!' he cries. 'Is it your mum? Is it Pat?'

'I can't... How could you do this to me? How could you... to us? To the children? For God's sake, Will, how *could* you? To me? I can't...' Her chest rises and falls, a terrible heaving that makes him think she's about to be sick.

He too feels sick. A premonition, a shape in fog, something moving towards him.

'Jess?' His scalp burns; his mind races. 'Come on, baby. Tell me, please, just tell me. Is it bad news? Are you ill?'

She stalks into the en suite, then back into the room. She is still crying with a kind of unstoppable fury. A second later, her iPhone lands on the bed beside him.

'I want you out of this house.' Her voice is low now, low and trembling, as if she has subdued it by sheer force of will.

'Out of this... What?'

'I want you out, do you hear me? Out. Get out. Get out of my house.' She is beating her fists against the sides of her head. He wants to tell her to stop, that she'll hurt herself, but every-thing is spinning, his senses tangling. 'I hate you for this. Oh God, oh God, this can't be happening.' She wails. It is a lonely, nocturnal sound, a sound of pain, appalling to hear.

Hot with panic, gut churning, he finds himself scrolling

through the WhatsApp thread. At the top there is a message: *Thought you should see these. From a friend.*

Below are photographs – a whole string of photographs. The first is him, quite plainly; the second...

Shit. Shit, shit, shit.

He closes his eyes. Opens them. To Margot. Himself and Margot le Fevre. Another, another. Him and Margot stepping into one of the hotels they went to. Him and Margot at Park Grand Hotel, Kensington – Margot in the narrow black ankle-length trousers she often wore, the short white jacket.

Hot with fear, he scrolls down: himself entering the door of the Barbican Rooms, Margot arriving a minute later, dressed this time in white ankle-length trousers, the large sunglasses she always wore that hid half of her tiny face; the dark brackets of her hair. Himself and Margot hugging on the South Bank on a bright London afternoon, oh God. Another picture – a couple, half undressed, in shadow at a hotel window, kissing – no, no, no. He continues to scroll up and down at random: expensive hotels, liaisons laid out indelibly, undeniably, *irrefutably* in front of him. Oh, and there they are again, walking in the gardens at Embankment, heads bent together, his arm resting lazily on her shoulder.

A final image, a gut punch: himself and Margot in each other's arms, kissing next to his rusty old people carrier. Heathrow Airport, almost a year ago.

Goodbye, dear William. I will never forget you.

Nor I you. Go.

Oh God. Oh God, oh God. All have been taken from some distance, but still, there is no way around it: he and Margot have been caught and somehow these images have been sent to his wife.

White heat flashes through him. Dark dots drop into his vision like rain into a black pond.

'Are you going to say something?' Jessica's voice has strengthened, a filament of steel at its core. 'Anything?'

He pushes a hand through his hair, fighting the urge to cry.

'It's...' he begins, flailing. How to make this right? How can he make this right?

'Will?'

'It's...' he begins again. 'It's not what you think, OK?' He cringes. That was not the right thing to say. That was not the right thing at all. Shit. He opens his mouth to try and correct himself, but something between a growl and a cry cuts him off.

'It's not what I *think*?' Jessica is shouting now. 'Really? *Really*, Will?' Tears are rolling down her face, but she doesn't appear to notice as the words continue to fall out of her. 'You're sitting there with a fucking photo documentary of your affair and you tell me it's not what I *think*?' She gestures towards the phone, disgust crossing her features.

'Jess!'

She turns away, apparently unable to look at him. *No*, he wants to say but cannot. *Wait*. If she could only wait while he figures out—

'Oh my God.' The crack in her high, quiet voice is unbearable, the pain that pours out of that crack. A fresh deluge of tears. He opens his mouth again, desperate, but the words won't form. He wants to jump up and take her in his arms, but his limbs won't move. A tight pain cramps in his chest. This cannot be happening. A mistake, yes. He crossed a line, but...

'I can explain,' he manages, his voice shaking with the wretchedness now filling him entirely. 'It's really not... I mean, she's not... She... she was a client, you see, and—'

Jessica roars, her cheeks deep pink; pink tracking down her neck.

'It's not what I think,' she whispers to herself, as if mad. She gives a cry, pacing, fists flailing about her. 'You've been meeting this woman in hotels *all over London*.' She picks up her bag, appears to be looking for something. 'Afternoon trysts while I was out working like a fool, like a *dog*. You kissed her at the airport, for God's sake. What was that, a romantic mini-break?' Her eyes widen, as if she has just that second understood something. 'Oh my God, was that the dads' ski trip?'

'No! No, I was—'

'All in on it, were they? Boys' club? Don't tell the missus?' Her voice has risen with every word, and now she is shouting once again. She never shouts. They don't shout at one another; it's not who they are. It is like being shot at. Rat-a-tat-tat. He can't get a grip on his thoughts, can't think how to phrase it.

Margot's voice comes to him: *Please, Will. You cannot tell anyone. No one. My life depends on it.*

Rat-a-tat-tat. Bullets of accusation. He's a kid, caught in one of his mother's tantrums, a rapid gunfire of criticisms puncturing him with holes, himself edging backwards, longing for it to stop. There is no room, no space to do anything but shield himself. He messed up, he crossed a line, OK, OK... Oh God, he needs to be careful, he needs to be so, so careful. He has to find the right words, absolutely has to.

But: 'No,' is all he hears himself say. 'No, no, no.'

'Will! For the love of God, just tell me the truth!'

'Daddy?'

The air stills. At the doorway of their bedroom stands Cassie, her white nightdress frilled at her little ankles, her blankie clutched in her tiny grip. Will's throat closes. She rubs one eye with her knuckles and yawns.

How much has she heard?

How much has she seen?

Jessica has turned her face to the window, hands pressed to the sill, fingertips white. Dust motes drift, glitter. Her shoulders rise, dip, rise, dip. Everything is happening too fast.

He pushes tears from his cheeks before holding out his arms to his daughter. 'Hey, poppet.' Dimly he is aware of Jessica scooping the phone from the bed and striding towards the bathroom. Cassie clambers towards him and throws her arms around his neck. She is warm. She smells of sleep, of herself. It is everything he can do not to sob into the glossy auburn hair she has inherited from her beautiful, beautiful mother.

'Daddy, are you crying?' Cassie asks with an innocence that makes his heart hurt. 'Is Mummy crying?'

'Mummy and Daddy were having an argument,' Will says softly, rubbing Cassie's back in reassurance. 'You have arguments with Charlie sometimes, don't you? And you love Charlie. Well, it's like that. We love each other; we're just cross with each other right now. It's nothing to worry about, OK?'

'It's all right.' Jessica is back, a weak smile failing to disguise the muscular clench of her jaw, her swollen eyelids, her red tear-stained cheeks. 'Why don't you go and wake your brother and the two of you can get dressed for school? Daddy'll be down in a minute to make your banana porridge.'

If Cassie perceives the quiver in her mother's voice, she doesn't comment on it, only hesitates a moment, her round green eyes meeting Will's.

He nods at her. 'Go on, love. It's OK. I'll be down in a sec.'

Sucking at the corner of her blankie, Cassie slides from the bed and disappears out of the door. A moment later, he hears her calling to her brother.

Like gas, silence plumes into the room.

'Jess,' he says, only now able to look at her. He brings his legs out from under the covers, plants his feet on the rug.

But Jessica's face is flint, her eyes half closed with what looks horribly, terrifyingly like hate. A soupy feeling of dread fills his gut, his lungs. He opens his mouth, but her hand comes up to stop him.

'You don't get to speak,' she almost whispers. 'There's no coming back from this, you must know that. I have worked myself ragged for *years*, while you've coasted along, chopping and changing, never sticking with anything. I've carried you, and for what? So you can have afternoon delight with your *client*? Fuck you, Will. And as if that's not bad enough, even when the evidence is right there in front of you, you tell me it's not what I *think*? How dare you? Do you think I'm stupid? Do you? You... you...' A sob overtakes her. 'I mean, who even are you? Really, who the hell are you? What's her name?'

He swallows hard.

'What's her name, Will?'

'I can't. I can't tell you that.'

'Client confidentiality? Really? You're really going with that? Who am I then? Only your wife. Only the mother of your children.' She laughs bitterly, closes her eyes, fingertips probing at her hairline. 'Just... just pack a bag, OK? Mum will pick the kids up from school. Or Lena. I'll text Lena. But I swear to God, if you don't do this one thing, if you... I can't... I... Do *not* make me into the monster here, OK? I'm not the monster. Just... just show me you have one ounce of sensitivity and be out of this house by the time I get back.'

'Jess, come—'

'Not. One. Word.' Jessica throws up her hand once again. 'You had your chance.'

'Oh come on! Jess! There's no need to—'

A blinding thump. Instinctively he pinches the bridge of his nose, which is already throbbing with pain. A shoe thuds on the rug. She... she has thrown her shoe at him.

'What the hell?'

She lunges forward, retrieves the shoe and marches towards the bedroom door. Will opens his mouth but closes it again. Fear pulsates in every part of him. He has never seen his wife like this. All he can do is watch, as if through glass, as if she were an accident, himself a horrified bystander. He does not dare speak. He barely dares breathe.

At the bedroom door, she stops and turns, so slowly his

stomach folds. Without make-up, her eyes are small, red and puffy from crying.

'The worst thing,' she says with a tremor that chills his blood, 'is you're only telling me now.' Her voice falters. She wipes tears from her cheeks, closes her eyes as if to summon courage. When she opens them again, it is to fix him with her cold blue gaze. With visible effort, she makes herself continue. 'And actually, you're not even telling me now, are you? We're not having this conversation because you love me or because you want us to be honest with one another or anything like that, but only, *solely*, because you've been found out. You've been busted, Will, and you don't even have the decency to look me in the eye and tell me the truth. And that right there, *that*'s why I'm not interested in a word you have to say. Not now, not ever. It's over. We're done.'

CHAPTER 3

JESSICA

All those hotels. All those dates. The mini-break. Where the *hell* did he get the money? Jessica's feet pound the pavement, her Nikes white flashes on the grey flagstones. Her hair is still wet, freezing in the mid-September morning. Tears are rolling down her neck; she can feel them soaking into her scarf. As she walks, she digs in her bag for a tissue, finds a used Kleenex to which a piece of hardened chewing gum is stuck. She tears off the gum, throws it back in her bag and wipes her face with the tissue of shame, which is at once soft and gritty.

The other woman must have paid for those hotels, she thinks, stuffing the sodden shreds of what now looks like ectoplasm into her coat pocket. His *lover*. She hears herself whimper at the word.

Is it even over? Or is there another *client booking* this week, in the middle of the day, while the kids are at school, herself at work? Jessica is walking so fast now she is almost running. The woman, the lover, must have paid for all of it. She must have. Because Will sure as hell didn't.

How pathetic.

But who sent the photographs?

She pulls her phone from her bag and calls the number at the top of the WhatsApp thread. She is crying so much she's unsure if she can even speak, let alone find what she wants to say.

The tone is dead.

She tries again. And again. Nothing.

The phone is switched off, its owner either busy or too much of a coward to risk a conversation.

It must be one of the school mums, some woman who doesn't know her well finding a way to communicate out of solidarity, out of sisterhood maybe. Out of spite – that's equally possible. Freya Gibbons? No, Freya's a prat, but she's not evil.

Who else knows? It would only have taken one person to see Will with this woman for the whole sordid affair to have spread like fire in a strong wind. Maybe it already has. Maybe she's the last to know.

Whatever, whoever sent those photographs did not want to be identified, that much is obvious. Which means it *must* be someone they know. *A friend*, the message said. Jessica doubts that means an actual friend, more in the sense of someone who knew Will was cheating and wanted to help her wise up.

But how did whoever it was follow him all over London to his sneaky little assignations? And, actually, *why*? Who would bother to do that?

Someone who has been hurt in love themselves perhaps? Someone who knows what it's like to be kept in the dark then brought shockingly, horribly into the light, only to realise they're the last to know. Perhaps some sad, lonely soul saw Will and this woman once, saw the body language and thought: *You lousy cheating bastard*. And took that first photo.

No. It has to be more personal than that.

A thought occurs to her, so awful it makes her stop in her tracks.

Could these photos have been taken by a former lover of

Will's? Bitter about being jilted for this rich, stylish woman, intent on outing him to his wife, exposing him for all to see?

Could Will have *form*?

Stomach roiling, she forces herself onwards, half runs towards the station. Makes the train with a split second to spare. It is astonishing that she has caught her usual train, that ending her marriage has not even made her late. How little time was needed, she thinks, to end the life she loved, the life she believed was hers. Mere minutes. Because that life is over, of this she is certain. One hundred per cent. She will not be married to a liar, even a lovely, funny liar like Will.

No thanks. She'd rather be on her own.

The carriage smells of soap and cologne, of coffee and foundation. In one of the seats, a woman holding a compact mirror applies an eyebrow, pausing, brush aloft, with almost psychic intuition whenever the train jolts. Around her, familiar early-morning commuters avoid Jessica's gaze. Small talk is the last thing anyone wants. They are all in their own worlds, mulling over their own problems or too spaced out with tiredness to think. Normally this would be perfect, but today it makes her feel achingly alone. Not that she wants to share any of it. God, no. She never wants to tell anyone, ever. It is so humiliating, so shameful and... Oh, the kids, the kids. The kids will be utterly devastated. Her throat hurts. Another wave of uncontrollable tears threatens. She should not be going to work. But she had to get away from him.

From her bag, she pulls out her sunglasses, though the sky is a brooding slate. She has no idea how she will get through the day. Her life, her entire life, has been upended like a shelf of crockery onto a tiled floor. It is smashing in pieces all around her. The noise of it is deafening, yet only she can hear it.

Will, a player.

Will, a liar.

Will, a gaslighting cheat – just like her father.

It cannot be. It just can't.

All Jessica's life, she has railed against the idea – proposed by the counsellor she saw briefly at university – that we are doomed to re-enact the traumas of our childhood. How depressingly fatalistic, she always thought. Surely we have more agency than that? Surely we don't simply sit back and let our past control us?

But: *It's not what you think.* How could he have said those exact words? She gave that information to him out of trust, out of love. *You show me your damage and I'll show you mine* – it was part of that exchange, how they became close, fell in love. He was supposed to keep it safe in his heart so that she didn't have to carry it all on her own. He was not meant to take it out and throw it at her. It's almost as if he was trying to hurt her.

None of it makes sense. The Will she knows and the creep in the photographs are two different people.

Except they're not. Isn't she just silently voicing the words of every single person who has ever been betrayed by someone they love? *I feel like I don't even know him.*

What a cliché she is. What a fool.

The day passes in a blur. She spends most of it in a toilet cubicle scrolling through the photographs over and over, weeping noiselessly, replying to emails with holding messages until she can get herself together. Around eleven, she texts her mum to see if she can pick up Charlie from reception, then later Cassie from primary. By some miracle, Mum is not on shift until the weekend and says yes, she can. A moment later, another text arrives: *Is everything OK, love?*

Her mother, ever the bloodhound, even over text.

Something's come up, that's all. Nothing to worry about.

Jessica texts Will: *Mum will pick up kids. Do NOT be there.*

In the next cubicle, a toilet flushes. The clatter of a door unlocking. Jessica holds her breath. A short blast of water from the tap, but no breath from the hand-dryer, only the squeak of the door, a soft thud. She is alone again. Her phone is buzzing incessantly. Mum calling. Too weary to pretend, Jessica picks up.

'Hi.'

'Is Will not well?'

'Oh, Mum.' And just like that, Jessica is sobbing like a child through everything that has happened.

Her mother tells her not to panic, that she is there, that they'll get through this together. 'My girl,' she says. 'My precious girl. I'll bloody kill him.'

'Please,' Jessica says. 'Please don't. Just leave it to me.'

'All right,' her mother says after a short silence. 'All right, love. If you say so.'

After she rings off, Jessica sees three missed calls from Will. A text: *OK, but can't you talk?*

She ignores it.

An hour later, he calls again. Two hours later, again. Clearly he cannot even respect this one, highly reasonable request: to leave her alone, give her some space. She lets all calls go to voicemail, deletes the messages. After lunch, an email from him arrives with the title: *EXPLANATION.* She sends it straight to the trash without reading, empties the trash folder.

At three, claiming a migraine, she leaves, bursting into a fresh flood of tears the moment she makes it through the revolving glass doors.

She has no recollection of heading down into Monument station, is on her own suburban street before she is aware of the journey. Her feet hurt. She sees that she has forgotten to change into her trainers, which must still be under her desk.

Mum greets her at the door with a hug, but Jessica finds herself as stiff as a chair, unable to accept it.

'Let's get you inside,' her mother says. 'Dear, dear.'

Later, she finds herself in the kitchen, half a mug of cold tea on the table in front of her. Mum must have made it. She must have made the kids' dinner too. Jessica has a memory of crying, Mum's hand on her shoulder, her brisk way of rising from her chair at the approach of either of the children. *Hey, hey, poppet, no, your mummy's fine, love, she's just had a bad day. Shall I put the telly on for you?*

Coming back to herself, she hears Cassie and Charlie upstairs, the sound of the bath running, the sing-song of her mother's voice, the high chatter of her children. The kitchen is immaculate; no trace of their dinner but for a savoury smell. Fish fingers. Oven chips. Mum has taken over with her nurse's calm, kind efficiency. Of all people, she knows what Jessica's going through, knows perhaps that it is too soon to offer words of comfort. There is no comfort, not today.

Later still, Jessica is in her own quiet living room, a glass of cool Pinot Grigio in her hand. It is a little unnerving how entire moments have dropped away like coins through a hole in a pocket. She has no memory of them whatsoever. At a certain point, her best friend Lena must have arrived, must have, since she is sitting opposite. Lena must have put the kids to bed, must have brought this wine with her. Did Mum ask her to come over? Or did she, Jessica, call her?

'So, what, he was wearing an old shirt?' Lena asks.

Jessica has no idea why Lena is asking her this, what she's even referring to. 'What?'

'Last night. For your anniversary. You were saying Will was his usual scruffy self.'

'Was I?' She must have been complaining about his lack of

effort. It has bothered her all day. Bizarre, she thinks, how last night she must have squashed her irritation into a dark corner, and now – poof! Out it has popped.

'Funny,' she says, wiping her nose with the tissue Lena has handed to her. 'You don't think these things get to you. But they do.'

'Oh, hon.' Lena pulls a sad face and takes a pensive sip of her wine. Thank goodness she's here. Thank God she didn't move back north after she and Ronnie split up, or to Scotland or Croatia or any of the places she's threatened to move to when some emotionally unavailable twat has broken her heart yet again. Thank God.

'I'm going to get Deliveroo,' Lena says, with purpose. 'Chinese?'

'Sure. Whatever.'

Jessica remembers she read Cassie a story earlier. Yes, she did, definitely. It was imperative not to let the kids down, all that kept her functioning. She remembers lying next to her daughter's warm little body, Cassie rigid with excitement at having a story read by her mummy, which in itself made Jessica feel sick with guilt. And then, of course, she asked where Daddy was. Jessica was grateful for the fact that they were taking turns to read aloud from *Charlotte's Web* and not looking directly at one another.

'Daddy's had to go away for work,' she lied.

'Daddy never goes away for work. Is that why he was sad this morning?'

Clever kids can be a curse. At six, Cassie is as sharp as a tack. And Will obviously did not make any effort to pretend everything was all right.

'Sometimes he has to go away,' Jessica improvised. 'He's gone to a...' Her mind is utterly blank.

'How long is he going to be gone for?'

'I'm not sure. I'll ask him when he calls, OK?'

'Why didn't he call to say goodnight?' Cassie's voice was so small it was barely there.

'He'll have been busy, darling,' Jessica said, stroking her daughter's gorgeous hair, thicker and a richer red now than her own. 'But you can talk to him tomorrow, OK?'

'OK.'

She flushed with shame, flushes again now just thinking about it. Will had called – at seven. She knew he was calling to talk to the kids, but she didn't pick up. Spite made her do this. Rage. She wanted to cause him pain. But in that moment with Cassie, she realised she had caused her children pain too.

'I feel bad about not letting Will talk to the kids tonight,' she says now, seeing that Lena has put her phone to one side.

'Don't beat yourself up. You're still in shock.'

'I just wasn't ready to hear his voice. I need to do better. I need to make sure the kids don't get upset.'

'Trouble is,' Lena says, 'that'll make it even easier for him, won't it? If you keep it all nicey-nice. Easier for him, harder for you.'

Jessica feels sick.

'Last night,' she says, 'I bought a new little silk number. I booked the restaurant, the babysitter—'

'Like you always do.'

'I did my hair, my nails. I looked nice, you know, for me.'

'What do you mean, for you? Sod off, you always look amazing.'

'And then he comes down in odd socks, one of which had a hole in, and I can't believe I'm thinking about that now. It's like I'm obsessing.'

'He'd obviously checked out of making an effort. When did that start?'

'Do you think? Do you think he'd checked out?'

'I think you're only noticing it now and putting two and two together.'

'Did I show you the photos?'

'Yes, babe.' Lena rolls her eyes, but a smirk plays on her lips. 'Can you divorce someone for wearing socks with holes in for a wedding anniversary?'

A laugh breaks from Jessica. 'Mental cruelty. Violence to the eyes.'

'A crime of fashion.'

'Very good.' She laughs again, grateful that Lena is not treating her differently, that she is not embarrassed into formality by Jessica's private humiliation. 'Thanks,' she says.

'What for?'

'For being normal.' She knows how hard it is to love a friend who is suffering, to not be able to wave a magic wand and make things right. She knows it from watching Lena's disastrous love life over the years.

'Will plays the idiot,' Lena says, finishing her wine with an angry flourish, 'but he's sponged off you your whole marriage, and now that he's found himself a richer model, he's off. You watch, next thing he'll be driving round in a sports car. I mean, it's classic midlife crisis.'

'He's not even forty yet.'

'You always see the good in him, but honestly, doll, he takes the piss. And now this. Will never gets out of bed without putting the heating on. Speaking from experience.' Lena's tone borders on resentful.

Jessica frowns. 'Did he cheat on you? I never knew that!'

Lena shrugs. 'Well, no, not exactly. But he barely had time to tie his shoelaces before he started going out with you, did he?'

Jessica sips her wine, unsure how to answer. She has forgotten how much Lena loves to tear into Will – so much so that she has often found herself coming to his defence even when she was in the middle of complaining about him. But Lena rarely brings up the brief, meaningless fling she had with him. Why would she? It's ancient history.

Lena leans forward and tops up Jessica's glass, whatever flashed through her a moment ago clearly gone, if it was ever there at all. 'You do everything. Literally everything. And now I'm thinking of all the times I covered for him when he said a session had overrun. I never thought anything of it.'

Jessica almost spits out her wine. 'What? When? A session can't overrun. It has to end on time. It's a boundary.' Boundary, she thinks. That ship has surely sailed. 'Oh my God, he must have been with *her*. Madame bloody X.'

Lena sighs. 'I'm so sorry. I didn't realise. I didn't think.'

'Why would you? Like you said, the signs were there, but I didn't see them. I just... I mean, he's a great dad, and he's funny and kind, so you roll with what you've got, don't you? He's just Will, you know? He's not Mr Alpha, I know that, but I never wanted...' Jessica can feel tears rising. A nanosecond later, Lena is wedged up against her, one arm around her shoulders.

'I hate him for doing this to you,' she says. 'He's an absolute bastard. I'll kill him.'

Jessica can't see for tears. 'He's... It's like he's thrown this bomb into our lives and it's carnage, absolute carnage. What am I going to tell the kids? *It's not what you think*. Did I tell you he said that?'

'You did.' Lena sighs. 'Like he was taunting you.'

'He won't tell me her name – can you believe that? She's a client apparently.'

'A client? Aren't they, like, vulnerable?'

'He's only a life coach, not a psychotherapist or anything.' Jessica's head drops back into her hands. 'I was so beside myself, I couldn't see straight. I... I just wanted him to tell me the truth and then when he didn't, I just – boom! – you know? I wanted him out. Just... out. There's no way back. I can't...'

Another crying fit sweeps over her. Will – lovely Will. Someone whose job it is to help people. And yes, maybe a bit anything-for-an-easy-life, but good, a *good guy*. She thought.

'Oh, babe,' Lena says softly, stroking her hair. 'Come here.'

'We were... balanced. Yin and yang. Opposites attract. We had our roles; there was enough for everyone to have what they needed, most of what they wanted. We're not greedy. Neither of us is greedy. I never thought... not someone like him.'

'But they say that, don't they?' Lena says. 'The quiet ones are the worst. That's what they say. Always the quiet ones.'

CHAPTER 4

WILL

The Travelodge in Brentford has to be the most depressing place Will has ever been. And it is raining, of course it is: the kind of apocalyptic bucketing that bounces off the pavements, carries merry crisp packets in sludgy rivers along the gutters, sprays brown fountains from under the wheels of passing cars, soaking you through. This is exactly what happened half an hour ago when he went to buy his wretched takeaway dinner.

He considers his trousers, steaming on the back of the vinyl-upholstered chair in front of the miserable plastic tea-making paraphernalia, the lone UHT milk sachet like some sort of metaphor for something he can't be bothered to think of. Apathy maybe.

How did this happen, and so quickly? The pain of it is so great, he feels like when he breathes, his lungs won't fill to capacity, like there is an obstacle there blocking his airways. Jessica's broken expression will not leave his mind. He cannot unhear her last words: *It's over. We're done.*

She is strong, always has been. She's had to be. But underneath that veneer of strength, he knows the other Jessica, the one others don't see, the one who bursts into tears at romantic

lines in TV shows, who buys *The Big Issue*, who always
leaves the waiter a big tip. He knows the Jessica who walked
in on her father cheating when she was too young to really
understand it, whose father continued to cheat over and over
again while her mother was on nights, Jessica plugging her
ears and fretting and praying for it to stop, until after a huge
blow-up on her fourteenth birthday, he left. He knows these
things because Jessica confided in him – a big thing for her,
which she did because she trusted him. Because she
loved him.

He checks his phone. Nineteen outgoing calls to her. Seven
desperate texts begging her to talk to him, to please read his
email, in which, free from her relentless verbal assault, he was
able to concentrate enough to tell her the truth.

Well, perhaps not the whole truth. But near enough. All she
needs to understand is that the whole thing with Margot was –
really, truly – not what she thinks. But her reply dripped acid: *I
have nothing to say and no interest in anything you might want
to say, certainly not in an email, for God's sake. Stop calling.
Stop texting. Stop emailing.*

And with a punch to the gut, he realised she had not bothered to read the email he had spent an hour crafting with
painstaking care. Thinking about it now, even though he cannot
deny she is right, her words cause in him a small, shimmering
feeling of injustice. All he's asking for is a chance to explain.
Yes, he messed up. Yes, he should have told her sooner, but it
was bound up with confidentiality, then with guilt, until one
day it became about fear. But this morning, he shouldn't have
compounded his mistake with cowardly lies. She deserved
better, of course she did, but he panicked.

Who could have taken those photographs? Who sent them
to his wife?

A friend, it said.

Someone they know then. But who would care enough to

follow him, photograph him, fuck up his life? Margot's voice comes to him, her frightened expression.

We have to be careful. My husband cannot find out.

It has to be him; who else could it be? Margot's husband was the reason she came to him in the first place, the reason he couldn't or didn't tell Jessica. A broken promise to Margot, Will knew, could mean danger for him and his family as well as for her.

He remembers her showing up at his office as he was leaving to pick up the kids.

'Excuse me,' she said, her French accent hitting him immediately.

He turned to see a small, thin woman standing on the pavement, her black hair tucked behind her ear on one side, a curl at her jawline on the other. She was wearing a plain white dress, her arms brown and thin. It was a summer dress, he thinks. It must have been the early days of summer, over a year ago now.

'Yes?' he said.

She took off her sunglasses and fixed him with her small brown eyes. Her mouth was bracketed by deep lines. Older than him, he thought.

'You are a life coach?' Her eyes flicked towards the little brass plaque above the intercom: *William Draper, Life Coach/Alan Fitzpatrick, Massage Therapist.* It occurs to him now that she must have been browsing in the exclusive boutique on the ground floor, must have seen the sign on her way out.

'I am,' he replied, pocketing his keys and pulling out his wallet, extracting a card with as much professionalism as he could muster. 'If you'd like to make an appointment, either call the number, email or use the form on the website.'

She took the card from him. 'You help people? You change people's lives?'

He couldn't help but smile. 'I help people to change their

own lives. I help them set goals, make plans, that sort of thing. Listen, I have to go and get my kids from school right now, but get in touch and we can set up a time if you're interested, OK?'

'OK. Thank you, William Draper.'

The way she said his name – so formal, so *French*. She never did call. Instead, she returned a week later in person.

'Margot,' he whispers, pictures her with her kids, smiling, laughing. Free. He did that too, at least. He is not a bad man.

But despite their caution, her husband must've been onto them almost from the beginning. Sending those photographs must have been an act of revenge, designed to destroy his marriage. Maybe Margot's ex thinks, as Jessica does, that it was an affair.

Well, it has worked, because now he's in this bloody Travelodge wondering if he will ever be allowed back into his home. All he can hope for is that the revenge will end there. Because if not, he is in danger. His family could be in danger.

From his lap, the feta cheese salad meal-for-one throws up an eyeless stare. One of his socks has a hole in it. They are the same socks he was wearing last night. Stubble scratches the palm of his hand. He needs a shave. His is not the kind of George Clooney five o'clock shadow women find sexy. It is uneven, with little bald spots. He is a mess. Everything is a mess, even work, which he has had to cancel for the rest of the week. There is no way he's in any kind of position to help anyone right now, isn't sure if he can even help himself. Diagnose himself, perhaps: post-traumatic stress. Severe bleeding idiot syndrome. I am a life coach, he thinks. I help people get their lives on track, and now mine has ploughed off the rails.

Idly he scrolls through his contacts, wondering who he can call. His mate Colin, fellow stay-at-home dad, would be understanding, he knows that, but he tells his wife, Freya, everything, and Freya would broadcast it quicker than a public service announcement. Graham, from his teacher-training days, would commiserate over a pint in a heartbeat. Any of the dads he played five-a-side with last year would be nice about it. But right now, Will can't face anyone. It is too embarrassing, too difficult to explain, too shameful... and possibly too dangerous. If he's right about who sent the photographs, he has to keep this to himself.

My husband is a violent man. He cannot find out about us.

No. Will cannot tell anyone. He cannot mention any names, for Margot's sake as well as his own. Jessica will have to respect that.

Outside the hotel window, sun leaks from between patches of cloud the grubby colour of their living room walls, a shade Jessica laughingly told him once was called Mole's Breath.

'There are one hundred and thirty-two shades of grey,' he remembers her saying, studying the colour chart. 'And here was me thinking there were only fifty.'

The thought of her in a happier time makes his heart hurt. He should have spoken to her the moment things with Margot changed to something risky. If he'd told her, who knows, he might not have got in so deep with Margot. But the betrayal Jessica will feel will be absolute. That's the crux of it. That is why she won't see him, won't hear him. At the time, like most people crossing a boundary, he convinced himself he wasn't infringing on their marriage, not strictly speaking. But the fact is, he couldn't have told Jessica without involving her. And something else, something he has always known: Jessica might have stopped him.

This is life and death, William. This is our secret. I need your word.

The rain has stopped. He's pretty sure he saw a McDonald's a block down. Jessica made them go pescatarian a year ago. Persuaded him, she would say, for health and for the environment.

Well, Jessica has kicked him out. And right now he could murder a Big Mac and fries.

Half an hour later, faced with the bright overhead menu, a Big Mac feels like yet another betrayal, so he orders a Filet-O-Fish instead. It's edible, he supposes. Tasty even, if you like mechanically recovered fish scraps moulded to look like a fillet. It is, at least, hot.

Outside, another shower passes. He watches it sitting on a red plastic seat screwed to the floor, the smell of fried food in his nostrils, the bitter aftertaste of artificial sweetener from the Diet Coke on his tongue. Six o'clock comes. Six fifteen. Six thirty. A group of teenagers enter – a rabble of arms and legs – lads in jeans with waistbands under their buttocks, logo underpants proudly on display; girls with tight elastic skirts, white legs, big shoes. They talk too loudly, swear at one another, affect constant outrage in a way that looks exhausting. These are the kids he could never cope with, the reason he left teaching. Another thing at which he failed.

Cassie and Charlie will be having quiet time before their bath at seven. He wonders if Pat is there, if Jessica has told her. Of course, and of course. His face heats. Northern matriarchs carry grudges to their graves. There will be no forgiveness from Pat.

At seven, he rings Jessica again, then tries the home phone, but no one picks up.

A new tightness spreads across his chest. He tries to remember a day when he didn't see his children. It must be four years ago now, the day his mum died. It was about a month after Charlie was born. He'd sat with her in the hospice, holding her hand. She was so small, so far from the stout, scary and, he knows now, deeply thwarted woman of his childhood. She told him he was a good boy, that he'd always been a good boy, which

made him cry despite everything. Slowly, her papery hand
cooled in his, and he choked on his words of reassurance and
love, knowing they had come too late.

Cassie was all over him when he got back: *Daddy, Daddy,
Daddy!* Charlie oblivious at Jessica's breast, Jessica pale, black
around the eyes, Pat keeping it all together, himself walking in
and feeling like an interloper.

His kids. His family. Oh God.

His hands clench into fists. It isn't fair of Jessica to keep his
children from him.

With effort, he straightens out his fingers, lies them flat on
the hard plastic tabletop. No. That's not what she's doing. She's
in pain. She needs space, that's all. Tomorrow she will come
round. Possibly the day after tomorrow. They'll talk. He will
apologise. Maybe they can see a relationship counsellor.

It's not like they're going to get divorced.

On the way back to the Travelodge, he passes the Express
Tavern pub. He knows it by sight, having driven past it
numerous times on the way to IKEA. He seems to remember
it's part of a chain of old pubs that have been modernised – a
middle-class pastiche of the kind of boozer Jessica's Uncle Neil
– Pat's brother – took him to when he and Jessica announced
they were getting married. There were pickled eggs on the bar,
a one-armed bandit, tobacco-brown Lincrusta on the ceiling.
Make sure you look after her was the message, delivered entirely
in subtext over four pints of Greenall's bitter. *I'm watching
you, son.*

Time crawls. The thought of the hotel room hangs like
doom over his head, like the black-as-death cloud he can see
hovering now over Kew. He cannot face that hotel room, not
yet, not alone, not without talking to another living human
being.

Inside, the pub is quite basic: floorboards, wooden chairs. Busy but not rammed. He orders the lowest-alcohol lager, a four per cent Pilsner, and, not wanting to take up a free table when there is only one of him, stands at the bar. The beer is good, clean-tasting; he closes his eyes briefly to savour it. Minutes pass. He exchanges a weather-based pleasantry with the barman, but that's it. Halfway down his pint, he sees the barman raise his eyebrows at another customer just out of Will's eyeline, hears a sonorous *Solaris, please, Bill* to his right.

A sideways glance reveals a man with thick greying brown hair pushed back and worn a little longer than a short back and sides. From the laughter lines making white bird's feet on his tanned skin, Will puts him at late forties, maybe early fifties. He is dressed in a good-quality wool coat, a fine dark sweater and dark navy jeans. On his feet are what look like expensive conker-coloured brogues.

It is, Will thinks, a well-heeled West London look: elegant brands without in-your-face labels or overly youthful fashions. It suggests the wearer has changed out of a good suit and into something comfortable yet smart for the evening, when a stroll and a quiet pint is in order for the sophisticated man about town who still enjoys the down-to-earth pleasures of a decent ale.

Will can feel his big toe poking through the hole in his two-day-old sock. He wishes, in a way he never would've thought himself capable of, that he wasn't wearing his hiking cagoule. Even if it is incredibly waterproof.

He lets the man sip his beer a moment before offering the brisk, near-imperceptible nod of men at bars.

'Evening,' he says, noticing as he does so the man's long black umbrella, which he has hooked onto the bar by its polished wooden handle.

The man returns the nod and goes back to his pint. It occurs to Will that he actually cannot bear to spend the rest of the evening alone.

He clears his throat. 'Filthy night,' he offers.

'It is indeed.' The man presses his mouth to the rim of the glass. The amber liquid tips.

'Pretty much a flash flood earlier,' Will adds. 'I thought I'd never get out of the door.'

The man stares straight ahead. Will wonders if he hasn't heard, or is ignoring him, hoping he'll go away. He is clean-shaven; his skin almost gleams, and Will can smell cologne or aftershave or whatever that woody scent is. Pushing at his stubble, he wishes that, as well as not wearing the cagoule, he'd bothered to shave.

He leaves the man to his drink. In his mind's eye, Jessica's angry face flashes, as if she has been waiting for him to return to his tortured thoughts so she can jump out at him. Her eyes are small and red and angry. *Get out of my house.* Rat-a-tat-tat. *My house.* It's true, she bought it. But it isn't like he hasn't pulled his weight over the years. OK, so his coaching practice hasn't quite taken off as he thought it might, but that's only because for the last two years he's had to be at the school gates at 8.30 a.m., midday and 3.15 every afternoon, barring Thursdays, when Cassie has football and Pat has Charlie and Will has an extra hour or two.

Thursdays – the days he saw Margot.

I contacted you because I am in a very difficult situation. Do you think you can help me, William?

Don't think about Margot and everything you haven't told Jessica – the hotels, the money, the risk you took. Think about how you being at home meant that Jessica could work unimpeded. Business trips to far-flung locations, late nights, Zoom meetings, client dinners – all of that was stress-free, at least on the domestic front, and that was because of you.

And now she won't even let you speak.

Like the end of a finger against his sternum, resentment pushes at him.

He looks up, almost desperate now to have a conversation, if only to save him from his own mind. The not particularly friendly man is almost at the end of his pint.

'First time I've been here,' Will tries. 'I often drive past, but I've never actually stopped.'

Finally the man looks at him, frowns as if to weigh up what he has said, as if, possibly, to weigh him up too. 'What's the occasion?'

'Occasion? I don't...'

'I mean, how come you're here tonight particularly?' He is well-spoken but with a hint of something earthier, something local.

'Actually,' Will begins, 'I'm staying in the Travelodge, but I didn't fancy being cooped up all evening.'

Again the man appears to be processing this information, taking a sip of his beer as if he's in a slow-motion film.

'Business?' he asks eventually and only after placing his glass with painstaking slowness on the bar.

'Not exactly. Just needed a bit of space. A break of sorts. Bit of a domestic, you might say.'

'Trouble in paradise sort of thing?'

Will laughs, fooling neither himself nor the man. 'You could say that. Not so much me needing space as the missus need-ing...' He widens his eyes and throws up his hands. 'I fucked up!' The flippancy shocks him. It is born of pure anxiety, he knows that even in the moment, but he still hates himself for it. It is another betrayal to add to his much larger one.

Ashamed, he lowers his hands. *I only joke*, he wants to say, *because otherwise I would break into a million pieces.*

'That's quite a shiner you've got there,' the man says. 'Been beating you up, has she?'

Will touches his fingers to his nose. It is still tender, has obviously bruised.

'Not exactly,' he says, trying to be light. 'She threw a shoe at me.'

'Ouch.' The man grimaces, reaches out his hand. 'I'm Ian, by the way. Ian Robbins.'

Will shakes his hand, bitter gratitude dripping inside him like damp into a cave. 'William Draper. Will. Pleased to meet you.'

'Likewise.' Ian's grip is firm. His pupils are as small as ball bearings, his irises palest blue ringed with indigo. His brow is heavy, his lips thin, his nose lean and straight, the nostrils flared like those of a racehorse. The combination of his features shouldn't be handsome, but somehow, it is.

He leans back, fixes his pale gaze onto Will's with disconcerting intensity. 'So, Will Draper, what did you do that was so bad you're stuck in Brentford's finest accommodation for the night?'

CHAPTER 5

JESSICA

Once Lena has left, Jessica finds herself restless, angry, a deep sense of injustice boiling in her guts. Lena was sympathy itself, but with all her ranting, she has unintentionally left Jessica feeling worse. Around her, the house howls with emptiness. The thought of going up to a cold bed is almost unbearable. She wants to text Will to come home, but, in a fit of misery, instead finds herself writing, *Just to let you know, I've contacted a solicitor.*

She almost deletes it. But the thought of the photographs pushes in, goading her. Lips pressed tight together, tears spilling, she sends the text. It isn't true. But so what? Let him suffer as she is suffering. She reads it back. Guilt washes over her. She has no intention of contacting a solicitor, of course she hasn't. But something Lena said has been burrowing into her: *Trouble is, that'll make it even easier for him, won't it? If you keep it all nicey-nice.*

Why should it be easier for him? And now he's chilling out in a hotel somewhere or supping beer in some pub with one of his mates while she is left to juggle the kids, the house, her job and everything else, not to mention a heart that feels like it's been smashed with a hammer.

She stares out of the window at the receding figure of her oldest friend, shoulders high against the damp chill of the September evening. Hours of heavy rain have left slick streets, a clear deep blue sky. There is a lightness in the air that does not match the heaviness she feels inside. She should not have sent that text. Fury made her do it. Rage. The deep desire to punish him, to cause him pain without causing the kids pain. She composes a second message.

Why don't you come over next Wednesday to see the kids? I know it seems like a long time, but I think we both need a break from one another. I'll make arrangements to be out so you can enjoy seeing them. Let's put them first while we figure this out. J.

She reads it again. Yes, that's softer without letting him think he can just move back after one lonely night. She cannot face him yet; she is too raw, too upset; he needs to understand that. She wonders whether he's staying with a friend – Colin maybe? Please God, not Colin and Freya. Freya would bloody love that; the excitement will send her into overdrive and by tomorrow the whole school will know.

But honestly? If Will came to the door right now, Jessica would let him in. Shameful, weak, but true. The house doesn't feel like home without him in it. But perhaps the ache inside her is in reality a desperate longing to go back to before those photographs. If she had never seen them, last night would still be a precious memory sealed with boozy butterfly kisses and whispered words of love. Will would still be here. They would still be happy, their problems no bigger than anyone else's.

In the kitchen, in a kind of stupor, she washes the plates and the two wine glasses, flicks on the kettle to make herself a herbal tea. While the kettle boils, she examines the photos yet again, zooming in, obsessing, a hard fist forming in her gut.

Would it really have been so bad never to have seen them? Is it essential to know everything in a marriage? Surely, in time, the affair would have melted away. He would have got over it. She knows him well enough to realise that it will have been in some way traumatic for him to betray her like that. And it's not as if she doesn't understand that a person can develop feelings for someone else. God knows, she's experienced it herself, briefly, when she went back to work after Cassie. She was exhausted, hormonal, still feeling bovine and unattractive, and her line manager had a way of looking right at her when he spoke, always seeking her opinion. He made her feel like she was shaking herself out of a cocoon, emerging bright with coloured wings.

She requested a move of department, got herself out of harm's way.

Will must have *known* he was developing feelings for this client, whose name he is so keen to protect. But he did not suggest she see a different coach. He did not get out of harm's way. He should have referred her to someone else, said he couldn't help her, whatever it took. Jessica wonders if this Madame X person has a job or if she is simply a woman with too much time, too much money, a rich person's flair for neurosis. Will would admonish her for thinking like that. It is part of why she's enjoying the thought now. A beautiful heiress with her Chanel jacket and her Gucci pumps. How could he have fallen for a woman like that?

Jessica, you know nothing about her. Nothing.

She knows only what this woman looks like: sharp hair, chic wardrobe, aristocratically thin. Magnified, the photographs are too blurry for her face to be clear, but Jessica imagines her as Disney pretty, with big doleful eyes.

You're so wise, Will. Only you understand me, Will. I love you, Will.

A thought occurs to her, so obvious she is amazed she didn't think of it before: he could have gone to *her* tonight. Madame X.

He might not be in a hotel or with a friend. He could be in her home. In her bed.

'God,' she whispers, disgusted, upset, frightened. She pours the herbal tea down the sink and picks up the bottle of Pinot Grigio, downs the remaining inch and returns to the living room. Staring out of the window at the graveyard that is suburbia late at night, fury rises again inside her.

Their house is on the curve. Will says he likes it because he can see her coming home from work in her smart clothes and the trainers she wears to speed-walk from the station. When the kids were little, he would lift them up and let them stand on the sill. Even now, he often brings them both to the window and she is greeted by the heart-swelling sight of her family welcoming her home.

She wipes away new tears. Her phone buzzes. Lena.

Back safe. Love you x PS it'll be OK

She replies: *Tks. Love you too x*

For the thousandth time, she scrolls through the photos, telling herself all the while that she should stop. Who could have sent them? Who would bother to take so many? *A friend.* But who?

She tries once again to call the number, but the line remains dead.

CHAPTER 6

WILL

Ian Robbins is at the end of his pint.

'Another one?' Will asks.

But Ian shakes his head. 'I'll get them.' He points to Will's glass. 'That Camden Hells or Pravha?'

Actually Will fancies a glass of Merlot, but he finds himself saying, 'Pravha, thanks. But only if I get the next one. Thank you.'

Ian hands him his umbrella and gestures to a table in the rear corner of the pub. 'Let's sit.'

Will makes his way over. The umbrella handle is smooth against his palm, the tap against the floor as he walks making him think of a cane, of Gene Kelly, of that old black-and-white series with Diana Rigg and Patrick somebody – the toff with the black umbrella. He had something else too. Will thinks it might've been a deadly bowler hat.

Above the table, dub reggae plays thinly from a wonky wall speaker. A vague smell of industrial cleaner pervades. Other smells too – bodies, clothes, perfume. In the etched mirror on the wall adjacent to his seat, his appearance is a shock: black puffy eyes, bloodshot whites, a swollen nose. Christ, he looks like he's been in a fight. He wonders if the shiner had come up before he dropped Cassie and Charlie off.

Don't think of Cassie and Charlie. Do not. You cannot cry in front of Ian Robbins – this polished man, this *gent*. He will think you're a wimp. Work out a plan. Some version of events that gives you a way back, an approximation of the truth that doesn't put anyone in danger. Think, Will.

'I brought snacks.' Ian places two pints on the table, digs two packets of crisps out of the pockets of his beautiful coat and throws them down. He sits opposite Will.

'Great.'

'Sea salt and balsamic,' Ian says, inspecting the packets. 'Cheddar and red onion. What a load of bollocks.'

Despite everything, Will laughs. 'I know. Why not say salt and vinegar?'

'Because then they wouldn't be able to charge silly money, that's why. It's all in the elevation of the humble potato.' Ian crosses his ankles. The shoes Will took for brogues are in fact ankle boots. Really, this guy is very dapper. 'So,' he says. 'You're in the doghouse then, yeah?'

Until this moment, they have managed to stick to small talk. Will has learnt that Ian also has two kids, and a wife called Jen. He lives in Kew.

He attempts a wry smile, but again it feels like he's betraying Jessica. There is no place for wry. What has happened is a total disaster.

'I don't want to pry,' Ian adds.

'No, it's OK.' Will lets his face drop into the sadness he actually feels. 'I am definitely in the doghouse.'

Slowly Ian pulls the coat from his shoulders. The lining is a green and blue two-tone, looks like it might be silk. His sweater is new, not one bobble. He is broad, with no middle-aged paunch as far as Will can tell – a good physique for a man his age. Will sucks in his stomach, which in these last few years has bloated from polishing off the kids' dinners before eating his own, from never quite finding time to exercise; from, he thinks, not caring.

'I had a mate who was going to start an app called *In the doghouse*,' Ian says and takes a pull on his pint. '*In the doghouse dot com*, or whatever apps are called.'

'Really?' Will cringes at how posh he sounds. As the evening has worn on, Ian's accent has become a little more South London. But Will is not about to start roughing up his own accent, is still recovering from having said *missus* earlier. 'What did it do?'

'My memory's shot, but basically I think you put in what you've done and it tells you what you've got to do to get out' – Ian pauses for effect – 'of the doghouse.'

'OK.'

'So let's say you've forgotten your wife's birthday. You put that in. The app asks you some questions, like, how long have you been married? Is this the first time you've forgotten? Sort of thing. You answer the questions then the app comes up with *bunch of flowers* or *take her out to dinner* or what have you.' He pulls an ironic face. 'Genius, isn't it?'

'It is.'

'So if, like, you've done the big one, say, had an affair with her best friend or whatever, the app will tell you a load of stuff you have to do and, I don't know, it's not my app, but it'll tell you how long it'll take you to get out...' He rolls his hand, picking up his pint with the other and drinking.

'Of the doghouse,' Will fills in, scalp tingling with discomfort at the light they are making of the subject.

'Exactly.' Ian claps his hands together and rubs them briskly. 'So, William Draper, what are we talking?'

'What are we... Sorry?'

'Are we talking bunch of flowers or dinner? What will you

have to do?' He raises his eyebrows, a trace of humour flickering across his face.

'To get out of the doghouse?' Will shakes his head. 'I think it's more than a bunch of flowers. A lot more.'

Ian scratches at his neck. 'That sounds more like Caribbean cruise territory.'

'I think it might be more like out of the house altogether. She's saying it's over.'

'I'm sorry, mate. I didn't mean to... I was just, you know, trying to—'

Will holds up his hand. 'Not at all. I got that. Completely. It felt good to smile. I've mostly been crying.'

'I can imagine. So, *was* it an affair?'

He stretches out his neck. It is stiff from too much time hooked over his phone, praying for Jessica to make contact.

'Forget I asked that,' Ian says. 'None of my beeswax.'

'It's complicated. I got... too close to a client. Helped her in a way I shouldn't have. Someone took photos of us going into hotels together and sent them to my wife. When she asked me about it, I didn't give her a proper answer and now she won't listen to a word I say. She says I'd never have told her if someone hadn't sent her the photos. She says she doesn't care what I have to say now because it's too late.'

Ian grimaces. 'When did she find out?'

'This morning.'

'And would you? Have told her?'

'I don't think so,' Will says, skirting around the solemn promise he made to Margot not to tell a soul, the fear he had for her, for himself. 'It wasn't an affair, but I didn't feel like I could explain it to my wife, if that makes sense. Plus, there were some other things, some things I did...'

'Such as?'

A noisy group of men in sports kit have come in, saving Will from admitting to any more. The air fills with the smell of sweat and nylon, raucous joking. Ian glances at the men, then turns back to Will, his eyelids heavy with what could well be disapproval.

'Will she take your kids?' he asks, breaking into Will's thoughts.

'Well,' Will begins, 'I mean, they're her kids too, but I'm a stay-at-home dad so I don't think… I'm not sure. Sorry, this is all very depressing.' He drinks his lager, partly to make himself shut up. He can feel the alcohol increasing his tendency to over-share. He's not a drinker, can't really take much more than a couple of pints, but knows he will have to offer Ian another and then he will have to get one for himself. Something about Ian makes him think he can't get a half, though he is supposedly far too emancipated, too old to think like that.

'Sounds like it's early days,' Ian says.

'And I don't want to drone on about myself. What is it you do?'

Ian leans back in his chair, adjusts his soft sweater with a pinching motion followed by a brush of his flattened hand.

'Property mostly,' he says. 'I've lived here since I was a kid, bought my first flat when I was twenty, did it up with my mate Dave and sold it on. Next one, same thing, except I rented it out and bought another place.' He shakes his head. 'Couldn't do that round here these days, but yeah, I've got a pretty decent portfolio. Puts food on the table.'

Will nods as if he understands. He doesn't, not really. Money is not something he's ever been great at, or interested in. But looking at Ian's smart clothes, hearing him talk, he has to admit to feeling scruffy and somehow small in comparison. When Ian says it puts food on the table, he is being modest. Ian is, Will suspects, very wealthy indeed.

Ian takes another swig of his drink and puts his glass back on the table. It is only an inch from being empty. Will's pint is still two thirds full.

'Let me get you another,' he says, standing. 'Solaris, yes?'

Ian frowns and checks his watch, looks up and meets Will's eye. 'Go on then. One for the road.'

Will tries not to notice that it takes him a lot longer than Ian to get served. He is passed over twice before the barman appears to even notice him. When he gets back to the table, Ian doesn't comment, only asks him if he minds going outside a moment while he has a smoke.

'Of course not,' Will replies.

They step out onto the busy road, where white-painted cast-iron tables are doing their best to make the rainy pavement look like some sort of Parisian terrace. Will is about to sit down when Ian tells him not to, that the seats are wet. Will almost laughs. Ian clearly hasn't seen his twenty-year-old jeans; he is too busy lighting up. He blows out a plume of smoke and offers the packet to Will, who demurs with a wave of his hand, although at this moment an illicit cigarette is a tempting prospect.

'Wise man.' Ian blows another jet of smoke respectfully away.

In front of them, car lights form a steady stream of reds and yellows over Kew Bridge. To the left, towards Chiswick, industrial cranes dangle great metal hooks into a hazy, darkening sky.

'I was thinking before,' Ian says, 'when you were at the bar. I reckon your wife has gone a bit nuclear.'

'Nuclear? How do you mean?'

'I mean, it's none of my business. You messed up, like you said.' His accent swings almost imperceptibly between South London and something classier, posher. 'Maybe she'll calm down, but she's gone a bit zero to a hundred, don't you think?'

'Zero to a hundred?'

Ian gesticulates with his cigarette, an orange sparkler in the night. 'The way she's thrown you out without letting you explain things. As I say, it's none of my business, but speaking as one who knows...' He puts the flat of his hand to his chest. There is a gold signet ring on his pinkie finger, the letters IR engraved at the centre. 'It's a big thing to lose your family. Not something to be taken lightly, know what I mean?'

Will finds himself nodding, understanding dawning. 'So you've been through something similar?'

Ian presses his mouth into a tight line before adding, 'Wouldn't wish it on my worst enemy.'

'I'm so sorry.' Will wonders if Jen, the wife he mentioned earlier, is his second wife, but to ask feels nosy.

Ian shrugs. 'Family isn't *an important thing*. It's *every*thing.' He fixes Will briefly with his pale eyes, a sad smile forming on his mouth. 'I didn't say that, Michael J. Fox did, but it's true.'

From the weed-ridden flagstones, silence rises.

'I've looked after the kids since they were babies,' Will says into that silence. 'I changed their nappies, took them to all the baby groups. Often, I was the only bloke singing "Row Your Boat" with a dozen sleep-starved women in a dilapidated Scout hut. I pick them up from school, make their dinner, put them to bed. Jessica isn't often home by then, you see. She works in Central London, so it's hard for her to be back before eight. She pays the bills, but I've supported her all these years in a practical sense. Every time they're ill, I'm at home with them, school holidays, all of that. She's not had to think about any of it.'

'Right.' With the toe of his boot, Ian pushes at a dandelion before looking up, meeting Will's eyes once again with his clear blue gaze. 'And you're sure she's not got someone else?' He doesn't blink, even when Will hears the sharp intake of his own breath.

'I hadn't even...' he begins but has to take a moment to collect himself. 'The photographs were of me, not her. There were so many of them, it was hard to... It's the photos that finished us, not anything she's done. We were happy before. Really happy.'

'What was her name, this other woman?'

'I can't tell you that, I'm sorry.'

Ian holds up a hand. 'No offence intended.'

'None taken.' Will thinks of Margot's eyes, small as hazel-nuts, wary as an animal's. *You're a good man, William Draper. I will pay you back every penny, I promise.* 'I... I got in too deep.'

'It happens,' Ian says, stroking his smooth chin. 'Just seems a bit convenient to me. Like these photos gave her the excuse to kick you out.'

'I don't think it's like that. No. No, I don't think so. Definitely not. She was devastated. I've never seen her like that. It was awful, just... awful.'

'Gotcha.' Ian lights another cigarette. 'So, you're a full-time dad, did you say?' His tone is lighter, a return to small talk, a metaphorical step back.

Will nods. 'I'm a part-time life coach too. I used to work with Jessica – graduate training scheme at a City bank – but I couldn't hack it. Then I trained to be a teacher and did that for a bit, but the kids walked all over me, the paperwork killed me and in the end I was signed off with stress. These days I help people organise their lives, which is ironic because I've never been great at organising my own.' He gives a brief laugh. 'And now it's turned to complete shit.'

'It looks that way tonight, but you'll pull yourself up.'

'Thanks. I love my work. I barely earn anything once I've paid the rent on the premises, but I'm hoping to expand once my little boy goes to school full-time next year. So if you know anyone who needs a life coach...' He raises his eyebrows, to show that he's joking.

'Life coach.' Ian chuckles darkly, shakes his head.

Will's face grows hot. 'That probably sounds ridiculous to you.'

'Not at all. If people have the money and they need someone to sort their lives out for them, that's their prerogative.

I'm more of a practical solutions man myself. I do, therefore I am. That's your man Descartes by way of Ian Robbins.' He grins, eyebrows raised, perhaps to mirror the surprise he assumes Will is feeling at the reference.

'Descartes,' Will says. 'Didn't he say I *think*, therefore I am?'

'He did indeed, but I've always thought the thinking part can be sorted down the pub with a few mates. The rest you have to do yourself. No one else can do what you've got to do except you, if you know what I mean. No offence to you, mind.'

'I do offer practical solutions.' Will hears the defensiveness in his tone. 'It's all about practical solutions actually. But I'm being rude, I've gone straight back to me. You mentioned your family. Jen, was it? And your kids. Are they...'

'They left,' Ian offers. 'Well, she did. Took the kids with her back to Dublin.'

'I'm sorry. That must have been hard.'

He throws down his cigarette butt and grinds it underfoot with more force than is needed. 'Went back to her old ma, bless her. Lucky if I see them in the summer holidays now. That's why I'm telling you, mate. Make sure she's not pulling the wool over, yeah? I know men can be bastards, but women are clever. They're sly.'

This seems like an outrageous not to mention sexist general-isation, but Will doesn't feel in a position to argue. And there is something about Ian that prevents him, something he cannot quite name.

'I'm sorry,' he says again. 'No wonder you think life coaching is for fools.'

'I never said that. And I don't, not at all. Funny. You'll never guess what my mates call me.' He shoots Will a by-now-familiar ironic grin. 'The therapist. Which is a similar thing to you if you think about it. I listen to their problems and I help sort them out. I mean, no offence, but it's just listening, and after that, as I say, I'm all about the practicalities, solutions, what have you. A well done is better than a well said sort of thing. That's Benjamin Franklin said that. But that's all it is, isn't it? You don't get involved as such, but you suggest, what do you call them, strategies?'

I did get involved, Will thinks. I *became* the strategy. That's why I'm in this mess.

'I try to facilitate people to help themselves,' he replies after a moment. 'But yes. Essentially. I help. Try to.'

'There you go.' Ian tips his glass towards him. 'Not so different as all that then, are we?'

CHAPTER 7

JESSICA

Jessica wakes to find herself on the sofa, the television frantic with some reality TV game show. She grabs the remote and switches it off. Her phone is ringing. After Lena left, she put on the television to fill the silence and lay on the sofa because the thought of the empty bed was too awful. Fell asleep.

She picks up her phone. It's her mother.

'Mum? Everything all right?'

'I'm ringing to see if you're OK. You seemed a bit out of it earlier. In shock, I should think.'

'I'm OK. Lena stayed for a bit. We got a takeaway. Not that I ate much.'

'No, well, watch that. It's easy to stop eating, but you'll need your strength.'

A silence falls. Jessica resists the urge to ask her mum to come and stay. They could sleep in the same bed like they did for months after her father left. Jessica has always thought her mother was comforting her back then, but now, in the light of the worst day of her life, she is unsure who was comforting whom.

'It'll get harder before it gets easier,' her mother says flatly.

'Yep.'

'But I'm only round the corner. You've got Lena five minutes away. And you've got so many friends. Don't forget that.'

'It's Will who has all the friends round here,' she says.

'Not for long. You'll see. The women'll cluck round you.'

'I'm not sure about that. The school yard brings me out in hives. They see me as the enemy.'

'No they don't. Those days are gone.'

'I'm glad you think so. Whenever I pick Cassie up, I feel like an alien. Lena overheard Freya saying she didn't know why I'd bothered having children if I was going to work such long hours.'

'Wouldn't say that about a dad, would she? Judgemental twit.'

Despite herself, Jessica laughs. The way Mum says *twit*, with such relish, as if it's the worst possible insult she can think of.

'There's always a Freya,' her mother adds. 'We take no notice of the Freyas.'

'Mottos to live by.'

'Anyway, shouldn't you be in bed?'

'Is that why you're calling?'

'You might be pushing forty, but you're still my baby. I'm going to stay on the line until you convince me you're tucked in for the night.'

'All right.' Smiling to herself, Jessica heads for the stairs. 'I'm going up.'

'I can read you a bedtime story if you like.'

'I think I'm past fairy tales. I'm putting the phone on my bedside table while I get my nightie on. Stay there.'

She gets changed and picks up the phone. 'Still there?'

'No, I've gone out clubbing.'

'Mum.' Phone held between shoulder and chin, Jessica

places her suit carefully over the chair. 'The night Dad left, was that because you'd caught him in the act or because someone told you what he was up to?' She reaches underwear out of her drawer, a fresh blouse from the wardrobe, and puts them on top of the suit for the morning. Down the line, she hears her mother sigh. They've never talked about that night, not really.

'I'd known for a long time,' her mother says. 'Knew it in my gut, and besides, I'm not daft. It sounds weak, but he was so nice to have around.'

'It doesn't sound weak. You're the least weak person I know.'

'He was a good dad.'

'He was.' With a cotton pad soaked in cleanser, Jessica wipes the grime of the day from her face. After all the crying, she looks like a vole.

'But I drew the line at him buggering about on your birthday. That I couldn't forgive.'

'I didn't know that.'

A silence pushes down the line.

'Are you going to clean your teeth?' her mother asks eventually.

Jessica laughs. 'You really are putting me to bed, aren't you? Hold on.' She puts the phone on the side of the sink and cleans her teeth before carrying her mother over to the bed. 'OK, I'm literally sitting on the bed now. I promise I'll do lights out. No messing about.'

'Hmph.'

'Mum?'

'Yes?'

'Did you ever regret kicking him out?'

Mum let out a long sigh. 'No. But I missed him. I missed him every single day. And I wish...' Her mother pauses, apparently searching for the right words. 'I wish I'd kicked him out the first time. You'd have been five or so. I wish I hadn't been so quick to forgive him and lie to myself that he'd stop. Maybe if I'd given him his marching orders that first time, the shock would've brought him to his senses. But I didn't.'

'It wasn't your fault.'

'I know. But I think I pretended I didn't know because I was desperate for us to be a family. I never wanted you to catch him in the act.'

'But I did.'

'I know you did, love. That's what I'm saying.'

The hair on Jessica's arms rises. 'You knew that I'd seen him with...?'

'You told me. Don't you remember?'

'No.'

'Not in so many words, but I knew what you were trying to tell me. I knew what you'd seen. You were always such a good girl, always wanting to look after everyone. I could see you were in knots about it, not wanting to tell on your dad but not wanting to let him carry on.'

Jessica's breath shudders out of her. 'What did you say?'

'I can't really remember. I might have said your dad sometimes had friends over to the house when I was on nights. In hindsight, I don't think that was the right thing to say, but like I said, I was just trying to hold it all together. In the end, though... well, in the end, I couldn't.'

'Oh, Mum. You could. You did. I always felt safe with you.'

Her mother falls silent. Jessica hears a sniff. Her own face is running with tears.

'Those women at the school gates won't be judging you, love,' Mum says gently. 'They're all clinging on by the skin of their teeth. Even the ones who look like they've got it all under control. Especially those ones, sometimes. We're all clinging on. Just like you are. Just like I was.'

After she ends the call, Jessica stands up to draw the curtains. Outside, on the corner, towards Oxford Road, she thinks she can see someone. She peers out, scrutinising the spot. The plum tree looks too thick. It moves. Separates. A person, definitely, too far away to see in any detail, but human. Her heart quickens. The figure looks like it's watching the house; something about the position of the head, though she can't be sure. She pulls the curtains closed, moves towards the edge, peeps out from the side. The person moves, heading away from the house, as if they had been waiting for her to go to bed. Another second and they have disappeared around the corner.

Shivering, Jessica pulls on her dressing gown and gets into bed with it wrapped tightly around her. In the darkness, the day revolves in her mind – the photographs, Will, her mum, Lena, the kids, the strange figure at the end of the road – round and round, until all she can see is a grotesque carousel of faces, herself a child, looking up, holding on tight to her father's hand.

CHAPTER 8

WILL

The bell for last orders takes Will by surprise.

'Is it that time already?' Ian asks.

'That's my fault,' Will says. 'I've kept you longer than I should have. I hope you're not in the doghouse.' Too late, he remembers Ian's wife has left him but, to his relief, Ian only gives a brief laugh.

'It's all good. My mate was meant to be meeting me here, so it's more a case of Dave in the doghouse, to be honest.'

'He'll have to buy you a bunch of flowers.'

'Good job he knows I like tulips.' Ian laughs again, but Will feels his head spin and has to close his eyes momentarily while it passes. The jauntily titled Filet-O-Fish has proved an inadequate stomach lining, especially as he's drunk more tonight than he has in years. When he opens his eyes, however, Ian looks as fresh as the proverbial daisy.

'I should probably head back to the Ritz-upon-Thames.' Will hears the slight slur in his words. 'But thanks so much. Seriously.'

'What for?'

'For the company. I can't face my friends right now.'

'I was the same when Jen left. A proper hermit I was. But it'll pass.' Ian reaches out, clapping Will on the shoulder and squeezing just a little bit too hard, fixing him with those strange indigo-circled eyes. Then, thankfully, he lets go and sits back.

'Listen,' he says as Will consciously refrains from rotating his shoulder to ease it. 'I was thinking before, when you went to the gents. I've got an attic space, down on the marina. It's nothing much. I was using it for storage until recently. It's only a bedsit, but you can cook a meal in it and there's a living room area so you don't feel like you're living in your bedroom sort of thing. As I say, it's not much, but it's yours if you want it. Not long-term or anything, just while you get yourself together. A few days, a few weeks, whatever. You can give your other half some space while you both work out what to do. What d'you think?'

'That's so kind.' Will shakes his head. 'Really, though, I can't possibly. It's too much.'

Ian gives a throaty smoker's cough. 'Trust me, I know what too much is and it isn't this place. I'm telling you, it's nothing special. It's just sitting there empty, that's all. Don't thank me till you've seen it. It's along the river, not too far. I'd show it to you now but I haven't got the keys on me. I can show you tomorrow if you like. What day is it tomorrow, Friday? Yeah, I should be able to move a couple of things around.'

'I... It's really kind of you, but I—'

'It's better with someone in it than standing empty, right? I hadn't got round to putting it up for rent, so why not take it for a bit, until you know how things are going to pan out? You can get back to work, get some sort of routine going while you sort things out with...'

'Jessica.'

'Jessica. When Jen left, someone helped me out. Dave, as a matter of fact, the bloke who stood me up tonight. Someone helps you; you help someone else – that's how it works. I'm helping you. Passing it on sort of thing.'

There is something about this man that soothes Will, something solid and reassuring, whilst at the same time making him feel insubstantial.

'I suppose I—'

'Tell you what,' Ian interrupts. 'I'll put my number in your phone. Sleep on it, and if you reckon it could work, give me a bell, yeah? I know it's hard to ask for help, but you haven't asked; I've offered.'

'I don't know what to say. Thank you.' Will passes over his second-hand reconditioned iPhone 6, tries not to feel embarrassed by it. He knows without seeing Ian's phone that it will be the latest model. Not that Will knows what the latest model is.

Ian hands back the phone. 'All done. If it's a no-go, no worries. I'll see you in here sometime. If I don't, I'll know you're back home and all sorted, yeah? No pressure.'

'Thank you. That's so, so kind.'

'Keeping the world turning, that's all it is. Be good to yourself, William Draper. Take care.' Ian makes a clicking noise with his tongue, points briefly at Will and leaves.

Once he's sure that Ian has gone, Will stands up shakily. The room sways, rights itself. He grips the chair backs as he makes his way slowly through the pub, holds on to the edge of the door a moment before stepping into the night.

Outside, the rain is still holding off, the car lights still hazing over Kew Bridge. The night smells fresh. With great concentration, he finds the pedestrian crossing and almost staggers across the dual carriageway and on down to the riverside. There is a bench. He perches gingerly on it, pushing his anorak beneath him so as not to soak his jeans. A bit of air, that'll do it. A bit of air to clear the head.

Between the banks, almonds of light undulate on the dark river. The thought of nameless bodies lying in the depths flashes: bloodless corpses, fish feeding on rotting flesh, empty eye sockets. Fear fills him. He closes his eyes, locks his hands together for comfort, to in some way hold on to himself. Ian Robbins' deep, rhythmic way of talking swirls around his head, sometimes South London boy, sometimes posh gentleman; the earnest furrow of his brow, his pale blue eyes, his dapper clothes. *Not so different as all that then, are we? My mates call me the therapist.* Will's breathing lengthens, deepens. His head is heavy, big; his neck feels as thin as a matchstick.

With a jolt, he opens his eyes. He is shivering, teeth chattering. Dark polka dots are spotting his old, faded jeans. The rain has started up again. Standing, he pulls up his hood before jogging along the river, back towards the hotel. It is not until he is safe in his room that he remembers to check his phone.

Jessica has replied. Finally! Hope surges in his chest, but the moment he starts to read, it plummets into an abyss.

I've contacted a solicitor.

CHAPTER 9

JESSICA

Jessica is woken once again by the buzz of her phone. In the fuzzy half-dark, the sight of Will's smiling face on the screen makes her swear under her breath. She has spent hours staring at the ceiling worrying about the kids, worrying about the figure out on the road, worrying about keeping it all together, about ending up bitter and alone – and the moment she finally drops off, he decides to call her.

It's almost two in the morning. In light of this, the sight of her husband's face irritates her even more. What the hell is he thinking, calling her at this time? This is sabotage, pure and simple.

The phone is insistent: *bzzz, bzzz, bzzz*. The sound conflates with Will's stupid smiling face on the screen, as if he's the one making this incessant, brain-frying noise.

The buzzing stops.

Jessica thumps the pillow, lays her head down and pulls the duvet up over her shoulders. Her eyes are on stalks. Her heart bangs with anger, her guts hard, thick knots.

But a moment later, he calls again: *bzzz, bzzz, bzzz*. No

matter how tightly she presses the duvet to her head, the noise reaches her, an intermittent bee she wants to whack with a bat.

With a cry of frustration, she sits up – and picks up. 'Will? Are you hurt?' *You'd better be.*

'Yes,' he says.

'Oh my God, are you?' Panic wipes away irritation like ink from a board.

'Course 'am 'urt,' he wails. 'You kicked me oudof our home. You won' even talk t'me.'

She can practically smell the alcohol down the line. Will never could hold his liquor. He sniffs hugely. A streak of rage rises from her toes to her head.

'Will,' she says. 'I'm going to put the phone down. You cannot call me like this, you just can't. It's the middle of the night. You're drunk. Go back to wherever you're—'

'Travelodge. I'm in a fuckin' Travelodge, fucksake.'

So, she thinks. He is not at *her* place. Not yet anyway. 'Whatever. Just go to bed and sleep it off, OK?'

'You've gone nuclear.'

'Nuclear? What? What the hell are you talking about?'

'I make one mistake, one, in all the years... and you – you've gone from zero to a hundred, thass wha' you've done.'

'Zero to... what?'

'You've compledely overreacted. You wouldn' lemme speak.'

'Oh my God, really? You're the victim now, is that it?'

'I go' too close, I know tha' now, bu'—'

'Will?' She elbows herself upright, her entire head throbbing. 'You slept with a client. You had an affair over several months. Why can't you just admit that and apologise?'

'Because iss no' wha'... iss no'... Why can' you jus' truss me?' He is weeping.

'You can't ask me to trust you.' The simmering undercurrent

in her voice almost frightens her, the cold revulsion at how pathetic he sounds. 'You won't even tell me her name.'

'I can't! Why're you bein' like this? A *solicitor*? It's like you don' even wanna work things out, like you're usin' this asn excuse to kick me out so you can... You're cruel. Cruel, Jess.'

Jessica closes her eyes and focuses on keeping her breathing steady, her voice low. She will not cry, she will not. She will not shout. Her husband, who is as pissed as a newt and drowning in self-pity, has lured her into this ridiculous conversation; her husband, who possibly won't even remember this conversation tomorrow when he eventually wakes up in a nice clean hotel bed while she will be on her knees trying to make it through another day so that the sodding bills can be paid. All of this she keeps in; how, she has no idea, but she cannot, *will* not let him turn her into a shrieking banshee.

Down the line comes a sob. She waits, gives herself the time it takes to breathe in and breathe out.

'*You* hurt *me*.' It takes all of her strength to say it softly. 'Let's be clear on that. You hurt me. Not the other way round. You threw our marriage into the trash. You, not me. I'm sorry if you think I'm a little frosty, but that's to be expected, don't you think?'

My heart is broken, she wants to say. *I can't eat. I can't sleep. I can't concentrate. My whole life has been turned upside down and the one person I most want to talk to about it, my right-hand man, my soulmate, is the person responsible.*

Despite herself, she is crying, trying desperately to suppress gasps and sniffs. She will not let him hear, no way.

'You're the one in a hotel,' she adds. 'You're the one with all the head space and all the time, and now you're drunk and wallowing. Do you know what? You're a... a poor role model for our children.' A pang of regret. She makes herself stop. That's not true and she doesn't mean it, not really. 'Look, I can't do this. I can't look after you as well. Please. Give me some space.

Come over on Wednesday and see the kids. But do not call me again.' She hangs up.

A moment later, still crying, she switches off her phone. Peace. She needs peace. She is shaking with distress, her teeth chattering. She tries to get her breathing to settle. Will is a good father. He's a good father. This mantra is all that has sustained her through this longest of days, sustained any hope of them getting back together.

The threat of a solicitor was a mistake, her pain toying with her, making her lash out. Wound up tight after talking to Lena, she was trying to shock him into acknowledging how serious his breach of trust is, something he doesn't appear to realise. She's not going to go through with an actual divorce, of course she isn't, but he has to believe she's thinking about it. A marriage is nothing without trust, nothing. Only a few hours ago, her mother expressed regret at forgiving her father too quickly the first time. Jessica will not make that mistake with Will. He will have to earn his way back slowly if they're going to have any chance of building a solid future together – surely he under-stands that?

But something has shifted, a hardening within her she does not like. Will has had almost twenty-four hours to reflect, and the net result is a pathetic, drunken, self-pitying phone call at a time of night he knows is a disaster for her. The one time she picked up, he could have talked to her, could have offered an apology. She would have listened. But all he had were accusa-tions. She has overreacted. She is cruel. It is somehow her fault. *In vino veritas*, she thinks. *I got too close* – a politician's rhetoric, designed to sugar-coat the facts when what it actually did was reveal how he feels about it: namely, that he doesn't think what he's done is that bad. *I got too close, I know that now, but...* Already there was a *but*.

But what? But I didn't mean to? But it didn't mean anything?

But I loved her?

'Oh God.' She heaves, hand flying to her mouth. That Will loved this woman had not occurred to her until right this second. Tears prick. Did he? Did he love this woman, this woman who is not her? This woman who could meet in hotel rooms in the middle of the day for glasses of champagne and casual sex in crisply laundered sheets? Who wore Chanel jackets and capri pants and Dior sunglasses?

Gah.

And if this woman really was a client, why didn't she go to the office on the high street? Why all the hotels? Really, this is such a poor lie. Because that, Jessica realises as she sits snivelling in the dark, is what it so plainly is. This woman was not a client. Will is not protecting client privilege. The only thing he is protecting is himself.

Jessica. Jessica, Jessica, Jessica. How did you ever think that this childlike man was so adorable? The responsible one, the grown-up, has always been you. You're so lucky, friends would say. He's so *sweet*. He's so *nice*. And he *adores* you. He's so great with the kids. And yet here you are, the adult in the room yet again while he affords himself the luxury of dissolving in a hotel.

'Fuck you,' she whispers, biting her lip because physical pain is easier than... than this unbearable ache in her heart, her belly, her bones.

Outside, the paling sky thins the curtains. In a few hours she will have to get up – sticky-eyed, tired to the marrow, a wreck. Because of him. Sleep is a non-starter now. Thoughts loop. But as the sun rises, a decision falls. She weighs it in her obliterated heart and thinks, *Yes*. She will not let him back in the house, not until this is sorted out. He can see the kids on Wednesday, but she will not talk to him, not yet. Lena was right. Jessica will have to find ways to make things nice for the children without making it easier for him.

CHAPTER 10

WILL

For the first few moments after waking, Will has no idea where he is. He fumbles for his glasses, puts them on, and then, like a landslide, as his surroundings spring into focus, it all falls on top of him. These cold white spotlights, this boxy little room, this garish bedcover belong not to his home but to the cheapest hotel he could find. He sits up, bones protesting, head throbbing. His tongue feels like the bottom of Charlie's hamster cage. Sense is falling. Last night. Christ, how much did he have to drink?

Too much.

Ian Robbins. The South London gent. The two of them philosophising outside a pub on the A315. Something about a flat. Is that right? Him handing Ian his phone.

His phone. Where is it? Slowly, groaning, he raises himself from the bed and goes to pee. God, he feels awful, just... awful. Suspects he smells pretty rank too.

Back in the bedroom, his clothes are strewn about, his trousers on the floor; beside them, his phone, which must've fallen out of his pocket. It is dead. He plugs it into the charger before taking the miniature kettle back into the bathroom. The kettle doesn't really fit under the tap; he can only fill it part way by tilting it awkwardly. How pathetic. How utterly wretched. He is trying to make a cup of tea and even that is a trial. He is crying without tears. Even his tear ducts are shit.

He makes tea still dressed in yesterday's T-shirt and pants. The phone blooms into life. He checks the contacts, sees, as he suspected in his foggy daze, that Ian has put his number in, notes that Robbins is spelt with two Bs. He has a spare attic. *It's not much, but it's yours if you want it. Just while you get yourself together.*

Will doesn't know this man, doesn't know anything about him apart from the fact that he deals in property, and that he is the sort of person Will admires in the way that people like him, who have only had to walk the path their parents laid before them to get where they are, admire people who have hurdled many more obstacles to get to roughly the same place. Except he is not in the same place as Ian. He is in a Travelodge in Brentford, that's where he is. Ian, meanwhile, is a successful, wealthy man, generous enough to offer Will a place to stay. The mythical kindness of strangers. Yes, it is the kindest of offers but it compounds his shame, presses it down with two great hands so that he can almost feel it physically: shame for what he did, shame for not telling Jessica the truth, shame for being skint and scruffy and for finding himself here in this miserable room.

He sips his tea. It tastes of UHT milk. It tastes, he thinks, of failure. He laughs at himself. Tea cannot taste of failure, Will, you absolute fool. It tastes of crap tea.

But something else is edging into the blurry view of his mind's eye. Jessica. A conversation. An argument? He checks his calls, sees that he called her at... oh God, he called her at 2 a.m. The call lasted five minutes twenty-four seconds. He has no memory of what he said or what she said but his gut tells him it was nothing good. His thumb hovers... but no, he cannot call her again now. She will be at work, somewhere beyond furious. And rightly so. Her job is tough enough on a full night's sleep, and she will be hanging by a thread because of him. Yet again, he has managed to throw petrol on an already inflamed situation.

You're a good man, William. Margot's eyes shining with tears. Her adorable accent. The second time she came to see him, she did not come up to the office, simply handed him a card, something furtive in her manner. On it was a number written in black ink, and her name.

'I cannot come here again,' she said. 'I will text you the name of a hotel and you will come there, yes?'

'I can't do that, I'm sorry.'

'I will pay for your time, your train fare, do not worry. But I cannot come here again. It will be only once, I promise. I will explain. Please, William. Tell me yes or no.'

'I...' he began, but she was already walking away, towards a Mercedes she had parked illegally at the side of the road. She got in. The engine fired. She drove away without a glance.

Minutes later, he received a text from the number she had given him with the name of a hotel, a request for a day and a time at his convenience. Again he found himself inclined to tell her no, that was not how he worked, but something, *something* stopped him – intrigue? The sense of himself as important in some mysterious story? Or was it simply how terrified she looked even then, his impulse to help her, no matter how inconvenient? Whatever it was, he replied that Thursday afternoons worked best. He would meet her once, he told himself. Just once. Find out if and how he could help.

A reply came seconds later: *Two o'clock? I will pay for three hours.*

He frowned at the message. Three hours would compensate him for the hours he would lose. She was, if nothing else, fair. He replied: *OK. See you there.*

When he arrived at the hotel, his phone pinged. It was a message giving him a room number. He made his way up, a sense of trepidation in his chest. He reached the room – he cannot remember the number, cannot even be clear which hotel came first – and knocked softly. A moment later, the door opened a crack.

'William Draper,' she said and opened the door wider to let him in.

He walked into the room, nerves jangling. There was a double bed, a small desk with one chair. It occurred to him only then that though the arrangement was clear, he had walked into something he didn't understand.

Margot offered him coffee, which she must've had sent up, since it was on a tray – a cafetière with two cups, real milk in a jug, sugar in a bowl. She handed him a cup and told him to sit on the bed. She took the chair, brought it close to him, their knees almost touching.

'William, I am going to tell you about my life,' she said. 'And afterwards, you will tell me if you can help me.'

Her vulnerability, that's what drew him to her from the start. It is not a pretty thought, not at all who he believed himself to be, but there it is. Later, he was afraid – for her, for himself, even for his own family. But at first, he was wrapped up in her: her frailty, the pleading in her eyes, her fragile direct-ness. Margot needed him in a way...

He passes his hand over his eyes and sighs.

Margot needed him in a way Jessica did not.

There is no way he'll be getting back home any time soon. He needs to let things settle, go along with whatever Jessica says. He checks his bank account and swears under his breath. There is barely enough to cover a week even in this place. He can't take it out of the joint account; Jessica will see it immedi-ately and freak. He cannot take any more out of the ISA; it is already two thousand pounds short. If she checks that, he'll have more explaining to do.

A thought cuts through his anxiety, his hangover, a thought

so terrible his hands fly to his face and he lets out a long groan: what if Margot's story was all a lie? She could have been a grifter, siphoning money off stupid men who fell for the whole mysterious-foreign-woman-in-trouble act. Men like him. If he'd told Jessica, this is what she would've said. She would've been appalled that he could be taken in by such an obvious scam.

But Margot seemed so genuinely frightened. So grateful.

And if she was an imposter, who sent the photographs?

His breath shudders out of him. The bottom line is… well, the bottom line. He's broke. He can't ask Jessica for money. And he'd rather die than ask a mate.

A few nights in Ian's bedsit would actually be a real help. It would mean he won't have the humiliation of having to ask someone for cash. Ian said the place was just sitting there empty.

Will brings up Ian's number. It takes him a dozen attempts to get the tone right, but eventually, he writes the text.

Hi. This is Will. Bit of a sore head this morning! No worries if you've had second thoughts or if it was the beer talking, but if the offer of the attic is still on, I'd be really grateful. Only for a day or two. As I say, no worries and see you around if not. Thanks again for the chat. I was in a bad place. Will.

CHAPTER 11

JESSICA

The next day, Jessica is so tired and upset she cannot function. Her boss is in New York, so she slips away after lunch and heads to the school to surprise Cassie. On the way, she texts Lena to let her know, and a moment later, Lena replies to say she'll go to the house to take over from Pat.

My team, Jessica thinks, with a surge of gratitude.

At the gates, she steels herself. Head high. Shoulders back. Sunglasses on. It will be OK.

Although there are a few men milling about, it is mostly women in the playground. Sports leggings and trainers, trench coats and baseball caps. Some mothers push buggies, some dangle small children from their hands, call after toddlers who run too far away. Well-cut salon-highlighted hair abounds. The women chat and laugh together in little groups.

Behind her sunglasses, Jessica hides what is now an almost constant urge to cry, aware that her dark business clothes make her stick out like a sore thumb. Her coat, which is perfect for chilly mornings and evenings, is too hot for the warm September afternoon. A line of sweat runs down her back. She watches the women, trying to figure out if they're actually friends or just being hysterically polite. Could one of them have sent those photos? She doesn't know any of them, but Will does, has been to their houses and shared chit-chat over tea or wine in their back gardens. All very cosy. Could one of them have had some sort of crush on him, somehow got her number from his phone? Maybe one of them is married to a man who never comes home. Bored and lonely, she went to see Will for some life coaching. Finding a man who would actually listen to her, she developed feelings for him, obsessive feelings that spiralled into a kind of madness.

Maybe.

A woman she vaguely recognises is heading towards her. As she passes through the crowd, she says hello to everyone, smiling, laughing, but not stopping. She is very slim, perhaps a little too slim, dressed in a seventies-style shirt and a brightly coloured silk headscarf. There is something funky and natural about her that splits Jessica in two. Half of her is jealous, the other half attracted. She racks her brains for the woman's name, tries to think how she knows her.

As the woman reaches her, Jessica braces herself for the inevitable *Not often we see you here*, the excruciating *I'm sorry, are you here to pick up a child?*

'Jessica,' the woman says. 'Good to see you.' She smiles and, to Jessica's surprise, gives her a one-armed hug – affectionate without being invasive. 'Haven't seen you since the Angel Gabriel debacle.'

It falls into place. Cassie's Christmas play, the poor kid who fell off the back of the stage during his big moment, the loud bang followed by some pretty violent crying. Jessica had become aware of this woman's shoulders shaking with suppressed mirth and had found herself giggling too, the two of them holding in snorts like naughty schoolgirls laughing at something forbidden.

'I had the afternoon off,' Jessica says, still trying to remember the woman's name.

'Cool. Nice day for it.' The woman doesn't sound like she has any inkling of what is happening with Will – why would she? Barely twenty-four hours has passed. News won't have travelled that quickly, not even here.

At the doorway to the infants' building, Jessica spots a couple of young teachers. The children, half hidden inside the school corridor, look like a boiling vat.

Penny. The woman's name is Penny. Jessica breathes an internal sigh of relief. Penny, yes. Definitely.

'Here they come,' Penny says. 'Brace yourself.'

Jessica looks about her. The other mothers are digging out muesli bars, packets of Mini Cheddars, chocolate raisins, fruit.

'Fuck,' she says, glancing at Penny, who laughs. 'Sorry. Shouldn't swear, should I?'

'I love swearing,' Penny replies. 'Keeps me warm at night.'

Jessica laughs. 'I haven't brought any snacks.'

'That's it. You'll be tried for failure to provide for a minor. Here.' Penny digs in her tote and pulls out a bag of apples. 'Have one of these.'

'Really?' Jessica is touched by this act of solidarity. It occurs to her that Penny might even have come over because she saw her standing on her own. 'Cheers, that's really kind.'

'No worries.'

By now the kids are filing out, bright in their red uniforms, their little white socks, all of them straining to spot their babysitters, carers, parents.

'Listen,' Penny says, 'before the tsunami, is your number on the contacts list?'

Jessica tries not to bristle. 'Ah, no. That'll be Will's. My husband. He's their main carer.'

'I only ask because me and a few of the other mums are

going for a drink next week if you fancy coming. They're a pretty good laugh. Only if you fancy.'

Jessica feels heat rise to her face. 'I don't really know anyone. Sorry. I mean... Do you work? Sorry. Sorry, I don't know why I said that.'

But Penny only laughs, shading her eyes with her hand. 'I do. The school gates are a shocker. First time I came to pick the kids up, I felt like a pariah. First coffee morning I spent ten minutes in my car crying, actually crying. I had to call my friend so she could counsel me into going in.'

Jessica gets it, totally. 'What were you afraid of?'

'Being judged! But it's not like that, don't worry. Most of them don't bite. I'd never even been here until three months ago.' Penny touches her headscarf. 'I'm over the worst, but I'm still on leave. Breast cancer. Absolute bastard.'

'Oh God.' Jessica feels like she's been kicked in the chest. 'That's shit. I'm so sorry.'

'Thanks. Thanks for saying it's shit. Really. It is, but I'll be back at work soon hopefully. Anyway.' She glances over towards the school. 'My number's on the contacts list. Penny Lane. Don't even go there. Scouse parents with a hilarious sense of humour. Text me if you want to come, or even if you just want to grab a coffee sometime.' She waves at the line of kids. 'Oop! That's mine.' She rests her hand on Jessica's arm for a second. 'See you later.'

Jessica watches Penny scoop up a cute little boy with black hair, something like excitement fluttering in her belly, before she turns to search out Cassie. She is there, jumping up and down and pointing at her. Jessica waves, love rising hot into her cheeks.

'Jessica! Oh my God, hi!'

She turns to see Freya, head cocked to one side, and feels her insides drop.

'Hi,' she says.

'Not seen you here for a long time. What's the occasion?'

Instant hate fires in Jessica's chest. 'Oh, just, you know...' Hardly eloquent, but better than fuck off, she supposes.

'That's my mummy,' she hears Cassie cry.

'Sorry,' Jessica says to Freya as the teacher nods her permission. 'That's Cassie.' She keeps her eyes on her daughter, pretends not to hear Freya suggest they grab coffee soon.

Cassie runs towards her, unbridled joy on her face. A moment later, she thumps into her with the force of a train and throws her arms around her.

'Mummy,' she says, breathless. 'Are you here because Daddy's gone?'

Once the kids have gone upstairs to play, Jessica offloads to Lena about Cassie announcing to *Freya* of all people that Will had left home. 'I can't believe he told the kids.'

'Did you ask him not to?'

'I can't remember. But you'd think it was obvious, wouldn't you? I can't believe he's done that. I'm trying so hard to protect them and he goes and blurts it out, probably trying to get them to feel sorry for him. There's no need to tell them anything at all! He could be back here in a week. And Freya'll be on the phone by now, probably fired it off into the WhatsApp group, barely able to keep her glee from showing.' Jessica sighs heavily.

Lena gives a little shrug. 'Who cares what Freya's doing? It's not your shame, it's his, and they'll all find out sooner or later. Anyone half decent will help you out. Most people have bigger things to worry about.'

'S'pose,' Jessica says, shrugging off the slightly barbed comment. She thinks of Penny, how lovely she was; of her mother's comment that most women were just clinging on.

It is only when the kids are in bed and they're about to head into the living room with the wine that Lena has brought round that Jessica takes in her friend's appearance.

'You look amazing, by the way,' she says. 'Have you had your hair done? New clothes? Lost weight?'

'All of the above.' Lena grins, her pale complexion pinking. 'I've had a glow-up.'

'Well, you look fab.' Jessica is about to open the bottle, but she knows without so much as smelling it that she cannot drink one drop. Her stomach feels raw. Everything feels raw. She can't believe Will told the kids.

'I'm sorry,' she says. 'I don't think I can manage any wine tonight.'

'Oh, don't worry. I only brought this as an in-case-of-emergency-break-glass option.'

'That's so thoughtful. You can take it home with you.'

'Stick it in your fridge, babe. I'm sure we'll drink it at some point.'

They share a smile. But something flickers across Lena's face.

'What?' Jessica asks. 'What's the matter?'

'Nothing.' Lena looks away.

'Lena?'

She hesitates. 'I need to tell you something.'

'OK.' Jessica's stomach flips. Her nerves are so close to the surface they are tingling at her skin.

'Let's get a cuppa first,' Lena says.

'OK. I'll make it. You go through.'

Alone in the kitchen, Jessica makes the tea, shoulders tight. What on earth does Lena have to tell her? What else can there be? What is this, hell week?

When Jessica enters the living room, Lena is sitting on the sofa biting her thumbnail. She looks up and smiles nervously. Nerves jangling, Jessica breaks eye contact, puts the two mugs

of tea and a plate of biscuits on the coffee table and sits opposite
her friend.

'So?'

Lena closes her eyes a moment before opening them again.
Jessica tries not to shout at her to get on with it.

'You know when you showed me those photos of Will with
that woman?'

Jessica nods. Thinks: *What other photos would they be?*

Lena sighs. 'I should have said something yesterday, but...

'But what?'

'I've seen Will with her. That woman.'

'*What?*' Jessica shoots out of her seat. 'When? Where?'

Lena holds up her hands. 'In town. I'm sorry. I should've
said.'

Jessica's face burns. 'Why didn't you *tell* me?'

'Because... because I couldn't be sure there was anything
dodgy going on. I had a feeling. The way they were talking to
one another was very... intense. But they weren't holding hands
or anything, you know, concrete, so I just thought it was none of
my business. But I knew.' She makes a fist at her belly. 'In here, I
knew.'

'Oh my God, Lena.' Jessica's voice is so quiet as to be almost
a whisper. 'You should've told me.' But even as she says it, she
knows exactly why her friend didn't.

Lena looks pained. 'I didn't think it was right to say something unless I knew for sure. I did follow them – to Tottenham
Court Road Tube station.'

'And?'

'They hugged. He went up Oxford Street and she went into
the Tube.'

'They hugged?'

'Yes, but it wasn't like a sexy hug or anything. I mean, I
couldn't tell. There were loads of people and I couldn't see

them clearly. It could have just been a friend. An old friend or his cousin or something, you know? It wasn't for me to—'

'It's OK. I get it.'

Lena's eyes fill with tears. 'That's such a relief. I'm sorry I didn't tell you last night, but you were in such a state, I didn't know what to do. I figured it wouldn't make any difference if I left it till you were stronger.'

'I understand,' Jessica says, despite her misgivings and despite not really feeling any stronger. 'I don't know what I would've done if I'd seen...' She peters out. She cannot use the example of seeing Lena's husband or partner with another woman because Lena is not married and does not have a partner, just a rather disastrous and ever-lengthening list of exciting but unsuitable exes.

'I didn't know what to do,' Lena says. 'It makes me so cross now to think about it. I could have saved you all this if you'd known sooner.'

'I don't know what difference it would've made. I confronted him with it and he tried to duck out of it, and all he's done since is get drunk and moan like a baby.' Jessica sighs. 'It's so depressing. If he'd just come clean in the first place, we could've tried to find a way through it, but now... oh, I don't know.'

'For what it's worth,' Lena says after a moment, 'I think once a cheat, always a cheat.'

'Well I'm not sure I'd...' Inevitably, Jessica thinks again of her father, of her uni counsellor. *Girl with daddy issues picks a wrong 'un.* Is this another cliché she's fallen into?

'He's got a cheek, if you ask me,' Lena is saying. 'Look at you! Beautiful, clever, successful. How dare he? Who the hell does he think he is?' Her face is flushed, the heat climbing her neck like pink ivy.

'I suppose he might have felt lonely. I do work long hours. Weekends sometimes. He has friends, but friends aren't the same, are they? He wanted me. He wanted me and I wasn't here.'

'What is this, the 1950s? I know loads of blokes who work all the hours, and I know him, remember? Getting him to go to the cinema or even out for a walk was like pushing an elephant uphill. I'd be like, come on! Move it, will ya?'

Jessica giggles. It is not the first time Lena has mined her brief fling with Will to make Jessica laugh. She loves her for trying.

'He might be free again soon,' she jokes, 'if you want him back.'

'Er – no thanks!' Lena laughs. 'Aw, he's all right, but sometimes I used to wonder how far that went, you know? That whole Mr Nice Guy shtick while somehow getting everyone else to run around for him, take care of him. I mean, when I look at you, out there keeping it all together while he slobs around like the cat that got the cream... No offence. But at the same time, I always thought, well, at least he *stays*, you know?' Lena looks down at her lap, presumably contemplating the ones – the many – who did not stay for her. 'But now,' she adds, recovering, 'I don't know what to think. If a slob like Will can do this, what hope is there for any of us?'

Jessica feels herself prickle. 'I wouldn't call him a *slob*. He would just rather use the money to buy the kids shoes, and kids' shoes cost a bloody fortune. I prefer that to some twat who rolls around town in all the gear like he's Jay-Z or someone. OK, yes, he wears those bloody awful joggers, but it's so he can take the kids to the park without getting his decent clothes dirty. I guess over the years he's forgotten he even has any decent clothes. It's all about the kids with Will.' Tears sting. She blinks over and over, fighting not to let them spill. 'Maybe I should be the one in a Travelodge. I can't be there for the kids like he is.'

'For God's sake, you need to get out of that time capsule, girlfriend.' Lena wags her finger and wobbles her head, in imitation of a sassy woman on a daytime panel show. 'Working mums are the best role models.'

Jessica coughs. 'I don't think we should pit mum against mum. We're all just doing our best, aren't we? Clinging on?'

'But what about Cassie? Don't you want her to see how kickass women can be? So you work! So what? You're devoted to those kids, every bit as much as him, and if you were a bloke, everyone would say, look at him, how hard he works for his family. You barely go out; you spend all weekend with them. Have you even got a social life?'

'You're my social life.' Jessica pulls a face, making Lena laugh.

The shared joke punctures the tension. A good thing; Jessica doesn't want to end up as she did last night – riled up, eyes popping.

'What I'm trying to get to,' she adds after they have both taken a reflective sip of their tea, 'is that maybe I'm focusing too much on my own hurt when I should be thinking of the kids. I mean, I think about nothing *but* the kids, but I've got to keep them out it, whatever happens. Maybe... maybe *I'm* too hurt and angry right now to make any real decisions.'

'No, babe. It's like you said, there's no coming back from this. He cheated on you over months. Months! It was an actual relationship.' Lena's mouth stretches around the words *actual* and *relationship*. 'And this is *your* house! You bought it. You had to buy it, didn't you, because he was' – she makes air quotes – '"changing careers". *Again*. If you ask me, he's been sponging off you for too long. What has he ever done, exactly?'

'He made a sarcophagus out of a cereal packet last week for Cassie's Egypt project. She was beside herself with excitement.' Jessica's eyes fill.

'I know. I know, babe. I get it. I'm just saying he has an easy ride, that's all. Compared to you. He swans about, going for his cheeky wine sundowners with the yummy mummies. And I know from when I pick the kids up that most of those women think he's a legend just for turning up. It does my head in. It's like, when men do the smallest thing, things that women do all the time, they're gods, aren't they? It's like he wants it all but he doesn't want to work for it, you know?'

'I'm not sure that's fair.'

'That's because you're too nice, my love. I didn't want to say anything, but I was talking to one of the mums the other week who said he's actually quite flirty. It's like he's been pushing on doors, waiting for one to open. And obviously one did.' Lena purses her lips. 'It just makes me so angry for you.'

Jessica edges forward. 'Hang on. Someone said that? Which mum?'

Lena shrugs. 'Dunno. Blonde bob. Peaked cap, activewear and, like, one of those belted macs?'

'Oh, that narrows it down.'

Once again the tension breaks as they share a laugh. But it is only a moment before Jessica's mind circles back, and back: to her father, to herself, to her husband.

'I'm not going to find myself on the wrong end of a MeToo campaign, am I?'

'It was just flirting, I think. Vibing, you know, by the sounds of it.'

Jessica's head feels like it's going to explode. 'So Will's basically a lech. He's had or is having an affair and he comes on to the other mums. I don't know how much more of this I can take. Maybe I *should* contact a solicitor.'

'I would. Find out what your rights are at least. Hopefully he won't fight you for the kids. Surely he can't take them off you, not after what he's done? I can pick Cass and Charlie up and give them their dinner while you get a childminder or whatever organised, it's no bother. And if I can't do it, your mum'll help. You don't need him, babe. You have options.'

'Thank you, love, but no, it's too much.'

'It's really not. I am their official godmother after all.' Lena's eyes are wet. It's as if she's pleading for a favour rather than offering a life raft.

'You really are a saint,' Jessica says after a moment, a little choked. 'It would only be for a week or two while I get myself sorted. That's amazing, Lene. Really. *You're* amazing.'

But Lena shrugs it off. 'I just think,' she says, 'the sooner you cut that man out of your life, the better.'

CHAPTER 12

WILL

A little after 2 p.m., Will arrives at the Black Hound. It is another trendy pub, this time at Brentford Dock, with dark floorboards, mismatched chairs and cask ales. There is a faint smell of stale alcohol, of new plaster. There are only two customers, both men, sitting by the window, the afternoon sun brightening their amber glasses on the shining wooden table.

Will is about to order a pint of lager by way of hair of the dog when Ian Robbins walks in. He is wearing a petrol-blue suit with a slight sheen and a sky-blue shirt. He looks, as last night, the epitome of understated elegance, though this time more formal, professional. And also as last night, Will feels acutely his own scruffiness, despite the fact that he is wearing the newest jeans he owns and a bottle-green hoodie he's pretty sure is clean.

With a nod of acknowledgement, Ian walks towards him, taking off his expensive-looking shades as he does so and slipping them into his inside pocket. Of a hangover, there is no sign – no red eyes, no sweaty pallor, just the same groomed, close-shaved appearance. The familiar smell of woody eau de cologne reaches Will before Ian does.

'Still suffering?' Ian asks with a lupine grin.

'Hanging by a thread.' Will stops himself from adding *mate*, but only just.

'What're you having?'

'No, let me. Solaris?'

'Coffee, thanks. Double espresso with hot milk on the side, if you please, sir.'

'Sure,' Will replies, now utterly at a loss as to what he himself wants. A coffee would, he fears, make him feel grim. Or worse, puke.

Ian gestures to the young woman at the bar, whose hair is dyed dark pink with two inches of black roots. 'Tiff, can you do us a Bloody Mary for this gentleman? Cheers, babe.'

The woman – Tiff – has already sprang into action, as if Ian is more than a punter, as if she has to be on her toes for him. Will wonders if he perhaps owns this place, whether 'property' extends to pubs. He can't think of how to ask, however, so says nothing – about this or about the Bloody Mary Ian has ordered for him without asking if it's what he wants.

'So,' Ian says but adds nothing more.

'I hope I wasn't talking nonsense last night,' Will offers, to fill the space. 'I can't remember a lot of what I said. I think I was in a state of shock.'

'Like I said, I've been through it and it's not for wimps.' Ian smiles flatly.

'Didn't Bette Davis say that about ageing?'

'That's not for wimps either. Still, not much to it. You just have to live long enough.' Ian raises his eyebrows. 'Groucho Marx.'

'I haven't heard that one. And was it George Burns who, when asked how it felt to be ninety, replied, "Compared to the alternative, pretty good"?'

Ian points at him and grins.

Will is still feeling pleased to have achieved decent banter whilst simultaneously knowing this is pathetic when Ian says: 'It wasn't George Burns actually. It was W. C. Fields. Although some say it was Jimmy Carter.'

With a soft clink of china, the coffee announces itself: a small white cup and saucer, a small jug of foamed milk and a white ramekin of sugar sachets on a circular black tray. Tiff returns a moment later with Will's Bloody Mary, also on a tray: a tall tumbler of thick tomato juice with a stick of celery, a bottle of Tabasco, another of Worcester sauce, two lemon wedges on a doll's-house-sized plate and a ramekin of salt and pepper sachets. Will can't remember having ever seen two more complicated drinks. He hands her his debit card.

'Take one for yourself,' Ian calls after her before meeting Will's eye. 'Don't mind, do you?'

'Of course not,' Will replies. 'You – er – beat me to it.' Never, not once in his life, has he told a bartender to take one for themselves.

'They call it the Brentford Marina,' Ian says once they've taken their seats, nodding to the river view outside the window. 'Used to be just the dock, you know, back in the day. Huge developments going up now. For the yuppies.' He grins at Will.

'Not me. I'd never be able to afford one of these apartments.'

'Maybe not. Nearer to Kew Bridge you've got your penthouses and all sorts, all mod cons, glass. Very tasteful. Beautiful if you like that sort of thing.' Ian adds half the milk to his coffee, carefully, so it makes a white circle in the toffee-coloured crema, a perfect tiny cappuccino.

'Do you miss how it was? Round here, I mean?'

He sips daintily, then places the cup carefully back in its saucer. 'People get all nostalgic about these things, but where I grew up was what you might call a shithole. Gentrification has its advantages. Take this place. Used to be a dive. Now you can order a coffee, and they put it on a tray and give you a little black serviette – sorry, napkin.'

Unsure whether to laugh or frown, Will goes with, 'Right.'

'And of course, where you've got modernisation, you've got spending power. Investment. You've got your pubs like this, which instead of getting boarded up get refurbed to how the people with disposable income want them. I'm not saying I like these identikit places with their grey walls and their arty pictures, but it's better than a smelly carpet that's been soaking up piss and ale for twenty years, know what I mean? And then you need your builders, your plumbers, your painter-decorators. Jobs. The world turns. Some call it capitalism, but I call it making sure everyone gets a piece. Unless you're one of these oligarchs who buys up ten properties and leaves them empty. What good does that do?'

'None,' Will says. 'None whatsoever.'

'You're not an oligarch, are you?' Ian grins.

'I don't think so. I feel like I'd know if I was.'

The feeling Will had last night returns: that he is talking to his father or a much older, much more powerful man. But also a kind man. Caught between wariness and attraction, he has the sense of being on his best behaviour. On a purely instinctive level, Ian is someone he doesn't want to cross. On a practical level, this man has offered him a home for a few days, maybe even a few weeks. And there is no way around the fact: Will is currently homeless. So he drinks his vodka and tomato juice like a good boy. He licks his lips. Feels better already.

Ian, he thinks, makes everything better.

The flat is neither an attic nor a bedsit. It is a first-floor one-bedroom apartment in an older brick block overlooking the water. Nor is it as run-down as Will had expected it to be. Quite the opposite.

'In good decorative order throughout, as the estate agents say,' Ian says in the tongue-in-cheek way Will is getting used to.

'With— no, not with; *boasting* fine views over the Brent River and good transport links into Central London.' He gives a slow wave across the view, his signet ring buttery yellow in the sunlight.

'It's so much bigger than I thought it would be.'

'It's bigger than I remember, to be honest. Dave's used it more than I have, and knowing Dave, the less I know about that the better.'

Ignoring the comment, Will follows Ian into a neat galley kitchen with glossy white units, gleaming chrome taps and what look like high-end white Corian work surfaces. They are the kind of kitchen fittings Jessica would love.

'I'd forgotten I got Dave to fix the place up,' Ian says, opening cupboards at random, peering inside the oven, while Will digests the fact that it's possible to forget you funded what must have been at least fifty grand's worth of refurbishment, more than he could spend on his own house let alone on one of myriad properties.

'This kitchen's brand new, pretty much,' Ian continues, inspecting the fittings as he goes. 'Dave's niece lived here for a few months last year, but apart from that...'

Will follows him into the living room, which is painted a neutral stone colour. Grey-washed wide wooden planks stripe the floor around a tasteful vintage-effect rug. There are two small dark grey sofas. Ian grips the back of one and pushes it so hard his knuckles whiten. 'I think this one is a sofa bed, so if you need to have the kids over, you'll be OK. I can get Dave to bring round extra bedding and a few more bits for the kitchen.'

'Oh no, I—'

'Don't worry about it. It's what I do. We've got tons of this stuff in the lock-up.'

'I do have sleeping bags for the kids. From our camping holidays.'

Ian narrows his eyes, scrutinising Will as if to figure out whether he's joking. 'What, like, an actual holiday in a tent?'

Defensiveness scuttles up the back of Will's neck. 'I had a career change, as I said... family of four, London mortgage. Holidays can get quite... I mean, it's only while they're little, you know, and they love it. They love the freedom of it.'

'If you say so.'

Will feels vaguely dismissed, but before he can reply, Ian is asking him what he thinks of the flat.

'It's amazing,' he reiterates. 'Really, truly amazing. But I have to pay something. You can't—'

Ian shakes his head. 'I don't need the paperwork, and as I said, you'll pass it on to someone else one day. You can bring your stuff over later or tomorrow, whatever works. I'll make sure Dave calls round before...' He checks his Apple Watch. 'It'll be before ten, I reckon. If that's not too late? I mean, you can think about it if you like, but what is there to think about?'

Will can't stop nodding. 'I'm sure it will only be for a few days. Really, though, this is amazing. I'll never be able to thank you enough.'

CHAPTER 13

JESSICA

Every night before she goes to bed, Jessica checks the spot at the end of the crescent, but there is no one there. On Monday and Tuesday, she has the impression she is being followed from the station, but on both occasions when she turns around, there is no one. On Tuesday night, as she is preparing to go to bed, she glances at the street from her bedroom window. This time, the figure has returned. Heart hammering, she runs downstairs, out into the crescent, squinting into the hazy evening. She runs all the way to the corner, but the figure is gone. He is not on Oxford Road, not on any of the front paths. Too scared to run any further from the house, she jogs back, finds herself, in her pyjamas, barefoot and shivering, arms wrapped around her waist, turning slow circles, looking for a figure in the shadows. The neighbours' curtains are closed. Lights make yellow stripes in blinds, hint at lives going on behind. There is no one out here, and yet she saw someone, she knows she did.

She wonders which is worse: someone watching the house, or imagining someone watching the house.

'Jessica?'

She turns towards the voice, sees a bright headscarf, a

particular way of walking she wouldn't be able to describe but recognises immediately. 'Penny? Is that you?'

'Hi.' Penny comes to a stop in front of her. 'Sorry, I forgot your house number. I was just about to ring next door when I saw you.' She smiles, as if her being outside Jessica's house at ten o'clock at night is completely normal.

'What are you...' Jessica begins, her chest tightening with unease. 'I mean, what...'

'What am I doing loitering outside your house? It's how I make all my friends.' Penny laughs, making Jessica laugh too. It feels like someone letting air out of a tyre, but as the laughter dies, the feeling of tension returns. Really, though, what is this woman doing here? Was she watching the house?

'Did you want to speak to me?' Jessica asks.

'Sorry. I know it's late. You're in your pyjamas, argh. Sorry, my body clock's all over the place.'

'Are you OK? Do you want to come in?' In truth, Jessica really wants to go to bed, but the weirdness will only increase if they continue to stand out here in the dark, and besides, her feet are going numb with cold.

'God, no.' Penny waves a dismissive hand. 'It's way too late. I wouldn't do that to you, don't worry. I'm sorry to rock up so late, but the evening ran away with me and I just thought, if I don't pop over now, I never will. I really just wanted to say I'm sorry to hear about you and Will.'

'You know about... Who told you?'

'I know it's none of my business, but when I was ill, I really noticed who checked in and who didn't, and I just wanted to...' She throws out her hands. 'I'm not here to rubberneck, but if you need help with Cassie or a chat or whatever... I couldn't remember if I'd given you my number.' She digs in her pocket, produces a slip of card. 'I was going to post this through your door, that's all.' She hands it over.

'Thank you,' is all Jessica can manage. She turns the card

over in her hand. It is a torn segment of a birthday card with a number and the message: *Give me a shout if you want to go for that drink or whatever. Penny L.* She stares at the words, but all she can think about is that the news is out. She thought it might be, thanks to Will and his inability to keep his mouth shut, to Freya's vampiric love of gossip, but the fact of it is undeniable now. She doesn't even know Penny, not really. Which means everyone knows.

'I'm sorry,' Penny says. 'I didn't mean...'

'No, it's OK. Can I ask – what have you heard?'

She shrugs. 'Nothing really.'

Jessica doubts this is true. 'Please. Look, are you sure you don't want to step inside a moment? I'm freezing.'

'OK.'

A little warily, Jessica leads Penny into the house, and they sit down in the living room. She doesn't offer coffee or tea or anything stronger. She has to find out what Penny knows, but she also has to get some sleep.

'You look tired,' Penny says, but her voice is tender. Her headscarf is a different one from the other day – sage and orange, beautiful. She has no make-up on. Her face is drawn and pale.

'I look like shit,' Jessica says.

'I don't think you could look like shit if you tried. I look like shit gone cold, not to be competitive.' Penny gives a crazed smile. 'Listen, I really was sorry to hear, that's all. I'm sorry if I've invaded your space. I didn't mean to, but I feel like I have.' Her face colours and Jessica feels for her, tries not to worry about the figure on the corner, the strangeness of finding this woman outside her house at ten o'clock at night.

'Were you standing on the corner before?'

Penny frowns. 'When?'

'About five minutes ago. Someone was standing there. Did you see anyone?'

She shakes her head. 'No, sorry. I was trying to read the house numbers. I wasn't really—'

'It's fine. Forget it. Just tell me what you've heard. I want to know what people are saying.'

'If they are saying things, they wouldn't say them to me. I can't stand gossip.'

'OK.' Jessica waits.

After a moment, Penny sighs. 'Freya put something on the parents' WhatsApp.' She pulls out her phone and reads: *Don't know if you've heard but Will and Jessica have split up. So sad.*

'Split up? We haven't split up! There is no split!' Typical Freya: adding two plus two and getting five. God, she must have loved being *she who imparts privileged information.* Jessica suppresses the urge to scream.

Penny is visibly cringing. 'As I say, I'm not here to... I just wanted you to know that I only live round the corner and am currently spending a lot of time watching *Loose Women* and eating Maltesers.' She meets Jessica's eye, her smile full of embarrassment, apology.

'There's no split,' Jessica says again, a little more sharply than she meant to. 'We just need a bit of space, that's all. Fucking Freya.'

'She was all over me when I first got diagnosed – lasagnes and chicken casseroles, you name it. I didn't want chicken casserole. I wanted someone to tell me a dirty joke. I had to tell her to stop in the end; my freezer couldn't take any more. I said it nicely, but she got all offended, and next thing I was getting the side-eye from the coven. It was so stressful.'

'Sounds horrendous.'

'It was. And I know I've turned up at an odd time like a total weirdo, but my number is there and I'm around.' She stands up.

'Well, thanks. And thanks for coming over.' Jessica gets to her feet to show her out.

On the front step, Penny stops. 'Listen, I don't know anything and I don't need to know, but check your bank account if you haven't already. I only say that because a woman from work's ex cleaned her out and disappeared off the face of the earth. They weren't married, but...'

'Oh, don't worry,' Jessica says, stifling a yawn. 'Will doesn't know one end of a banking app from the other.'

On Wednesday, Jessica wakes with a feeling of dread. She is not at all sure she can face Will later. She expected to feel better, but he has not been in touch other than to speak with the children. Which is exactly what she asked of him. But still.

At quarter to four, she almost texts Penny. In the end, she doesn't. It is too soon to get close to anyone new. If they go for a drink, the alcohol will loosen her tongue, and as funny and kooky as Penny is, Jessica doesn't know if she can trust her. She remembers what Penny said as she left, some bizarre advice about checking her bank account. It has been a kind of low rumble in her subconscious all day. How Will managed to pay for the fancy hotels was, after all, her first thought before she assumed that Madame X must have paid.

But maybe she didn't.

She checks the joint account. She goes back, back again, back a little more. There are the usual payments: Cassie's football club, the supermarket, Charlie's nursery fees. Starbucks, Starbucks, Starbucks – these little debits irritate her despite herself; they should have come out of his account, not the joint one. Petty, she thinks. Stop it.

Further back are a couple of cash withdrawals for £200 each, a payment of £47.50 to a florist. Flowers. Jessica cannot remember Will giving her flowers. And what did he need two hundred in cash for?

Blood thrumming in her temples, she checks the ISA. She

doesn't think Will even knows the password, but then she doesn't really know *him*, does she? Not any more.

And there it is. She suppresses a gasp, hand flying to her mouth. A little under a year ago, there is a withdrawal of £2,000.

'What?' Her heart is hammering. 'What the *hell*?'

Lena. She needs to talk to Lena. This morning Lena texted to suggest they go to the pub later, kindly anticipating that Jessica would need somewhere to be while Will visits the kids. Lena she can trust, one hundred per cent. She finds the text and replies. *Pub later great. The Fox? 7?*

Lena's response is immediate. *Great. Make sure you look hot. Give him something to think about x*

Jessica tries to settle to her work but finds she cannot. Her mind is all over the place. The affair, Will's flirtations, payments for flowers, cash, and now two thousand pounds from the ISA. They were saving for a new kitchen! Where has the money gone? He's had ample opportunity to tell her, so why hasn't he?

It's all too much. Her head cannot contain it, feels like it's going to explode. Unable to focus, she pulls up a blank Word document and types, hoping the act of writing will help her to articulate how she feels, if only to herself.

Dear Will,

Thank you for respecting my wishes and not contacting me this last difficult week. I needed time to think. It has come to my attention, however, that in addition to the affair, you have made cash withdrawals from the joint account and a large withdrawal from our ISA, without my knowledge, and that you have told the children that we are no longer together. I cannot begin to express my anger and disappointment. I have no real idea how to put any of this down in words. What are the words?

She looks up, checks that no one can see her crying through the glass panels of her office. She pushes her tears into her hair and continues.

I have worked so hard to build a life with you, but for the last few years, my feeling is that your heart hasn't always been in it. It is a feeling I have chosen to ignore, but now I know why I felt it. You let me believe everything was OK. You continued to take everything I had to offer, all the time knowing your affections lay elsewhere. You took my money and used it to pay for the object of these affections. I didn't ask you not to tell the kids, but I would have thought, in the interests of us working things out, that it would have been obvious. You know how difficult things were for me growing up. You know how hard it was for me to trust and how I finally found trust in you. You have destroyed that trust and part of me with it.

My belief is that I can never feel safe with you ever again. That's why I will be filing for divorce. I wanted to be clear and to give you fair warning. I wish to have custody of the children and to keep the house.

Don't fight me on this. Don't damage me more than you have already. Let's do what's right for our children and try and keep them out of it.

For the record, I am deeply sad that things have ended this way. I loved you so much.

Jessica

She sits back, weeping uncontrollably now. The letter is so cold, so far from who she is, but if she even starts to try and tell him how she really feels, she will break.

In her desk drawer, she finds a packet of tissues, pulls out two and presses one to each eye. Her body shudders with sobs. It is all she can do to stop herself from wailing. Only the fact that someone might hear makes her stifle her devastation. She never wanted this. She thought there was a way back. But there has been too much betrayal, too much dishonesty. She can never trust him now. And without trust, for her there is nothing worth saving.

Later, at home, brittle as blown glass and nursing a mug of tea, she waits for the kids to call her upstairs for bath time. She has rearranged their routine so that if she scoots in by seven, she can give them their bath and read to them. In the evenings, without Will here, she can catch up on her work.

As is her habit now, she wanders to the window and checks the corner of the street. There is no one there, only the thin silhouette of the plum tree. But then both times she saw the figure, it was nearer ten at night. The time Penny appeared yesterday. She denied it, but could the figure last night have been her, building up the courage to come and say hello? It can't have been Penny last week, though, can it? Last week was too early for the news to have spread.

Someone else then. But who?

'Mummy!' Cassie breaks into her thoughts. 'Charlie's trying to get in the bath on his own! He's not waiting!'

'Coming!'

Leaving her mug on the windowsill, she fills her lungs and breathes out. She repeats this twice more before arranging her face in a mask of good cheer and heading up to the kids.

'Hey, hey, hey!' The sight of them, their little bodies, Charlie's chubby hands gripping the side of the bath, his expression of anticipation, waiting for permission to climb in, moves her beyond words. 'Look at you two,' she says, her voice wobbly, 'all ready to go! How brilliant is that? Shall I test the water?' She checks the temperature – not too hot. The water is fluffy with bath foam.

'Good job on turning off the taps, Cassie.' She scoops some foam into her hand and blows it at Charlie, who giggles; scoops some more and pushes it onto her own face to make a beard. 'I am Captain Jackson,' she says, in a gruff voice somewhere between pirate and farmer, 'and I say it is time to sail to... Where are we going?'

'France,' says Cassie, one leg already over the side.

'Dorset,' says Charlie.

'Let's call in at Dorset on the way,' Jessica says, lifting him in. 'And then we'll set a course for Normandy.' Cassie's face falls. 'Which is in France,' Jessica adds. Cassie's face lights up again.

Twenty minutes later, leaving the kids to drink their warm milk in the kitchen, Jessica wanders into the living room and looks out of the window again. It has become a nervous habit, a tic. A figure at the end of the crescent startles her momentarily – but it is only Will, who continues towards the house. Her stomach flips. She thinks of the letter she has printed off and left for him on the coffee table. Her feelings have abated since she wrote it. She no longer knows if she wants a divorce, whether she can come to trust him again, only that, if it's even possible, it will take a long time. She should rip the letter up. It is too strongly worded, too distant.

Should she?

He will feel so awful when he reads it. He will be scared. But isn't that the point? That he will wake up to the consequences of what he has done? Yes, he did call, did try to talk to her the day she kicked him out, but the thought that she would be anywhere near ready to have some sort of calm conversation when she was raw and reeling was laughable. It was insulting, insensitive. She wonders now if she was right to delete the email he sent, whether she should have saved it to read when she was ready, but the fact is, in that moment, it felt so hurtful that he'd contacted her in such a ridiculously formal way. She wasn't in any kind of state to read some sort of prepared statement. No. The only way he will know how wretched she feels is by feeling wretched himself. He needs to feel, as she does, the hurt, the hopelessness, the devastation. The fear. Maybe if he is in as much pain as she is, they can be equals. As equals, they can come back to the table and begin an honest dialogue face to face, eyeball to eyeball.

She retreats to the back of the room. He cannot catch her looking out for him, no way. She realises she is hunched over, hiding. A sick feeling hits her. It is the same queasiness she feels each time she thinks about the whole town knowing about her collapsing marriage, about the horrid argument that caused that collapse, about the photographs that caused that argument. She has tried to call the number every day since, but there is never any reply. Now, she tries to philosophise, to tell herself that it isn't about the photographs, it isn't about whoever sent them – it is about what was already happening before.

She slides her feet into the high heels she only ever wears in the office and calls to the kids that Daddy'll be here in a minute. Their shouts of glee send her back into the dark hall, blinking back tears. Flattening herself against the wall, she fights to compose herself. She must regain control before Will knocks on the door. He can't see her like this, he just can't. She has dressed up, like Lena told her to. She has no intention of asking him about the money, the fact that he has broadcast their private business to everyone at the school, let alone about the woman in the photographs. Let him read the letter; that way her emotions won't get the better of her. She will leave the house the moment he steps in. She must, or she will shout at him or burst into tears. Or worse: fall to her knees and beg him to come home, a recurring dream spilling into humiliating reality. For strength, she makes herself focus on Lena's words when she called half an hour ago to give her a pep talk.

'You're going to swan out of there looking fabulous, OK?

Fabulous and in control. You're going to leave him with his mouth hanging open, longing for the woman he's lost.'

She cannot bear to be here when he reads the letter; she will crack, take it all back. But he needs to feel shocked. That's all she wants: to shock him. He needs to feel like she'll go through with it, that he might lose her. Because he might. And because at the moment, he appears to be coasting along, waiting for her to come to her senses.

And hasn't he always been like this? Since that awful morning, she has been trying to figure out when things started to slide. Under the less forgiving lens of infidelity, of stealing money, of payments made with that money for flowers she never received, the scruffiness she had passed off as dedication to his kids has taken on a different hue, as has his failure to shoulder an equal load, his lacklustre career. All she can hope for is that the letter will frighten some sense into him. God knows, it frightened her to write it.

His key rattles in the lock. Jessica's lungs fill. The kids thunder into the hall. Will steps inside and wipes his shoes on the mat. Jessica pretends she is just coming through from the kitchen, that the sight of her children clinging on to him and saying *Daddy, Daddy* over and over is not a knife through her already broken heart.

'Hi,' he says, in a near whisper, meeting her eye before looking down at the kids, ruffling their hair, asking them what they've been up to. He looks smarter, certainly smarter than he has these last few years, and noticeably thinner. He is wearing the jeans she bought him for Christmas two years ago but which disappeared to the back of the wardrobe, never to be seen again. With effort, he looks back up, gives her a trembling, apologetic smile, which should make her feel some sympathy but instead makes her want to scream.

'I'll be back around ten,' she says, unable to prevent an imperious tone that is all armour, all fake. She strides past the heartbreaking love knot of her children and her husband, a knot in which she should be deeply entangled, and calls out a cheerful goodbye. On the front step, it is all she can do not to trip in her high heels. What she does not miss is the glimpse of an appraising glance from her husband. She too has lost weight through stress. The dress she is wearing is one she hasn't been able to fit into in years. That she's only going to the pub with Lena is for her alone to know.

'You don't have to rush out,' he says in a plaintive voice.

'I'm late, sorry.' It takes everything she has to get the words out. She closes the front door quickly before bursting into tears on the front path. She carries on walking, doesn't stop to brush away the tears in case he is watching. She will clean herself up when she gets out of sight. He will not see her cry. No way.

By the time she reaches the end of the crescent, she is hobbling as well as weeping. She hardly ever wears heels other than to walk from her office to a meeting room, and has forgotten how bloody uncomfortable they are over more than fifty paces.

'Shit,' she whispers but carries on until she is around the corner. Once out of sight of the house, she removes her shoes and carries them one in each hand, the tarmac cold against her soles.

At the Tesco Metro, she puts her shoes back on, cleans her face up and pops in to grab some Band-Aids. On a whim born of sod-it, sod-it-all adrenaline, she finds herself at the tobacco kiosk asking if they stock menthol cigarettes. The kiosk server is a trainee and tells her she'll have to go and check.

'I don't think they sell menthol cigarettes in the UK any more,' comes a man's voice from her left shoulder. She turns to find an attractive – my God, a *very* attractive – well-dressed man standing behind her, an ambiguous smile on his lips. A little older, she thinks, tries not to notice that his ring finger is without a wedding band, curses herself inwardly. Ridiculous,

Jessica. Absolutely ridiculous. She's not looking for that, can't face even the thought of...

'I might be wrong,' he says. 'There might still be the ones that you crack the filter or something. The thin ones. For women.' His eyes widen; his attempt to communicate irony, she thinks.

'Ah yes,' she says, smiling. 'Tiny cigarettes for our tiny lady hands.' And then, 'I don't actually smoke.'

He smiles a little wider now, as if what she has said has amused him. He has nice teeth, an immaculately clean-shaven chin, no nicks like Will gets when he shaves. The collar of his white shirt is thick, pristine, especially for this time of day. 'Neither do I.'

'No, I really don't. I absolutely don't.' She is laughing, despite herself. Possibly *at* herself. 'I've just had a hell of a week, that's all. I need a small act of rebellion.'

'Oh, we all need those from time to time.'

Flustered by his flirtatious tone, she smiles politely and turns back, is saved by the kiosk girl, who tells her they have no menthol cigarettes but, when Jessica asks for Vogues, is pleased to the point of triumph to produce a packet from behind the blackout screen drawn down to hide the shameful habit.

Jessica pays for the cigarettes, a lighter and the Band-Aids and drops the lot into her bag.

'Goodbye then,' the man says as she steps away as nonchalantly as is possible with your heels screaming in pain. 'Enjoy not smoking.'

And someone, she has no idea who, lifts her hand and makes it do a little feminine wave. This same person lifts her mouth at the corners and trills, 'Sorry! Miles away! Yes! Bye now!'

Out on the pavement, face aflame, she succumbs to a girlish attack of the giggles.

· · ·

Lena is looking more glamorous than ever. She's even had her hair done again, the dark locks now chopped to chin length and highlighted with warm auburn streaks. In the dim light of the low-ceilinged pub, it looks thick and rich. A leopard-print shirt dress draws attention to her newly slim waist while showing off her still enviable cleavage.

'Wow,' Jessica says. 'Is that a new dress?'

'It is.' Lena beams.

'You look really gorgeous. I love your hair like that.'

Lena laughs, already pouring white wine from a frosty bottle that has been chilling in a silver ice bucket. 'I got Sauvignon Blanc – that OK?'

'God, yes. Anything. Turps. I've just left Will a letter saying I want a divorce.'

Lena makes a face. 'Oh God.'

'Found out he's taken money from our savings. A lot of money.'

'You're joking?'

Jessica shakes her head. 'I'm not. There's payment for flowers I never got, cash withdrawals for hundreds, thousands.'

Lena gasps. 'Oh my God.'

'Exactly. I don't know if it's final, but I need some sort of reaction, you know? So I've put a rocket up his arse. But let's not talk about Will. You must be sick to death of the subject.' Jessica holds up her glass. 'Here's to you looking hot. Cheers.'

'Don't look so bad yourself.'

'I took your advice. Gave Will something to think about.' It didn't stop the pain, though, did it? Was the letter too a subconscious act of revenge?

'Good move,' Lena says.

They clink and drink. The wine is dry and cold. Jessica feels a shiver of pleasure, a sense of something illicit, something like a sense of herself as something other than a victim, lost and alone. Putting her glass back down, she takes in her friend's appearance. It is more than new clothes, she thinks. More than new hair and the loss of the half-stone Lena always complains will never budge. Lena is *glowing*.

And then it hits her.

'Lena,' she says, 'have you met someone?'

Lena blushes a deep pink and throws back her head. 'Might have.'

'Lena! Why didn't you tell me?'

'I was going to, but... it wasn't exactly the moment, was it?'

'Well, no, but... No, actually, you're right.' Jessica's laughter comes easily, as if the earlier flirtation in the supermarket has loosened it somehow.

'I met him a while ago.' Lena titters into her hand and takes a large swig of wine. 'We were just friends at first, but in the last six months it's become a bit more than that.'

'Tell me everything!'

Lena tells her everything. How she met John at the gym. How he is not her usual type. A shy accountant, who fell apart after losing his wife in a horrible car accident nine years ago and is only now coming out of that shock.

'Going to the gym was part of his decision to try to get his life back together again,' she says. 'He's still seeing a therapist and says she saved his life. He doesn't drive too fast, doesn't do drugs or drink much, and he hasn't come in heavy with the love-bombing.'

'Wow.'

'He's not tight though,' she adds, holding up her finger for emphasis. 'He's generous but sensible... without being boring. You see? I do listen to you. I mean, sometimes when he talks about money I glaze over, but so what if he's not Mr Exciting? He's a good guy and at least he hasn't pissed all his savings into the wind. And most of all, he's kind.'

Jessica feels tears prick. 'You won't go getting bored of him, will you? Just because he's nice?'

Lena shakes her head, her eyes brimming. She appears to be wrestling with whether to say something, but after a moment she adds: 'He says he wants a family. He never got to have kids before...' She meets Jessica's eye with a vulnerability that is almost painful. 'Do you... do you think I'm too old?'

Jessica hits her friend on the leg. 'You're not too old! You're only just over thirty.'

'We're thirty-eight, babe.'

'As I said, only just over thirty.'

Jessica reaches for Lena's hand and squeezes it. For a moment, all her problems fade away. For years she has counselled her friend against falling for fancy restaurants and extravagant gestures, to no avail. Seeing that her unsolicited advice wasn't always welcome and scared of coming across as smug, she has tried to limit herself to hoping privately that Lena would find someone who would love her and be good to her long-term.

'I'm so happy for you,' she says now, meaning it.

Lena gives an excited little shrug. 'He wants me to move in with him, but I've told him we need to take it slow.'

'You did *what*? Who are you and what have you done with my friend?'

Lena gives a coy laugh and rolls her eyes. 'I know, right? Me, playing it cool, like you always told me. And it only went and worked. It's made him keener, if anything. At this rate, I'll have a perfect man and a perfect life, just like...' Her face falls. 'Shit. Sorry.'

'Not so perfect, as it turns out.' Recovering, Jessica reaches for the bottle, tops them both up and returns the wine to the bucket. She wants to say more, really, ask who the hell has a perfect life, but she can see from Lena's face that she is already mortified.

'So,' Lena says a little shakily, 'you seem a bit better tonight.'

'Funnily enough, I've just had a romantic encounter

myself,' Jessica offers, to lift the cloud. 'At the tobacco kiosk in Tesco of all places.' She pulls the cigarettes from her bag and shakes them. 'Fancy one of these, for old times' sake?'

In the pub garden, shivering beside an electric heater, she tells Lena about the attractive guy and the rather flirtatious conversation.

'Did you get his number?' Lena asks.

'God, no! It was just nice, you know? Nice to be noticed, I guess. In that way.'

'Oh, come on. You always get noticed – you know you do. Half the time I feel like Beyoncé's assistant walking into places with you. It's like I'm not even there.'

'Don't be silly. You're a goddess.'

They are both tiddly, Jessica thinks. The cigarette has made her a little nauseous, but apart from that, this is the best she's felt since Photogate.

'To goddesses,' she says, holding up her glass.

'To goddesses.'

As she approaches the corner of the crescent, Jessica screws up her eyes to see if there is anyone there. There is no one, only the plum tree shaking its leaves in the breeze. Her shoulders drop with relief. At the front door, she steels herself. She is a bit tipsy. Only half a bottle and two cigs, but she can't take it like she used to. Why, oh why, didn't she eat before she went out? Why didn't they drink water? Why didn't they order some chips? What is she, eighteen? That reminds her: she needs to find somewhere to spit the spearmint chewing gum she bought from the twenty-four-hour garage on the way home so that Will wouldn't smell the smoke on her breath.

At the bottom of her bag, she finds an old receipt, wraps the gum in it then unlocks the door. Inside, the house is silent. On the floor of the hallway are two hulking shapes, which turn out to be holdalls. Will has packed his bags then. Her stomach churns. From below the living room door leaks a thin line of cream light.

The nausea, which had abated, returns. She wishes, deeply, that she had not left the letter. She should've vented to Lena then arranged to meet Will somewhere public to talk. Maybe the letter will provoke a conversation. Maybe, when she goes inside, he will apologise and explain. Maybe it is too late.

She braces herself and opens the door. Inside, she finds Will flushed and tear-stained on the sofa. On the coffee table is the bottle of single malt they've had for five years but never touched and one of the Edinburgh Crystal glasses they got for a wedding present and have used about as often as the whisky. The bottle is still all but full, thank goodness. Will would never get drunk with the kids in the house. But he clearly needed something to settle his nerves, something strong.

Beside the bottle lies the letter.

Guilt washes over her. Will looks haggard.

'Hey,' she says softly.

He looks up at her, eyes so full of pain she cannot hold his gaze. 'You're going to take the *kids*?' His voice is barely a whisper. 'You'd do that to me?'

There is no apology. No acknowledgement of the pain he has caused her, only of the pain she has now caused him. She makes herself take a breath.

'I'm not *taking* anything,' she says. 'I'm their mother. I love them just as much as you do. You're the one who threw us into the fire. You, not me.'

'But I'm their main carer. Me, not you.' Childish. And still no apology, no attempt to acknowledge that he is the reason they are here. She knew this would happen. That was why she had to write him a damn letter.

'I'm not going to talk about it now,' she says as firmly as she is able. 'I need to go to bed. I haven't slept since you left and one of us needs to work. To get money. To pay for all the things.' She bites her lip, too late. 'Sorry,' she says. 'Sorry, that was... I've had a drink. I just don't want to talk about this now.'

'I've made one mistake, a mistake you won't even let me explain, and you've made up your mind. It's like you'd already decided.'

One mistake. He makes it sound like he scratched the car – lost the house keys, perhaps; shrank her knitwear on a hot wash. And what about the other 'mistakes' – the flowers, the missing money, not to mention chatting up the yummy mummies? She holds up her hand, as much against her own rising anger as his pathetic insistence on glossing over the facts. She thought the letter would force him to step up, to come out fighting for her, for their family. But no.

'Please,' she says. 'This... this whole thing has made me realise we were just going through the motions. I'm too young to... Look, I don't want to be married to someone who can't be bothered any more, OK? Especially if I can't even trust you. You need to hear that. Go back to your hotel and let's progress this like grown-ups.'

Her feet are killing her. She sits down and pulls off her shoes, the mundanity of the task bringing her back to herself. She can't look at Will. She doesn't need to look at him. His self-pity infuriates her, but she cannot let herself shout at him again. She wants the shouting to stop, the blame to stop, the whole damn drama of it all.

She senses Will stand up. Hears a huge sniff.

'You're absolutely heartless,' he says. 'Do you know that? And don't tell me you went out with Lena. Since when do you go out with Lena looking like that?'

'Since I decided to regain my self-respect,' she replies acidly, without looking at him. 'Since you betrayed me in the most humiliating way with someone you won't even tell me the name of and I had to hear about it from someone who won't even tell me who they are. Since then.' She stands up. Will is on the far side of the living room. He will have to walk past her to leave.

These petty logistics, she thinks. These mundane practicalities.

'You don't even want to try,' he says, his voice thick.

No, she thinks. *You* don't even want to try.

'Please,' she says. 'I have work. I can't lose my job as well as...' *As well as you.*

She sits back down and bows her head, covers her face with her hands. If she stops speaking, he will go. He must. He takes a step, another. He is level with her now. For a second, two, she can feel him standing over her, his worn-out trainers flat and filthy on the rug they chose together.

Everything, everything in this house has a story that belongs to them both.

It is unbearable.

He moves. She keeps her head down. Another few seconds pass. The front door slams shut.

CHAPTER 14

WILL

Back at the flat, Will makes himself a strong whisky and Coke and reads Jessica's letter once again, to torture himself.

It has come to my attention, however, that in addition to the affair... cash withdrawals...

He knew this would happen, and instead of pre-empting it, he left it. And instead of asking about it, she's thrown it in his face, in a letter, so he cannot defend himself. He cannot defend himself. Margot needed that money. She needed it to buy the plane tickets to get her and the kids to France. She will pay him back. She will. He had to believe that. Has to believe that.

You have told the children that we are no longer together...

No, he did not. He did not tell them anything. He told them he was going away for work, that was all. Whoever it was that started that rumour, it wasn't him. It is not his fault that fucking Freya Gibbons broadcast it on Cassie's class WhatsApp group. But again, he couldn't defend himself because his wife was out with... well, let's face it, it's looking like she must have been out with some guy.

And since when did he check out of their marriage? That's bullshit. He's the one who keeps everything afloat, everything, while she's off pursuing her fabulous career. He gets that she's hurt, humiliated, and yes, that's on him, but she hasn't let him explain. The truth is hard, yes, he's not proud of it, but he hasn't slept with anyone else and he hasn't stopped making an effort. Yes, he should have told her about the money as well as every-thing else, but they can work through that, can't they? He loves her. He could make things right if only she would let him. And now she's saying she loved him, past tense? That she wants the children?

Will necks the rest of his drink. The sofa has sucked him into its cushions. He cannot get up, cannot move. His bones ache like those of an old man.

He cannot think about this now. He just can't.

Today is Wednesday. He knows because today he saw his kids for the first time since his life slid sideways and everything fell off. Since Jessica kicked him out, the days have melted into one another. Ian has called twice to ask if he needed anything – small kindnesses that Will appreciated deeply. Colin sent him a message when he left the class WhatsApp group after Freya's foghorn message – *Hey mate, you all right?* He replied that he was lying low, that he'd be in touch. Friday, the day he moved in, Ian's friend Dave dropped off some extra bits and pieces for the flat. Every bit as handsome and well turned out as Ian, Dave was more softly spoken, almost fey. As he carried two large cardboard boxes into the flat, Will asked him if he wanted help. No, he was fine, thank you. Will asked if he wanted a drink, a cup of tea perhaps, or coffee, but again Dave demurred.

'There's bedding for the kids and some stuff for the kitchen,' he said finally, gesturing to the boxes. His voice and manner were so polite as to be almost deferential, but his hands and wrists looked preternaturally strong – capable of wringing a neck, Will thought, a dark aside for himself alone. Like Ian, he wore a signet ring on his pinkie finger, his with the letters DS engraved into the gold oval.

The boxes were the kind you'd find in a factory: new, closed with shiny brown parcel tape, Will's name scrawled in marker pen on each one, as if there were many other men like him, all receiving these charity packages from a central warehouse somewhere. Because charity was what this was, and the shame of it burnt somehow more sharply in that moment, because not only Ian but now Dave had witnessed Will's rather pathetic dire straits.

'Thank you,' he said simply, helplessly, wondering what *stuff for the kitchen* could possibly be, since the cupboards were already well stocked with everything you could conceivably need except, maybe, a blowtorch.

He did not share this thought with Dave.

'This is amazing,' he said instead. 'I can't thank you enough.'

'It's just spare stuff from the lock-up. Need anything else, tell the boss, all right?'

'Do you mean Ian?'

'Unless you know any other bosses?' Dave's mouth twitched with the trace of a smile. Sarcasm, but not malicious. At least Will didn't think so.

'Ha, no. I mean—' Will stopped himself. He had no idea what he meant. 'Well, thanks again.'

Dave nodded. 'See you later.'

Once Dave had left, Will felt his lungs empty with relief. After a stern word with himself, he made a hot meal, mindfully, a way of staving off the despair he could feel coming for him. Making a meal was a conscious act of self-care, something he would advise his clients to do in times of difficulty. But the moment the food hit the plate, his throat closed up in refusal.

Nights, he has slept fitfully, waking periodically in a strange room in a strange flat in a strange life. Mornings, he has found himself in this same strange life, the sense of how he got there either vague and dreamlike or flashing with a terrifying clarity.

He has done a lot of walking, eaten little, slept less. At

some point, he informed his clients that he would be back to work within the month, referred any emergencies to another life coach he knew. Not that he deals in emergencies or anything, really, of great importance. Hasn't since Margot anyway. Sometimes he curls up on the bed, hands over his ears, eyes closed. He thinks about Margot a lot. Dreams about her. If only there was a way to make contact, ask if she's all right, find out how she and the kids are settling in. Once she's up and running, he's sure she'll contact him somehow, ask him how she can transfer the money. It takes time to set up a life, especially with kids. Even longer to save a couple of thousand pounds. He doesn't really care about the money, not for himself. But Jessica does.

That's why he didn't tell her.

He thinks about Jessica all the time. Dreams about her too. Sometimes Margot and Jessica are both in his dreams, in his house. They are drinking wine, gossiping. They are laughing at him.

Then this morning – so long ago now it seems like yesterday – he woke with a pit in his belly. He would be seeing his kids after almost a week away. He had to rally. He had to be strong. Seeing their father crumble would be traumatising for them, and he didn't know what Jessica had told them about his absence, only that they knew their father had left. To keep his anxieties at bay, he walked up the Thames path towards Kingston and back again, tiring himself enough to slow his looping thoughts, his heart. His life had become something he no longer recognised. His life was not his; it did not belong to him.

Now, Jessica's letter lies on the coffee table. His Fitbit shows 32,425 steps. His legs ache. An old disc injury worries at the base of his spine. He pours another whisky and Coke, but it is warm and he has difficulty swallowing. He feels hot. His forehead is hot. Is he coming down with a cold? His eyes are sore.

He had to take out his contacts the moment he got in. His glasses are filthy.

To think that earlier he showered and dressed in his newest clothes. He thought she would at least notice how smart he looked, the effort he had made.

But no.

My feeling is that your heart hasn't always been in it...

Fitbits and smarter clothes. The passing suggestion that he join a gym – as if being a stay-at-home dad meant he had that kind of time. What did she think he did all day, lie about? He had all the work of running the house and all the work of his practice. He didn't get to drop everything and disappear into London for twelve hours a day, eat club sandwiches in glossy boardrooms, go for cheeky drinks in glamorous City bars. He was oblivious to his wife's attempts to improve him, to slim him down, smarten him up. Well, now he is slimmer and smarter, but it is apparently too late.

I wanted to be clear and to give you fair warning. I wish to have custody of the children and to keep the house.

So hard, so unfeeling. Resentment pulses through him. Jessica has made up her mind. Could it be as Ian said: she already had, his infidelity a convenience, not the disaster she claims it is?

She looked incredible tonight. Did she know he would guess she wasn't really meeting Lena? Was the whole performance a kind of taunt? She didn't even warn him about the letter, simply left him to find it: *Read it and weep, sucker.*

Fortunately he had the sense not to open it until he'd put the kids to bed. Their overjoyed faces on his arrival – *Daddy! Daddy!* – brought the ache of tears to his throat, but he smiled through it for their sakes. He made them laugh, made them hot chocolate, read them both Charlie's stories, the three of them cosied up in his single bed: *The Gruffalo, Hairy Maclary from Donaldson's Dairy, We're Going on a Bear Hunt.* When Cassie asked when he was going to come home, he told her soon, that he and Mummy were just working it out, that sometimes grown-ups did this. Mummy and Daddy loved them very much. Not to worry. He cuddled them as if he hadn't seen them for months. It felt like he hadn't seen them for months. It felt, somehow, like he was seeing them for the last time.

Later, after he'd read Jessica's letter over and over, he crept upstairs and stared at them, at their soft apricot cheeks in the hazy dusk of their night lights. When he leant in to kiss them, he inhaled the damp smell of the baby hairs stuck at their hairlines.

How could she do this to him?

How could she be so cold?

How could she destroy their family like this?

Grimly, determinedly, he packed his holdall along with another, older one he found in the loft space. He packed his dressing gown and slippers, his sports kit, even his wedding shoes. If she could act like it was over, then so could he. He would make her agree to him having the kids at the weekend. He had somewhere to host them, thanks to Ian. Perhaps a weekend all on her own would wake her up to the reckless damage she was doing. She would call him and tell him she regretted that letter, that they should talk.

Downstairs, he succumbed to an attack of the shakes so violent he had to pour himself a finger of whisky to calm his nerves. Margot came to him: her frame brittle, her body fraught with fear. When he held her, her ribcage pressed against the inside of his arms. When she laughed – it was wonderful to make her laugh – her clavicle bone protruded so much he feared it would break through the skin. It was never about sex. She had no one else to turn to. He had to help her. Theirs was a connection he couldn't explain even to himself other than the magnetism of her helplessness, her reliance on him, his counsel, the promise of his silence. For Margot he had crossed lines that should never have been crossed. He knew it was risky. But he never thought it would cost him his marriage.

When Jessica appeared at the living room door, he could tell by looking at her that she'd had a few drinks. The smell of cigarette smoke drifted from her, but he felt at a gut level that he no longer had the right to ask if she'd been smoking. Either she had or someone she had been with had.

But Lena didn't smoke.

Ian's words came to him: *And you're sure she's not got someone else?*

Since when, he heard himself say in a tone dripping with bitterness, *do you go out with Lena looking like that?*

These same words return to him now as Wednesday ticks into Thursday, as it becomes a full week since he was happy. He has been so desperate to explain things to Jessica. Now, with this excoriating letter in front of him, he discovers that inclination has gone.

He no longer wants to tell her anything at all. After the way she's treated him, she doesn't deserve to know.

He sends a text: *If it's all right with you, I'll take the kids this weekend. I have somewhere for us to stay. W*

To his surprise, she replies: OK.

Will's phone buzzes.

He blinks, eyes sticky, finds himself on the sofa in the flat. It is light outside. Not a moment later then; it is morning. On the coffee table is Jessica's letter, a half-empty tumbler of whisky and Coke. He takes a sip. It is flat, warm. He picks up his phone. The time reads 11:37. The text is from Ian.

Wotcha.

Wotcha yourself, he thumbs. He can permit himself this, he thinks. He and Ian have reached the level of banter. *Everything OK?*

The phone rings – Ian calling.

'Just checking you're OK,' he says, his usual refrain. From the background noise, Will can tell he's driving. 'I'm actually about two minutes from your place and was going to drop by, see how you're settling in.'

'That's very kind of you.'

'I'm actually checking you haven't been having a rave on my property.'

Will laughs. 'I have, but I've tidied up. Come over.'

Ten minutes later, Ian enters the flat and takes off his shades, performing both actions so simultaneously and smoothly he makes it look like a dance move. He is wearing a navy suit and a white shirt but no tie. He looks so. Damn. Clean. Will is glad he had the presence of mind to at least pull last night's jeans over his boxers and clean his teeth. Not possessing a pair of socks without holes, he has remained barefoot.

'Double espresso, milk on the side?' he asks.

'Well remembered.'

'Dave brought a coffee machine. I've just about managed to figure it out.'

'Good old Dave.' There is something heavy in Ian's tone, but when Will glances at him, his face clears. It feels odd to have Ian Robbins in the flat, the flat itself too small somehow. It is not Will's property of course. It is Ian's. And yet it is Will who is preparing the coffee. Perhaps that's all it is, this palpable weirdness: the reality underpinning the surface of Will as host, Ian as guest. Then there is Ian and Dave, these two old friends, now business partners – still friends? *Tell the boss. Good old Dave.* There is something between the two men, Will thinks. Something he can't put his finger on.

'I'm not on suicide watch or anything,' Ian says as they sit, one sofa apiece. He picks something invisible from his thigh, which is thick with muscle and which presses against the fine fabric of his trousers, making the knee into a huge shining blue knuckle. 'But I know it don't do to be alone too much, especially in the early days.' He taps a forefinger to his head, presumably to indicate mental health.

'I saw my kids last night,' Will says, shaking his head. 'It was... upsetting.'

Ian sips his coffee pensively. 'The first time after they've left is a real killer.'

'Jessica didn't even talk to me. She just left as soon as I got there. I was going to write her a letter to explain everything, to tell her how sorry I am. I was going to leave it for her. But I didn't. I've been too... spaced out. Anyway, turns out she wrote me one. She got there first.' Will glances up at Ian, who is watching him with a patient listening expression.

'She seems to be saying she wants a divorce,' Will says into the silence. 'She wants the kids.' He puts his hands over his face. 'And last night she said she was meeting her friend Lena for a drink, but she was... much more done up than she would be usually. Lena's her oldest friend. They went to school together. Lena used to come and visit Jess at uni. I was at uni with Jessica, you see. We weren't together then, just friends. Sorry, not got this in order, have I?' He half laughs. 'I went out with her for a bit actually. Lena, I mean. Nothing serious. It was before Jessica and I got together, but it was only a fling. Anyway, to get back to the point, when Jess came home, she smelt of cigarettes. But she doesn't smoke. And neither does Lena.'

Ian narrows his eyes. 'I knew there was more to it.'

To his embarrassed annoyance, Will feels his eyes fill. He cannot cry in front of this man, he cannot.

'I feel like I don't even know her.' His voice sounds like he's being strangled. 'Like I never knew her.'

'Mate,' Ian says. 'I'm gutted for you.'

The sympathetic look on Ian's face almost brings the tears

out, but Will rubs his face, hard, and stands up. 'I need to get back to work. I need to keep moving. I'll be OK.'

'I'm sure you will. But in the short term, you're not. It's OK not to be OK, but you shouldn't be on your own. Have you got any mates you can call?'

'I can't really face anyone at the moment. I know what the school gates are like. That's another thing she's accused me of – telling the kids. Which I didn't. But someone did. The news has spread like wildfire. The other mums will hate me by now. Hell hath no fury like the outrage of the sisterhood.'

'What about older mates? From back in the day sort of thing?'

'They don't live locally. And I'm not... I'm not up to it. Weirdly, it's easier to talk to you.'

'Told you they call me the therapist.' Ian too stands up. For a moment they are eye to eye, too close. Ian's irises are so pale, almost white, his pupils so small and black – the distant speck of a bird in a cloud.

Will steps back and bends to pick up the cups and saucers, mostly to break the intensity. He hears the clink of keys.

'Tell you what,' Ian says. 'Why don't you come to mine for dinner later? Six? I know it's early, but I'm not a late-night person. I'll text you the address. Actually, I've got a meeting in Isleworth at four thirty, so I'll pick you up about half five, quarter to six. It's not far. Just over in Kew.' He raises his eyebrows, his mouth set in the familiar promise of a mischievous grin that never quite comes. 'Unless you've got plans?'

On the dot of 5.30, Ian calls. 'I'm in the car park.'

'Great,' Will says, but the line is already dead.

In the forecourt, he finds an enormous black Land Rover, the familiar blunt silhouette of Ian at the wheel. As Will walks towards the vehicle, he notices that it is not shiny but matt, a

finish he has never seen before. Butterflies move in his belly. He
is out of his comfort zone. That's all this is. This last week has
left his nerves jangling. But Ian is not the cause. Beneath his
alpha maleness, he is quite the softie. Will has never known
anyone like him.

Ian greets him with his trademark gruff affection. 'All right?
Belt up.'

To Will's surprise, Ian drives within the twenty miles per
hour speed limit – something Will himself struggles to do. Not
that there is much opportunity to speed. The rush-hour traffic
carries them at a painstaking crawl back towards the Travelodge. At the Express Tavern, Ian takes a right, over the river to
Kew. A minute later, another right, then right again into the
driveway of an enormous detached Victorian villa. The iron
gates open automatically. On the gatepost, the bulging black
eye of a security camera stares down at them as they drive
inside.

At the grandeur of the place, a new feeling of foreboding
rises in Will's gut. But he smiles through it, commenting
politely on the beauty of the house, the manicured gardens with
their round-edged and perfectly green lawns, the copious, well-
tended mature shrubs at the borders. There is a glass car port
coming off the left-hand side of the house. Beneath are two
vintage sports cars, one blue and one red, but there is still room
for the humongous Land Rover. Ian kills the engine and gets
out. Will jumps down, the gravel giving a satisfying crunch
under his trainers. He follows Ian around to the double front
door, which is painted a dark Victorian green and adorned with
a tarnished brass ring. The air smells fresh; autumn hinting at
its arrival as the sun sinks out of sight.

'Drink first,' Ian says once he's unlocked the mortice at the
bottom of the door and the chest-height Yale. He steps up ahead
of Will into an immaculate vintage-tiled porch where he
unlocks an inner door, half of which is paned with etched glass,

the lower half painted white. This he pushes open and with perfect manners moves aside to let Will enter first.

The hallway is vast. The carpet is spongy underfoot. The ceiling reaches up to the top of the first floor, creating the kind of atrium Will has only seen in hotels. Heavy Victorian wallpaper lines the walls: scenes of wildlife repeat over and over in long ovals – deer, rabbits, badgers, the background a dense forest design. The wallpaper appears to have been varnished, possibly to preserve it. Will wonders if it's original. To the left of the space is a slender antique table – mahogany? – with elegant carved legs and, on top, a cream Bakelite phone next to a white vase of blowsy freshly cut flowers.

'From the garden,' Ian says and sniffs. 'They're the last of them. Cut them this morning. I like to have hydrangeas in the house when they're in bloom. They remind me of Jen and the kids. Come through.'

He leads Will through to a kitchen that is twice, maybe three times the size of his own. The floor is stone and the grey units are hand-made. Like a heart, a dark red Aga sits at the centre. The house is not showy, as Will has been anticipating, although he has no idea why he would think that – Ian's own personal elegance is, after all, understated. Like its owner, this kitchen is tasteful, simple, low-key, the grey tones and the Aga giving a warm, traditional look that suits the house.

'Beer?' Ian asks, opening a concealed fridge. 'IPA?'

'Sure. Thanks.' Will stops himself from asking if Ian hired an interior designer. He is not sure if the question would be a compliment or an insult. He is, he realises, really quite nervous.

Ian throws him a can. 'Good stuff this. Gluten free. Let me get you a glass.'

A moment later, they are pouring India pale ale into glasses while Ian tells him all about the local brewery that makes it, in which he invested a few years back. They supply the Black

Hound, which, as Will suspected, turns out also to be owned by Ian. And then he is being taken, glass in hand, on a tour.

'I'll show you the boys' room,' Ian says, throwing open a thick white door to a flight of stone steps leading down to a basement.

Will hesitates.

'Go on,' Ian says. 'I'm not going to lock you in. It's not that kind of party.'

Will hears the jitteriness in his own laugh but, out of nothing more than politeness, heads down into the dark. To his relief, he has only descended a few steps when a light goes on. The walls are white, the basement floor the same stone slabs as the kitchen. Not a spider-infested coal cellar then. Not a torture dungeon, though why he would think this, he doesn't know. From the white hall, two doors lead off to the right and left. Will tries the handle of the door to the left. But it is locked.

'Storage,' Ian tells him, pushing past.

Will wonders why he would lock a room in his own house if it's only for storage. But then the wealthy are often security conscious. Quite simply, they have so much worth stealing.

Ian is opening the other door, telling him that this is where he *chills out with the boys*. Inside is a long rectangular games room with French windows giving onto a green garden.

'The back lawn is lower than the side one,' Ian explains, walking slowly between the full-size pool table and the full-size table-tennis table. 'In case you were wondering. So we don't feel like we're underground.'

On the left, at the top end of the room, is an open dartboard with scores chalked in white on the black inner doors: two columns headed *Dave* and *Mitty*.

'Mitty's a space cadet,' Ian says. 'Bloody good darts player though. Do you play darts at all?'

'I have done. And I used to love pool at uni. This is amazing, absolutely amazing.'

'We've had some good times in here. It gets a bit messy.' Ian grins. 'The back faces west so we get the sun in the evenings. A few beers. It's great.'

Completing his circuit of the pool table, he heads out of the room and leads the way back up the stairs. Will stays close, unsure as to why beyond an irrational fear of the door slamming shut, the turn of the key, himself in the dark. Really, he thinks, Ian Robbins could be anyone.

But Ian leaves the door open, of course he does; this is not a film. And as they make their way back along the hallway towards the dining room and sitting room respectively, Will's anxieties subside a little. Everywhere is decorated in sombre colours appropriate to the Victorian era, furnished with what look like antiques or good replicas, not that Will knows the first thing about any of it. Respectable is the word that comes to mind. There are old portraits and landscapes on the wall. Again, he isn't sure if they are vintage, maybe even members of Ian's family, or vintage-style. He does not permit himself to ask.

In what Ian calls the drawing room, a collection of framed photographs adorn one wall. They turn out to be mostly of Ian: skiing on a snowy mountain somewhere, in a rickshaw in what looks like the Far East, on a white beach with turquoise sea, in a restaurant holding a fishbowl goblet of red wine. There are a couple of Dave. In most of these pictures, both Ian and Dave are younger. There are only two photographs of Ian's wife and children. In one, Ian stands with his arm around Jen, who is blonde, good-looking, holding the hand of a pretty girl of about nine or ten, who in turn holds the hand of a handsome little boy of seven or eight. The photograph looks like it has been taken in the garden of this house. In another photo, Ian stands in a similar pose with the children, all of them eating ice creams in what appears to be a European resort – Spain possibly, or Italy.

Looking at the family portraits, Will's heart contracts for his new friend. There are almost imperceptible spaces on the wall, he notices then, barely visible grey outlines where other pictures once hung. He understands. Cannot imagine having to look at a wall full of photographs of Jessica with him and the kids, doesn't want to even think about all the photographs he has taken over the years, the happy memories they contain. This house is made for a family. Once contained a family. Now, it is too big, almost empty. Maybe it is better if Jessica keeps the house, he thinks. He is not sure he could live in it without her. To live in it without her or the kids would be absolutely unthinkable.

He stares at his shoes, composing himself.

'This wall used to be full of Jen and the kids,' Ian says quietly, as if reading his mind. 'Wedding photos, baby photos, you name it. I just can't really deal with...' His voice breaks. 'Whatever you do, hold on to your family. Hold on to them tight.'

Will does not respond. He has no idea what to say, and besides, he would not get the words past the fist in his throat.

A moment later, the spell appears to break.

'I'm doing chicken jalfrezi,' Ian says, turning to him. You're not veggie, are you?'

Will hesitates. A bird is not so far from a fish, is it?

'Of course not,' he says, with a false cavalier laugh. 'Chicken jalfrezi sounds amazing.'

Back in the kitchen, Ian throws him a second can. On an empty stomach, Will can already feel the first. The beer is strong, he thinks, and he is not used to it like Ian is. But to check the percentage would be... he doesn't quite know. Weak maybe? He opens the can, still processing the size of the house, Ian's naturalness in it – neither boastful nor apologetic. Despite the humble beginnings he hinted at in the pub that first evening, Ian Robbins is at home in this impressive, almost intimidating property, every bit as much as the original owner might have been.

'So,' Ian says, tying an apron at his waist with an oddly effeminate flourish, 'tell me about this missus of yours. This Jessica.'

Will takes a slug of his beer. 'Well, I met her at uni, as I said. But we didn't get together until after. We did a graduate training scheme together. Jessica was fast-tracked and I dropped out. It wasn't for me. She's made of strong stuff. She works hard, really hard. She's stoical, clever, funny. She's beautiful. I... I love her.'

'But you had a thing with someone else.' The dismissiveness with which Ian says this almost winds Will, but he absorbs the punch. 'What did you say her name was?'

'I didn't. I won't give her name actually, if you don't mind. She was a client.'

'Fair enough.' Ian nods and slides chunks of chicken breast into a pan. A violent hiss rises into air already fragrant with fried garlic and chilli, cumin and possibly garam masala.

'Sorry,' Will adds.

'Not at all. I respect it. And where do you live now?'

'Twickenham way,' he replies, keeping it vague for reasons he can't name.

'Nice. You a rugby man?'

'Not really. I don't follow sport. Wimbledon occasionally. And by occasionally, I mean the singles finals.'

'I love Wimbledon. I'll take you sometime.' Ian empties a can of tomatoes into the pan and stirs. 'And you said this morning you think she's seeing someone else. Do you have any idea who?'

Will shakes his head. 'I don't even know if she is seeing someone.'

'Or if she was all along?'

His scalp tingles. 'I don't know. But it would make sense. I feel a bit... gaslighted.'

'Gaslighted? How d'you mean?'

'In the letter, she seemed to be saying she was unhappy before. But that's not true. We were happy. She sees those photographs and... that's it.'

'And you think when the photos came in, she seized her opportunity?'

'Opportunity? What do you mean?'

'Like, she's throwing all the shade on you so she can come across as the wronged woman sort of thing, when actually she's been playing away herself.'

'I...'

Could Ian be right? Could Jessica be somehow capitalising on Will's mistake? Was she poised, waiting for the opportunity? But that's... that's horrible. It's devious and calculating and manipulative, which is not the forthright, straight-talking Jessica he knows.

'It doesn't matter either way,' Ian says. 'She won't get the kids or the house; you will.'

'But she bought it. I haven't really contributed much financially.'

'Don't make no difference. Trust me, I've been there. I only have this place because Jen left me. Doesn't matter what you did or she did. If you're the kids' main carer, you live in the house and it's all split down the middle. Personally, I think she's trying to put the frighteners on you. It was a mistake to let her kick you out. But she's in for a shock when she finds out your rights aren't affected.'

'Really?'

'If I were you,' Ian says, gesturing at him with the spatula, 'I'd get my arse down to a solicitor and file before she does.'

The curry is delicious. Ian is a consummate host. Will loses count of how many cans he catches, how many Ian sets before him when he can no longer catch. At some point, they switch to red wine. Ian is obviously someone who enjoys looking after people, and having no wife and kids any more, he looks after his friends.

'Where did you say your wife was now?' Will asks, aware of feeling dizzy.

'Outskirts of Dublin,' Ian says, pouring him another large glass of red wine. 'She gives me the kids once a year, like crumbs from her table, and I have to pretend like that's OK.'

'I'm so sorry.'

'Marcus and Kirsten. My kids. I was never at home. Classic workaholic. I had no chance. But you? You're a stay-at-home dad. You've got to fight for your rights, son. Do you hear me?'

Will nods. Thinks, did he just call me *son*?

'Tell your solicitor,' Ian goes on, 'that she never came home from work till late, that she ignored you, that it was mental cruelty.'

'But that's not true.'

'It's whatever you say it is.'

'I miss them so much I feel sick.'

'There you go. It's your health at the end of the day. Listen, do you want me to put someone on her? See what she's up to?'

'I... No. No. I don't think so.' The room is spinning.

'And I'm thinking you could do with somewhere better to take them at weekends.'

'What? No, the flat is great. I'm so grateful for all you've done for...' Will grips the edge of the chair, fearing he might fall off.

'I think you might be a bit worse for wear, mate,' he hears Ian say. 'Here.'

'Sorry. Not really used to drinking.' Will lets Ian help him to his feet, is dimly aware of his arm around Ian's thick shoulder, a sense of beast-like strength, of the two of them hobbling up the wide staircase. There are brass feet on the carpet runner. Oak edges. They don't make staircases like this any more. They don't make houses like this any more. He feels sick. They are walking on the flat now – shoes sinking into a red patterned carpet. A door opens. The carpet is blue now, plain.

'I'm going to put you in here,' Ian says. 'You can't go home in this state.'

He is sitting on a bed. An older, more tired version of him is staring at him. It is himself. It is a mirror. He groans.

Ian returns with a white towel and some pyjamas. 'Can you manage? There's an en suite through there.' He points towards the far side of the blue room. 'I'll bring you some water. Just lie down, yeah? Can you take your shoes off? Will? Mate? Can you take your shoes off?'

CHAPTER 15

JESSICA

On Thursday evening, Jessica leaves at four – her boss is being super-understanding, having been through a divorce himself. He has also agreed to her working from home once a week, on Fridays, which means tomorrow morning won't be quite so much of a scramble.

She gets home before six, but the house is empty. A chill shoots through her.

'Hello?' she calls out, unease gathering in her gut. 'Lena? Cassie? Charlie?'

Her heart quickens. Will flashes into her mind: his tear-stained face, the whisky glass. That letter. How she wishes she hadn't left it for him. It helped her to write down her rage and have him read how she really feels, but she wishes she hadn't. Wishes she'd arranged to meet him instead, somewhere outside the house, somewhere neutral. If he would only call, she would pick up. But it has to be him who makes the first move, and he has to be ready with a proper apology for the pain he has caused her.

But now the house is empty. And Will hasn't called. He

wouldn't do anything desperate, would he? He did send her a text this morning with an address on Brentford Marina. Claimed to be renting a small flat, though how he is paying for it is anyone's guess. It must belong to *her*. Must do. He's supposed to be picking up the kids tomorrow, but he still has a key to the house. Has she pushed him too far? Has he stolen them in an act of defiance? You hear about that sort of thing, read about it in the papers sometimes.

'Hello?' Her voice is too loud in the silence. 'Anyone home?'

Swallowing nausea, she hangs her coat by the front door, her bag over the banister rail, and heads towards the living room. Sweat pricks on her forehead. She tells herself she is being ridiculous. There will be a perfectly reasonable explanation. She folds her fingers around the door handle, opens the door and steps inside.

No one. There is no one here.

'Hello?' she calls, her voice quieter now.

At the far end of the room, behind the sofa, a blanket has been thrown over the dining room table. A suppressed giggle comes from beneath.

Jessica exhales shakily, her hand flat to her chest, the other gripping the back of the sofa. She wants to laugh but is too far along towards crying. She pushes her hands to her knees and makes herself breathe. The last thing she wants to do is frighten them, no matter how badly they've frightened her.

'No one home?' she says in a puzzled tone once she's got herself together. 'I wonder where they've got to. Cassie? Charlie?'

More giggles. At four, it will be killing Charlie not to shout, *I'm here, Mummy!*

'Where *are* they?' she asks with pantomime intonation as she paces around the room. 'Cassie? Charlie? Auntie Lena? Hmm. I wonder if they're behind the television. No-o. Under the coffee table? No. Wait! What's this strange tent? Who put a *tent* up in the living room?'

By now, Cassie is giggling too: barely audible nasal exhalations, a squeak. Swallowing her laughter, Jessica creeps towards the home-made den. God bless Lena. She's such a sport, knows exactly how to entertain the kids. She finds the edge of the blanket and pulls it aside. Underneath the table, three faces in shadow, all in fits. 'There you are!'

The kids throw back their heads, lost in peals of laughter. Both are cross-legged, Charlie's hands clasped at his chest, his little milk teeth white in the gloom. Cassie's wrists are loose, hands floppy with hysteria. Lena is lying propped up on her elbow, grinning, her face flushed. She looks like she's overheating. In the middle of their little triangle, on paper plates, are cocktail sausages, crisps, sandwiches, cherry tomatoes, chunks of cucumber, a bowl of sliced-up pear. Lena is the fun aunt, doing things with them Jessica is too tired to do after a hard day at work. The sight of the three of them having so much fun is wonderful, of course it is, but something stirs within her, something more than the usual waves of guilt – a dark and unwelcome feeling that is uncomfortably close to jealousy. Possessiveness perhaps. Inadequacy. Shame.

Forcing all of this from her, she gives a wide smile and crawls into the space. 'Is there room for me?'

'Yes!' Cassie's tremulous euphoria brings a lump to Jessica's throat. 'Lena said we could have an indoor picnic! We went to Tesco!'

'Well, it is nearly Friday.' Jessica smiles at her friend. Mouths, 'You're a legend.'

'I know,' Lena says. 'I am the living shizzle.'

Charlie gasps, claps his hand over his mouth.

Jessica giggles, meets Lena's eye. 'Mr Outrage over there.'

'Mummy.' Cassie is tugging at her sleeve, a plate of sandwiches in her other hand. 'Do you want a sandwich? I made them. It's egg and cress. Auntie Lena let me boil the eggs.'

Jessica never usually eats before eight. Often, dinner is a noodle bowl or something picked up at Waterloo station and guzzled without thought on the train. It feels like the middle of the afternoon, but Cassie wants her to eat a sandwich, so she picks one and bites into it and closes her eyes in rapture.

'Yum!' She opens her eyes wide at her beautiful daughter, whose ecstatic smile is almost too much to bear. 'You didn't make this, did you?'

Cassie nods approximately seventy times in a couple of seconds. She is as serious as a judge.

'I made the ham sammiches.' Charlie is holding a sandwich out to her, his fingers squashing the bread.

'I'll have to try one of those too then, won't I?' She takes the offering and bites so that now she has a sandwich in each hand. 'Good job I'm starving. Delicious!'

'I'll get out of your hair,' Lena says, lifting herself up but banging her head on the underside of the table. 'Ow!'

The children fall about laughing. Charlie snorts water through his nose, which makes Cassie spit her sandwich into her hand. Pandemonium ensues momentarily.

'Charming,' Lena says, pinching Charlie on the waist. 'That's hilarious to you, is it? Thanks a lot.'

Cassie is deep pink, her eyes still wet. 'Sorry, Lena.'

Lena meets Jessica's eye. 'I can't actually figure out how to get out without dislocating one of my limbs.' She drops down and wriggles backwards, commando-style, towards the exit. 'Oh no,' she says. 'This is giving me a wedgie.'

The kids collapse, utterly hysterical. Cassie looks like she's going to laugh herself sick.

'Don't go,' Jessica says over the giggles but then remembers Lena has a life, a new boyfriend. She, Jessica, is the lonely one with the bastard ex now. 'Unless you have to?'

'I thought you'd be sick of me by now.' A meaningful gaze communicates that she is not seeing John this evening.

'Never. Stay. We can open that bottle you brought, watch some crap telly?'

'Mum!' Charlie's eyes are plates. 'You said crap.'

An hour later, kids bathed and ready for bed, Lena offers to read them a story while Jessica orders a takeaway, resolving to resume healthy eating next week.

The blanket is still on the table, and as the phone rings out, the warmth Jessica had been feeling cools. Will should be here for these moments. These are the moments that families are made of – these silly nothings, the giggling fits over a few sandwiches eaten under a table just for fun. But he is not here. He is with his lover.

Does she greet him at the door in a silk kimono?

Does she cook for him, pour him a glass of Merlot, listen to his troubles while she strokes his back?

What is her trendy dockside apartment like?

Does she have a sense of humour?

Is she funny?

Gah. It is horrid to feel so curious about someone you are trying desperately not to care about. It is a bug beneath her skin that will not stop burrowing. Towards four this afternoon, she even called Will's practice just to see if he was at work. Alan answered, tried to chat her up as he always does, making her skin crawl, before telling her Will had taken two weeks off.

'How've you been anyway? Not seen you for ages.'

'Good, thanks. Got to go.' With indecent haste, she closed the call before pushing her forehead against her desk until the urge to upend her office furniture had passed.

'Take a holiday, Will, why don't you?' she whispered with flashing fury into the sleek padded leather. 'Take a break, you lazy cheating bastard. Take a break while I work to pay back the money you've stolen. Pour yourself a drink while I bath and feed our children.'

And that was when she put on her coat and, with all the dignity she could muster, strode out of the office.

CHAPTER 16

WILL

Will wakes in a blue room. Something about the light suggests it is late morning. He is not in his temporary flat. He is... he is in Ian's home. Yes, he crashed here last night, drunk. How embarrassing.

He raises his head but immediately lowers it back onto the pillow. Someone has clamped a vice to his head is how it feels. He is wearing pyjamas that are not his. They are navy blue with white piping, so soft he fears they might even be silk. Did he put them on himself? Yes. Yes, he did, he remembers. Oh, thank God – not blackout drunk then, but drunker than he is comfortable with. He looks about him, resolving to not let this happen again. He cannot match Ian drink for drink, simply does not have the capacity. Below the coving, there is a football motif running around the top of the room. On the wall, a framed signed poster of a football player in a red-and-white-striped kit.

Gingerly he rolls to his side and slowly levers himself up. The duvet cover is emblazoned with a circular red crest with the words Brentford Football Club running round the perimeter. In the middle is the image of a bee. This must be Ian's son's room. What did Ian say his name was? Michael? Martin? The room is immaculate. But what brings a pit to his stomach is that, unlike the rest of the house, it is not impeccably tasteful. The football theme is very much about the boy, not the house. Ian has forgone his classy taste solely to make his son happy. And his son doesn't even live here any more.

Is this what lies ahead? Pouring love into an empty room for an absent boy?

Whatever happens with Jessica, Will thinks, she cannot move away. She will have to stay in the area; he will insist on it.

His head falls into his hands. How can he even be thinking along these lines? They will not be getting divorced. They will not, they will not, they will not. This is just a blip.

But he has left Jessica space and she has not called him. And now she is planning to consult a solicitor. She wants the kids. Ian could be right. She might have met someone else. And Jessica can more than provide, of course she can. She can provide in a way he can't.

I'd get my arse down to a solicitor.

No. No way. They will talk. She isn't with someone else. She can't be.

But who was she with on Wednesday evening? Because it sure as hell wasn't Lena. And if it was a date, it is far too soon for her to have launched herself on Hinge or Bumble or whatever the latest dating site is. Which means that whoever he is, she must have known him *before* – was possibly seeing him *before*.

Shaking the thought away, he staggers out in search of the bathroom. On the landing, he opens a door to find a similar bedroom but for the fact that the duvet cover is floral, the walls pink, and there are flowers running along the coving. Cassie would hate a room like this. She would prefer the boy's one. The pit in his stomach returns, the idea of Cassie coming to *visit*, of him not being across her latest craze, getting it wrong.

Heart in his throat, he closes the door silently, careful not to wake the ghost of a girl he has never met, the spectre of his own lost daughter. Ian Robbins is one broken-hearted man, he thinks. This fact lies at the heart of the connection they have made despite their superficial differences.

The bathroom when he finds it is marble, with a sunken bath, shining gold taps, fluffy white towels like a hotel. It feels wrong even to use it, but he does. It is only when he is back in the boy's room that he realises there is an en suite there. His chest sinks. Everything here serves as a reminder of all that he cannot provide, has never really provided, for his children.

Their house is tiny. The dimensions of the rooms are so small that every time someone moves, someone else has to get out of the way. It will be years before they can think about converting the loft so the kids don't have to share a bedroom, let alone extending the kitchen. His bank balance is pitifully low. If Margot doesn't send that money, if it turns out she was, after all, a con artist, he will find a way to pay Jessica back. He *must* return to work, and when he does, he will book the kids into after-school club and take on more clients. Jessica will soften once she realises how hard it is to hold down a demanding job without his support. Maybe she will ask him to be with the kids in the afternoons until she gets home, and from there they can rebuild the friendship that has always been the bedrock of their relationship.

But why should he? Why should he make it easy for her when she's doing everything she can to destroy him? Why should he play childminder to his own kids?

No. No way. Either he goes back as their father or not at all.

The tantalising smell of bacon drifts into the room. He becomes aware of Ian moving about downstairs, singing to himself – a John Coltrane song, he thinks. The man is full of surprises.

In the en suite, Will showers and dries himself with the

ridiculously soft white towel. At the corner, the initials IR have been embroidered in navy cotton. He smiles to himself. Coming from nothing, it makes sense that Ian should want everything. Jessica has a little of this in her too, often buys herself *House Beautiful* or *Elle Decor* for a treat. She says she only buys them to get ideas, but he has seen how longingly she looks at those perfect houses. Ian's home could feature in one of those magazines. But he has no one to share it with. It is quite stratospherically sad really. Perhaps his paternal energies have been channelled into being a saviour of others.

But then didn't he, Will, appoint himself Margot's saviour the day she fell sobbing into his arms, surrounded by the luxury of an elegant hotel room? He remembers how, without warning, she reached up and caressed his face, stared into his eyes with such fear and sorrow. How he felt himself being pulled towards her.

'William,' she whispered, close enough that he could feel her breath on his lips. 'You are a good man.' She closed her eyes, her own lips parting.

He almost kissed her. Almost. Startling, he found himself there as if he had left and re-entered his own body.

'I'm sorry,' he said, edging away. 'I'm married. I love my wife.'

'No, I'm sorry.' Tears ran in thick threads down her thin face. 'It is my mistake. I don't know myself. My children are shadows. I am a shadow. I need to get to France. It is the only way. My only hope is a stranger, William. You. Can you help me?'

The kindness of strangers. Will has thought many times since about that almost-kiss. He doesn't think she was trying to seduce him into helping her, not exactly; more that in some warped way born of desperation and confusion, she was trying to offer him something in return for his help. He will never know. He would never have asked. He helped her because she was frightened and alone and because it was the right thing to do. The only thing he did wrong was not tell Jessica. But he didn't think she would ever agree to giving someone they didn't know two thousand pounds, would think he was soft in the head, a pushover. But Jessica never saw the terror in Margot's eyes when Will got her and the kids to the airport that day.

His rusty old people carrier was the perfect disguise, Margot said. When he pulled up outside Departures, his heart was beating fast with fear. Margot looked left, right, behind her – wide-eyed, electric with paranoia.

'No one has followed us,' he said softly, to calm her.

A watery smile, little more than a twitch of her lips, her eyes hidden by black sunglasses. He got out, ran around the front of the car and opened the passenger-side door.

'Thank you,' she said, lowering herself out like a fragile queen. 'Thank you, William.'

'Get the kids. We need to be quick.'

'First I need to say goodbye.' She caressed his face for the second time, pulled him to her and kissed him, hard and for no more than a second. It was not a romantic kiss; it was the sealing of a bond only they understood. He did not resist. She stepped back, still holding his arms tight in her bony fingers. 'Goodbye, dear William. I will never forget what you did for us. I will never forget you.'

'Nor I you. Go.'

In the back seat, the kids were mute with fear. Margot dipped down to retrieve her bag from the footwell, looking around like an animal leaving its den. The bag overturned, spilling their passports against the kerb.

'It's OK,' he said. 'I'll get this. You get the kids.'

Yes, he thinks now, dressed in another man's silk pyjamas, he is hardly a stranger to the saviour complex himself, is he?

Downstairs, he finds Ian in the kitchen in front of the stove. He is dressed in beige chinos and a long-sleeved navy T-shirt. Around his waist is a grey chef's pinny. Jazz plays softly from invisible speakers.

'Thought you might need a fry-up.' He meets Will's eye and grins.

In the pan, fat sausages spit and crackle. Last night, Will said he wasn't vegetarian. It is, he realises, too late to change that now. Besides, he thinks as the near-intoxicating smell fills his nostrils, the whole no-meat thing was Jessica's idea, not his. It is about time he stood up for himself.

'That's so kind of you,' he says. 'I hope I'm not stopping you working.'

'I'm the boss, mate.' Another grin. 'There's coffee in the pot. Milk in the jug. Sugar in the bowl. Help yourself.' With a deft flip of tongs, Ian lifts the sausages onto a plate inside the oven. A moment later, he has cracked four eggs – one-handed and unbelievably quickly – into the frying pan.

'Won't be long,' he says. 'How's your head?'

'Fuzzy.' Will pours himself some coffee. On the bar are two white plates, gleaming cutlery, thick linen napkins.

'Paracetamol?'

'I'll see how the coffee goes.'

'Put the toast in, will you?' Ian gestures towards the chrome Dualit toaster, where four slices of bread are waiting to go. 'Hope you like sourdough. There's butter in the dish. I don't have it myself. Watching my cholesterol.'

Glad of a task, Will busies himself with the toast. A minute later, Ian places a long white platter and a pair of silver tongs on the bar. On the platter are browned button mushrooms, black pudding slices still bubbling with heat, and crispy bacon to add to the sausages and eggs. He pours orange juice into two crystal tumblers. A life full of beautiful things.

'This is incredible,' Will says. 'You're such a good cook. You have everything so nice.'

'Something I've learnt. Didn't want to go down the baked beans on toast every night road like a loser, know what I mean? It's nice to have someone to cook for, to be honest. Do you cook?'

'I try. I make a mean lasagne. A passable roast.'

'Good man.'

They tuck in. After a moment, Ian announces that he has been thinking. He holds up his fork for emphasis. 'The way I see it is this: you're in a proper spot. I was in a spot, as I might have mentioned. Dave helped me out of that spot. I'm going to help you out of yours.'

'But you've been more than generous,' Will says. 'I already don't know how to repay you.'

Ian shakes his head, raises his hand, chewing a mouthful of food. 'Like I said' – he swallows – 'one of these days, you'll be in a position to help someone. It might be a mate; it might be a stranger. It might even be me. I like you. Don't know why, to be honest. Your clothes are crap and your hair needs a cut, but you're all right.'

Will laughs. The sausage is spicy, and so delicious he wonders how he ever let himself be cajoled into thinking smashed avocado with a poached egg on top was just as good.

'The flat is OK,' Ian says. 'But you get your kids later, don't you? Weekends I go to my flat in town. It's near London Bridge, South Bank. I like to ring the changes, see things, get a bit of culture. Jen introduced me to all that stuff and it stuck even if she didn't. I go to the galleries. I see films at the BFI, the theatre sometimes. Long and the short, this place is empty most weekends. I don't need the house or the cars. You'll have your kids, what, every two weeks?'

The words are a kick in Will's chest. Every two weeks.

Fourteen days. Unable to speak, he builds a small tower of egg, mushroom and sausage on the scaffolding of his fork.

'I guess,' he manages.

'So bring them here. Boy and a girl, you said?'

'Cassie and Charlie,' Will says.

'Cassie and Charlie. Boy and a girl. Gentleman's family, like mine. They can have a room each.' Ian looks down a moment, coughs briefly into the fleshy roll of his fingers. 'If I'm going to be here, I'll tell you. If it's not convenient. But, like I say, this place is usually empty and the kids'll go mad for the games room. You've got Richmond down the road, the river; they'll love it. Plus, you can keep the burglars out for me. House-sit sort of thing.'

Will shakes his head but already he knows he will not be able to refuse. Just as an origami artist takes a sheet of paper and makes a tiny swan, so Ian folds his huge generosity so as to make it small and pretty enough to accept – a gift, a token. It is a killer combination with the propulsive, masculine energy he possesses, the sheer force of personality or charisma or whatever it is that means he gets served immediately at the bar, is successful in his business dealings, is someone others recognise immediately, jump to attention around. Will has been going to the same branch of Starbucks for the last eight years and not once has a barista remembered him – and there, they write his name on the paper cup, for God's sake.

'Listen,' Ian says with an air of weary resolution, running his tongue over his gums and sucking his teeth, 'I'm offering partly as a bit of an apology. I need to tell you something.'

'Oh?'

'Don't throw a wobbly. I know you said not to, but I am as I am and I do as I do. And I did something. You might think something I shouldn't have.'

Will's scalp tingles. 'What?'

'Last night when I asked you if you wanted me to put

someone on your missus, I was hoping you'd say yes.' Ian sighs. 'The fact is, I'd already got one of my lads to have a look and see what she was up to.' He throws up his hands. 'He didn't go anywhere near her, just had a look, that's all. Nothing intrusive, but the long and the short of it is it looks like you might be right. She might have someone.'

'*What?* How did you know where I live? I mean, where she lives?'

'He followed you there on Wednesday evening.' He grins. 'Didn't notice, did you? Told you he was discreet. She was with this geezer in Tesco's. My man said they looked like they were on... intimate terms, I suppose you'd say. Giggling and what not. I was going to tell you last night, but you were a bit worse for wear. I'm sorry, mate.'

Will lays down his knife and fork, feels the slap of the chair against his back. He covers his face with his hands and makes himself breathe.

'I hope I didn't do the wrong thing, but I have a spider sense for when someone's having the wool pulled over their eyes, do you know what I mean? Years dealing with sharks. Her reaction to your... thing... it just seemed off. I'm sorry.'

'It's OK,' Will says. 'You were acting out of kindness – I can see that. It's just... it's a shock, that's all. The idea of having someone followed. Having Jess... I never thought she'd— I mean, were they shopping together? As in, for a meal?' A meal they would prepare together, eat together, accompany with a nice bottle of red. Smoke an after-dinner cigarette, or maybe they smoked after... Oh God. While he was with the kids.

'... but I do know what it's like to lose your family,' Ian is saying. Will tunes back in. 'I'm not going to stand by and watch you lose yours. I know I only met you last week, but I have a sense for these things. You're a good bloke, I can tell. You messed up, but we all mess up sometimes, and I can't stand by and watch you get taken for a ride. Because that's what she's doing, mate. She's taking advantage of your good nature. She's taking you for a ride.'

'She's... No. It won't be that.' *Jessica, lying in bed with a man he can't picture beyond a dark shape, her hair falling loose over her naked shoulders, laughing, smoking. He does not know this woman.*

'You don't want to believe it. I get that, I do. I didn't either. But like you said, she was all dolled up and it didn't feel right, and when something doesn't feel right, in my experience, it usually isn't. You've never been done over; it's only natural you're not suspicious. I get that. But whether you believe it or not, you need to start thinking ahead. Don't let her blindside you like Jen did me. If you want to keep your kids, you need to get your act together. I'm telling you because you need to hear it from someone. You need to think of your kids. If she wants to live the life of a twenty-something, sleeping around and such, she can do that from a flat, not the family home. That's... it's inappropriate.'

Will says nothing. His breakfast is going cold. *Jessica lying in bed. With another man. Laughing. At him.* He picks up his fork, makes a desultory stab at a piece of sausage. Stares at it.

'You've got the use of this house for now,' Ian says. 'You've got the flat. It's called making adequate provision, if I remember rightly.'

'Adequate provision. Yes.'

'If you need cash, give me a shout. I've got a thousand errands need doing that I don't have time for, and you'd be helping me out. Meanwhile, let's get you a solicitor.'

'Yes. OK. OK. I've got one actually.'

'Not like this one you haven't. Hugo is the dog's. I'll text you his number and I'll let him know you're going to be in touch.'

'I'm not sure I can afford—'

'Don't worry about that. Hugo owes me one. Don't worry about it.'

'Oh. I... If you're sure.'

'I'm sure. We don't let her take your kids, all right? No way.'

'No.'

'We fight, yes?'

'OK. OK, yes. We fight.'

'Right. Now, let's get you down the barber's. You don't want to be turning up looking like that.'

CHAPTER 17

JESSICA

On Sunday evening, Jessica is staring out of the window, waiting for the kids to come home, when a huge black Range Rover or Land Rover, whatever it is, turns into the crescent. Either one of the neighbours has won the lottery, she thinks, or someone has a rich visitor.

She turns away from the window. The living room is immaculate. She has spent much of her first weekend without Cassie and Charlie cleaning. On Saturday, Lena took her into town for a light lunch and a glass of fizz, *because this is the sort of thing you can do now, babe,* then browbeat her into having her brows, well, beaten – or microbladed, to use the correct term. Then she took her to have some acrylic nails put on. Jessica is not at all sure about them, nor about Fall Wonders, the gaudy red colour Lena pleaded with her to choose. Jessica is not much of a shopper – she buys her clothes online and over the years has built up a professional wardrobe that is good quality, plain and practical. At weekends, she's in jeans and a hoodie. But it was fun, in a way, trying on clothes, holding up horrible dresses and calling each other silly names just like they did in their teens.

The moment she found herself back home, though, she felt like she wanted to scratch off her own skin. When Will used to take the kids to the park, staying home was a break, a moment to catch up with herself – she was usually asleep within seconds. But this was different. She was alone, starkly, painfully, not out of choice. And now her hands are raw – Will's Marigolds are too big. Her back aches from an overenthusiastic bout of sweeping the patio after she mowed the lawn. Yes, even the garden is pruned and primped, and when she finished, she stood with her hands on her hips and waited for the satisfaction of a job well done to hit. But instead, all that hit her, squarely and with the force of a hammer, was the fact that this labour was not for her at all. It was for Will. For pride, perhaps, but mainly for Will. She had nearly killed herself so that he would see she could manage perfectly well without him.

The doorbell rings. Jessica checks the crescent. The hulking black car is parked in front of next-door, their own house fronted by the dilapidated people carrier Will said he'd replace and never did. When he picked up the kids on Friday afternoon – sporting a trendy new haircut and a beard flecked with red and trimmed to perfection – he said he didn't need the car, that he would take them on the train. Jessica didn't ask why, wanting only for him to leave as quickly as possible so that she could close the front door, slide down it and burst into tears.

She makes her way into the hall, where the excited chatter of her children reaches her. How strange that she did not see them wandering down the close a moment ago. When she opens the door, Will is there with them of course. His clothes are smart – the dark jeans she bought him for Christmas again and his best green hoodie. He looks... attractive, frankly. Another kernel of resentment forms. Now that they are no longer together, he has smartened himself up? For whom?

His lover. Of course.

'Hi,' he says, his smile strange.

Hooked over his forefinger is a car key with a silver fob. The fob has the Land Rover logo on it. Knowledge falls, lands. Lena's words return to her: *Next thing he'll be driving round in a sports car.* And here he is. The pimpmobile was not a lottery winner; it was her husband. Will, penniless Will, has dropped the kids off in a car that costs twice what most people earn in a year. Madame X has let him borrow her ridiculous overpriced SUV. For God's sake.

'Hi, gang,' she manages through gritted teeth and bends to hug the kids. 'Have you had a lovely time?' She will not ask about the car. She will not. No way. Standing up to meet his eye, she asks: 'Whose is the car?'

A smug grin she would never tire of punching clean from his poncy new beard spreads across his – well, across his poncy new beard. 'It's a... a friend's.'

She averts her eyes. Cannot bear to look at him. Focuses instead on Cassie and Charlie, who are chattering nineteen to the dozen. *A friend's.* Hers then. No doubt about it. She could scream.

'We stayed in a mansion,' Cassie almost squeals.

'It had a ping-pong table and a home cinema,' Charlie says. 'We watched *Jumanji* and had popcorn from the popcorn maker.'

'*We* have a popcorn maker,' Jessica says, hating herself instantly. She crouches down beside the kids. 'I tell you what, if you guys get your pyjamas on right now, we can watch a movie tonight, OK? Why don't you say goodbye to Daddy and run upstairs?'

'Can Daddy stay and watch the movie?' The way Cassie is looking at her is a brutal and penetrating torture.

Jessica blinks back her tears. 'I think Daddy's got to—'

'Remember we talked about this in the car?' Will interrupts, lowering himself down and tucking a strand of hair behind

Cassie's ear. 'Mummy and Daddy are having some time apart for a bit, OK? But we love both of you very much.'

They are both crouching now, and when Will's eyes meet hers, what Jessica sees there shocks her: a hardness that is new. Will does not want to stay and watch a movie. He is not pleading with her, even silently, to let him come back. He is *happy* to drop the kids and leave. It is as if they have been separated for months, as if divorce is inevitable. Oh why did she let him read that damn letter? Why are men so bloody *literal* about everything?

But of course, this is not about the letter. It is because he has someone to get back to, someone waiting for him, someone he loves. That is why he has not tried to call her, to meet her, to talk.

Unable to bear it, she stands up but has no idea where to look, where to put her hands. She feels like a child stuck in a car rolling towards a cliff edge.

'Bye, guys.' Will's overblown good cheer rings false, almost sinister. Time has speeded up; it's going far too fast. 'See you on Wednesday, OK? If you're really good for your mum, I'll make popcorn again, all right? *And* you can ask for your favourite dinner. Just tell Mummy and she'll text me and I'll buy the ingredients on the way, OK?'

'Like, even lasagne?' Charlie says, eyes round.

'Deal,' Will says, as if he's American. 'But only if you get those PJs on super quick and be good for Mummy for three whole days, OK?'

'Yay!'

Will has pulled out his trump card – his delicious cooking. Jessica curses herself for agreeing over text that he could pick the kids up from school on Wednesdays from now on. She only did that because it helps her – her, not him. But he has immediately turned it to his advantage. He pulls the kids into his arms. Jessica turns away, tears winning out. She wipes her face with her hands. *Stay*, she wants to say, so badly she has to press her mouth tight shut. *Let's stop playing these games. For God's sake let's just work it out and live our life.*

'Go on upstairs then,' she hears him say. 'See if you can put your jim-jams on in record time.'

Giggling, the kids rumble past and up the stairs. Jessica turns to face her husband, whose effortless ability to get them to do things and be cheerful about it is a dagger in her chest after all the bargaining, whining and blackmail of the last week. She wants to be the bigger person and say *thank you, thank you for asking them to be good for me*, but it feels humiliating, and besides, he is already walking away. He has not noticed the garden. Has not even stepped into the house. Halfway up the path, he turns and raises a hand briefly before continuing to the car, the extortionate army tank that Madame X no doubt won in her last divorce settlement. No goodbye, no self-pity, no *hey, can we talk?* Something has calcified in him. His diamond-hard affability has given her a pain in her chest.

The car bleeps and flashes. Will gets in. A second later, he roars away, and Jessica finds herself standing at the open door, hand on the catch, as if she's waiting for someone to come home.

She shakes herself, checks her watch. Five minutes have passed since Will roared away in his lover's car and she is still standing at the front door, holding on to the catch. From inside, the sound of the kids drifts out. They seem happy to be back at home, and she doesn't know how she feels about that, about any of it. On impulse, she texts her mum: *Kids are back. Fancy coming over? I can make us a simple pasta supper.*

Fifteen minutes later, her mother is sitting with Cassie and Charlie while they gabble to her about the magnificent house, the home cinema, the sickening amazingness of it all. Over their heads, her mother catches Jessica's eye and they share a conspiratorial glance of exasperation.

'Is it OK if I pop to Tesco quickly?' Jessica asks, thinking she will grab some Prosecco, Mum's favourite, to share.

'Of course it is. Off you go, love.'

Inside the supermarket, she picks up a basket. She shopped earlier today but must have been distracted, because when she got home, she realised she'd forgotten half of what she went for.

Slowly she tours the aisles, trying to block the thought that one of the other shoppers might be the guy from the tobacco queue. At the fresh section, she picks up a box of grapes, considers the blueberries for longer than is necessary, stares at the herbs as if mesmerised. That guy won't be here, of course he won't, but if he is, she will talk to him. Why not? Her cheating, stealing husband with his midlife-crisis car and his fancy lover can go and jump in a lake.

In the fridge at the end of the third aisle, she finds some Prosecco on offer. She reaches to the back to grab the coldest and is lowering it into her basket when a voice she recognises says, 'Fancy meeting you here.'

She feels herself blush. For God's sake, what is she, twelve?

'Oh,' she says, turning to face the guy from the tobacco queue, whose good looks have not faded since the last time she saw him. 'Hello.'

'I could follow that up with *do you come here often* if you like?' He grins. He is really very attractive. Not in the same way that Will is – almost the opposite in fact. Where Will has a kind of shambolic charm, this man is very put together. And there is no way Will would approach a woman he didn't know without some sort of introduction.

Or would he? What does she know?

The man glances into her basket. 'Any good?'

'God knows. It's on offer, that's the main thing. I'm having a cosy night in with my... my friend and just realised I was out of booze.' *Too much information, Jessica.*

'Sunday is the new Friday sort of thing?'

'Oh, I'll be doing Friday too, don't worry.'

He laughs, his eyes crinkling gorgeously at the edges, his fingertips touching his forehead momentarily. His nails are clipped, manicure-clean, the backs of his hands tanned. His shirt cuff is pale blue, new-looking. Jessica fights the urge to lean in and smell him.

'And then there'll be another weekend,' she adds. 'At which point I will probably do Saturday and maybe even Sunday again, just for kicks.'

He rolls his eyes, but good-humouredly, and reaches into the fridge. 'A bottle of this sounds good. I think I'll do the same. Alone, alas.' He cocks his head to one side, pulls a rueful face.

Jessica feels heat climb up her neck. God help her.

'Well, enjoy.' She moves away, tries to remember how she usually walks, rounds the nearest corner so she can breathe.

It is so long since she has even entertained the idea of flirtation, she thinks as she picks up some Petit Filous for the kids. There has been an invisible wall between her and other men. She has bricked herself up – consciously or subconsciously, she is not sure. Some Babybel cheeses are thrown into the basket, a tub of Philadelphia. But the bricks are falling and the effect of realising that she is still there, that she can still be seen, is not unpleasant.

She is loading her bags into the boot when she sees the man crossing the car park towards her. He breaks into a jog, his easy fitness obvious even in his lovely suit.

'Forgive me,' he says. 'I don't do this. I really don't do this, I swear. Maybe it was the tragedy of the cosy night in for one, but I was wondering if I could possibly get your number?'

· · ·

A plaintive wail sails down the landing.

Cassie. Jessica rubs her eyes, checks her phone: 02:33. Her head aches – she and Mum finished the bottle while they chewed over the latest developments with Will.

'Mummy! Daddy!'

Jessica jumps out of bed and rushes along to the kids' room.

Cassie is sitting up in bed. She is hot and damp to the touch, possibly still asleep.

'Hey, hey, darling. It's OK. Mummy's here.' Jessica pulls her daughter into her arms. I hate you, Will, she thinks. I hate you for what you've done to us.

'Where's Daddy? When is he coming home?' Cassie's eyes are pools of sadness. Jessica doesn't know if she's asleep or awake.

'I told you, lovey. Daddy and I are having a break from each other. Grown-ups do that sometimes. I'm the lucky one because I get to stay with you and Charlie while Daddy is staying with his friend. Did you... meet them while you were there at the weekend?' Them – gender neutral. She should not pump the kids for information. She should not she should not she should not.

'Daddy's friend wasn't there. There was a home cinema. We watched *Jumanji*.'

'Yes. You told me.' Her scalp shrinks to her head. She too feels hot, sweaty; the room is stuffy. On the far side, Charlie is curled up, his hand a soft fist against his cheek.

'When is he coming home?'

'Let's talk about it in the morning, OK?' *Please have forgotten this conversation by then.*

'But you always have to go to work. And then we have Lena or Granny. Why can't Daddy pick us up any more?'

'He's going to pick you up on Wednesday, OK? That'll be nice, won't it?'

Jessica stands and opens the window a crack, holds her face

momentarily against the chill air before returning to her daughter. She straightens out her bedclothes. 'Shall I get you some water?'

Before Cassie can reply, she walks out and heads for the bathroom to fetch a glass. But there is only the plastic toothbrush beaker, grey scum at the base. She is too tired to go downstairs, so tired she could weep, and now she has lied to her daughter, more than once. She cleans the scum from the beaker with the end of her finger, rinses and fills it.

Damn you, Will, she thinks. Damn you to hell.

Back in bed, eyes dry as dust, she rakes through Will's departure earlier in his girlfriend's ridiculous status-symbol car. She wishes she'd pushed Cassie a little more. Asked for a name, casually. But if the woman had made herself scarce, and Cassie didn't volunteer a name, that means Will hasn't been so crass as to introduce her or tell them anything about her.

Her hands close into fists. Madame X. The woman with whom it is all supposedly over. The Chanel jacket. The car. The mansion – big enough for a games room and a home cinema. She has let her hapless lover live in her flat, use her house to host his children, to save him from having to beg to return home. She has used her wealth to ensnare him, quickly, while there is a crack of light through which she can squeeze her manipulative skinny bones. Will cannot afford rent; Jessica should have known he'd moved in with someone. My God, he must have called Madame X the moment he walked out the door, told her not that he'd been kicked out but that he'd *left*, that he couldn't live without her, that he'd told his wife everything. Wooed by this grand gesture, weeping with the romance of it all, she took him back instantly. Typical Will, always landing on his feet.

'Bastard,' she whispers, feeling utterly unhinged, and bursts into tears.

CHAPTER 18

WILL

Almost four weeks have passed in relative calm. A hiatus, a breather, a ceasefire. A routine has been established, a civil exchange. But if Jessica thinks Will has been sitting at home twiddling his thumbs while she gets ready to take everything from him, she is wrong. Will has been busy.

He makes his way to the Express Tavern, self-conscious in his new-found smartness. But he is meeting Ian, and as he has learnt, Ian likes his friends to be well dressed. There have been hints: one scathing comment on the age of Will's jeans, laughter at his trainers, and the bag of clothes Ian dropped off at the flat. In the bag were three shirts, two pairs of jeans, one pair of chinos, a suit jacket, two cashmere sweaters, all unworn; a pair of brand-new Nike Air trainers and a box containing a pair of dark brown Red Wing ankle boots, also new. All items Ian was apparently giving to charity.

'Thought you might like a rifle through first if you're short on clobber. You a size ten shoe? Same as me. There's a couple of pairs in there. I buy stuff all the time and then I either don't like it or don't get round to wearing it but can't be bothered to take it back. Too busy. Have a look. Pick out anything you fancy and take the rest down to the FARA shop for me, yeah? If you don't mind, that is.'

Will said that no, of course he didn't mind. He kept everything of course, doubling his wardrobe, not to mention giving it a serious upgrade. The trousers were a little too big, the collar size on the shirts one up from his own, but so what? He pulled his old belt from his jeans. He could wear the shirts with an open neck. The sweaters were a large but looked fine over the shirts. *Beggars can't be choosers*, his mother chimed in, goading him even in death.

What must that be like, he wondered as he held the fine knits and the cottons against himself, took in the designer logos, the pristine cardboard, even tissue paper; what must it be like to have the money to buy shoes in multiples and never even get them out of the box? To order sweaters and trousers and throw them away before they pill or sag, sometimes before they've even been worn? The last time Will bought shoes, he left the old ones in the shop for the shop assistant to put directly into the bin.

The clothes are not really his style – their quality embarrasses him even though they are not ostentatious – but now, walking down the street, he has to concede that he feels different, that he felt different last week when he returned to work. It is the same difference he feels when he drops the kids off in Ian's car: a kind of power that makes him walk taller and with more purpose. The look on Jessica's face that first time was priceless. He half wishes he could be there when she receives the letter the solicitor drafted for him this morning. What Hugo had to tell him was a surprise, to say the least. He informed Will, with all legal certainty, that as the main carer, he did indeed have the right to live in the family home. Jessica must know this. Which is why there has been no solicitor's letter from her, why she has gone quiet on that front. Perhaps she's not quite ready to move in with her boyfriend yet.

Perhaps she is still working hard on making *adequate provision*.

'But it's her house,' Will said to Hugo in his lovely office in Barnes. 'She bought it before we got married. I moved in with her.'

'But then you got married. The fact that your wife bought the house is irrelevant.' Hugo peered at him through two thick-framed windows of trendy tortoiseshell. 'You're married. You're entitled to half of everything. That's the law. And if you've looked after the children all this time, then custody will go to you.'

'Really? Even if I'm the one who... if I'm the one in the photographs?'

'Irrelevant. The law is the law. Blame doesn't come into it. There would have to be criminal activity or abuse or something of that sort. An extramarital affair doesn't affect your rights in any way.'

They proceeded to brainstorm possible grounds for divorce. With devastating skill, Hugo fired question after question, teased out strands of information and fattened them into ropes to tie Jessica in knots. He promised, in carefully chosen words, to compose a letter that would make Jessica's lovely auburn hair curl.

Will left the solicitor's office reeling, a little sick. Jessica had made him believe his life was over, that he would be banished to a one-bedroomed flat, allowed to see his children only once a fortnight. He only agreed in order to keep the fragile peace for the children, for fear of Jessica making things even worse for him. He was trying to get her to a place where they could talk, where he could win her back even. But now he knows that if things break down irreversibly, he has rights. Ian has given him so much more than shelter and fine clothes, not to mention a palace for him and the kids at weekends. If it hadn't been for him, Will is pretty sure he would have suffered a complete nervous breakdown. Ian's confidence in him – yes, this is what lies at the heart of things, the firm belief that he can not only survive but somehow come out on top – is all that has propped him up since that dreadful day.

But soon, officially, he won't need Ian's house or his dock-side flat. The family home will be his. The children will live in it with him, and Jessica can sing. It's not like he even wanted this divorce, not initially. He only wants it now because why would anyone want to stay with someone who clearly doesn't love them any more? Because she doesn't and she's proved that. One look at those photographs and she went from nought to a hundred. She pushed the nuclear button. You don't do that if you love someone. And now, through Ian's man on the ground, he knows why. She was already seeing someone and was wondering how she could leave when an exit plan landed – *boom!* – on her WhatsApp.

A thought hits him: what if Jessica's boyfriend is behind the photos? What if, sick of being her bit on the side, he took and sent those pictures to make Will look like a cheat so that he could coax her away from her husband and family?

He wishes he had more details on this guy. But if they were filling a basket together in the supermarket, chatting affection-ately, they must be dreaming of a future together by now. Will pictures them wandering the aisles, the basket hooked over the crook of this bastard's arm, Jessica making suggestions, holding up bars of chocolate and making puppy-dog eyes, him laughing and saying *oh go on then* while Will sat there weeping over the letter she had written him – my God, the cruelty.

Well, let her read his solicitor's letter and cry him a river.

Ian is already at the bar. It occurs to Will that they are simi-larly dressed. Of course they are. He is wearing Ian's cast-offs – not even cast-offs; his unworn rejections.

'Pravha?' Ian says.

'Great, thanks.'

Ian orders the beers and the two of them sit at the same table as the night they met.

'Did you go and see Hugo?' Ian crosses his feet and takes a gulp of his Solaris. His brogues look bigger than a size ten, Will thinks. 'Will? Hello?'

'Sorry.' Will takes a sip of lager before filling Ian in on his conversation, how pleased he is, how the letter will be with Jessica tomorrow or the day after.

'Good,' Ian says. 'Good. Work?'

'Back to it. Taken on two new clients.' It is an effort to concentrate on the conversation. Ian told him their feet were the same size. Why would he lie about that? Did he buy those shoes for Will? And if he bought the shoes, did he also buy the clothes? That would be quite weird, wouldn't it? Very weird.

'Good man,' Ian says. 'Did it go OK?'

'What with?'

'Your new clients. Work. What planet are you on, mate?'

Will makes himself meet Ian's gaze, forces himself back to the moment. 'It went well, yes. I don't know whether it's the new clothes or the haircut or what. Maybe I'm just running on rage or something, but I was more... assertive, I suppose you'd say.'

Ian licks the foam from his top lip like the cat that got the cream. 'How so?'

'Well, there's this one client. She always takes off her glasses and her bangles and her rings, even her shoes, so she can tuck her feet under her and get comfortable. Then when the session ends, it takes her an age to sort herself out. We always overrun. Always. But yesterday I ended the session five minutes early, and when she asked why, I explained that I was allowing time for her to put her things back on. She looked shocked but I explained it was a boundary for me, that it was important to respect the timings of the session.'

'What did I tell you? Clothes maketh the man.'

'I'm guessing you know who said that?'

Ian grins. 'Mark Twain.'

'I've never really thought too much about it,' Will says. 'My job isn't an office job, so a suit is too formal – not that my old work suits would fit me any more – but I'd never have believed what I wore would make so much difference. Thank you.'

'There's no greater feeling of ease than knowing one is suitably dressed.'

Will waits.

Ian shakes his head. 'I've forgotten who that's from. Might have been David Mamet, but don't quote me.'

Will smiles. 'Do you often give away your clothes brand new like that?'

'They know me very well in FARA, I'm afraid. It... assuages my guilt, I suppose you'd say.'

Perhaps the clothes *were* Ian's. They were, after all, too big. Perhaps his feet look larger in those chunky brogues.

'Well, thanks again,' Will says, for something to say.

'You'd let your wife take all the power, that's all. It happens. You've been left holding the babies, quite literally, while she's gone from strength to strength. I bet she's got some decent threads, hasn't she?'

'She needs them. For work.'

Ian throws out his hands, as if what Will said proves his point.

'There you go,' he says. 'And if your suits don't fit, we need to get you enrolled in a gym, get that beer belly sorted. She'll be begging you to come back.'

'I think I'd lost confidence,' Will says after a moment. 'Being at home with the kids is great and everything, but you don't access your professional persona with any real regularity.'

'Access your professional persona.' Ian raises his eyebrows, pushes his bottom lip up against the top and nods. 'Nice.'

Will gives a modest shrug. 'You can quote me on that.'

'I might.'

'No, but you know what I mean. Your work face or game face or whatever it is kind of withers, that energy, that way of being. You go back to work and try and focus, but you're so used to hanging out with under-fives that next thing you know, you're in a meeting room and it's all you can do not to jump out of your seat and shout *Bus!* when a double decker goes past the window.'

Ian laughs.

'That's why,' Will goes on, 'I mean, maybe that's why I... with Mar— That's why I let myself cross the line. She only met the professional, confident version of me. She saw me differently. Sometimes Jessica makes me feel like I'm surplus to requirements, you know? She's so strong, so independent, sometimes it felt like if I wasn't there, she would manage perfectly well. I guess we all need to be needed. And maybe I...'

'Let yourself go.'

That wasn't what Will was going to say, but he presses on. 'I've spent so much time wiping bums, watching kids' TV and bargaining with a four-year-old who doesn't want to eat his broccoli, and meanwhile she was heading up high-powered meetings and travelling the world. And then she'd ask me to do something like buy a new car, but I didn't know what she wanted and I felt like I would be pestering her by asking. Worse actually. I didn't know what *I* wanted. I wasn't able to pay for it with money I'd earned, so it didn't feel like my decision. It never felt like my decision. Same with booking holidays, restaurants. The rare occasions we went out, say, for our wedding anniversary, she always booked. Nothing felt like my decision.'

As he talks, he feels himself getting angrier. Jessica has let him become this person, and now she's throwing his shortcomings in his face as the reason for ending their marriage, claiming that she carried him, that he checked out, stopped making an effort, when his whole existence was effort, for her, for the children, his own professional life pushed so far to one side he had to squeeze it into the short periods of time when he wasn't tending to his family's needs.

She carried *him*? Ha!

'You raised those kids,' says Ian. He picks up his glass. 'Sounds like you did a great job. And now they're a bit older, a bit easier, she wants them to herself. Probably thinks she can make a new family with this other fella.'

Will's stomach churns. 'Maybe.'

'She's threatened you with a solicitor, but she hasn't done it, has she? She knows she's on dodgy ground. And now you've got there first.'

Will picks up his own glass, a dark thrill blooming in his chest. 'When she opens that letter, she's going to get the shock of her life.'

CHAPTER 19

JESSICA

Two days later, Jessica gets in from work already feeling frazzled due to an insidious text from Freya, which arrived while she was on the train.

Hey hon. Just to say, am here if you want to chat. Hugs xxx

It was the third such text from her. The first two Jessica left unanswered. Seething, she could practically see Freya's cocked head, her faux sympathy, her thirst for misery, her mental notepad, her glee, her... Oh God, the smug mumzillas would no doubt be attributing St Will's departure to having a wife who worked hard. *Poor Will. So neglected. No wonder.*

She is still concocting a reply to Freya with a deep subtext of *piss off* when she spots an official-looking letter waiting for her on the kitchen table. The envelope is franked but she can't read the company name; the ink is too faint. Upstairs, she can hear her mother bathing the kids – her jolly voice, her gentle cheer. Jessica has bust a gut to get home early, leaving a task she should really have completed by close of business, but she has still arrived too late to sit with them and catch up on their day. At the moment, it feels like she's failing in every part of her life.

She thumbs open the envelope, a small fist of anxiety closing in her gut.

H. S. Cairn & Co. Solicitors
27a Barnes High Street
SW13 9LN
Hugh.Cairn@SSC&Co.com
Tel: 020 869 3876

Our ref: HC/WD
28 October 2023

Dear Ms Jackson

Subject: Mr William Draper

We write to inform you that we have been instructed by our above-named client regarding the breakdown of your marriage. Our client has come to the unfortunate conclusion that the marriage is at an end and has instructed us to initiate divorce proceedings.

'What?' A blow to her belly, hard, like a kick. A ringing in her ears. Jessica bends double, arms across her waist. For a moment, she can't see, the room no more than dark swirls. Slowly, her vision clears. She straightens up, one hand on the kitchen counter for balance. She can't lift her head. Pots and pans lie upside down on the draining board. Her mother has washed them up as she always does instead of using the dishwasher. The folded dishcloth hangs draped over the tap. On the surfaces, not one crumb. The smell of lemon cleaning spray.

She cannot read on, she cannot.

Eventually she manages to raise her head. In her hand, the letter shakes.

Our client has instructed us to file for divorce on the ground of unreasonable behaviour. This appears to be the only ground open to us at present since you have not been separated for more than two years. We shall forward you a copy of the divorce petition in due course. We trust that you will cooperate with the divorce process in order to ensure a swift resolution.

Our client is keen that the children are affected as little as possible and that the matter is processed in the most amicable way possible.

We advise you to seek independent...

She feels the letter slip from her grasp, hears the *plack-swish-swish* of it on the linoleum, fumbles blindly for the back door, finds the handle, staggers through. Outside, rain clings to the dark air. On the wet grass, her suede wedge-heeled boots darken at the toes. She finds that she is biting down on her fist, suppressing a scream so that the children won't hear.

Unreasonable behaviour.

My God. Can Will have done this? Can Will, her Will, have resorted to such *violence*? Apparently yes, he can. He has. Unassuming Will, *innocent* Will, who claimed he could explain everything, has shown he cannot explain anything at all. Those who can explain do not attack. Those who can explain do not say: *It's not what you think.* They do not refuse to give the name of their lover. His modus operandi is clear: he has taken her at her word like the literal-minded fool he is and is attacking her before she attacks him. Could he not see her letter was written when she was blind with pain? Surely he has that much emotional intelligence?

But no, he is thinking only of his own crimes, trying to minimise what he's done. He is already living his new life, with *her.* He cannot face his own wife honestly, cannot claim his actions. He is firing a shot then dipping behind the parapet. He is either not able or not prepared to save their marriage, even though he is the architect of its destruction. He will not fight for them and all that they have built together, only for himself.

The bastard. The coward.

The stranger.

Yes, she kicked him out, told him she wouldn't hear another word. And yes, she mentioned a solicitor, but obviously that was an empty threat. If she'd actually meant it, she would have sent a letter by now – surely that's obvious? Was she not allowed a *moment* of rage?

Not letting him come back immediately, acting proud even though she had shattered into a million tiny pieces was meant to give him time to reflect. It was not meant to make him take up arms against her! How can he not realise this when he knows her better than anyone? Apart from Lena and her mother, he is the only one who knows about the night she walked in on her father, how she had to watch him leave in front of all the neighbours, suitcase swinging from his hand; the years of scraping a living, the constant threat of losing their home, the financial help she gave – was proud to give – her mother. He knows her damage just as she knows his. It is part of their bond. Isn't that how intimacy works? He is the only man she has trusted. Surely he must know that in betraying her, he has ruined her for anything more than the most casual encounters from now on? She will never throw herself into love again, ever. She would not dare.

Through the kitchen window, she can see her mother fixing her children's bedtime snack. She shrinks back. None of them have seen her standing out here like a wet rat in a drain. She cannot go into the kitchen now; she will frighten them, vision of madness as she must be. All she can do is stare, on the outside looking in. The children's hair is tracked where Mum has combed it, damp at the edges behind their ears. They are so beautiful. They are golden. They are oblivious, drinking their glasses of milk, nibbling at their biscuits, chattering away. Her mother's eyebrows rise, her mouth makes an O of amazement. Children just want to be seen, for their worlds to be acknowledged as real, valid. They do not want to be told that what they know is not so. No one does, not even grown-ups.

It's not what you think.

I can't tell you.

Unreasonable behaviour.

Weeping silently, she takes cover under the sparse shelter of the apple tree and calls Will.

'Jess.' Even in that one syllable, there is an unemotional firmness that is not him.

'I got the letter,' she says, blinking away raindrops made fat by the branches above. 'Is this really what you want to do?'

'I thought it was what you wanted to do.'

She closes her eyes in frustration. 'Unreasonable behaviour? Really?'

'That's what he advised.'

Classic. Not his doing, not his responsibility. No communication, just another bomb thrown into their family. She pictures Madame X at his back, listening in, arms circled round his waist, head resting between his shoulder blades: *I'm here for you, honey.*

'And you took his advice,' she states, her own preternatural calm frightening her a little, her shaky distance from herself. 'But what the hell have you chalked up as unreasonable behaviour?'

He clears his throat. 'You closed me down. You kicked me out without hearing what I had to say. You physically assaulted me with your shoe. I could have lost an eye! You ghosted me and prevented me from seeing our children for nearly a week. I was traumatised.'

'*You* were traumatised?' She can see herself as from above. Through the sopping branches of the apple tree, the white circle of her crown in her rain-darkened hair. 'I kicked you out after I'd seen twenty-seven photographs of you with your lover.'

'She's not my lover!'

'What then? I'm sorry, "the person you were sleeping with in fancy hotels" doesn't exactly trip off the tongue. And I find it very hard to believe she was your client, by the way. A client would have surely come to the office.'

The rain is pouring now. She moves further under the tree, the last of the apples clinging on, the rest abandoned and browning in slushy lumps on the lawn.

'Do you know what? You don't deserve an explanation,' Will says with chilling quietness. 'You've blocked me at every turn and now I'm afraid I'm no longer inclined to tell you anything at all. You've made it clear that my shortcomings are many and that you've *carried* me all these years. You're cold and you're cruel, and I can't spend the rest of my life making up for your father's bad behaviour.'

'My father's... What? Oh my God! Right.' She breathes deeply, but the air is thin. 'You've made your position incredibly clear. But, Will? Are you listening? You will not win this, not over my dead body.' She ends the call, forces herself to put the phone in her pocket and not throw it into the forsythia.

The light in the kitchen goes out. A moment later, a soft glow blooms from Cassie and Charlie's bedroom window. They have no idea of the pain she is in, of what a shit their father really is. They think the world of him. They love him more than me, she thinks, the thought as sharp as a blade. I have not put them to bed, again. I am working so hard to be *nothing*, invisible, inaudible. I may as well not exist.

She pulls the phone from her pocket, finds the man she has hidden away in her contacts under *Supermarket*, the man who thus far has been a harmless fantasy in a moment of despair. Well, maybe a harmless fantasy is what she needs right now. She texts: *I'm free for dinner at the weekend if you are. I'm free even if you're not.*

Witty, she thinks. He will enjoy that.

CHAPTER 20

WILL

Will is waiting for Ian at the entrance to Selfridges. It is almost six weeks since Jessica kicked him out. Their routine is not one he would ever have chosen, but he can stand it – just – because he knows it is only a matter of time before he returns to the family home, and that even if all hope of Jessica being his is gone, he will at least get his children back. He is biding his time – for the children, for himself.

The weekends spent at Ian's magnificent Kew home have been bittersweet. Watching Cassie and Charlie's joy is overshadowed by the thought of the Sunday-afternoon drop-off, which makes the minutes with them tick by like a countdown. And there's the fact that Jessica isn't with them. She would love that house; they would have giggled together over the sheer grandeur of it. Plus, she's a mean pool player, used to beat him every time at uni. But when he dropped the kids off last time, she seemed more distant than ever. She has not mentioned the solicitor's letter since that angry phone call. That she has not formally responded yet unnerves him. In front of the children, they interact as strangers might, or acquaintances who loathe one another without really knowing why and cover it with a veneer of politeness.

Jessica might be the ice maiden, but he too is keeping his cool.

Are they both acting?

Who knows?

All he knows is that Ian is a little late and that they have a boys' day out in town planned. Will is not sure what this entails. But in his campaign to return Will's self-respect to him, Ian is determined that as well as looking smart, he will also smell good. Along with the flat, the clothes and the gym – he has some free guest passes and has booked Will in for a session with his own personal trainer – he has advised that Will adopt a grooming routine. Ian did not have a famous quote for this aspect of male maintenance, and Will can't think of one either. *Cleanliness is next to godliness* perhaps.

London is busy. It is a mixed early-November day – full sun but black clouds over Hyde Park. He thinks of Pat, the way she would say in her strong northern accent: *Eh, it's a bit black over by Bill's mother's.* His heart pinches. Like her daughter, she has no words for him now, only a flat mouth and eyes that would freeze fire. Her silence is worse than anything she could say. He did try to talk to her last week when he bumped into her on the high street, but she only raised her hand and said, *It's none of my business.* It is all so heavy. He loved Pat, loved her fierce loyalty to Jessica, her calm and funny way with Cassie and Charlie, and with him too. When he and Jessica announced they were getting married, she didn't gush or fuss, said only: 'That's it then.' Her face an image of suppressed joy. 'You're my son now.'

Over Marble Arch, the black clouds creep forward. The effect is ominous, the *raison d'être* of black clouds everywhere, he supposes, and of course everything is ominous at the moment. Songs on the radio, snatches of news; everything seems to pertain to the shitshow in which he finds himself. A permanent stone has taken up lodging in his gut, his shoulders are tight, his breath shallow. Ian tells him he is winning, but winning was never something Will thought about before all this. Winning means someone has to lose. He wants to call Jessica and say: *Please. Let's stop this. No solicitors, no animosity, no war. Let's sort this out and try again.* Things could be better than before, he thinks. He could be more honest about feeling a little taken for granted, frustrated professionally. Jessica could get things off her chest too – like whether she really feels like she carries him, what she thinks he should be doing differently. They should have got all this on the table years ago. If they had, he would never have fallen so hard for Margot and her plight.

The one blessing is that, in all the stress, he has almost forgotten to worry about who took and sent those photographs. Whoever it is appears to be happy with their handiwork. If it is Margot's ex, he can rest assured that he has destroyed Will's marriage – tit for tat. This, apparently, has been enough. If it is Jessica's boyfriend, the same applies. Still, Will wonders now who else could be behind it. Jessica's number is not on the class WhatsApp. Her friends would have it obviously. Freya would have it. Which means Colin could access it. More than once, Colin commented on Jessica's attractiveness in a way that felt a bit uncomfortable. But that's a stretch, isn't it? There was that other woman too, the one who was ill. He remembers her asking him for Jessica's number once. What was her name?

'Wotcha.' Under the covered doorway, Ian is shaking out his umbrella.

'Is it raining?' Will considers his own new black golfing umbrella, which he bought last week on a whim.

'It was,' Ian replies. If he notices Will's umbrella, he doesn't comment. 'Let's do this,' is all he says before taking Will's elbow and guiding him into the store, where all is glass and shine, doll-like assistants behind gleaming counters.

'I've never been here before,' Will says as they step onto the escalator.

'Of course you haven't,' Ian replies.

In the men's cosmetics department – who knew there was such a thing? – Ian introduces Will to a world of products he had no idea he needed. The most urgent thing, apparently, is hair wax.

'Your hair looks like one of my daughter's fluffy toys, mate. You need to get it under control. And it'll need cutting again soon. Every six weeks at least. We're not hippies.'

Will laughs. There is something enjoyable about the way Ian gently bullies him. Perhaps because he knows Ian has his best interests at heart. His advice on everything from legal matters to the ins and outs of the male toilette is a kind of avuncular education, the kind of life advice Will never got from his father, who never taught him to shave, never took him to the barber's, never really showed him how to do the things that men are supposed to be good at. Will has always assumed men who can put up shelves and change tyres are able to do this through some innate gift. But no, they have been shown, just as Jessica was shown by her mother how to earn and look after money, how to paint a room and hem a pair of trousers, how to survive.

Clutching a bag of toiletries costing over a hundred pounds he was too embarrassed not to spend, Will finds himself perched on a high stool at the champagne bar, where Ian has ordered two Veuves.

A moment later, the flutes of champagne arrive, are placed on dainty paper coasters. A small white dish of crisps follows.

Ian holds up his glass. 'Here's to your renaissance.'

'Well, I have to say, *you* are quite the renaissance man.' Will picks up his own glass and chinks it against Ian's. 'I think this might be the first time I've drunk champagne in a public place.'

'There's loads of good places to drink champagne in London. I'll take you to Claridge's sometime. The Corinthia is pretty good too.'

The Corinthia Hotel. Margot. Room 217. Second floor.

'Cheers,' Will says, recovering himself. In the mirror behind the bar, he catches his reflection. His hair is pushed back with something called *fudge*, his new beard thicker and glossier due to a transparent goo the tanned and incredibly worked-out shop assistant with a strip missing from one eyebrow referred to as *balm*.

'You heard from the missus?' Ian asks, popping a crisp daintily into his mouth. His white shirt cuff is as stiff as cardboard. From a gold cufflink, a red jewel flashes.

Will sips his Veuve. *Veuve* means widow in French, he's pretty sure.

'She got the letter?' Ian presses.

'She did.'

'I'm guessing she wasn't happy?'

Will laughs without really knowing why. Despite the fact that Ian will pay for this no doubt heinously priced glass of champagne, the sense of being pushed around persists, though less enjoyably than before. He cannot afford to spend a hundred pounds on toiletries. He could get Cassie three pairs of trainers for that, buy Charlie several hamsters. He will have to take it all back when Ian isn't here.

'Come on, mate,' Ian says. 'It's like getting blood out of a stone.'

'Sorry,' Will says. 'She, er, called me the night she got it. She was angry. Apparently, I will not win, not over her dead body. I haven't heard from her since. Not sure what that means.'

'It means she'll need a bloody good lawyer.' Ian sniffs, glances about briefly, as if to check for spies. 'She will if what Dave's seen is anything to go by.'

'Dave?'

Ian only nods.

'Dave's been watching her?'

'You didn't seem too keen on having her followed, so I told him to keep his distance. But I can assure you he's smart, a smart geezer.'

The thought of Jessica being followed makes him feel ill. But still, he is unable to stop himself from asking: 'Has she seen him again? The guy from the supermarket?'

'He took her to the theatre last weekend. The matinee of *A Streetcar Named Desire*. Afterwards they went to a Japanese restaurant. Very nice, a very nice place.'

'While I was with the kids?' Will's head throbs. 'Any idea where they went afterwards? Did they go on somewhere or...?'

'Mate.' Ian shakes his head, his expression sorrowful. 'I hate to be the one to tell you this, but she took him home.'

CHAPTER 21

JESSICA

At the sight of Will's silhouette in the doorway, Jessica slips on her wedge-heel ankle boots and opens the door before he can ring the bell. Without heels she is the same height as him. With them, she is taller.

'You look nice,' he says, his tone snarky.

'Thank you,' she replies tersely. She is wearing the new dress she bought for her date at the weekend, careful make-up, perfume. It is her armour, her defence, her flailing grip on her slippery pride. Without looking him in the eye, she moves past him, determined to leave the house as quickly and cleanly as possible. She has until the end of the week to respond to the solicitor's letter and will make him wait to the very last second. Meanwhile, if he wants to think she's dressed up for a date, let him.

'The kids are upstairs,' she says over her shoulder. 'They're ready for bed.'

But as she steps over the threshold he says, 'Going anywhere nice? Theatre? Sushi?'

Skin aflame, she makes herself continue walking. Don't reply. Do not reply.

'I won't be late,' she manages, her voice sounding strangled even to her own ears. Pretending she hasn't heard isn't ideal, but it's all she's got. How the hell does he know about her date? She hasn't even told Lena.

Behind her, the front door bangs shut. It is fantasy, she knows, but the sound is somehow triumphant. Will is winning. And he knows it.

She stops on the pavement, winded momentarily by a thought. If Will spied on her on Saturday night, he must have left Cassie and Charlie with Madame X. Unless... unless the figure at the end of the crescent...

'Oh my God,' she whispers, hand over her mouth. She feels sick.

By the time she gets to Lena's, she has chewed up half her cheek. Lena must read her expression, because her face immediately softens.

'Hey,' she says, stepping back to let Jessica inside. 'Are you OK? You look shaken.'

Jessica meets her eye. 'I know we said just tea tonight, but do you have anything stronger?'

'So.' Lena has fixed them both a Campari spritz, a new drink she's learnt from John. They are settled in the small but cosy living room of her first-floor flat. 'What's happened? What's he done now?'

'I...' Jessica begins but can get no further. Lena knows about the solicitor's letter. Jessica called her the moment the kids were in bed that night, cried down the phone for over an hour. But she is almost afraid to tell her friend what just happened. She can't tell her without telling her about the weekend, and she fears, she realises, being judged. Will has only just left and already she has had a liaison that may well prove to have been very dangerous indeed.

'Jess? Come on. Whatever it is, you can tell me, you know that.'

'I met someone.' Jessica takes a large gulp of her drink, feels the hit almost instantly.

'Supermarket Guy?'

Jessica nods. 'I... I bumped into him. Anyway, whatever, he asked for my number. I wasn't going to do anything. I'm not looking for a relationship. But after I got the solicitor's letter last week, I was just so furious and so humiliated. And I... I texted him.'

'And?'

'We did a bit of texting. Then at the weekend, we went out. It's not serious. He came in for coffee afterwards, but he didn't stay... I mean, nothing happened. It's just, the weekends are so lonely and he's attractive and intelligent, and I just thought, sod it, you know? It was only a date.' She glances up and, seeing Lena's grin, allows herself a brief smile. There is no judgement. Of course there isn't.

'So why are you beating yourself up?'

Jessica sighs. 'Because I think Will knows.'

'How can he know if he was with the kids?'

'I have no idea. Unless he... unless he got her – his girlfriend – to babysit?' She doesn't mention the figure on the road. He has not been there for weeks and she really doesn't want to get into it now. There's enough going on, frankly.

Lena's jaw drops, actually drops. 'What a shitty thing to do. Oh my God, that is absolutely outrageous.'

'The more I think about it, the more I think that's what's happened. How else would he know? But to use his lover to look after the kids while he spies on me?' Jessica's head falls into her hands. She feels overwhelmingly tired.

'How do you know he knows?'

'He asked me if I was going to the theatre,' she says through her fingers. 'Just now, as I was leaving. And for sushi. That's exactly what I did with...'

A shocked silence falls.

'I think you could have him for mental cruelty,' Lena says after a moment. 'He's gaslighted you, saying he wasn't having an affair when he was. He's framing you kicking him out as unreasonable behaviour, which, by the way, is straight out of the narcissist's handbook. And now he's following you when he's supposed to be looking after your kids. That's so insidious. It's stalking technically. What is he thinking, that he'll use it against you to get custody? I suppose he'll be adding adultery to the unreasonable behaviour file.'

'I don't know. I don't know I don't know I don't know.' Jessica looks up, meets Lena's gaze. 'What am I going to do?'

Lena shuffles forward to the front of the sofa cushion, her newly bony knees at the hem of her dress. The dress is tight, tighter than anything Jessica has ever seen her wear. 'I hope you don't mind,' she says, 'but I spoke to John about it. Not in detail.'

Jessica waves a hand: don't worry.

'Right. Listen. John does the accounts for this absolute hard-nosed solicitor. She's handled celebrities and all sorts. He says if he puts a word in, she'll give you a discount.' Lena picks up her phone from the coffee table and thumbs it. 'I'm texting you her email now. If I tell John you're going to contact her, he'll tell her to expect your email. He said to put your name in capital letters in the subject box then she'll see it.'

'I don't know. I don't want to escalate it even further.' Jessica's phone pings.

'Too late for that, babe. He's going to ruin you if you don't up your game. Email her. Sasha Coulson. She's a killer. An absolute shark. She won't let you lose.'

'Are you sure?' Her phone pings again.

'Trust me. Look her up. Will is going to wish he'd never been born.'

· · ·

On the way home, Jessica checks her phone. There is the
WhatsApp from Lena with the email for Sasha Coulson. And
another.

Hey. Miss you. Next Wednesday?

Sender: Supermarket. She laughs at the nickname, the
ridiculous and, as it turns out, ineffective subterfuge of it. She
didn't even tell Lena his name, passed it off as a bit of fun.
Which it is. Absolutely. But now Will knows. How she's not
sure. But if Will's at home with the kids next Wednesday, he
won't be able to follow her, will he? He wouldn't dare bring *her*
to the house, no way. When it comes down to it, he is too much
of a coward. From what she has gleaned from the kids, they
haven't yet met his mystery woman.

Hmm.

So that blows her babysitting-for-them theory out of the
water.

Unless... Oh my God. This is getting more and more awful.
Unless Madame X did the following?

Stop! Stop thinking, stop overthinking. It certainly wasn't
Madame X watching the house; she is tiny. Stick to what you
know. What you know is that Madame X clears out when the
kids go and stay. Probably goes to her penthouse in Kensington
or something, or maybe to the Brentford Marina apartment.

Jessica sighs. She wishes she had a drone so she could
watch her husband and this woman's every move. She stares
at the message. *Hey. Miss you.* Impossibly sexy. His lips on
hers for that one slow goodnight kiss, the smell of sake, of
expensive eau de cologne. In all her years with Will, he never
bothered to wear any of the aftershaves she bought him. It
was heady to be with someone who smelt so good, who wore
such beautiful clothes, who booked the theatre and the restaurant without asking her what she wanted to do. *Next Wednes-*

day? Sod it. It isn't as if the game can be more up than it already is.

Sure, she replies, knowing somewhere deep inside that she is on some kind of edge. *Where?*

She finds Will in the living room, shoes off, feet crossed on the coffee table. His socks are new. There is a pink logo embroidered into the navy cotton of the sole.

Get your brand-new designer socks your lover bought you off my damn coffee table, she thinks.

'Hi,' he says, withdrawing his expensive feet and putting them on the floor, slipping his feet into his... is that yet another pair of box-fresh Nikes?

'Everything OK?' she asks. 'Kids OK?'

'Fine.'

'Good.' She can smell something fresh, pleasant. It can only be coming from Will. Cologne. Oh, the irony. For Madame X, he wears it. For her, he dresses well. For her, he wears the ridiculous Three Musketeers facial hair of a Lothario.

On her tongue, resentment pools its bitter juice.

'I need your address,' she adds.

'This is my address.' Still, he does not look at her.

'I mean where you're living now,' she says. 'I need to direct my lawyer where to send the letter of response.'

'It's the same one I gave you the last time you threatened me with a solicitor.' He is tying the laces with more care than is necessary.

'Right,' she replies. 'Right then. Good.'

He stands up, pulls at his gorgeous navy cashmere jumper and gives her the briefest, most perfunctory smile. 'Bye then.'

'Bye.' She waits, rigid, rooted to the spot.

With no move to kiss her cheek or hug her, he leaves the

room. She is about to call after him, to call his name, with no real idea of what she could say next.

But the door slams shut.

CHAPTER 22

WILL

A little over a week later, Will finds himself in Smithfield. He is having dinner with Ian in a restaurant called St John. It is November, and cold. Street lamps haze in a charcoal sky; the smell of meat mingles in the air with detergent, traffic exhaust. Ian has called this meeting in response to Will's desperate phone call this morning. He had just received a solicitor's response from Sasha Coulson on behalf of his wife. Upon googling the name, he found a catalogue of articles and images featuring a celebrity divorce lawyer whose slicked-back hair and bright red lipstick appear to be some kind of trademark. On Wikipedia, a list of actors, directors and musicians she has represented. A panicked perusal was enough for him to ascertain that Sasha Coulson never loses. She doesn't look like a woman who loses, that much is certain.

'This calls for a real restaurant,' Ian said after a moment's pensive silence down the line. Minutes later, a text arrived giving Will the time and the place.

He steps into the restaurant, an elegant space with high ceilings, white walls and tablecloths, simple wooden chairs: understated and stylish, like Ian Robbins himself.

'You ever done nose-to-tail dining?' Ian asks now as they study the menu, his black designer reading glasses enlarging his pale cloud eyes, deepening his laughter lines. On the table, two glasses of claret, ordered, tasted and approved by Ian of course. The rest waits in its bottle, napkin folded around the neck like a cravat.

'Er, no,' Will replies.

At the top of the menu is a diagram of a pig divided into the various cuts. A list of dishes follows: roast bone marrow, fried tripe, something called Mangalitza loin.

'Good. I like introducing people to new things. They use everything here. Literally everything. There's no waste. I like that. Can't stand waste.'

'Me neither.'

'And there's none of that nouvelle cuisine nonsense where they pile it in a stupid tower. It's good food, but like a lot of the best dishes in the world – your paella, your pizza, your trusty old hotpot – it has its roots in the soil of your honest working man. But it's sophisticated.'

'Sounds amazing.' Will could not be less hungry.

'I can order for you if you like.' For some reason, this sounds less like a question than a demand.

Will raises his eyebrows to show he is open to the idea. 'I guess if you've been here a lot, you know what's good. Maybe not offal though.'

As if summoned, the waiter arrives, as immaculate as the rest of the place. Dealing with so much blood and guts behind the scenes, Will thinks, it must be important to keep the workings out of sight and out of mind with this front of starched cleanliness.

'Mr Robbins,' the waiter says and smiles. He is young, tall and skinny, with bright ginger hair.

'Darren,' Ian replies, leaning back in his chair, taking off his glasses and letting them loll from between his pinched finger and thumb. 'Shouldn't you be back at uni?'

'Reading week. Picked up a few shifts.' Darren blushes deep pink.

'Well, make sure you get back to those studies.'

'I will.' Darren laughs, his colour still high. Will thinks he detects a hint of nerves. 'Thank you. Thanks so much.'

'Now,' Ian begins, sliding his glasses back onto his nose, 'for starters, my good friend here will have the terrine and I'm going to go for the roast bone marrow.'

Darren waits, hands behind his back.

'Then for the mains,' Ian continues, 'I'll have the grilled ox heart and my friend will have the devilled kidneys. Give us a side of potatoes, will you? And one of greens.' He looks up, holding out the menu. But when Darren takes it, Ian does not let go. 'Remember, I've always got errands for smart kids. Let me know if you need anything extra, yeah?' He lets go, causing Darren to take a step back.

'Thanks,' he says again. 'Thanks for everything.' And before Will can form a question involving the words kidneys and offal, Darren vanishes.

'Nice kid,' Ian says, removing his spectacles again and placing them on the white tablecloth.

It is too late to protest about the kidneys. Will opens his mouth to ask instead why Darren kept thanking him just now, but Ian claps his hands and rubs them together.

'Down to business,' he says. 'Have you brought the letter?'

Will nods, hands it over.

The spectacles slide back onto Ian's nose and he proceeds to read. He frowns, makes almost silent little grunts as his eyes travel slowly back and forth across the page. It's a long time before he looks up, over the top of his black frames.

'Gaslighting,' he says. 'Mental cruelty. Infidelity. Stalking.' He rubs his chin and grimaces, takes off his glasses and returns the letter. 'Strategy,' he says. 'That's what we need. That solicitor your missus has got is a tiger. Someone's giving her good advice. We need more material.'

Will opens his mouth again to speak, but Ian hasn't finished.

'What I can tell you is that last night, when you were with the kids, she was in Soho. The Groucho. With the fella. Dave couldn't get pictures without blowing his cover, he said, but this guy's trendy-looking. Tall.'

'That's why she was so late back,' Will says, racking his brain for any clients she might have mentioned from the world of theatre or television. He heard the cab pull up outside a little after midnight and put on his shoes so as to get out of there as quickly as possible. Jessica seemed tipsy, pleased with herself. She did not even try to suggest she'd been with Lena. But then Will didn't give her time to say much at all. She must've known he'd receive her solicitor's letter the following morning, but she chose to say nothing.

'More on that,' Ian says grimly, pausing while Darren sets their starters carefully before them. Will stares in dismay at his own, which looks like a wall made of pink fat bricks. He realises he has no idea what kind of terrine it is, that he never asked.

'You left,' Ian is saying, 'what, about a minute after she got back?'

'I didn't stay to chat.'

'That's right. Then once you'd gone, he goes in.'

'*What?*'

Ian is chewing. He swallows. ''Fraid so. He must've got out of the cab when she did and gone to hide round the back of the house or something.'

The terrine blurs. Will closes his eyes, feels the room spin.

'The kids.' It is all he can think to say.

'I'm sorry, mate.'

He opens his eyes. He is aware of his fingers tight around the cutlery handles. 'The Groucho is a media club, isn't it?'

Ian nods. 'Media types, yeah. It's nice enough if you like that sort of thing. Not really my scene. Too many bullshitters. People either pretending to be important or looking over your shoulder to see if they can see someone more interesting to talk to.'

But Will isn't really listening. He draws his knife through the terrine, lifts a mouthful to his lips. It will not pass.

'I'm sorry,' he says, laying down his fork. 'I don't think I can eat.'

'Understandable.' Ian waves his hand: not to worry. He has tucked his napkin into the neck of his shirt and returns now to spreading the bone marrow thickly onto the toast and delivering it into his mouth. He chews vigorously, washes it down with a gulp of the red. 'How are you for money?'

Will shakes his head. 'Pretty terrible.'

'You're going to need it. A lot of it.' Having finished his starter, Ian pulls the napkin from his neck before leaning over and helping himself to a forkful of Will's terrine.

'Shame,' he says. 'It's bloody good.'

'Sorry.'

'Don't worry about it.' He switches their plates. 'But listen. I've got things I need doing and I don't have time to do them. If you want to earn a lot in a short time, let me know, OK?'

'I... I'm building up my practice.'

Ian shakes his head. 'That'll take too long. You need cash and you need it now. I can lend you the money tomorrow, but if you earn it, there's no debt.'

'I'm already so indebted to you.'

'It doesn't work like that – I told you that. But I know you're a decent bloke so that's why I thought you might prefer to earn it fair and square.'

Darren arrives to clear their plates, which he does swiftly and without a word.

'What kind of work would it be?' Will asks, once the waiter is out of earshot.

Ian throws out his hands. 'Simple stuff. Drop-offs, handovers, nothing taxing. I mean, obviously, when the money is this good, it's more than an errand as such, but we trust each other now, don't we?'

Will swallows. 'Of course.'

Ian chuckles, points at him briefly. 'Your face,' he says. 'It's all above board, don't worry. I mean, it's not illegal.'

'I wasn't—'

'Yes you were.' But Ian is laughing, so Will laughs too. 'I'm not a criminal. If you're looking for a criminal, that'd be Dave. You do *not* want to be dealing with Dave, trust me. I might move it about so the taxman doesn't take it all, but who doesn't? I'm no more a criminal than these Tory bastards with their offshore investments and billion-pound contracts for their mates.'

'Dave is a *criminal*?' Will's voice sounds high, feminine. He clears his throat. 'What kind of criminal?'

'Oh, don't worry. He won't hurt your missus. Not unless I tell him to.' Ian chuckles, winks.

Will grips the edge of the table. The lights dim a fraction, though he can't be sure it's not his own eyesight. His heart is beating hard, his throat thick. It is an effort to stay in his chair.

The mains arrive. The kidneys are shiny, plump and purplish on the white plate. He cannot eat them. He doesn't like kidneys or liver, never has. He's almost certain kidneys count as offal. Even the smell nauseates him.

Ian is still chuckling at his little joke. 'Your face,' he says. He picks up his knife and, with great relish, slides it deftly through the bloody heart of an ox.

·   ·   ·

Ian drops Will off in a cab. As he makes his way carefully up the stairs to the flat, his claret-soaked mind works its way through the evening's conversation, trying to take stock. His wife is sleeping with someone else. He has allowed it in only as a thought experiment to wind himself up, but there is no denying it now. And somewhere along the line, he, Will Draper, life coach, stay-at-home dad and all-round nobody, agreed to having her followed by a criminal, an actual criminal.

Or was Ian joking? It is so hard to tell sometimes. His generosity has been endless to the point of unnerving at times, but tonight it felt as if the air supply had been thinned – the nervousness of the waiter, his out-of-context thanks, Ian's odd chuckle when no one had said anything amusing.

Nothing is amusing any more. There is nothing funny about Will's life.

He lets himself into the flat and sits on the sofa in the dark. It occurs to him that he has known Ian Robbins only a couple of months. Throughout their short friendship, Ian has always insisted he is someone who believes in making the world turn, not someone who records a balance sheet of favours given and favours owed. But that wasn't how it felt this evening. Something about the waiter, the reference to university, as if Ian was somehow invested. The thank you. Is Ian involved in paying towards the lad's education? Is that what that was about? He used to run errands for Ian was Will's understanding. Is that how he earned his college fees? Will wonders what will be expected of the lad once he finishes his degree.

Then there was the allusion to Will needing to get his hands on a great deal of money. Errands again, something about running them for cash because Ian didn't want him to end up in too much debt. But Ian has always insisted there is no debt. And yet they both know the debt is already fathomless. When Ian paid the bill, Will did not even offer, knowing that Ian would insist it was his invitation. And hard as it is to admit, Will knew this when he accepted that invitation.

Towards the end of the second bottle, talk had turned to women. The details are hazy, but they were talking about sex, the getting or not getting of it – veiled terms, innuendo.

'I could introduce you to some nice women,' Ian said. He definitely said that. 'Attractive, available. For the night, I mean. Just say the word.'

Realisation dawning, Will fought to hide his mild panic.

'It's OK,' he said. 'I'm fine, thanks.'

'Suit yourself.'

He pushes his hands through his hair. It is sticky with hair gel. Now his hands are sticky. He wipes them on his jeans. On the coffee table, his clients' notes are fanned out where he left them. Like them, he needs to get his life together. Ian is right: he needs money, lots of it. He cannot let Jessica bully him like this.

Dave is the criminal, not Ian. Ian's a businessman, that's all.

How hard could it be to run a simple errand?

CHAPTER 23

JESSICA

Over pasta al pomodoro in an Italian restaurant near her office, Jessica confesses her suspicions about Will to Lena. She has held off, partly because Lena's glee at Will's failings makes her feel a little queasy, but now she lets rip: the lover, the flat, the house, the clothes, the kids coming home full of table tennis and Deliveroos and 3D films in the home cinema.

'It's like nothing touches him,' she says. 'He's swanning around while I'm sweating blood trying to keep all the balls in the air. Do you know what? Half of me wishes he'd come back. Just on a practical level. Last night we had to have fish and chips because there was no food, and the bedding hasn't been washed for a month.'

'Fish and chips never killed anyone. And kids don't care about fusty bedding.'

'Where he's getting all the money from?'

'From her surely?'

'Maybe. I mean, yes, I know he is, I just don't want to know, you know? But it's the *only* thing that makes sense: the bottomless pit. People like us struggle to even imagine how much people like that have, what it must be like to never have to choose between one thing and another, to be able to just have all of it, all at once, without even having to work. I'm trying not to feel resentful, but it's hard, it really is, and I'm so bloody tired.'

'Oh, love.' Lena lays her hand on Jessica's arm.

'He hasn't even responded to Sasha's letter. It's like he's playing some sort of game of chess. Well, of course he is. But he's acting as if he's sure of getting custody, like it's a done deal, no rush. I don't think that letter frightened him at all.' From nowhere, Jessica bursts into tears. Embarrassed, she grabs the napkin and presses it to her eyes. 'I never even wanted a divorce,' she sobs. 'I was only calling his bluff, for pride as much as anything. I thought if I met fire with fire, it'd scare him into picking up the phone. I just feel like if we could talk to each other now, we could sort it out. We've calmed down. There's some distance. But he's... unreachable. I just wish I hadn't...' She looks about her, but the restaurant is busy, noisy. No one is taking any notice of her thankfully.

'Hadn't what?' Lena asks.

'I've messed up.' Jessica sighs. 'I swore I wouldn't let Supermarket Guy come to the house when the kids were there.'

'OK.'

She leans forward to avoid anyone eavesdropping. 'He ended up staying over.' She glances up. Lena is watching her intently, listening. 'The kids were asleep obviously. I would never... He was only meant to be coming in for coffee. But he was so... persuasive.'

'And why shouldn't you have some fun? It's not the fifties. Was it all good?'

Jessica hesitates. The question is direct, but the answer feels complicated. Smoky.

'I think,' she says, 'with hindsight, I felt a bit pressured. He'd really spoilt me and we'd had a few drinks, and one thing led to another. He was quite... passionate, I suppose you'd say, and then... I asked him to go, but he said he was too tired. I couldn't just kick him out like that, so... so I agreed he could set the alarm on his phone for five a.m. But we must've slept through it, and the thing is... God, I feel terrible, but Cassie saw him.'

'In your bed?'

'God, no! He was in the kitchen. He said he wanted a quick coffee before he left. We were whispering, but she must've heard us, because she came downstairs and saw him.'

Yes, Cassie saw them, and for that awful moment, Jessica saw herself, a child in the half-light, standing at the open door of the kitchen trying to make sense of her father's trousers around his ankles.

'Oh no.' Lena wrinkles her nose.

'I wouldn't mind, but normally I can barely get the kids out of bed at seven, and there she is at six thirty, bright-eyed and bushy-tailed, saying who are you?'

Lena giggles. 'You have to laugh, don't you?'

Jessica is not sure. None of this strikes her as funny. 'What if she tells Will? It's not like I can tell her not to. I can't make my own daughter complicit.'

'There's nothing to tell. What did you say?'

'I said it was my friend from work and that he was just calling in for a quick coffee because he'd had to drive in from far away.'

Lena pulls a face.

'I know. Rubbish. Oh God, I've made one mistake, one, in all this stress and I feel wretched about it. I swore I'd never lie to my kids, but the thing is, you just want to protect them, you know? From life, from all the bad stuff, from making mistakes. You can't. No one can. But I never thought I'd end up protecting them from *my* mistakes. Deep down, I think I'm still hoping Will might come to his senses. I never thought we'd... I never thought it would go this far. I worry we've just dug in our heels and now neither of us can find our way home. And now

I've let this happen. I can't believe I've done that. It's a reaction, I do know that. I was just desperate to claw back some dignity. Maybe I thought if I wallowed in something shallow it wouldn't have the power to drown me, but now I'm choking and I don't know what to do.'

'I'm sure it's fine.' Lena sounds like she thinks 'fine' is the last thing it is. 'It's only once. As you say, a mistake. People make mistakes. You're all over the place. Maybe he took advantage. Sounds like he came on very strong, and you're vulnerable right now. You didn't *mean* for Cassie to see him. But maybe...' She twirls the glossy spaghetti strands on her fork, but her lips are pressed tight.

'Lena?'

She lets the fork drop. She has barely eaten half her meal; it is so unlike her. She wipes her hands on her napkin and takes a sip of her sparkling mineral water. She is wearing a loose blouse of soft fabric, and Jessica cannot help but notice that her chest bone is visible beneath the skin. Her shoulders are squarer, angular in a way they have never been.

'Lena,' she says again, 'are you OK? You're not ill, are you?'

Lena shakes her head. 'It's just something John said. Suggested really. Will's been spying on you, yeah? He's been gathering all this stuff on you.' She glances up, meets Jessica's eye. 'Have you thought about hiring a PI?'

CHAPTER 24

WILL

Four days later, Will is waiting at Exit C on the second floor of a multistorey car park in Kingston-upon-Thames. He has rushed here directly from his last session – a newly retired schoolteacher at a loss as to how to cope with her free time and wanting to get fit and embrace her creativity. If only his own life were so simple. He has taken the 285 bus from work in order to get here by 6.30. Public transport can be like trying to hit a small target from miles away, and not wanting to be late, he has inevitably arrived forty-five minutes early, forty-five minutes he has spent getting progressively more nervous, his imagination conjuring ever more fantastic scenarios in which the errand Ian has given him has become everything from smuggling guns to human trafficking.

'All you have to do is memorise the number plate,' Ian said yesterday evening, handing over a black Alcatel phone in the privacy of Will's living room. 'Don't be late.'

'Why are you giving me a phone?'

'So I can call you.'

'Why not use my normal phone?'

'Because you'll be leaving that at mine, remember?'

The BMW belongs to Dave, Ian explained. Dave had been called away to Birmingham on business and couldn't pick it up from its service. He didn't want to cancel the service or have his precious motor left in the garage overnight, so the garage agreed to drop it off in the nearby multistorey and hand the key to Will.

'I'll let you know where to drive it once I've heard from Dave,' Ian said, nodding towards the phone. 'I'll call you on that.'

Will did not ask why again. Ian had told him any errands would be above board. This cheap phone, he knew, was what they called a burner. He wasn't completely naïve; he'd seen *The Wire*. There was something dodgy going on. But the money Ian offered was more than Will could have earned in a month. Two months actually. Besides, Ian did not use the word *errand*; he asked if Will could do this *favour*. Refusing did not feel like an option. Will does not want to find out what happens when you refuse to repay a favour to Ian Robbins.

He tries to breathe through the butterflies in his belly. Once he knows where to drop the car, he is to put the phone in the bin. He must not forget. He must not mess this up. There is no actual evidence that Ian is asking him to do something illegal, he tells himself, is still telling himself when he hears the screech of tyres on ramp. A moment later, a silver BMW, registration S1L VMN 45, speeds onto the second floor and performs an emergency stop. The driver – wearing shades and a buzz cut – looks about fifteen. He flings open the door as if the car were on fire and strides with great swagger over to where Will is standing with his fists clenched like a little boy on his first day at school.

'William?'

'Shakespeare,' Will replies, as per his rehearsal with Ian. 'Florida.'

'Keys,' the lad says, somehow managing to lace the short word with sarcasm.

Startled, Will holds out his hand.

The lad drops the leather fob and key into his waiting palm and pulls a car-park ticket from his pocket.

Will takes the ticket and attempts a businesslike nod of acknowledgement. But the lad is already marching away towards the stairwell, his macho gait rolling with the giddy sway of a tall ship caught in a storm.

Heart thumping, Will waits for Ian's call – until it dawns on him that he should park the car before it blocks the way and draws attention.

He gets in. There is no ignition. A fire of nascent panic kindles in his belly. But it's OK. It's like Ian's Defender, a button, not a key. He pushes the button, and to his near-ecstatic relief, the engine fires. The dashboard lights up like a spaceship. Will breathes shakily. Thank God.

There is also, thank God, a gearstick. Painstakingly slowly, sweating with fear that he might scratch the paintwork, he reverses into a parking space. The BMW is at least smaller than Ian's massive tank. There are no cellophane sheaths on the seats; no evidence whatsoever of a service, but Will pushes this from his mind. He cuts the engine, his heart still quick, swollen in his chest. Minutes pass. The panic subsides a little. His breath deepens. Fright fades into something nearer exhilaration. This is exciting. He is a player, albeit a bit player, in a world so far from his safe suburban existence. He feels... edgy.

It's only one favour, one highly paid favour. His first and last.

The phone rings, startling him. He answers.

'Hello,' he whispers, glancing about him. 'Who's calling?'

'What?' comes Ian's gruff voice. 'Who do you think? Listen. I'm going to give you the address. Do not write it down.'

'OK.' Will's armpits prickle.

Ian tells him the address. 'You got that?'

'Yes.'

'Repeat it back to me.'

Will repeats it.

'Good. Now bin the phone. Grab a cab over to mine when you're done.' The line dies.

Will sits for a moment, repeating the address over and over until he's sure it has stuck. It's easy – a street in St Margarets, twenty minutes away, give or take. He's almost done. This is the home straight.

He starts the car and edges it out of the space. The paint marks on the concrete walls make him feel sick with anxiety. As slowly as a hearse, he clears the first ramp, glimpses through his rear-view mirror the nose of another vehicle at the top. A dark grey Ford. He continues, the Ford in pursuit, the world's slowest car chase. He is not being followed. There is only one way out of a multistorey, that's all.

At St Margarets Roundabout, his nerves settle. He finds the street, which is like any other in this postcode: semi-detached Victorian villas, neat stripes of garden with neat little paths, spindly trees, new-looking cars. A wealthy, well-cared-for neighbourhood; the essence of respectability. Dave's house is more modest than Ian's but in this area still worth more than a million. Will parallel-parks, more confident behind the wheel now, locks the car, strides up the terracotta-and-black tiled path of number 37 and drops the keys through the letter box. The door is olive green, as Ian said it would be. In the front garden is a hydrangea, the blooms faded now that autumn is fully here. A car drifts by, a grey Mondeo. It disappears into the T-junction. Will's senses tingle. Was that the Ford from the multistorey?

Eyes round, breath shallow, he walks towards St Margarets High Street. At the junction, he waits. The car has gone. It won't have been the same one that followed him out of the car park. Probably wasn't even the same model. Jesus, this world is not for the faint-hearted. He feels like he needs a stiff drink.

. . .

Ian greets him with a smile and throws open the door.

'I was about to send out a search party,' he says. 'Cheers for doing that. Really appreciate it.'

'Sorry, I just fancied a walk.' Adrenaline still pumping, Will walked all the way here. The phone he wiped and dropped into a bin near Kew Gardens.

They head towards Ian's kitchen. Ian is telling Will he can't be everywhere all at once, when it comes to Dave he has to say yes, does Will know what he means?

'Yes,' Will says, thinking that he really does know exactly what Ian means. 'Of course.'

'Did you bin the phone?'

'Yes.'

'Good man.' Ian hands him a can of IPA. 'Hungry? I was going to order pizza.'

'Sounds great.'

'What's the matter?' Ian is staring at him. 'You look like you're having a breakdown.'

'I'm fine. I... I mean, it was all above board, wasn't it? The car thing?'

Ian's brow furrows. 'What? Yeah. Course. That car means more to Dave than his niece. Manner of speaking. I would've done it myself, but I don't have that kind of time.'

'Why the burner phone?'

He shrugs. 'Force of habit. Don't like people snooping on me and my business. And I suppose when it comes to Dave, I never know what's in the trunk, know what I mean?'

'What?' Will's heart thuds, but Ian laughs and shakes his head.

'Don't worry about it. It's all good.' He points at Will. 'Do you like pepperoni?'

CHAPTER 25
JESSICA

The following day, at 1.30, Jessica calls her assistant and tells her she's popping out for a quick lunch. Canary Wharf is busy thankfully; the café a chain, full enough for a degree of anonymity. In the far corner by the window, she immediately recognises Lena's private investigator. Actually, John's PI, via Lena: a Martin Duncan, one of those Christian-name surnames. Lena said John had told her he was balding, as tall as a lamp post and skinny, with a beak for a nose and a full set of luggage for eye bags – the kind of unflattering picture you'd paint only if the person in question was not present but which makes recognition incredibly easy.

So far, Jessica has only spoken to Martin over the phone: once when she called him with the job and again when he rang her yesterday late in the evening to say he had information for her. He offered to email it, but not wanting it on her work email and knowing that Will would see it on their shared one, Jessica asked him to meet her here to hand over a hard copy. She could have set up a new email account, she thinks now. Her brain is in bits and subterfuge is really not her strong suit.

So here she is, like something from a film noir. All it would take is Martin to be wearing a trilby and a dirty trench coat, herself red lipstick, a fascinator and a sultry expression of misery. If it weren't so horrific, it would be amusing.

How is this her life?

'Martin?' she asks, one hand on the back of the chair opposite.

'Yes.' A perfunctory smile, his nose less prominent face-on. What is left of his hair is close-cropped. His eyebrows are blonde. He half stands and shakes her hand: firm, dry. Eye contact. All good signs.

'Can I get you another coffee?' she asks.

'I'm fine, thank you.' He pulls a cardboard file out of a cross-body bag while Jessica sits down. 'It's all in here.' He slides the file over the table. It is astonishing how quickly he has come back to her.

Jessica opens the file. At first she does not understand what she is seeing. Martin talks her through the images even though there is an accompanying report, telling her in neutral tones that her husband took the 285 bus to Kingston-upon-Thames yesterday evening where he alighted and entered the Bentall Centre car park at 17:23. Pretty unglamorous, she thinks, her eyes following the report as Martin continues to speak. Apparently, he did not enter the shopping centre itself, only took the staircase to the second floor of the car park and waited there for forty-seven minutes for the silver BMW pictured here...

Jessica listens, flipping over the photographs, some blurry, some less so, but Will utterly identifiable.

'I traced the registration,' Martin says. 'The car is registered to a David Silverman, possibly why it's silver and has the reg S1L VMN 45. Strong ego.' He allows himself a smirk. 'He's a known drug dealer.'

'*What?*' Jessica feels herself flung back against the plastic chair. She swallows hard.

'Will,' she whispers, tears pricking. 'What have you done?'

All this time, she'd thought the conspicuous wealth was from Madame X. It had not, not for one moment, occurred to her that drugs could be the source.

'Mr Silverman is a well-known member of the South West London criminal community. He's also well known to the police. Your husband delivered the car to an address in St Margarets and walked from there to Richmond. From there he appeared to be heading to Kew, at which point I'm afraid I lost sight of him due to roadworks at the roundabout.'

Wordlessly Jessica stares at the photograph of her husband walking towards Richmond Bridge, a haunted expression on his face, his shoulders high, his dark wool coat one she doesn't recognise. The idiot, she thinks. The absolute irresponsible, stupid idiot.

'I'm sorry to say,' Martin interrupts her thoughts, 'whatever your husband is involved in, it's not good.'

CHAPTER 26

WILL

Will wakes up in Ian's son's room, where he crashed after a late night playing *Call of Duty* turned into an early morning playing *Grand Theft Auto*.

His phone is buzzing. He fumbles for it, finds it in his trouser pocket. Only five per cent battery. Enough to see that it is after two in the afternoon and that there is a text from Jessica, sent at 1.30 p.m.

Call me the moment you get this. Urgent. J

A wave of anxiety-induced nausea rolls over him. That doesn't sound good.

He wanders out onto the landing, towards the stairwell. On the ground floor, all is silent. There is no sign that Ian is awake, that he is even in the house. It is so late. He is probably at work. Wherever that is.

Will makes coffee in a pot, enough for Ian in case he is at home. There is fresh soda bread in the bread bin. He makes toast. The butter melts, makes the toast chewy, toffee-like. He closes his eyes while he eats. Sustenance. Fortification. He will call Jessica once he has eaten this toast, drunk this coffee. He just needs a—

In his pocket, his phone vibrates. Another roll of anxiety; he doesn't know the source of it – Jessica or Ian?

He glances at the screen. Jessica. 'Hello.'

'Will?'

'Mm-hm.' His voice is a croak. He sips his coffee.

'Have you lost your mind?'

'Wh-What?'

'Consorting with *criminals*?'

'What? What are you going on about?'

'You have children, Will! We have children!'

'I know that. I should be there looking after them. It's you who kicked me out, don't forget.'

A pause. He hears her breathe. Can see her expression even down the line: eyes closing momentarily while she gathers herself against him.

'If I'm so irritating to you,' he adds, 'if I'm so stupid, I fail to see why you married me in the first place.'

'Will,' she says quietly. 'Yesterday afternoon, you picked up and delivered a silver BMW on behalf of a known drug baron.'

'*What?*' His head spins. Too much. Too much infor—

'David Silverman,' Jessica continues. 'Ring any bells? Or did they not give you his name? He's a criminal. Known to the police. A bad, bad man. What the hell do you think you're doing? Who the hell are you mixing with, you fucking fool? This is... this is dark, Will. This is some dark shit. I knew there was something to it, with the designer clothes and that *ridiculous* penis extension of a car.'

Her words land. David Silverman. Dave. Dave is into bad stuff. Will knows this. Ian told him. He was perfectly honest about it. Will knew, not even deep down but further up. He chose to pretend – to himself! – that he didn't know so he could get hold of some easy money.

He pushes his hands through his hair. He wants to cry.

I never know what's in the trunk.

Drugs. What else would it be? That's why Ian wouldn't touch it. Did he, Will, unwittingly make a drug delivery?

'He's not—' he begins but cannot get any further.

'He is.'

'How do you... how do you even know? Have you been *following* me?'

A bitter laugh. 'Excellent. Some more top-quality gaslighting from Will Draper. Listen while I tell you something. You will not get the kids. You will not get the house. I have photographs of you and your girlfriend and evidence of cash withdrawals made without my consent, and I will use all of it against you – not because I want to win or because my pride is hurt or anything like that, but because you are not fit to be a father to our children. I could have you put in prison. You've shacked up with your gangster sugar mummy and put all of us in danger. I will never forgive you for this, never.' She bursts into sobs.

The Mondeo, he thinks. It was following him. He saw it. Dismissed it. Gah. 'Jessica...'

The phone dies. He finds Ian's charger in the drawer and plugs it in. He is still muttering her name, still trying to make sense of what she has told him when the phone reawakens, a second text from Jessica on the screen.

I will need to move away. Mum too. I can't live like this. Thanks a lot.

'Jesus.' With shaking hands, Will pours the rest of the coffee. 'Jesus Christ.'

He puts the plate and cup in the dishwasher. On the window ledge is a plain brown envelope, his name written on the front. He can tell just by the bulging shape that it is full of cash. Knows by the handwriting that it is from Ian: payment for putting the lid on the coffin of his marriage and nailing it shut, for endangering everyone he loves, for losing his family.

He folds his arms over his head and crouches, then sits on

the floor, his back against the cupboard. The urge to cry persists, but he makes himself breathe through it. Dave is not a petty criminal but a bigger fish entirely. He is Ian's close friend, his employee, and he is a known drug dealer. Dave does not simply bring coffee machines to Ian's new friends and watch Ian's friends' wives have affairs. Dave is a bad man. A drug baron, Jessica said. Whatever that even means.

Will bangs his fist against his forehead. 'Idiot,' he whispers. 'Idiot, idiot, idiot.'

Last night he felt the thrill of being involved in an operation that was like something off the television. Last night, laughing and joking with Ian, full of self-congratulation, he felt almost proud of himself. With his tough new mate, playing on the Xbox, he felt like a ten-year-old boy allowed to stay up late with the grown-ups. Jessica is right: he is a fool. Bored at home and professionally thwarted, he has let himself be seduced, first by Margot le Fevre with all her mystery and intrigue, a woman who took two grand from him and disappeared without a trace, and now by Ian Robbins and a world that seemed so glamorous, so other. He still wants to believe that Margot didn't take him for a fool. But what about Ian? Is he a criminal too? It doesn't necessarily follow. Ian told him Dave was into bad stuff but that he, apart from hiding from the taxman, was strictly on the straight and narrow.

He picks up the envelope and peeks inside at the thick wad of notes. Ian has paid him far too much – Will knows this somewhere inside himself. When Ian asked for this favour, Will thought he could somehow even up the score sheet, clear the debt. But there is too much money here, and so the debt still stands. Ian has been endlessly kind to him out of some world-view that what goes around comes around, a back-scratching philosophy where favours are king and men are brothers who support one another in hard times. And yet he never seems to owe anyone anything. Perhaps it is better for him if he keeps his friends beholden. Yes. Of course it is. There is more power for him that way. Dave is involved in nefarious activity. Ian doesn't judge him because of their age-old friendship, those common roots, but that's not all. If Ian knows Dave's business, he can hold this knowledge over him. Ian keeps his nose clean, keeps the advantage. He is wise enough to stay friends but steer clear of criminal activity.

Ian is clever. He is not like Will. He is not stupid.

Calm down, Will. Think logically. Even if Dave is the wrong 'un in this scenario, there's nothing, nothing whatsoever, to say there was anything illegal in that car, and there is certainly no proof. Ian wouldn't use him to run drugs. He wouldn't do that. Jessica has jumped to a wild conclusion.

Will breathes deeply. When he feels able, he makes himself stand up. This kitchen is so clean, so beautiful. This is not the house of a gangster. It is a family home whose heart has been ripped out, that's all. Just like its owner. Ian has put into this home everything he never had growing up. Will knows this on a gut level, and from piecing together all that Ian has told him and not told him. OK, so he has possibly been involved in shady dealings in the past, but his drive for respectability is palpable, tangible in everything he possesses, everything he does, everything he is. Ian Robbins is more of a life coach than Will is!

Still, Will wishes he had never accepted anything from this man. Even if he himself is cleaner than clean, Ian Robbins still mixes with dangerous people who move in a world Will has no idea how to negotiate. That night at the Express Tavern, he should have refused the offer of a flat, told Ian thanks but he'd be fine. In letting Ian help him, he has made the relationship unequal, he can see that now. And now Jessica has so much dirt on him she can take him to the cleaners to wash it off. She can move his children far away. He let Ian's solicitor persuade him that unreasonable behaviour was the way to go. He felt uncomfortable about it at the time – Jessica is a saint – but he was

desperate not to lose his kids. Blinded by anger, he let himself
be swayed. Typical. Typical Will. A reed in the wind, a lost
cause, always relying on others, never himself. And that word,
the word his father always used before digging him out of yet
another scrape: pathetic.

Jessica must have had him followed. She has done this not
because she is sly but because he pushed her to it. Didn't he do
the same to her? Didn't he insinuate that this was what he had
done? Couldn't help himself, dropping in *theatre* and *sushi* like
a spiteful kid who can't keep his mouth shut. His pain has made
a coward of him, a tiger of his wife. And now her claws are
bared. She is out to kill him.

How did they get here?

He picks up his phone and, unable to think of anyone else,
calls Ian.

'Yo.' The noise of traffic rushes in the background.

'Is Dave a drug dealer?' Will hears the girlish pitch of panic
in his voice. 'Did I deliver a car for a—'

'Mate. Stop. I don't know what you're on about, but not on
the phone, yeah?' Ian's voice is fuzzy. A siren wails, fades.

'OK,' Will says, stunned into silence.

'I'm driving, mate.' Ian chuckles. 'Meet me in the Brewery
Tap. On the canal. Uber it. I'll be there in half an hour, maybe
forty-five minutes. The traffic's terrible.'

The Brewery Tap is tucked away in a small business hub on the
canal. There is a vintage car garage, a pizza van, other small
enterprises. At the foot of some stone steps leading up to the
pub door, chairs and tables have been arranged – rather opti-
mistically, given the cold night. Beyond, a pathway runs along-
side the water.

Will climbs the steps to the door. Inside, a man who must be
at least a hundred is playing a piano that sounds like it's about a

semitone off. His back is a curve, his fingers bent twigs bouncing on the keys.

Will orders a Bloody Mary from a handsome boy with a crew cut, which he nurses propped up at the bar, watching the door. He has stopped matching Ian drink for drink, but still, he is drinking too much. He has had more hangovers since he's known Ian than his whole time at university, certainly since the kids were born. Ian, however, never seems to be affected.

The door squeaks open once, twice, three times. The customers bring the frigid air in with them, chafing their hands, blowing into their gloves. Autumn is turning to winter. Will has on a woollen scarf and hat with the slightly too big Crombie coat Ian passed on to him. Now, in the heat of the pub, he takes them off. The door hinge squeaks again. It is Ian finally: smart, in charge as always. He has on a long herringbone coat, no hat, his black scarf tied in a sort of cravat shape.

'Pint of Pride, please, Ali,' he says to the barman, and turns to address Will. 'How's your head? You hit the red a bit hard last night, didn't you?'

Will attempts a smile. 'I think it might have been the doobie we smoked after that.'

'You have to smoke a spliff when you play *Call of Duty*. It's the rules.' Ian laughs, accepts his pint from the barman with a nod of thanks and a *get one for yourself*. The cursory tap of credit card on reader. There is no sign that this man had less than four hours' sleep.

'I'm having a nightmare,' Will says. 'Jessica called me. Please tell me I didn't...' He looks about him, lowers his voice to a whisper. 'Please tell me I didn't run a drug delivery yesterday.'

Ian shakes his head. 'Let's go outside. I need a smoke.'

He leads Will back out into the cold, down the stone steps to the tables. On the pathway, the water has begun to lap. Another couple of hours and it will flood where they are now sitting. Will shivers, pulls his coat tighter and folds his arms.

Ian's herringbone is buttoned up, the collar popped. He takes out his cigarettes and offers Will the pack. Will takes one. Not like he can feel any worse.

'Jessica's onto me,' he says, letting Ian light his cigarette. 'She knows about the delivery.'

'She doesn't know anything.'

'She knows who the car belongs to, and she has photographs of me getting in it and dropping it off.'

Ian says nothing, only screws up his eyes while he smokes with painstaking slowness. Will takes a pull on his own cigarette, feels the nicotine calm and nauseate him in equal measure.

'Did you tell her?' Ian asks finally.

'No!'

'Did you tell anyone? Anyone at all?'

'I haven't seen anyone.'

'She must've paid a private dick.'

Will has already thought of this possibility. But it is so... so un-Jessica. It is outside any kind of realm of reality. But maybe it isn't. Jessica is a very successful woman. To be successful, you have to play the game, and the game is not for the faint of heart. Where he has fallen on the easy kindness of a stranger, Jessica has been independent, proactive, cool from the outset.

'She's going to leave me with nothing,' he says into his pint. He is almost crying. 'She's cleverer than me, harder. I can't do this. I wish she'd drop dead. I wish I was dead.'

Ian raises his eyebrows. It is the slightest of facial expressions, but it makes Will's blood slow.

'I mean, I don't obviously. But she's got all this stuff on me. She's got photographs, documents. She's got this lawyer, this absolute ball-breaker, and I'm... I mean, I could end up in prison. She's saying she's going to move away. Says she doesn't feel safe here any more. She'll probably go back north with her mother. She will too. I've seen what she's capable of. I hurt her.

I hurt her in the worst way, and they say that, don't they? A woman scorned? She said she was going to kill me and she meant it. Metaphorically, but still. She's already killing me. I want my kids back. It's killing me not seeing them. I can't sleep. I'm going mad. I wish she would just fucking disappear, leave me alone so I can go back to my kids and put this whole thing behind me.' Realising that he sounds hysterical, Will makes himself shut up, sucks at the acrid cigarette.

Ian is watching him. 'Disappear,' he says after a moment.

'I mean, no. I'm just venting, you know? My life would be so much simpler, that's all I'm saying. I could have my kids and all this would just... go away. As it is, she's got me on a hook so big I don't know how to get off, and all I ever did was help someone who needed me. That's all I did. It just feels like too much punishment. It's too much.'

'Does she have life insurance?'

Will doesn't meet Ian's gaze. He knows that if he does, he will have to admit what he knows – that Ian is asking a serious question; that if he answers it, he is damned.

'I think so,' he says. 'I mean, yes.' It's just words. They're only *talking*. 'I know because her mum insisted on it. Her and her mum, they're savvy. They've had to be. Her dad left them, you see. He was a... a philanderer, I suppose you'd say.'

'That's why she's gone so mental with you then.'

'Yes,' he says, sadness filling him. He sips his drink. The tomato juice is all but gone; what remains is watery, insipid. He puts down his glass.

'Listen to me,' Ian says. 'No one is going to jail. I'll admit you're in a spot. Never reckoned on her having you tailed. But I've got a proposition for you. If you're serious about putting it all behind you. You ever seen that film *Strangers on a Train*?'

'I've read the book. Patricia Highsmith.'

'So you know the set-up.'

'I think so. Two men agree to commit each other's crimes.

One kills the other one's wife, the second man kills the other one's father-in-law or stepfather or something, whatever. The perfect motiveless crime. Except it all goes wrong.'

'It does,' Ian says. 'But only because one of them is never really on board. He never agrees to it. The other fella forces his hand by going ahead and killing the guy's wife because he's a lunatic.' He leans forward, steeples his hands. 'Listen to me. I need to tell you something. I've known Dave since we were kids, that much is true. We go back a long way. But he's involved in stuff I don't want to be involved in. He's dangerous, a dangerous man, a very dangerous man.'

Will thinks of the softly spoken, well-dressed, almost subservient gent who delivered the boxes, how he had felt uneasy in his presence but had not been able to say why.

'To be honest with you,' Ian says, his face for the first time registering something like worry or fear, 'I don't like saying this, but Dave's not a good bloke. I bend the rules, sure, but there isn't a businessman in the land who doesn't. Dave's something else. It's unlucky your wife hired a private dick, but we are where we are and you're right, she's got you by the bollocks. And Dave has got me by the same. Dave has stuff on me, do you hear what I'm saying? Sometimes it's not so easy to shake off the people we need to shake off. I'm just trying to be a decent bloke, trying to keep my nose clean, and all the time Dave's got this thing over me.'

'Would he use it against you? He wouldn't, would he? You're friends.' Will wonders what the thing is, but he doesn't dare be so direct.

Ian sucks hard at what is left of his cigarette then throws it to the ground. It is so cold out. The water has covered the path, is only a couple of metres away now, but the two of them make no move to go back indoors.

'He did me a solid,' he says. 'A year or so ago. I tried to pay him back, pay him money, but he didn't want it. The more time goes on, the more I realise he doesn't want me to pay him back. He prefers me to owe him big. He likes to see me squirm because what he has on me would be of interest to the police.'

'The police?'

'Like you, I made a mistake. Like you, I'm in the doghouse. And like you, it'll take more than a Caribbean cruise to get me out. Are you getting this?'

'Yes.' Will does not move, feels like he could not move even if he wanted to.

'We're not all born with silver spoons in our mouths. Sometimes you have to do things. I try to be a good boss, a good landlord. I try to be a good person.'

Will swallows. 'You are a good person.'

'Why do you think I'm so busy? I'm running around checking boilers, batteries in smoke alarms, making sure fire doors are fitted. I fired a tenant last month because they were dealing. I keep my nose as clean as a whistle because I don't want any trouble from anyone. But lately, Dave's started leaning on me. He wants me to come in with him on something and I don't want to. He says I owe him. I want to stay on the right side of the law, but he...' Ian shakes his head, winces as if tasting something bitter, 'he's got me like your missus has got you. She's going to take your kids God knows where, and trust me, I know what that's like. She'll say she'll let you have them whenever you want, but it won't work out like that. They'll be busy. The train fare will cost too much, you name it. You'll see them summer holidays if you're lucky. And meanwhile Dave is pushing me to do things I don't want to do. He's squeezing me like a lemon, and like you with your wife, it'd be easier for me if he... disappeared.' He looks up, his eyes milky ice in the floodlight. 'Now do you get what I'm saying?'

Everything stills. Understanding is sinking, settling. Ian is asking him for something, something that goes beyond all reason, beyond humanity.

'I'm... I'm not...'

'I know you're not. Neither am I. But Dave's an evil bastard. He's a psycho. I've known him since we were kids but I need him out of my life just like you need your missus out of yours.'

'I'm sorry.'

'Don't be. I'm the therapist, remember. I find practical solutions. And I'm thinking we might have a practical solution here. A perfect crime, but with both of us on board from the off. What do you say?'

'What do you mean, what do I say? What?'

Ian rolls his eyes. 'Don't make me spell it out. We'll both stay out of prison. You'll get your kids and her life insurance. I'll get Dave off my back so I can stay regular. I want to go into politics, serve my community, do some good on a bigger scale. But I can't do that while Dave walks this earth, do you know what I'm saying? What do you think? Neither crime could be connected to us. No one knows we're linked.'

'What about your flat?'

'It's not traceable to me.'

'But...' Will is flailing, 'Jessica knows I'm linked to Dave.'

'She won't know anything once she's dead, will she?'

Will stands up so abruptly his chair falls over, clatters on the damp ground. He backs away, almost trips. 'I'm sorry, I'm not cut out for... I couldn't. I can't. Sorry.' He turns on his heel and walks as quickly as he can without breaking into a run, doesn't turn even when Ian calls after him.

'Think about it.'

CHAPTER 27

JESSICA

Jessica and Lena are snuggled under the duvet with Cassie and Charlie watching *Encanto*. On the coffee table, a mixing bowl once full of home-made popcorn is now empty but for two hardened corns that refused to pop.

Half an hour into the film, Will rang. Knowing she would only hurt the kids if she ignored his call, Jessica paused the film and told them to take the phone upstairs so she and Lena could chat.

Now she closes her eyes. It is hard to relax knowing that Will might have put their family in danger. Since her initial panic, she has tried to rationalise it. If Will *is* involved with drugs, it does not follow that these people will come after her and the kids. A great many people buy and sell drugs these days; you only have to go to the riverside of an evening to know that. But if Will insists on being part of that world, she will move the kids away. The figure watching the house all those weeks ago must have been something to do with that world. Was it even this Silverman guy? Whoever it was, Will's actions have left her afraid of her own shadow. She feels watched, constantly, almost trapped. It would break her heart to move away from her job and her friends here, but she will not live in the shadow of fear. That Will has done this to them is unbelievable. Every time she thinks about it, fury fires in her, violent and visceral, making her want to punch things, shout at the top of her lungs. Quite simply, she could kill him with her bare hands.

The film ends. Jessica yawns, the forty-eight-hour week shivering out through her aching limbs. She tells the kids to clean their teeth and jump into bed while she sees Lena out. At the door, Lena gives her a long hug. Feeling her friend's ribs against her arms, Jessica pulls back, holds her by the shoulders and looks into her eyes.

'Don't lose any more weight, OK? At our age, there's a line.'

'I'm fine.' Lena shakes her head, but her smile is too wide, her eyes too big. 'I'm loved up, that's all. I'll get my appetite back once he moves in and starts leaving his dirty socks on the bedroom floor.' She laughs, but Jessica is not convinced.

'John's not making you lose the weight, is he? You said you met him at the gym?'

Lena flaps her hand. 'He's not like that. He doesn't care either way. Honestly.' She lurches forward, kisses Jessica on the cheek. 'Give me a shout if you need anything over the weekend, OK?'

Jessica closes the door, unease in her gut. Lena has never been thin. She loves her food and her wine too much. And the last few times they've met up, she has seemed a bit subdued – no, not subdued exactly, rather excessively cheerful but in a way that felt hollow, like someone trying to hide a serious illness for fear of being treated differently. And then there are the flashes of aggression these last couple of months, which isn't like her either. When Jessica asked her how work was going earlier, she replied quite coldly that not everyone has a blue-chip career, which really stung. She apologised immediately, said she'd had nothing for a couple of months and that she was starting to get a bit stressed. Jessica offered to lend her money, to pay her for picking up the kids every day from school, but Lena waved her off: no way. They were friends; it was what friends did. She was fine. Don't worry. Feeling like she was coming up against a brick wall, Jessica tried asking if she could meet John sometime soon, but again Lena blocked her, told her that she wanted to take it slow this time.

Jessica hopes Lena hasn't swapped out one kind of bastard for another. Bastards, after all, come in infinite varieties.

Upstairs, Charlie is cleaning his teeth. Cassie is peeing.

'Her Royal Highness is on the throne,' Jessica says in a posh voice, making Cassie giggle. 'Come on, guys, let's get you to bed. We need sleep if we're going to go swimming tomorrow.'

Charlie spits the toothpaste foam into the sink. 'Are we going swimming? Are we actually?' He is beaming. You'd think he'd been offered the moon. After Will left, Jessica continued to take them to the pool out of a determination that they would not miss out on anything. At first, she hated it – the changing rooms with their clumps of other people's wet hair, their sodden Band-Aids, the lockers that are always broken, the freezing gust that comes from who knows where when you return to the cubicles from the poolside. Now, she loves taking them. Afterwards, she always feels so alive, work well and truly chlorinated into oblivion. She is getting better at simply hanging out with them. They don't need fireworks, only constancy. And whatever energy they appear to take, they return with interest.

'When is Daddy coming?' Cassie asks as Jessica tucks her into bed.

'He'll be here on Wednesday.'

'Is he ever going to come and live with us again?' Her eyes fill.

Jessica feels her heart crack down the middle. 'Not just yet, lovey. But next weekend you'll go to his friend's super-duper house again, won't you? Have you... met them yet?' Her cheeks burn. She vowed she wouldn't do this again.

Cassie shakes her head, no, but is unbothered. 'It's only us. But his friend leaves us lasagnes and garlic bread and Daddy said we could have chicken curry next time if we want.'

'Wow!' Jessica makes a little fist in the air, feels herself die inside. A woman definitely. Is she part of the drug cartel? Do they call them cartels? Whatever, Will's girlfriend is looking after her man, finding the way to his heart through his stomach. There's no way a man would cook and leave meals for another man. For a moment, she considers asking Martin Duncan to follow Will with the kids this weekend. But no, she has gone far enough, further than she ever dreamt she would. When she looks in the mirror, when she thinks of some of the things she's done since seeing those photographs, she doesn't recognise herself.

Besides, she's not sure she dares find out any more.

She changes into her PJs and watches the news with a herbal tea. At 10.45, she turns off the television and the room dies. There is no one on the corner, the houses all in darkness. She draws the curtains. On the coffee table, her phone lights up. Supermarket Guy.

Are you awake? X

She should pretend she hasn't seen this message. She should tell him it's over.

I'm awake, she replies.

Can I come over?

No! It's late.

A GIF: a kitten with big pleading eyes, the caption *Please?*

Not tonight.

I don't need to stay, just want to see you.

You can't stay. The kids are here.

Does that mean I can come over?

Jessica sighs. He is really very pushy. *Not tonight*, she texts. *Sorry.*

I guess I'll go to bed alone then :(Miss you. When can I see you again?

If she doesn't give him something, he'll keep texting. She holds the phone to her chest a moment before composing a reply.

Maybe this weekend?

CHAPTER 28

WILL

Will arrives at the flat sweat-soaked and panting hard. His clothes too are drenched. His smart coat and new umbrella were useless against the wind and the rain, the floods that bounced up from the gutters. His hiking cagoule and old wellies would have been better.

At the door, his fingers won't coordinate. He can't get the key in the lock.

Yes he can. That's it. Breathe, Will. Breathe. Calm down.

Inside, he closes the door and collapses against it. His chest heaves.

'Oh my God,' he whimpers. 'Oh my God, oh my God, oh my God.'

He strips off his coat and shoes, carries them to the bathroom and throws them, along with the umbrella, into the bath. There, shivering, he takes off the rest of his clothes. There is nothing that isn't wet, even his pants. He runs a hot shower and lets the water warm him through, though he cannot stop shaking.

In the bedroom, he puts on his old jogging bottoms and

hoodie, his socks with the hole. He slides his feet into his slippers and gives his head a good rub with the towel. He is starting to feel calmer. With effort, he is managing to control his breathing, his trembling limbs.

Ian's proposal circles and circles, winds itself around him, tighter and tighter.

Don't make me spell it out... Neither crime could be connected to us... You'll get your kids and her life insurance... We'll both stay out of prison... Neither crime could be connected to us... We'll both stay out of prison.

What was he thinking? Was he even thinking at all?

Jessica knows I'm linked to Dave.

What the hell did he mean by that? That his reason for not agreeing to have his own wife *murdered* was that he would be found out? Surely those words did not pass through his rational brain? It was a panic response. A holding device while he worked up the nerve to get the hell away from Ian Robbins and his horrific proposal. Something forced him out of that chair. Something pushed him beyond his limit.

She won't know anything once she's dead, will she?

That was it. Then, yes, he had bolted. Finally. As he should have done at the first insinuation. Because that was how Ian did it: by stealth. Polished it up slowly until malice gleamed on its shiny surface in the form of Will's own face, reflected back at him: *Monster.*

There is no way he will say yes. No way he ever would have. But that doesn't change the fact that he is in what feels increasingly, horribly, like a trap.

He has to think of an exit strategy. He has to get the hell away from Ian Robbins and the world he has somehow lured Will into. Because he has been lured, gradually, from the moment they met that first night. Why? Why him? Is there some link with Margot? Because that's where this all began.

Could Margot herself be behind this, pulling the strings, the whole damsel-in-distress thing an act?

Whatever the link, Will has to extricate himself from Ian quickly and without offence. Because, as he has always known somewhere inside himself, Ian Robbins is not someone you offend.

But how? How in hell?

It is seven o'clock. Time to call the kids. He has to get himself together or he'll cry down the phone. In the kitchen, he eats a Kit Kat, makes a mug of tea, into which he heaps two teaspoonfuls of yet more sugar. He settles himself on the sofa as best he can and calls Jessica's mobile.

'Daddy?' It is Cassie. He closes his eyes, almost sobs. She must have been waiting by the phone. Jessica must have let her hold it so that she could pick up the moment he rang.

'Hey, buddy,' he manages. 'How're you doing?'

'We're watching *Encanto*. Lena's here. We made popcorn.'

Three statements. Three knives through his heart. *I'm so sorry, my darling girl*, he wants to say. *I've got involved in something I don't really understand and I don't know how to get out, and I've let you, your brother and your mother down.*

'That sounds great,' he manages, brushing tears from his cheeks. 'Where are you now?'

'I'm walking upstairs. Mummy paused the film. She said to come upstairs so she can chat to Auntie Lena.'

A pain in his chest, easy to name: the fathomless ache of love.

'Good girl,' he manages. 'And is it just you and Mummy in the house?'

'And Charlie!'

'Yes. And Charlie! Can't forget Charlie! Where's Charlie?'

'He's doing a wee.' She giggles. 'I'm in our room now. Auntie Lena's here too.'

'Oh yes, you said.' Good old Lena. Who spends more time with his kids than he does. He coughs into his hand. Hates himself for what he's trying not to ask, what he knows he is about to ask.

'And have you seen any of Mummy's other friends?' Subtle as a brick, but she's only six.

'I went to Angelica's for tea yesterday and for a playdate. We played Jenga. It was hilarious.'

'Was it?' Angelica. Colin and Freya's daughter. He hasn't reached out to Colin, doesn't really know why. On Wednesdays, he arrives late at the school gates, practically runs out of there with Cassie on his back. She loves it, thinks it's a game.

'What about at the house?' he tries. 'Has anyone else come to the house?'

'Granny Pat.'

God, this is like pulling teeth. Still, it sounds like the kids haven't met Jessica's boyfriend. Which is good. She must sneak him out of the door in the mornings before they wake up. But that won't last. She will relax into it, let her guard down. The thought makes him feel physically sick. 'Mummy doesn't need anyone else, does she? She's got you and Charlie!'

Cassie giggles. 'Her friend from work came.'

'Did... she?' The hair on Will's arm lifts. 'What was her name?'

'It was a he, Daddy!' Cassie giggles. 'He came for breakfast!'

Will swallows, hard. 'He came for breakfast, did he? Did you all have breakfast together?'

'No. It was too early. He only had coffee.'

'Right. Right.' Disgust at himself covers his skin in a sticky sheen. He needs a damn shower. He needs hosing down with disinfectant. 'And what did he look like, can you remember?'

'He was tall.'

'Tall, eh? Did he have any hair?'

Cassie giggles again. 'Yes, Daddy!'

'Tall with hair, eh? I think I know him.'

'Do you? Do you actually?'

'No! I was only joking.' Christ, this is so awful he can barely go on. But he cannot stop himself, even while self-loathing gathers and hardens in his chest. 'What was his name, can you remember?'

'I can't remember his first name.'

'OK. Can you remember his second name?' He waits, tries to think of her colleagues' names. What's Doug's last name? She claims to find him obnoxious, but that's the classic cover.

'It was two birds,' Cassie says with triumph.

'Two birds?' he asks, his throat almost closed. 'What do you mean, two birds? Like starlings? Thrushes?'

'No, Daddy!' She is giggling hard now, enjoying their little game so much. 'It's robins!'

A whimpering sound comes out of him. His hands are over his face. His elbows dig hard into his thighs. The air thrums.

'Fuck,' he whispers. 'Fuck, fuck, fuck.'

Robins. Robbins. Ian Robbins is sleeping with his wife. He is... he... Oh God.

Will holds on to his head with brittle fingers. He tries to breathe, feels the shudder in his airways. This whole nightmare isn't about Margot at all; it's about Jessica. Jessica's lover is where this all starts, and Jessica's lover is Ian Robbins. Will digs his fingers into his scalp until it hurts. How the hell didn't he see? Ian is the boyfriend who has been on the scene the whole time. He took the photographs or got someone to take them so her could lever her away from Will. He then engineered a chance meeting so he could suss Will out, hide in plain sight while he assessed the competition, making sure he had a little fun while he was at it, before coldly, methodically annihilating him.

Ian has played him, utterly. Toyed with him. Why didn't he see? *How* didn't he? How? How did this happen?

He makes himself stand up. Paces back and forth in front of the window, the boat lights bright stars in the evening, yellow squares from other apartments, other lives.

No. It's too far-fetched.

Is it?

Yes. No one goes to those lengths. Will is spiralling. Ian hasn't been after him since the beginning. That night, in the Express Tavern, it was Will himself who initiated the conversation. He had to work hard to get Ian to talk to him. Ian is a businessman, an opportunist, that's all. He asked questions, lots of questions, kept the conversation off himself. That's how he operates. Information is power. Dave has a hold over him because of what he knows. Ian knows about Dave's criminal activity. Knowledge. Power.

That night, Ian Robbins saw a man in pieces – overfriendly, desperate for company. At first he resisted, but as Will spilt his guts, Ian listened closely, started to think there might be an advantage after all in talking to this scruffy nonentity nursing a pint of weak lager and a broken heart on a miserable rainy night in Brentford. *This man's wife sounds nice*, he must have thought. Ian's wife had left him some time before. Ian is a busy man, no time to search for a woman. Which means he wasn't seeing Jessica before. Which means he didn't take or send the photographs.

But that night, Ian took control without Will even realising. He has stayed in control of every second of every minute since. Will handed over the dumpster of his life to a complete stranger. All Ian had to do was pick through it for valuables. He had Will followed – immediately and without permission. Will led him to Jessica. Really, it could not have been easier.

Is that what happened? Did Ian have Jessica followed because he was curious to see who Will was married to? Except he didn't have her followed, did he? He did it himself. Or did he? Was it, as Will thought a moment ago, that he was seeing Jessica before?

Oh God. It is mind-boggling.

Think, Will. Slow it down. Either Ian was seeing Jessica before and had Will followed and photographed to get rid of him, met up with him to make sure he never came back; or he was genuinely nursing a broken heart when he met Will quite by chance. He knew that Jessica too was heartbroken, devastated and vulnerable, because Will told him so. Seeing that she was also incredibly attractive, he swooped in with all his charm, all his elegance, all his substantiality. A chance meeting in a supermarket caught her off-guard. All he had to be was all that Will is not. Which is exactly what Ian Robbins is: the opposite of Will. And for Jessica, in the full tilt of violent humiliation, filled with fury and disappointment and disillusion, the opposite of her pathetic, cheating husband must have been so appealing.

Something like that. But whatever the timeline, whatever the sequence of events, Ian has used both of them. Used their anger and bewilderment against them, to seduce each of them in different ways, to turn them against one another.

And now what?

Now what?

Jessica will have no idea what Ian is capable of. Ian, who only hours ago proposed killing her himself, claiming to have no link to her. But Lena must know his name; Jessica must have mentioned him. The police would only have to question her to find out that Jessica had been seeing him.

Unless that's not his real name?

I don't know, Will thinks. I don't know him, do I? I don't know a thing about him.

He digs his nails into his scalp until it hurts. He has to get out of this. He has to get Jessica out. But how, if she won't even listen to what he has to say? Even if she did let him speak, she no longer trusts a single thing that comes out of his mouth.

CHAPTER 29

JESSICA

After their text exchange, Jessica decides to edit Ian's contact details in her phone. Despite her concerns, he has become more than a moment of madness, a warm shred of comfort, a boost for a bruised ego. He's a little rough-edged but he's also polished. He's uneducated but cultured, pushy but playful, considerate but always in charge. He is unlike anyone she's ever known. From now on, she will take it slow, yes, but... She deletes *Supermarket*, types in: *IR*.

Next weekend, he's taking her to the ballet. Now that Will is picking up the kids from school, she won't even have to see him; she can go straight from work.

'He loves the ballet,' she told Lena yesterday when she got home from work, sounding even to herself like a schoolgirl with a fat crush. 'He listens to opera in the car. *Madame Butterfly*'s his favourite. And theatre. He came from a poor background but he's worked so hard, really made something of himself.'

'So have you, babe.'

'So have *you*. Do you know, he never swears? I need to stop swearing.'

'He sounds great,' Lena said, but her frown belied her feelings.

'What?'

'Nothing.'

'Lena, what?'

Lena sighed, her shoulders rising in an apologetic shrug. 'I... I don't want to be a Debbie Downer, but you'd say it to me, wouldn't you? You know, about the love-bombing? You'd tell me to watch it, wouldn't you, if a guy was treating me like a princess?'

Jessica laughed like a fool, smug and silly as a llama, but she didn't care. 'I actually think it's just the way he is,' she said. 'He's determined to enjoy every minute of his time on earth. He thinks people who have money and don't spend it are ridiculous. I so admire that. Every little thing, he knows how to do it, you know? Booking tickets, buying a drink, ordering food, he just knows, knows how to be. Will was always so awkward, so indecisive. He used to ask what I was having, as if he couldn't decide on his own. It really used to ruin the mood. Ian *always* knows what he wants. Always. When a guy takes you out, you don't want him dithering about like an old lady, do you? You want to feel like he's looking after you. Like the sky's the limit.'

Lena's smile was doubtful. There were black circles under her eyes; Jessica is only remembering this now and thinking she should have asked about that.

'If you're sure,' she said.

'I'm not.' Jessica cackled, actually cackled. 'I just know that when I'm with him, the time just disappears. I find him... I find him absolutely fascinating.'

CHAPTER 30

WILL

The canal is flat and black, the moon white and round in its depths. It is late – after midnight – and cold. Unable to sleep, Will has come out here to think.

On the pathway, there is no one, no one on the riverside, the barges dark, their inhabitants asleep behind blank porthole windows. Do the boat-dwellers dream of owning a house? Or are they committed to the freedom of life afloat? Could *he* live on a barge, release himself from all but the essentials?

Without question, he would've said two months ago. Jessica and the kids are all I need. The rest is window-dressing.

Would he say that now?

He has let himself be lured by a glamorous stranger he met in a pub. How did he let that happen? How has he got in so deep? And at what point did Ian betray him?

It occurs to him that whatever he is feeling now, it is a fraction of what Jessica felt when she saw those photographs. No wonder she lost her head. He feels like he is losing his mind. And then, when she wouldn't talk to him, he took offence, gave up. That's what he does. He gives up.

Pacing down the dark riverbank, he rakes through his

conversations with Ian these past months. The rooms in his home – one for his girl, one for his boy, rooms they only ever occupy during the school holidays when they visit. His beautiful wife pictured in happier times. His family gone, leaving an empty home waiting to be filled. An empty heart waiting...

Whatever you do, hold on to your family.

In another conversation – he can't remember exactly where or when – Ian admitted he worked too hard, was the *classic workaholic*, left his wife alone too much. So she left him and took his kids. How old these kids are now, how long ago they left, Will has no real idea. All he knows is that losing his family is Ian's greatest regret, that it was this pain that bonded him and Will together, or so Will thought. In Will's drunken moment of self-pity, Ian heard all about Jessica, how wonderful she is. He found her. Watched her. Spoke to her. Liked her. Made his move.

An empty home. An empty heart. Jessica and the kids could fill that home, that heart. They are the ideal ready-made family, would fit perfectly into the life Ian could offer them.

An opportunity then – like a run-down flat, a boarded-up pub – an investment for the right kind of cash, the right kind of attention. *The world turns... everyone gets a piece.* Ian had only to step in with his nice suits and his money and his easy man-of-the-world charm. To step in and capitalise.

But why pursue a friendship with Will? Why not simply seduce Jessica, move her and the kids into his family home, if stealing Jessica was his aim? After all, it is Will who has been moved into Ian's properties, not Jessica, Will who is now trapped in Ian's flat like an animal in a cage.

And why suggest killing her? And what does Dave have over Ian that Ian needs him disposed of? Surely it's too risky to send a man like Will to dispose of a psychopath like Dave? Will is hardly made from the right kind of material.

Unless...

On the dark, lonely waterside, Will stops. His hand closes over his mouth. His breath quickens.

Unless Ian has no intention of killing Jessica.

Unless it is not Dave he wants dead but Will.

'Oh my God,' he whispers through his fingers, heart hammering now.

Could that be right? Ian Robbins sends soft, educated Will Draper – a boy, by his standards – to kill a known gangster, a drug dealer, a psychopath. Ian knows Will has little or no chance of coming out alive. Dave will be stronger, quicker, wily as a fox, brutal, unhesitating. Even if Ian arms Will, Will has never used a gun before, doesn't know if he could even pull a trigger.

It's a theory. Run with it, Will. See where it takes you.

So.

Dave has nothing on Ian; that was a lie. Dave is meant to kill Will. Will arrives like a chump thinking he's the hired assassin, but Dave is waiting for him – *bam*. A classic double-cross.

'Oh my God,' he whispers again. 'Oh my God, oh my God.'

What about the perfect crime?

The thing is, if Will dies, it is *still* a perfect crime; he and Dave are no more connected than they would be if Will kills Dave, are they? It is a simple job. Dave will know how to murder someone without leaving a trace. Ian meanwhile gives himself an alibi – possibly even Jessica. Jessica has no idea what she's involved in. Ian is with her when she gets the terrible news, there for her in her grief. She comes to rely on him, comes to love him. Ian gets a new family and Will is six foot under. Bingo. A golden opportunity not to be missed. No comeback. No consequences. No ripples in the canal.

Could that be right?

Because what lies at the bottom of this particular version of events is that if Ian is involved with Jessica, he has no intention of keeping up his side of the bargain.

The suggestion of killing Jessica was a bluff – to get rid of Will.

Yes. The more Will thinks about it, the more this makes sense. Ian has played him for a fool, but he is not a fool; he has simply trusted someone who was kind to him in a vulnerable moment, that's all. Nothing, no experience in his life, could have prepared him for Ian and what he is capable of. This is not his world. He neither knows its customs nor speaks its language. But now he has wised up. Now he can take a step back, think carefully about how he might get himself and Jessica out of this man's reach.

Unless...

Another possibility dawns; it is incredible how much can be discovered simply by slowing everything down. Doesn't he say this to his own clients? Take a step back. Think.

Ian is double-crossing Will, of that there is no doubt. But perhaps he genuinely wants Will to kill Dave. He doesn't ask Dave to kill Will; Dave arrives quite unsuspecting. It's possible that Ian truly believes that a hapless life coach with a loaded gun and the element of surprise will work. It's a risk, yes, but a calculated one.

Let's go there, play it out.

Will lies in wait. Dave arrives. Will shoots Dave, who succumbs to a bullet between the eyes. Will shudders at the thought. Ian still won't kill Jessica, because he wants her and her children to fill the void at the heart of his wealthy life. Dave is dead, the threat of blackmail along with him, leaving Ian to be a model citizen, an MP, Mayor of London, whatever. Coldly and calmly, Ian informs Will that there has been a change of plan, that he's taking Will's wife and family to live in his Kew mansion. Like coins from an open palm, Ian Robbins lifts everything Will holds dear from him. Will can do nothing because Ian has only to go to the police to land him in prison. Maybe Ian goes to the police anyway, or gets someone, one of his contacts, to lead the police to Will. Will tries to tell them Ian is behind it all, but Ian is untouchable, a paragon of respectability.

Ian Robbins gets his family, his gleaming reputation intact.

Will is behind bars.

So far, so clear.

'Fuck,' he whispers, chewing now at his thumbnail.

How to get out? How does anyone win against Ian Robbins?

He could tell Jessica the truth about her new boyfriend. But she won't believe him because all trust between them has been lost. Jessica will assume he's trying to show Ian in a bad light to somehow win her back. She has more than proved that a woman scorned is a woman unwilling to listen. And now she is not only scorned but frightened – again, because of him. He could try Pat, but she's about as likely to listen as a brick wall. Besides which, to tell Jessica or Pat the truth about Ian Robbins is to put them in danger. Because beneath all of this, one thing is becoming painfully clear.

If Will refuses to kill Dave, Ian will turn nasty.

If Will kills Dave, Ian will turn nasty.

If Ian gets any inkling that Will or Jessica are onto him, Ian will turn nasty.

In any scenario not to his liking, Ian will turn nasty.

Choice is an illusion. The only option is mortal danger.

Will feels the singeing creep of fear across his skin. His anger is draining away, his theories, his logic. No amount of stepping back and thinking clearly can help. Dread expands within him, solid and terrible. Raw with hurt, alienated from one another, turned against one another by the same man, he and Jessica have been caught in Ian Robbins' spiderweb. It is a cliché, but it is horribly true. With extravagant gestures and gifts, with the warm, flattering glow of attention, Ian has been slowly wrapping them both in silk, turning them around and around, turning Will against Jessica, turning Jessica against Will, making both of them prey.

How he wishes they could go back to the way they were. He would sit her down, he would tape her mouth shut if necessary, and make her listen to the whole story of him and Margot. Because it is not a story that can be nutshelled, not one he could have told her while she was verbally machine-gunning him. He must tell her and she must listen. If he is to save her and the kids, he must find a way. That he could ever have thought two thousand pounds would matter in the grand scheme of things is laughable.

But even if Jessica does listen, if she decides she can forgive him and that they can move on, how can they walk away from a man like Ian Robbins, a man whose reach Will can only guess at?

The path lightens, chips of gravel picked out by the moon drifting from behind a cloud. Will feels the ache of his legs, his knees, the tiredness in his shoulders, his neck. He is chilled to the bone, shivering now as he comes back to himself. With no solution, no plan, no decision beyond getting some sleep, he turns back towards the flat, capable of nothing more than watching his bright trainers pace left, right, left, right. His Nike Air Max, of which, despite himself, he felt as proud as a teenager. A toxic present from a wicked man, one of so many, a drip from a feed of pure poison. And Will fell for it all, like a child falls for the offer of sweets from a stranger, only to find themselves deep in the dark wood with no one to hear them cry.

Head down now, he marches, bound for his borrowed home. *Neither a borrower nor a lender be,* his mother would have said, harping on after the fact, glorying in yet another of his mistakes. *Never be beholden to anyone. Ever. Didn't I tell you? A thousand times I told you, but did you listen? Did you? Honestly, William Draper, I waste my breath, I really do. You don't think, do you? You just don't think, child.*

Could it be that he has spent his whole life a borrower, beholden to friends, to his wife, out of some long-buried instinct to act out, a childish *fuck you* to his mother, a woman who died over four years ago? Is it possible he is only understanding this now? Then Margot. Margot was perhaps the first person who really needed him, the first he felt he could truly help. *She* was beholden to *him*. He appointed himself her saviour not out of goodness, but, he sees now, out of a desire to be a benefactor, to be that most slippery of terms: a man.

Looking about him, he realises he is much further from the flat than he thought. He no longer recognises any of the buildings. And actually he has paced and turned and stopped so many times he is not one hundred per cent sure which way is the right way back. His mouth is dry, his eyelids are heavy. After a moment's deliberation, he decides that if the river was on his right when he set off, if he keeps it on his left, he will eventually get back. Hopefully.

He sets off once again, moving more like a sleepwalker now, dragging his feet. There is no sound save for the vague rush of traffic somewhere to his right. Fearing hypothermia, he tries to ignore his exhaustion and keep moving. He must keep moving. He must keep thinking. If he keeps his mind on the problem, a plan will appear. It must.

The problem is one of inevitability. It's like *We're Going on a Bear Hunt*, Charlie's favourite of all the books Will reads to him at night. This insurmountable obstacle is like the grass, the river, the mud: he cannot go over it, he cannot go under it; he's going to have to go through it. Because what is becoming apparent is that at some point in the next week or two, he will very probably find himself confronting Dave, a known gangster and drug dealer, with, he's guessing, a gun, since he can't imagine Ian trusting him to somehow take Dave with his bare hands.

He, Will Draper, is going to have to do this.

He pictures himself, puts a gun in his hand, sees it shake. The gun is black, but that's as far as he can get. He has never seen a gun up close, only on television, in movies like *Pulp Fiction* and anything with Bruce Willis, films he and Jessica would watch with a takeaway, for fun. So there he is, William Draper, ex-banker, ex-teacher, life coach, house husband, father, holding what looks a bit like the plastic pea-gun he had as a boy, confronting David Silverman, gangster, psychopath and owner of a personalised-number-plated silver BMW on a maybe moonless night, on the riverbank, in the dark.

As he walks, Will makes a gun with his hands.

'Put your hands up above your head where I can see 'em.' He laughs, staggers, rights himself. 'Don't shoot. Please don't shoot,' he mutters, tittering to the black trees. 'I wasn't going to kill you, honest, guv!'

His head lolls backwards. A fit of the giggles. He has to stop, sit down on a bench while he gets himself together. This is madness. This is how madness starts. Maybe it's how it ends: a man laughing at himself, a dead man on the riverbank, a man who didn't have the balls to tell his wife straight to her face that he'd lent a woman money he'd never earned, helped her escape, knowing perhaps deep down that he had been scammed. And that is where it would have ended. But no. Instead, Will hid from telling the whole truth. Opted instead for the quick fix, the kind stranger, then later, believing himself by then to be the wronged party, he fell for... what actually? Power? The chance to play at grown-ups? To win? To be in some sort of Guy Ritchie movie?

'Christ,' he says, wiping at his eyes. 'Don't shoot, guv! Ha! Hahahahahahaha!'

A confrontation in the dead of night, a desperate conversation in, say, an abandoned warehouse somewhere he has never been. Rain drips from ruined rafters. The moon glints through a ragged hole in the roof. Somewhere a crow caws – why not? Bring on the clichés; bring them all on. Moons glint in films, don't they? Crows caw. The hour is always midnight. The trap is a spiderweb. A shot rings out, because that's what shots do, don't they? They ring out. A man cries – argh! Clutching at his chest, he falls to his knees, onto his front, his face plants itself in the dirt.

And – *Cut!*

The hysteria abates. Will's hands close into fists. Something is edging in, some cloudy start of a solution. Could he...? It is the same scene but played out differently. Himself and David Silverman, but this time...

Is there a catch? A flaw? A plot hole?

No. No, he doesn't think so, but then what the hell does he know?

One final scenario: the abandoned warehouse, the midnight riverbank, wherever. Will has the gun. Dave turns, his face registering shock.

'Wait,' Will says. 'Ian sent me. I'm not going to kill you, but we need to talk.'

Will tells Dave that Ian wants him dead. Will wants no part of it, is letting Dave go. Dave is grateful. He does not knock the gun from Will's hand. *Thanks, man*, he says. *I owe you one.*

Will calls the police. Does he?

Dave calls the police? Not likely.

Will bites at his bloody cuticles. A plan, the beginnings of a plan. Will tells Ian he's up for Operation *Strangers on a Train*. He will go first. Why? To... to prove his commitment, yes, that could work. Ian will agree. Because Ian isn't going to kill Jessica.

'Yes,' he whispers. Yes, this is genius. The key here is to make Ian think everything is going his way.

What comes next? Dave is alive and Will's friend now. Ian is not intending to kill Jessica but is still wooing her, still moving in on Will's family, and now that Will has betrayed Ian to Dave, Ian will be angry. He will want Will dead.

So no. That won't work.

Think.

Dave has something on Ian. That much must be true. Dave tells Will what it is. Will can go to the police in a way Dave could or would not. Dave will not want the police anywhere near him. But he will want Ian put away.

OK, so the plan needs a little refining. Calling the police now is out of the question. Without evidence, they will let Ian go. Will risks getting himself murdered and leaving Jessica, his kids, even Pat at the mercy of Ian Robbins. At the moment, it looks like betraying Ian to Dave is all he has. It's got to be better than killing him, and besides, he could not kill anyone, not in cold blood, no way. He could barely stomach *Call of Duty* without copious amounts of booze and dope; there is no way he could cope with taking a real, actual life.

In a flat on the ground floor, a light comes on – amber stripes in a venetian blind. He wants to rap on the window, call to whoever is in there, still awake.

Help! Help me!

But instead he climbs the stone stairwell to the first floor and lets himself into the apartment Ian Robbins offered him two months ago. He throws his keys on the coffee table and makes his way over to the window. Outside, pink pushes against the graphite sky. He is shivering with cold, trembling from head to toe. He puts on the heating, stands against the radiator as it warms, pressing his legs to it, blowing into his hands. A hope glimmers, small but persistent. If knowledge is power, then maybe he has just enough knowledge to untangle himself.

He peels off his shoes, throws them one by one towards the bedroom and lies on the floor in a starfish next to the radiator, still in his coat, hat and scarf. The ceiling is fuzzy, greyish white. His limbs are water, his chest a rock. He is melting into puddles on the hard wooden floor. Think, Will. One last bit of focus. One last push. Dave must have more than knowledge. Knowledge is not enough to put Ian away. There must be evidence somewhere. Dave must tell you where the evidence is hidden.

You call the police. They arrest Ian. You drive over to Jessica's and tell her everything – about Margot, about Ian, about Dave. Dave will not come after them because Dave is glad, grateful. Ian is locked up. No one has to die.

Could that be it? Could that be his way out?

Whatever happens, keeping Jessica and the kids safe is all that matters now. He will go to prison, risk his life, whatever it takes. His family's future is in his hands. The only choice he has is to throw it all up in the air and hope to God he can catch it.

The sun is rising. He pulls out his phone. And texts Ian Robbins.

I'm in.

CHAPTER 31

JESSICA

Along the landing, Jessica can hear Mum and the kids chatting. She leans in, brushing mascara onto her lashes. Nothing too heavy. Ian doesn't like her to wear too much make-up; he prefers a more natural look. For this evening, she has chosen a maxi dress. The plan was to wear her little black number, but some instinct told her not to. It's a little short perhaps. It's not that she's too old to get her legs out, just...

She doesn't know. A feeling.

'They're all tucked in.' Her mum is smiling at her from the bedroom door. 'You look lovely.'

Jessica meets her eye in the mirror. 'Thanks.'

'He's a lucky chap.'

'It's just a casual thing.'

Her mum nods. 'Do you good. We all need a bit of a boost.'

Mum's footsteps recede. Jessica listens to them pad downstairs, wonders briefly about her mum's love life. There has been no one, as far as she knows. A shame, she thinks. Her mother is a total catch.

She pushes her lipstick around her mouth, blots it on a tissue, wondering now if her mum thinks she and Ian have yet to sleep together, whether she'd be shocked if she knew they had, even if it was just once. Jessica doesn't know now what came over her beyond a post-traumatic-stress-related moment of madness, a buried sense that she didn't quite know how to say no. But it's too late to go back now, despite a tiny niggle she has yet to tease into the light and examine. She will, just not yet. When she's stronger, she will. For now, they are not a couple, not exactly, but... something.

She considers her reflection a moment. It's possible she should stop dyeing her hair soon. Rich auburn is the colour of her youth; she should ask her hairdresser about toning it down now she's approaching forty. She pushes it back from her face, lets it fall. Frowns. Smiles. Better. Her eyes are still nice, she supposes. A few lines at the corners, but she doesn't mind those. Her face is thinner than it was two months ago. The stone she has lost since Photogate appears to have come off her cheeks and breasts, leaving her looking tired but still wearing jeans a size bigger than she'd like.

Will wouldn't care. He wouldn't even notice. Will loved you exactly as you were.

She shakes her head, shakes the thought away.

Why should she care what Will thinks? He is not her husband any more, despite the fact that neither of them has progressed the divorce beyond one solicitor's letter apiece. They have reached a kind of stalemate, she thinks. As if they both know that to go any further would mean they have no way back. Sasha emailed the other day to ask her what was going on. Jessica has not yet replied.

She rubs her lips together, eyeing herself, thinking of the way Ian looks at her, the slight appraisal she feels under his gaze. But it's only a feeling. She's not used to dating, that's all. It has been a lo-o-ong time.

Downstairs, her mother is already settled in the corner of the sofa, legs tucked up beneath her, crossword on her lap.

'All set?' she asks, her strong reading glasses making her eyes look huge. Her once long red hair is cut short these days and has faded to a washed-out coral. Jessica feels a rush of love. Her mother has offered not one word of judgement about her seeing someone else, is on her side at the deepest possible level. Her rock.

'I won't be too late,' Jessica says now, nerves fluttering in her belly.

When she refused Ian's offer of a lift this evening, he said he would send a car. A car, for goodness' sake. Jessica flatly refused: *No way. I mean, thanks, but I'm a grown woman.*

'Hold up the Spanish within twenty-four hours,' her mother mutters to the newspaper. 'Delay.' Her hand clenches briefly before she inks the answer into the boxes.

Jessica orders an Uber to take her over to Esher, where Ian has booked a Chinese restaurant he likes. They're meeting in the Bear first for a drink. She will not let him pay for everything again. It's flattering but it makes her uncomfortable.

'Be as late as you like,' her mum says, looking up again from the paper. 'I'm not on shift till next week.'

'You *can* stay over, you know.'

'I like my own bed.'

Jessica smiles – it was the answer she was expecting. 'I'll text you when I'm on my way and you can jump in my cab.'

'Don't be silly. I'm only round the corner.'

'Mum.' Jessica frowns at her until she relents.

'All right. You can put Granny in a taxi.'

'I don't like the thought of you walking in the cold, that's all. Why didn't you come in the car?'

Her mother holds up her arm, her new Fitbit on her wrist. 'Got to get my steps in.'

Jessica laughs, checks her phone, sees that the Uber is a minute away and bends to kiss her mum. 'Bye then.'

'Go on, bugger off, you're putting me off my crossword.'

Jessica is still giggling when she gets into the cab.

She finds Ian in the pub lounge. He has ordered a pint of beer for himself, a gin and tonic for her. She tries not to bristle. Gin and tonic is what she would have ordered, but that's not the point. She might have wanted something else. He does not know her *that* well; it feels a little like he is staking his claim.

'Hello, gorgeous,' he says, in his low, sexy voice. 'You look good.'

'Thank you.' Not wanting to get the evening off to a sour start, she offers her cheek for him to kiss before lifting herself onto the bar stool beside him. 'It's just an old dress. Ancient really.'

'I'll buy you a new one.'

She laughs, though he is not smiling. 'You don't need to buy me clothes,' she says. 'I have plenty of clothes.'

'But I like giving gifts. What size are you?' He looks her up and down with a dispassionate frown.

She narrows her eyes at him. '*What?*'

He stops, thank God, and sips his drink. 'Ten on top, twelve on the bottom?'

She lifts her glass and takes a large gulp of her gin and tonic, stalling. She has no idea what to say. Uncomfortable is the least of how she feels. Frankly, she wants to tell him to piss off.

'And you're a thirty-two waist,' she says after a moment, scrutinising him as he did her. 'Sixteen-inch collar? And your boxers are, what, a medium?' She glares at him, right into his eyes. 'Definitely not a large.'

He throws up his hands. 'No need to be touchy.'

'In no rush to give me your measurements, I see. And for future reference, can you wait until I get here before you buy me a drink?'

'Didn't you want gin and tonic?'

'I don't know what I wanted. I don't usually decide until someone offers.'

He blows air through his lips, his eyebrows raised. 'You're the boss.'

'I'm not. But neither are you.' She slides off her stool and pulls the strap of her bag over her shoulder. 'Actually, I'm really tired. I'm going to head home. Sorry, I shouldn't have come out.'

He reaches for her, his fingers circling her forearm. His expression is earnest but not quite apologetic. 'Don't go. I didn't mean anything by it. I was just trying to be nice.' He searches her face, his brow furrowed. He is still holding her arm, his grip tight. 'Come on. Sit down. Tell me about your day. Don't let me and my clumsy manners put you off.' He slides his grip down to her hand, holds it tightly in his.

'All right,' she says, feeling herself flush. 'All right.'

He loosens his grip, lifts her hand to his lips and kisses it.

She rolls her eyes. 'For God's sake.'

'My queen,' he says, eyes playful before they darken into an expression she cannot read.

She breaks free and gives a merry little laugh. Sips her drink, thinks about her mother on the sofa at home, muttering crossword clues, making that little fist pump in the air when she gets the answer. She thinks about the kids upstairs, angelic in the glow of their night lights, their eyelashes, the way their heads smell when they're asleep, how she longs to inhale that smell, down, down into her lungs. Her feet are killing her. This bar stool is making her back ache. She has no idea what she's doing here.

'Are we OK?' Ian asks her, his gaze soft.

'Sure,' she says and, despite herself, smiles.

CHAPTER 32

WILL

'You just point it and press the trigger. Simple as that.'

Ian is turning a black semi-automatic pistol over in his hand. Will has just discovered what is behind the locked door opposite the games room in Ian's basement, and why the contents did not form part of the tour the first time he came here. It is a soundproofed corridor, a little like a ten-pin bowling lane. It smells dusty in here, like damp plaster, and it is cold, the kind of breezeless chill you only feel in basements, the kind that seeps into your bones, makes you feel like you'll never warm up again.

At one end of the room, hanging from clips like oversize washing pegs, is a black fifty-centimetre square with a white cross marking the centre; at the other, two sets of ear defenders on hooks on the wall and a locked cabinet containing four firearms. He was expecting Ian to give him a gun, but this? It is all he can do to stop his voice from shaking, stop himself from shaking. In fact, he can't. For the moment, he is standing as still as he can, his mouth tight shut, trying not to think of all the times he brought his kids to this place, how close they were to this room.

'These are only for my personal use,' Ian says, gesturing

towards the gun cabinet. 'I like to fire a few rounds now and again. It's like going to the driving range. A sport. Me and the lads come in here sometimes, but mostly we're happy with a game of darts and what have you next door.'

'I didn't...' Will begins but can get no further, is not even sure what he was going to say.

'This is a Glock,' Ian says, nodding to the pistol in his hand. 'Standard handgun. I keep another one upstairs for protection. It's easy to use. Does the job.'

Does the job. Will feels colder still. He shivers, reminds himself that this is nothing more than a dance. Ian has no intention of killing Jessica, and Will has no intention of killing Dave, but the mere thought of it, of what this small black lump of metal can do, is enough to make him feel sick.

Ian places the gun into Will's palm with the kind of care you'd use to hand over a wounded bird. It is not as heavy as Will thought it would be, but it is heavy. He lowers his hand a fraction, attempts a knowing smile.

'Is it loaded?' he manages.

'Not yet.'

Ian takes the gun from him. 'This is the mag release,' he says, pushing a small button on the... the word 'handle' comes to Will's mind, but he's pretty sure that's not the right term. Whatever, an inner section pops out of the bottom of the gun.

'That's the magazine,' Ian says, pulling out the inner section. 'Now' – he fixes Will with his pale blue eyes – 'just because you've taken the mag out don't mean the gun isn't loaded, OK? There could still be a round in the chamber. You won't need to know any of this because I'll load it for you, but I'm telling you anyway. It's better if you know your way around your weapon.'

Will swallows, nods. *Your weapon.*

'You slide it back.' Ian demonstrates, then turns the gun upside down. 'You check for or empty out your round like so.

Always, always make sure you're not pointing it at yourself or anyone else, yeah? I mean, it's common sense.'

'Common sense. Yes. Absolutely.'

'Then you load the mag. This one's a double stack. It's pretty quick. Means if you miss, you've got plenty more chances.' He hands the empty gun to Will, keeping hold of what Will now knows is called the magazine, putting a whole new spin on *Woman's Own* and the *Angling Times*.

Ian digs in his pocket and pulls out a gold-coloured bullet.

Will's breath catches in his chest. He knows what a bullet is, of course he does, has seen one a hundred times in films, on TV, but this one is right in front of him, this capsule that looks a bit like, well, a bit like a suppository, a rather beautiful golden suppository. It occurs to him that any notions of Ian not being a criminal are long dead. This room, these guns, this golden bullet are not the preserve of a regular law-abiding guy. But who is the bigger criminal, Ian or Dave? Who is the boss?

'You push it into this spring thing here,' Ian is saying, frowning with concentration as he pushes the bullet to the mouth of the magazine. It lodges. He digs again into his pocket. 'Then you push the next one in and up against it, then the next one, and so on. You want the numbers towards you, the front away. As I say, you don't need to know this. I'll make sure it's full. All you have to do is shoot.'

'OK.'

In the terrible silence, Will watches Ian load the magazine. The silence extends, punctuated only by the soft clicks of bullet after bullet being slipped into place. Will tries to regulate his breathing, to keep it from juddering out and giving him away. He focuses on keeping his heart rate steady, though he is not sure he has any control over it or, for that matter, his bowels, which feel like they're on the move. How has this become his world? Surely he could stop this right now and say, *Actually, Ian, thanks for everything but I'm going to go back to my wife and kids now. I'm going to put my arms around them and never let them go.* But he can't. On a visceral gut level, he knows that Ian is not a man from whom you can simply walk away.

For the thousandth time, he mentally berates himself. He should have stayed and fought; he knows it so acutely it hurts. He should have made Jessica listen. She would have understood, eventually, about Margot. They could have had counselling. Who knows, their relationship would probably be better now if he had only fought for it. He just never thought things would escalate the way they have. He thought a night in a hotel and a good talk once the dust had settled would be enough. If only he could go back to that morning and raise his hand and say: *Stop.* Play the whole thing differently. Be brave, braver. Be the person she deserved him to be, the person she thought he was.

'There,' Ian says, taking the empty pistol from Will's open palm. 'Then you put the mag in like this, rounds facing forward.' He slides the magazine into the handle of the gun. Will hears it click into place. 'Then you push this little button to chamber the round.' Another click. 'As I say, you don't have to worry about it. All you have to do is make sure you kill the bastard. If you can't do it with seventeen rounds, you don't deserve to come out of it alive.'

A jet of air escapes Will's nose. He cannot speak, does not trust his voice at all.

'Right.' Ian is holding the ear defenders. He places them over Will's head with a gentleness that feels paternal. He moves behind Will as a dancer might, a moment later puts his hands on Will's shoulders, pushes them down and positions him opposite the target. He lowers the loaded pistol into Will's hand before closing his other hand around it, and Will is reminded once again of a bird – a sparrow at the roadside, fallen out of a tree, dying but still warm.

'There,' Ian says. 'Get a good grip. Thumbs together but not crossed. Keep your finger straight – that's it – until you're ready to shoot. Keep it nice and steady.'

The gun trembles.

'Sorry,' Will says.

'It's all right. Normal to be a bit shaky at first. With power comes great responsibility – that's Winston Churchill said that. These are blanks, but you can still do a lot of damage at close range. Now.'

Will aims at the target, aware of Ian close behind him, of his hands over his own. It is incredibly intimate, like an embrace. He can smell Ian's cologne, feel his warmth, his solidity. Ian removes his hands, steps back and tells Will to spread his feet slightly and to hold the gun a little higher. He touches Will again once on the shoulders. Obediently, Will lowers them.

'Basically, you just have to go for it.' Ian's voice is quiet through the headgear, but Will can tell by the tone that he is shouting. 'The main thing is to take him down, then you can finish it at close range.'

This cannot be happening. It cannot be happening.

Will widens his stance and takes aim. Shoots. The gun gives a dull bang. His hands jolt, sending him backwards a step. He has clipped the edge of the target. Encouraged, he steps forward, tries again, this time hitting the top-right corner. Adrenaline fills him. He shoots again and again, misfiring, landing almost on target, misfiring. From behind him, Ian shouts words of encouragement, tells him to go on, that's it, he's a natural. Will fires again but the trigger is loose.

'I'm out of ammo,' he says, raising the empty gun and turning to Ian.

'Whoa.' Wide-eyed, Ian pushes the black tip away before lifting Will's ear defenders from his head. 'Never point the gun at anyone unless you mean to. Never. There might be a round left in the chamber. OK?'

'Sorry.'

'That's OK. Let's go again. This time you can load it. We'll have you shooting like a pro in no time.'

Will feels a weak smile spread across his face. He could have shot Ian just now. At close range, he could have caused him damage, maybe even killed him. Could he have done that? No, he could not. Besides, what would it achieve?

But if it did come down to it, could he kill to defend himself? Defend his family?

He is not sure.

He reminds himself as Ian loads the gun again that he is *not* going to kill anyone, is he?

No one is going to kill anyone.

Later, in the kitchen, Ian makes small talk while they wait for a home-made cottage pie to come out of the oven. On the table is a jar of pickled red cabbage, also home-made. There will be steamed broccoli too, which Ian tells him is for iron and vitamin C. The whole scenario is so surreal that Will wonders whether he is in fact awake. He has the feeling that if he were to push his hand against a wall, his fingers would sink into it as if into marshmallow; if he were to throw his can of beer to the floor, it would bounce back into his open palm without spilling a drop.

'Talk me through it,' Ian is saying.

'Sorry, what?'

'Talk me through it.' The meal is on the table. Ian is taking off his apron and sitting opposite Will at the kitchen bar. 'I need to hear you say it so I know you've got it. Talk me through what you're going to do.'

Will clears his throat. Before him the mince and carrots, gravy and mash, the bright green broccoli steam. The cabbage is pink, acid.

'Tuesday afternoon.' He glances up, into Ian's waiting eyes. 'I pick up the Glock. You won't be here because you'll be in town creating your alibi. You'll leave the gun in the left-hand drawer of the table thing in the hall.'

'The credenza.'

'The credenza.' Will coughs. Something is tickling his throat. 'I drive to the storage unit. You're going to leave a car for me. It'll be parked up on the road. A black Nissan. The key will be in the drawer with the gun and a phone. The lock-up key will be there too. At the lock-up, I park a short walk away, out of sight. I unlock the unit, go inside and wait there.'

'You close the shutter.'

'Sorry, yes. I close the shutter.'

'You hide behind the boxes.'

'Yes. I hide behind the boxes.'

'The light?'

'I keep the light on so it doesn't blind me when Dave gets there.'

Ian chews, swallows, drinks water from a tall glass. 'Then?'

'At around six thirty, Dave will arrive, thinking he's picking up some stuff for you. When he comes in, I shoot him before he knows what's happening. I make sure I... erm, make sure the job is finished before I send you the text: *All delivered.*'

'You make sure he's dead.'

'Sorry. Yes. I make sure he's dead. I text you. I go back to yours.'

'What do you do with the gun?'

'Sorry. I wipe it and leave it at the scene.'

'Where's your iPhone?'

'It's in my flat.'

Ian nods, forking a mouthful of the pie and delivering it into his mouth. 'All you have to do is lock the unit, wipe your prints and throw the burner in the bin.'

'Gotcha.'

'Say it.'

Will repeats it: lock unit, wipe prints, phone in bin.

'Now tell me again from the top.'

After three run-throughs, Ian appears satisfied.

'I can't help you,' he says. 'Not with this one. If there's the slightest chance I could've made it there and back, they'll have me. Dave tells me your missus is seeing her mate in the evening – Lena, is it? Her mother's babysitting the kids. I'll be in the area nine o'clock-ish, in case she leaves early. I've got her phone on my tracker so I'll know exactly where she is.'

'You've...?' Will stops himself. 'How does Dave...?' Again he stops himself. How does Dave know? He doesn't. Ian knows Jessica's arrangements because Jessica is his girlfriend. Jessica will have told him herself. She will not know he is tracking her phone.

He fakes a smile and taps his nose. 'Intel,' he says, like an absolute fucking idiot.

'The more you learn about everything, the more you learn that everything's fixed not in your favour. That, my friend, is the mighty Lemmy.'

'As in Motörhead?'

'The very one. Point being you have to *make* favour for yourself. You came to me and I did you a couple of solids. I don't need anything back, but it just so happens we find ourselves in the position to help each other out. And that's what we're doing. Strangers on a train, that's what we are. You don't know me; I don't know you. You've got no connection to Dave. I've got nothing to do with your Jessica. Once it's done, you'll move back in with your kids and you'll have a hefty insurance policy to keep you in bread and butter. We'll keep our distance, then maybe one day, in a year or two, you can buy me a pint of Solaris.'

He makes it all sound so reasonable, so easy, almost like a song. All Will can do is watch and listen at what feels like a distance, fascinated by how easily the lies fall from Ian's mouth. It is as if he himself believes them. Here they sit in this cosy domestic tableau, bare-faced lying to one other, plotting double murder with smiles on their faces, home-cooked food on their plates. As far as Ian is concerned, Will won't get anywhere near his kids, might never see them again. They will be in a new family with Ian and Jessica playing mum and dad while Will is either six foot under or rotting in police custody for the murder of David Silverman. Ian will have killed two birds with one stone. Or so he thinks.

Will supresses a smile.

'All you have to do,' Ian goes on, 'is leave the car where you found it, return the keys, then pick up your iPhone and make your way to the Express Tavern around nine, nine thirty. Your phone will tell the story that you were in the flat all the time then you went out for a quiet drink. Make sure you chat to the landlord. Do something memorable if you have to. Spill your pint, whatever. But be there so you can't have been anywhere near your missus, yeah? You won't hear from me obviously. Common sense.'

'Common sense.'

'Not hungry?' Ian gestures to Will's full plate.

'Sorry, no. It's really delicious though.'

'You've got lovely manners, I'll say that for you.' Ian gives a smile that does not reach his eyes. 'Too sensitive for your own good though,' he adds and swaps their plates around.

'Tuesday then?' Will says.

'Tuesday. I'll intercept her on her way back from this Lena's place.'

'How will you...?'

'Don't think about that. Just do your bit and it'll work out perfectly.' Ian gathers up a forkful, opens his mouth wide and delivers the lot onto his waiting tongue.

CHAPTER 33

JESSICA

On Tuesday evening, Jessica tells her mother she won't be late at Lena's, just an hour or two. She'll be back around ten, half ten.

'Are you all right?' her mother asks. Really, there is no hiding from her.

Jessica blinks back tears. 'I'm fine.'

Mum lays her newspaper to one side and folds her hands in her lap. She pats the sofa beside her, but Jessica knows if she sits there, she will not get up. She can't cancel Lena at the last minute; Lena said she's going to cook, and if Jessica is honest, she's more concerned about Lena than she is about herself right now. Her newly slim figure has passed into worryingly thin, which can mean one of three things: physical illness, mental illness or John. Although the last two could well be bound together. Whatever, Jessica is determined to get to the truth this evening.

'Where've you gone?' her mother asks.

'Sorry.' She laughs. 'Too many plates spinning. I can't stop worrying about... everything actually. Everything and everyone.'

'You need to worry about yourself.'

'Oh, I do that too.' Another laugh, though why she laughs in these moments it's hard to tell. 'I just can't keep it all going. I'm losing touch with my friends, I'm forgetting birthdays, I get ratty with the kids, I run out of food *all the time*, even with a supermarket delivery. My roots are showing. My toenails need cutting. I picked off all my nail extensions because I didn't have time to go back to the nail bar. Cassie needs new trainers. Charlie's Jurassic creature things died on Friday, and if I pull back at work, I'll lose my job and then we'll be homeless.' She sighs. 'It's... hard. I miss... I...' She stops herself. If she goes on, she will admit too much, will cry and not be able to stop, and then her mum will be worried, and then Jessica will worry she's made her mother worry.

These endless loops of love.

'Oh no, no, no,' her mum says with feeling. 'None of that. You're doing brilliant. Absolutely brilliant.'

Jessica smiles at her mother's gorgeous aversion to adverbs. Her hair is sticking up at the back from where she's been lying with Charlie reading *The Three Little Pigs*. There are dark shadows under her eyes from her shift yesterday and yet here she is, as she has always been. Earlier, while Jessica read to Cassie in the next room, all she could hear was her mother's voice: *I'll huff and I'll puff and I'll...*

Charlie almost shouting: *Blow your house down!*

Blow your house down. That's what blindsided her. The thought of her house as no more than tinder-sticks, the life she thought so solid now this fragile thing. She had to lie there pretending she wanted to hear Cassie read the rest of the chapter when in reality she couldn't have read aloud for fear of her daughter hearing the break in her voice. Another loop. As Cassie read haltingly from her mindless fairy adventure book, Jessica lay there brainstorming accommodation solutions: *sell up, buy a two-bed flat, sleep on the sofa; pool resources with Mum; move to a cheaper area.*

There is no way she can voice any of this to her mother. She will insist on dipping into her savings, on working extra shifts, and she has worked hard enough, all her life. At sixty-three, she looks ten years older. What a shame. What a mess it all is. A set of photographs has blown her house down and everything with it.

Jessica swallows hard.

'I think,' her mother says, shuffling forward to perch on the edge of the sofa, 'you need to think about what you *have* done, not what you haven't. When you walk to Lena's, I want you to list everything you've done since you gave buggerlugs the heave-ho. What's he done? Shacked up with his fancy woman in her big house. Oh, well done, I don't think.'

Jessica feels the watery smile on her lips. Mum doesn't even know about the money, about the drug dealer. It would kill her.

'Will you do that?' Mum insists.

Jessica nods. 'Make a list. Check.'

Her mum stands up and throws out her arms. 'Come here.'

They're not huggers, never have been. But since Will left, they hug every time they see one another, hello and goodbye. They hold on tightly, for long seconds. Right now, Mum smells of fish fingers and the Chanel No. 19 Jessica bought her for Christmas. Jessica pushes her nose to her mother's shoulder and inhales.

'A chat and a few giggles,' Mum says when they break apart, holding the flat of her hand against Jessica's cheek. 'That's what you need.'

In her mother's eyes, Jessica can see herself reflected: drawn, drained, tired. She cannot hide from her, no matter how brave a face she puts on. Her mum will worry, will pretend not to, all of this transparent in its turn to Jessica. 'Tell Lena I said hello,' she says now, pushing Jessica's hair behind her ears.

'Will do.'

. . .

Jessica walks the short distance over to Lena's flat. It's a cool, dry, windless night, the first Christmas decorations hanging in windows and porches, brown leaves wet and stuck to the path.

As she leaves the crescent, she remembers her promise to her mum.

Number one. Crucially, at base level, she has survived – not really a tangible thing, but an achievement nonetheless. She has not gone under.

She breathes deeply, fills her chest, squares her shoulders as she walks.

Number two: she has kept her job.

Three: she has kept her professional shit together.

These aren't really specifics, though, are they?

OK. OK.

Four: she has interviewed three nannies and has found one she really likes.

Five: she has learnt how to build a den with a blanket and a table.

Six: she has learnt how not to stress out when the sofa cushions are being used as a fantasy water park, how to make a meal from a seemingly empty store cupboard, how to get two kids in and out of the public swimming baths before she's had coffee without having a breakdown.

That takes her to about nine, she thinks.

One more: she has learnt how to ask for and accept help.

This last has been the hardest.

A figure is walking towards her. A young boy, she thinks, but when they pass under a street lamp, she sees it is Penny, without her headscarf. Her hair is short, like a pelt, and pale grey. In the short moment before she notices Jessica, Jessica sees that she is crying.

'Hey,' she says softly, so as not to startle her. 'Penny?'

Penny stops in her tracks. Her eyebrows rise. She pushes at

her face with her hands, is clearly discombobulated. 'Sorry. Just came out for a bit of a weep.'

'Oh no!' Instinctively Jessica pulls the other woman into a hug, holds her there until she feels her shift.

Penny straightens up, sniffs. 'Thanks. Sorry.'

'Don't be sorry. Are you... Can you talk about it?'

She closes her eyes momentarily and shakes her head. 'It's fine. Just... men. They're a different species.' She gives a shallow laugh but doesn't appear to want to say anything more.

'They're from Mars,' Jessica says. 'Or is it Venus? No, Mars. Definitely.'

Penny smiles, a lone tear leaking out of each eye. She gives another huge sniff.

'Listen,' Jessica says, placing a hand on Penny's arm, 'I'm going to a friend's for dinner right now, but do you fancy getting together sometime? I'm free on Wednesdays and every other weekend, or we could do something with the kids?'

Penny nods, still smiling, wet-eyed. 'I'd like that. Next Wednesday? A drink?'

Ian flashes through Jessica's mind. And in that moment, with the sudden clarity she remembers from her younger years, she knows that the thing with Ian, whatever it was, is over. She will tell him tomorrow.

'Wednesday's great,' she says. 'I'll ask around the office, see if anyone knows any dirty jokes. The Eel Pie on Church Road? Seven-ish?'

'Done.'

As Penny is swallowed by the darkness, Jessica turns away, adding one more achievement to her list.

Ten: she has made a new friend.

Smiling now, despite everything, she continues to Lena's.

CHAPTER 34

WILL

Will reaches the storage unit half an hour early. It is already dark, winter nights encroaching ever further onto the shortening days. The darkness is welcome. More fitting for killing someone.

Will. You're not killing anyone. No one is killing anyone. Keep it together, for Christ's sake.

Terrified of Ian reading his thoughts these last days, he has focused hard on not letting anything slip. He has a plan. Well, most of a plan, and all plans require improvisation. Much depends on how Dave reacts, whether he will be on board when the time comes. Will simply has to take it from there. He knows he's not cut out for any of this, but if he doesn't do it, who will?

Ian is in town until later, that much is certain. He will not risk being anywhere near the murder scene. Except, in Will's plan, there will be no murder scene.

The sky is all but black, the storage unit deserted. Not a midnight riverside after all, nothing so poetic. Not a dilapidated warehouse with a hole in the roof. No moonlit caw of crow either; only concrete rows of lock-ups and the hum of the A316.

The shutter rolls up with a rattle so loud it puts his teeth on edge. He finds the light switch next to the one for the shutter and presses both at the same time. The strip light flickers on, a strobe, making the shutter appear to jump downwards. Once established, the light is white, harsh. Looking about him, Will chafes cold and dust from his hands, chewing his cheek, tasting blood. He pulls down his woolly hat, digs his gloves out of his pockets, tightens his scarf. Christ, it's colder in here than outside, and the whole place smells of concrete, plastic wrapping, boxes, if those things even have a smell. There are so many boxes. At the far side, what appear to be coats hang from a rack under a clear cellophane sheath. In front of the rack stand six or seven larger boxes labelled with photographs of what look like gaming chairs, more plain brown boxes to the left. Three dozen shoeboxes with the Nike logo are stacked against the wall. A roll of brown tape lies on the floor, a tape gun.

Did Ian's cast-offs come from here? Some of them, at least.

Will checks his watch, shivering. Less than half an hour to go. He moves behind the stack of gaming chairs. He won't need cover for long, just long enough to tell Dave he's not going to shoot, that he's here to talk. Dave is due to pick up some goods, whatever that means, although judging by the stock in here, not drugs but merchandise, possibly stolen, who knows? Will doesn't believe anything Ian has told him any more.

The minutes pass slowly. For the fiftieth time at least, he pats the pocket of his Crombie. The Glock is there, solid, safe and sound.

I know the word for the type of coat I am wearing, he thinks. I know the name of the gun I am carrying.

Who the hell am I?

After what feels like hours, the sound of a car pulling to a stop comes from outside. The engine dies. Will's heart quickens. He has parked Ian's Nissan about half a mile away, though he suspects it is not registered to Ian, just as the flat on the marina is probably not in his name either. Discreet, Ian said. Untraceable. Whatever that means.

Tuneless whistling. The bleep of an expensive car locking system. A cough. Will takes off his gloves and pulls the gun from his pocket. His teeth chatter. Nausea rises. The urge to cry like a child. Should he pull back the chamber now, be ready to shoot? He needs to be ready to fire if there's even the smallest chance of Dave being sent here to kill him. But then it might go off by mistake. And then what? Disaster.

With its nerve-shredding rumble, the shutter rises.

'Hello?' Will calls from behind the boxes, his voice thin as a reed.

'Who's there?' He recognises Dave's perplexingly soft voice. Apparently he has not come here to kill him.

'It's Will Draper. Ian's friend from the Brentford flat.' Will steps from the shadows, realising too late that he has not pulled back the chamber in readiness. Somehow Dave has moved forward, is right there, right in front of him.

'What the fuck?' Dave's eyes widen; Will's close.

Something knocks against his hand. The gun flies out of it, cracks on the concrete floor. Another thump across his face. His glasses bang into his nose, fly off, skitter. The pain is unbelievable. He cries out, but now Dave has him by the neck and is pushing him backwards. A moment later, he feels the thud of the wall against his back. He blinks. The storage unit is a blur, Dave's face horribly clear.

'Wait,' he says. This is where I die, he thinks. I will die without telling Jessica how much I love her, how sorry I am. Without the chance to make it right.

'Talk,' Dave almost whispers, his breath warm and smelling of cigarettes.

'You can let me go,' Will says, half his voice lost to the chokehold. 'I don't fight. I can't. I'm a life coach.'

Dave loosens his grip but keeps his fingers around Will's throat. 'Talk to me.'

'Ian sent me to kill you,' Will says. 'The gun is his. He taught me how to use it and sent me here because you've got something on him. I wasn't going to kill you. I had no intention... I came to talk.'

Dave's eyes narrow.

'I'm telling the truth. Could you... can you see my glasses at all? I just... I can't see. I won't do anything. I wasn't going to shoot you. I told Ian I would, but I came to warn you. I don't want to kill anyone.'

Dave takes a step back, aims a deft kick. Will winces at the scratch his glasses make on the hard ground.

'They're by your feet,' Dave says. 'Pick them up. Slowly.'

Will crouches, one hand raised. With the other, he pats the floor, humiliation complete, until he finds the glasses. He picks them up, inspects them. One lens is cracked – the left one – but he puts them on. The storage unit returns to focus, a great split down the middle, a world fractured in two. Dave is holding the gun; that much is terrifyingly clear.

'You really should talk,' he says with that same unnerving gentleness.

'Ian sent me,' Will repeats, hands raised in surrender. 'He claimed he was going to kill my wife in exchange for me killing you. He said it was the perfect crime. He said no one would be able to trace the murders because I don't know you and he doesn't know Jessica. That's my wife. I didn't want to do it. I would never do something like this, but he's got me trapped. He's in London now, making sure he has an alibi.'

Dave says nothing. Under his left eye, a vein twitches.

'I'm not lying.' Will hears the panic in his voice. 'I never wanted him to kill Jessica. But he is so... somehow he's... I... I didn't know what the hell to do. So I pretended to agree. He thinks I'm here to kill you. But the thing is, I found out he's

having an affair with her. Jessica. My wife. So then I realised if I
could just talk to you... because he's not going to kill her, you
see. He wants her and my kids for himself. I'm guessing he was
going to have your murder pinned on me. I didn't mean to get
involved in any of this. Ian was kind to me and then I got kind of
trapped. I wish I'd never met him.'

Dave grunts. 'Yeah, well. Quite a few people wish they'd
never met him.'

'I know that now. I get it. But he said he'd done something
bad that you know about and that he needed you dead. I was
hoping that you could tell me what it was and where the
evidence is, and I'll tell the police for you. You see, I know he
isn't going to kill my wife because... because he's sleeping with
her. I thought you wouldn't mind helping me and we can both
benefit.' He can hear his words coming out faster and faster,
running into one another. 'All you'd need to do is give me what
you've got on him and I can do the rest. Then he'll be out of
both our lives, won't he? You want to stay alive, and I... I want
my life back. Please.' He makes himself stop, is aware of
himself pleading, of the wall of impassivity that is David
Silverman.

'No.' Dave frowns, shakes his head.

'No, you won't help me?'

Dave gives a half-laugh and finally lowers the gun. 'No, he's
not going to steal your wife.'

'He is. My daughter told me. Jessica doesn't know I know.
Ian doesn't either. He told me he'd had Jessica followed. He
made out he was helping me by gathering information to use
against Jessica so that I'd get custody of my kids. He tried to get
me to think she was already seeing someone before, before we...
separated.' Will knows he's gabbling but cannot stop himself.
'He said he'd had her followed but he followed her himself, do
you see? He told me my wife was seeing someone but it was him
the whole time. He wound me up against her and her against

me so he could have her for himself. Sorry. I'm a bit nervous. I'll stop talking now.' He exhales shakily.

A smile is spreading across Dave's face. Will is not sure why. Dave laughs, but this time it's a proper laugh. His hands go to his hips and he shakes his head over and over, still laughing, the gun held loosely at his hip. Will wonders if he's ever felt so frightened in his life. This guy will stop laughing any second now. Stop laughing and either shoot him through the head or strangle him just to shut him up, set him in wet cement, whatever it is these guys do. Even now, it is possible Dave and Ian are in cahoots, have played him for the fool he is.

But, 'You think Ian's getting it on with your wife?' is all David Silverman has to say.

'I *know* he is. My daughter told—'

'Ian did put me on your wife. Jessica.' Something in Dave's eyes, something about the way he says her name makes Will's skin creep.

'It was me who followed her,' Dave goes on. 'Very attractive. Very. Likes a nice restaurant, someone who knows how to take charge. Not used to it, is she? Someone booking a classy place, being able to afford it, someone who doesn't worry how much things cost.'

'What do you mean?' Will's scalp is burning. Somewhere within himself, he knows what Dave means.

'Ian Robbins hasn't been sleeping with your wife. He's never met her. I'm the one who's been... on intimate terms, shall we say.'

'*What?*' Will reels. 'But Cassie... Cassie said...'

Another grim, mirthless laugh. 'Not going to use my real name, am I? Call it my insurance policy. Good job too, especially as she found out you'd delivered my car. That would have gone down like a cup of cold sick, wouldn't it?'

Understanding is falling. 'Jessica...'

'We met at the supermarket. Bumped into her, as you do

when you're tailing a target, and it went from there. She's a bright woman. A lot about her. I think she likes me.' Dave smiles.

'Ian didn't betray me.'

'Oh, I wouldn't go that far. Ian Robbins is a very dangerous man. He's a psychopath.'

'But he said you were the psychopath. You have a hold over him, he said. Information he doesn't want the police to get hold of.'

'I do. I do indeed. Do you want me to tell you what it is?'

Will says nothing – he does and he violently does not – but Dave continues to speak, every word burrowing further and further under Will's skin.

'He told you his wife left, did he?' Dave begins. 'Jen and the kids? She did leave, manner of speaking. He had her followed – by yours truly, until he took over. He knew she was leaving him, knew exactly which day she was going to take off. That day, when she thought he was at work, he watched her through a hole he'd had made in the bedroom wall. Watched her put a few clothes in a bag, watched her get into a cab with the kids. He'd been biding his time. And then he caught up with her. He caught up with her and the kids and he... let's say he *persuaded* them to come home. Do you know what he did then? Your mate who thinks *I'm* the psychopath?'

Will shakes his head. He could not reply even if he wanted to. Can barely breathe.

'One by one,' Dave says with quiet relish, 'he took them down to his basement. Into the soundproofed room.'

'No.'

'All three of them.' Dave draws closer, speaking the words into his ear. 'One by one. Like they were target practice.' An unreadable smile passes over his lips. 'Couldn't have them for himself. Couldn't stand anyone else having them, could he? Ian's a solutions man. He always was possessive.' He cocks his head, fixes Will with his dark eyes. 'Who's the psychopath now?'

Will steadies himself against the wall. Coldness fills him. Saliva pools in his mouth.

'He called me,' Dave goes on. 'Afterwards. To be fair, he was in a state. Very upset. Crying, what have you. I went straight over and I... I helped him. You know Ian. He has this way of giving you no choice. Only I know where they're buried. Is that the kind of evidence you mean?'

'I... I can't...'

'Well, I'm going to give it to you. I accept your terms, shall we say. They're under the hydrangea. The big pink one in the back garden. He always loved that plant, was very particular about putting it back properly. Worried it might die for ages afterwards. Jen never went to her mother. They were estranged.'

Will makes himself look up at Dave, who seems to be studying him, waiting for a reaction. Another sly upturning of his mouth – not quite a smile.

Bile rises thickly. Will swallows it down. He is panting, his hand still pressed against the wall. The image of Jen and the kids blooms in his mind. The perfect family, smiling for a photograph, very possibly inches from where they were to be buried.

'Poor woman,' he whispers. 'Those poor children. My God.'

'Playing God, more like. Thought he was a nice guy, did you? Ian *is* a nice guy. Always helping others. Until he isn't. If you don't play along, he isn't nice any more. But he's not sleeping with your wife.'

'Because you are. Thank you, I get it. But if he's not with Jess...' Will tries to grasp his thoughts, but they fall away.

'If he's not sleeping with her,' Dave says, rolling his hand, his eyes dark beams, 'it means your plan still stands, doesn't it?'

'It means...' Will is searching, searching in the cold, cracked room. And then, 'Oh *God*. It means he *is* going to kill her.' He turns towards the exit, but Dave grabs his arm, tight. 'I need to call the police. I need to warn her. Now.'

'I wouldn't do that. If you call the police, what are they going to do? He's made no threats. He'll deny everything. Ian never touches anything – don't you get that? He's smoke. It's your fingerprints on the gun, not his. It's never his fingerprints. Not on anything. The cops will release him without charge. And then he'll be after you.'

'But I need to warn her.'

'Again, no. If you warn her, she'll change her plans and he'll know. He'll know you haven't killed me, that we've spoken, and he'll kill her and the kids and come after you before you or anyone else can stop him.'

Will can't get his breath. Can't think. 'Oh my God, oh my God. What am I going to do?'

'You're going to calm down for a start. Calm down and listen to me. I appreciate you not killing me, do you hear what I'm saying? I appreciate it. I'm going to help you because that's what works for me. I've given you the information, haven't I? So trust me. This is what you're going to do. You're going to pretend you've killed me, as per. If he calls me, I won't answer. I'll leave my mobile here – I'm guessing he told you to leave me here, did he?'

Will nods, too quickly, too many times.

'So, he'll ring me. He'll know my phone is here, but he'll still check. I won't answer. He'll think it's all gone to plan. First things first – you're supposed to text him about now, yes?' Dave nods to Will's pocket. 'So text him exactly what you said you would. Exactly.'

Will pulls out his burner phone. With trembling hands, he thumbs the agreed words: *All delivered.*

He presses send, looks up at Dave, who is still holding the gun. 'Now what?' His voice is strange, strangled.

'What were you supposed to be doing?'

'I'm supposed to drop the car and the keys back at his place. Then I have to pick up my phone from my flat and go to the pub where we first met. But that was when I didn't think he was going to kill my wife. I was expecting him to... I don't know what I thought was going to happen. I was just trying to stop anyone from getting murdered. For God's sake, this is not my world, it's not my world, it's not my world.'

'All right, all right. Calm down, will you? Keep your shit together. What time did you say he's meeting Jessica?'

'He said he was going to intercept her on her way home from Lena's. Her friend Lena's. He said he'd be in the area by nine but no sooner because he needed to create an alibi.'

'Lena. Yeah, I've followed her there a few times.'

'The timings were important.' Will swallows hard, blinks back tears. His chest rises and falls, rises and falls. 'Oh God.'

'So there's no rush, is there? I'm dead. He's up in town. It's barely seven o'clock. Listen to me while I tell you what to do. You take the gun. You wait it out. You get yourself outside this Lena's place for, say, nine-ish to be on the safe side, but for Christ's sake don't let him see you. Don't take your phone. He'll have put a tracer on it, sure as anything. Leave it at your flat or drop it at the pub if that's where you're supposed to be, and use that burner. You need to follow your wife and you need to wait for Ian to make his move.'

'What? What if he shoots her?'

Dave shakes his head. 'Ian never uses a gun. Not since. He'll be wearing gloves.'

Ice reaches up Will's spine. He does not ask Dave what he means.

'I need to call the police,' he says, but his voice has lost all resolve.

Dave shakes his head. 'This is one battle you're going to have to fight on your own. He won't have a gun. He'll think you're having a breakdown somewhere in a Brentford pub.

You'll be armed. And if you want your wife and kids alive, you're going to have to fight him, end of. You don't have to kill him; you just have to bring him down. Shoot him in the leg or something, but shoot him so he can't run. Then and only then do you call the police, all right? No police until the bastard's down. And leave me out of it. If it goes wrong, you never saw me. You never came to the unit, yes?'

'There has to be another way. I can't use my own wife as bait. I can't let Jessica walk into a trap.'

'I think it's a bit late for that, don't you?'

Through the fog of panic, understanding lands. The only way out of this is if Ian Robbins goes to prison for a very long time. And the only person who can put him there is Will.

'But what about the information? Can't I call them and tell them where the bodies are buried?'

'You can, but you'd be a fool to rely on that. Do you know why? Because I wouldn't put it past the bastard to have moved them. Keep me thinking I know where they are so that if I ever tip the police off in some plea bargain or whatever, I'll look like the pillock. Even if they're still there, it would take longer than you've got, mate. Your best chance is to let him try and do what he's going to do, stop him in the act and call the cops after. There's no other way. Like I said, the man is smoke.'

'Oh God.' Will feels his guts sink. He thought he'd dug as deep as he could, down, down into the darkest depths of possibility, but still, he realises, he was not able to dig this deep, this dark. Quite simply, it is beyond the reach of his imagining.

'If I were you,' Dave says, emptying the gun, 'I'd look in his study. There's a tall cabinet thing by the door, two drawers at the bottom. There's something in there you need to see. If it's still there. The key is in his desk, right-hand side, at the back. Trust me.' He passes Will the gun and drops the bullets into his other hand.

Will frowns. He is about to ask Dave why he's being cryptic

all of a sudden, but Dave has turned away. With an almost preternatural calm, he pulls his iPhone out of his pocket and places it on top of a cardboard box. He turns back, meets Will's gaze and smiles.

'What are you going to do?' Will asks.

'I'm going to wait for you to put the boss in prison.'

CHAPTER 35

JESSICA

Lena peeks around the door before opening it fully, her eyes huge in her thin face. From behind her, the smell of spices drifts out.

'It's you,' she says.

'Who else would it be?'

'No one. Come in.'

There is something awkward about this exchange, but Jessica affects normality, breeziness. She holds out a bottle of chilled Sauvignon Blanc, which feels in that moment like a peace offering. For the last week or two, she has felt something, something like a thorn, between them. She has been wondering if Lena is getting sick of picking up the kids, will tell her tonight that a nanny will be starting next week. There's a voucher for a spa weekend in her bag – a thank-you gift: the promise of luxury and long chats in fluffy white robes by the pool. Lena will love it.

She follows Lena up the tiny hallway. Tantalising aromas drift from the kitchen. Through the floor comes the dull bang of a bass line, a tinny vocal – music from the downstairs neighbours' flat. Lena is wearing a new baggy denim jumpsuit. Actually, no. It's an old one. But she used to fill it. Her cleavage was quite magnificent in it. Now it hangs off her like an overall.

'Wine?' Lena asks.

'Oh, I can whine for Great Britain.' The joke is a bad one and makes Jessica feel a bit sick.

Lena doesn't even smile to make her feel better, only opens the cupboard to reach a glass. On the worktop is a large ceramic bowl of salad. Beside it, Lena's glass, half full.

'This is so kind of you,' Jessica says. 'What's for dinner?'

'Veggie balti saag. I've done it in the oven.'

Lena isn't looking at her. Jessica tries to think if she's met her eye at any point this evening. No, she doesn't think so.

'Are you all right?' Jessica asks. 'You seem a bit... I don't know... out of sorts.'

Lena's shoulders rise. 'John's coming over later.'

'It'll be nice to meet him.'

Lena stiffens. She pushes a glass towards Jessica before lifting her own, draining it and pouring herself more. They haven't even said cheers.

'I don't have to stay,' Jessica adds when Lena doesn't reply. 'We can easily reschedule.'

Lena shakes her head. 'He's not coming till later.'

'What time do you need me gone?'

She wrinkles her nose. 'Ten-ish? Is that OK? I didn't think you'd stay late anyway.'

'Absolutely fine. I'm determined to be in bed before half past. You weren't worried about telling me to go, were you? It's only me.'

Lena takes another large gulp of her wine, her glass almost empty already. She blushes. 'He said he wanted to ask me something.'

In the silence that follows, the penny drops. 'Oh my God,' Jessica says, trying to sound excited. 'Do you think he's going to pop the question?'

'It might not be that.' Lena turns away, tops up her glass.

Jessica has the sense that the conversation is closed, which is weird because Lena opened it.

'I have news,' she offers. 'I'm trialling a new nanny next week. She seems lovely, so hopefully you won't need to hold the fort much longer.'

'Sure.' The way Lena says it, Jessica can tell she hasn't listened. She was expecting her to protest that she loves being with the kids, that she's their chosen auntie after all. But she doesn't.

'They're going to miss you,' she says. 'You'll have to promise to visit once a week at least.'

Lena presses her hands on the worktop, the knuckles white. Jessica was intending to give her the spa voucher, but the mood is really not right.

'Lene? Are you OK?'

'I'm fine.' She bends to open the oven door. The smell is so delicious, Jessica's mouth waters. 'You go through. I'll bring it in.'

'If you're sure?' Sensing that Lena truly wants to be alone but utterly confused, Jessica leaves her.

In the snug living room, the *thump, thump* from downstairs isn't quite so loud. Tea lights flicker on the mantelpiece, among the house plants on the little shelf unit, on the window ledge. On the coffee table are two place settings with white plates and flowery paper napkins folded into bishop's hats, a jug of iced water with lemon slices floating at the top, two tumblers, two little bowls, one of mango chutney, one of lime pickle, a plate of poppadoms. Lena has gone to so much trouble – the candle-light, the detail, it's almost romantic. Jessica sighs, moved. Maybe Lena's invited her over to get something off her chest. Whatever she's going through, hopefully she'll feel able to talk about it after a few glasses of wine.

'Here we are.' Lena appears at the doorway carrying a tray,

her face set in concentration. Onto the table she transfers the bowl of salad, one of rice and one of the curry with chopped coriander fresh and green on top.

'Wow,' Jessica says, clapping her hands. 'You're spoiling me. I should be spoiling you.'

'I wanted to.' Finally Lena meets Jessica's eyes, her own glossy. 'I love you – you know that, don't you?'

'Of course I do.' Jessica's ears feel hot. There is such intensity in Lena's eyes, she has to look away. 'I love you too, silly. This is so lovely, thank you.'

'It's nothing. Dig in.'

As they serve themselves, Jessica resolves to give the voucher to Lena after they've eaten. Hopefully by then the atmosphere, which has swung so violently from one kind of weird to another, will have returned to normal. But another silence has fallen and Jessica has no idea how to fill it. They concentrate on eating, perhaps both of them pretending that this is why they are not chatting away like they usually do.

'This is so good,' Jessica says, and, 'Wow, so tasty,' and, 'You can really taste the cumin,' and, 'Yum, so delicious.'

Lena says nothing. She hasn't eaten more than a couple of mouthfuls. She is sipping her wine as if she's on some sort of challenge to see how much she can imbibe in an hour. She tops Jessica's glass up, although there is really no need, and fills her own. The bottle is almost empty. She must have been drinking in the kitchen.

Jessica says nothing. Lena is presumably having doubts about John but doesn't quite know how to talk about it. She wonders if, after all the years of waiting for commitment from a guy, now that she finally has it, she no longer wants it. It is often the way. She hopes it's just the usual misgivings everyone has and not something more sinister. There is Lena's weight loss, the fact that she's not eating now, only helping herself to some salad leaves. Since when did anyone serve salad with a curry?

In an attempt to fill the silence, which has begun to press in, Jessica tells Lena a little about her date with Ian the other evening, how it started badly but ended up fine. She does not add that she has decided not to see him again. Ian, she has always known deep down, is a reaction to Will. He is everything her husband is not, and for a few dates, that has felt good. When Lena gives little by way of response, Jessica tells her about her day, that her mum says hello, anything she can think of. She doesn't ask after Lena's mum, as they don't really speak. Sometimes friendship is knowing when to ask, when to back off. This is definitely a moment to back off. Lena will confide about John if she needs to and when she is ready. As soon as Jessica stops speaking, however, the muffled bass of downstairs' stereo beats time to yet another pregnant pause.

Lena disappears to the kitchen and returns with another bottle. Jessica isn't counting, not at all, but her own glass is still almost full; she has mostly been drinking water. Lena must have drunk most of the bottle, plus whatever she'd had before. Jessica tries to think of something funny, a story from work or some classic quote from Cassie or Charlie, but cannot.

They finish their meal accompanied by downstairs' music selection, the constant slamming of doors, the apparent need to shout conversations through those doors. Jessica attempts more small talk, tells Lena a story so boring she almost can't finish it, but as the clock ticks towards nine, she begins to think about making her excuses and heading home. She cannot leave before half nine. Lena has gone to so much trouble. Jessica needs to sit with her in whatever it is she's wrestling with, even if she can't talk about it. After all Lena has done for her, it would be rude to simply eat and leave. And more: it would be to acknowledge that something is very wrong.

After another half hour of strained conversation, Lena shakes the bottle at Jessica. Her eyelids look heavy, her eyes red at the corners.

'I'm going to stick with water,' Jessica says. 'Day from hell tomorrow.'

'Suit yourself.' It's a little sharp. Lena has been letting the odd caustic comment slip out lately. She pours herself yet another glass.

Jessica takes a sip. 'Is everything really OK? With you and John?'

'What do you mean?'

'I don't know.' She falters. 'You're very quiet. You don't seem yourself. It's none of my business, but I'm your best friend and I'm a bit worried about you. Is it him? You've been seeing him for a while now and you won't let me meet him.' Or he won't let me meet him, she thinks but doesn't permit herself to say.

'We're taking it slow, that's all.' Lena's words are slurred. 'That's what you told me to do, isn't it? We can't all go straight from one committed relationship to another.'

'*What?*'

'Nothing.'

'It doesn't sound like nothing.' Jessica sets her glass down and turns to face her friend. 'Have I done something to upset you?'

Lena either won't or can't look at her. She shrugs. More than anything, she looks desperately, unbearably unhappy. Her jawline flexes.

'Just,' she begins, 'I mean, you've hardly waited five minutes.'

'Right.' Jessica hears her own shocked in breath. 'Ian's not serious. In fact, I'm going to end it. I was going to tell you, but you seem to have a lot on your mind already. He was just a... a rebound thing. After Will, I was in hell, you know I was, and maybe Ian wasn't the wisest decision, but...' She stops. Why is she justifying herself?

'He was just a *rebound thing*.' Lena's imitation of her is

filled with sarcasm and feels wantonly mean. 'But like every other man on the planet, he's obviously mad for you. You get the love-bombing *and* the commitment, whereas I...'

'Is John not returning your calls or something?'

'Oh, John never *stops* calling me, don't you worry.' Lena laughs, pushes her plate away and runs her hands through her hair.

'Lena? Is there a problem with John? Is he being overbearing? Controlling?'

She shakes her head. 'John loves me. He wants to marry me. We're going to have a family. It's just you... you always get to have everything, that's all. You always have. It all just falls in your lap. Will, the kids, even your mum. She's the mum everyone would want.'

'I know things were tricky for you,' Jessica says, carefully skirting around Lena's nightmare narcissist of a mother. 'But Mum loves you, you know that. She loves you like a daughter. Will loves you. The kids love you.' Her eyes fill. 'I love you.'

The glance Lena gives her is full of something – hurt, rage? 'Pat's not mine, though, is she? You're not mine. Will isn't mine. None of it is. And your kids... God knows, if they were mine, I wouldn't leave them to someone else to look after. I'd be right there, not missing a second, not one second.' Two tears track down Lena's face, her mouth an ugly grimace.

Certainty hits Jessica square in the chest: she is being judged by the one person who always claimed she would never do that to her. Her best friend. She has been judged by her best friend for a long time, possibly for their entire friendship. Her throat closes, the sudden ache of tears. She shuts her eyes, feels like she's falling from a tower.

'You don't know what you'd do,' she says quietly, opening her eyes, fixing Lena, who is blotchy and wretched in the candlelight. 'You have no idea.'

'No, I don't. Because I don't get to have any of it. Because I can't even pick a man correctly. I don't want John, not really. I just want a fucking family. So I'll marry John, because you took the man who should have been my husband.'

'*What?* What are you saying?'

'Nothing. I wasn't meant to...' Lena tails off, shrugs, her face a mask of utter misery.

'You barely even like Will,' Jessica insists. 'You do nothing but slag him off. What the hell are you...' But something is dawning. Lena's constant readiness to do Will down, her eagerness to point out his failings, her venomous outrage at his betrayal. *The sooner you cut that man out of your life, the better.*

'That's what you tell yourself,' Lena blurts, crying now. 'But you *knew* I was in love with him. Back then. You couldn't help yourself, could you? You just... you just took him. Why? Because you could.'

'*What?* This was years ago! What the *hell?* You and Will were together for about a week and you'd already split up when... For God's sake, where is all this coming from? Why now?'

Lena laughs. It is a horrible, bitter sound. 'You're so blind. So self-obsessed. It took you weeks to figure out I was even seeing someone. You'd have known straight away if you'd bothered to make an effort. And when you finally, finally asked and I finally got a word in, you came straight back with Supermarket Guy. Couldn't even let me have two minutes in the sun, could you? And then Supermarket Guy turned out not to be a onenight stand but another fucking boyfriend, Ian fucking Robbins, another man totally besotted with you, yawn. You always had someone dancing to your tune, always, since forever. Do you even know who you are without a man? You just couldn't let me have my own bit of news, could you? Couldn't let me have my moment.'

Jessica's head is spinning; her heart feels like a boulder. 'I can't believe what you're saying. It's like... it's like you hate—'

'You never appreciated Will.' Lena's voice quivers with tears. 'You just took him and you never appreciated... Not like I would have.'

They are both crying. Jessica cannot speak, cannot remember ever having had a cross word with this woman who she has loved for most of her life. Longer than Will. How can Lena be in love with Will? How is this even possible? Lena loves Jessica, loves her kids, her mum, loves Will, yes, but not like that. Will isn't her type. Lena likes bad boys, charmers. This is what Jessica has believed for so many years she'd have to stop to count.

'You hate me,' she says now, through sobs. 'You actually hate me.'

'I don't.'

'I think you do. I think you've hated me for a long time. Why didn't you tell me you loved Will? Why?'

Lena throws out her hands. Her face is crimson, her eye make-up smudged. 'What would've been the point? He was so obviously in love with you. And I loved you too. I still do. It's all just... My head is... I don't know what I think any more. I wanted to do something nice tonight, but it's all too late. I can't... Being near you, that's the best I could have. Second best. As usual. Waiting for a place at the table. Before you got those photos, I hadn't seen you for weeks! The moment you needed me, suddenly you had all the time in the world for me. You treated Will the same, like an unpaid servant. No wonder he had an affair. Probably desperate for someone to take some notice of him for once.'

'Wow.' Jessica wipes her cheeks with the backs of her hands and stands to go. She picks up her phone. 'I'll get out of your hair, since I'm so obviously to blame for all of it, not John, obviously not John, who clearly prefers his women psychotic with starvation.'

She regrets the words the moment they leave her mouth,

but it is too late. Boiling, she strides out of the living room. Another two seconds and she's opening the door to the flat. She stops on the threshold, desperate for Lena to call her name, tell her to come back. From the living room, she can hear her crying, almost howling with what sounds like pain. The urge to go back and throw her arms around her is as old as their friendship; it is within her like her heart is, her kidneys, her lungs. She takes a step back towards her broken friend, a sob breaking from her.

But no. What is left of her heart is cracked down the middle. She turns back towards the dark night. There is nothing for her here. There is no one for her here any more.

CHAPTER 36

WILL

Ian's house is in darkness. Will digs out his keys and finds the one for the front door, the one Ian gave him weeks ago with his casual trademark generosity – *Just let yourself in. Let me know if you need anything* – when Will believed him to be a magnanimous and miraculous benefactor wanting to help a chap down on his luck. Another one of his mother's told-you-sos comes to mind: *If something seems too good to be true, it usually is.*

Pithy. It could have come from Ian's quote bank.

He opens the door and steps inside. Listens. There is no way Ian will be here. But still. He wants, desperately, to call Jessica. But his iPhone is at the bottom of the paper towel bin in the gents at the Express Tavern, where he has put it so that it won't betray his whereabouts to a man who is on his way to kill her in cold blood, a man who shot dead his entire family to stop them from ever belonging to anyone else. My God. He should have sent her another text, one last try, something more explicit, something that would alert her, something stronger than a rather milky *Call me when you get this.* But if, if by any chance Ian had seen the message, Will might have triggered the murder he is trying so desperately to head off at the pass. It was stupid of him to try and call her. What the hell would he have said if she had already been with Ian? Dave said not to contact Jessica or the police and Dave is, after all, part of this world. He knows how it works.

Pocketing the keys, Will continues down the vast hallway towards the stairs. Passing the credenza, he sees the white jug, empty. That first time he came, it was full of pink flowers. *I like to have hydrangeas in the house when they're in bloom*, Ian had said. *They remind me of Jen and the kids.* He had cut flowers from the bush under which he had buried his family. He had arranged a welcoming posy, a posy of death, for the family he had murdered. Something else too. Another thing Ian said once, though Will can't remember exactly when or where.

The first time after they've left is a real killer.

'Christ,' he whispers to himself.

It is as if it has all been a joke, a game. Perhaps it has been.

Tears prick. His chest tightens. For a moment, he considers going into the sitting room to pay his respects to Ian's family, to touch his fingers to their photograph and give them some sort of blessing. He is not a religious man, but still.

Instead, aware of time ticking, he climbs the familiar staircase with its thick carpet, brass stair rods and oak banister. It is all so unbelievable, so surreal. In all the dark thoughts Will has had since Jessica kicked him out, there has never been a day, a minute, a second in which he has wished her dead. Realising her life is in danger has given him the clarity he was sorely lacking. It is like the sun coming out after the clouds of rage and resentment, the dead ends and the stubborn position-taking of people in terrible pain. They have done one another so much damage, the kind of damage that can only come from love. Quite simply, he loves her. He wants her and the kids back with a depth of feeling that is physical, a rock in his chest. If he can't have them, he thinks he might die. What is certain is that he will never forgive himself if he doesn't fight with everything he has to save them.

As for Margot, he hopes he can convince Jessica that yes, she was a client, and yes, she was in need, and yes, he was drawn into that need like air into a vacuum. Margot saw him, appreciated him, at a moment when he was feeling invisible, a little taken for granted. But by keeping how he was feeling from Jessica, he never gave them a chance to talk about it. And by not telling her about that, or about Margot, he effectively withheld his love; he sees that now. He did not tell Jessica because he did not trust her to understand that he was losing himself, that he was in trouble. He didn't trust her with it. If he had, she would have understood. He would not have got himself mired so deeply in that trouble.

William, you are the only person who can help me. Can you help me?

I can. Just tell me what I need to do.

The kiss at the airport had been their only one. A kiss of farewell, of relief perhaps, after he delivered her to safety. He didn't see it as a betrayal of Jessica. It was something private, something meaningful, something that belonged only to him and Margot and the danger they had put themselves in, the risk they were taking, their shared sense of victory that she and her children had escaped.

The couple kissing in the hotel window was not him and Margot. He has no idea who they were, but he can see how Jessica, faced with twenty-six other incriminating photos, would make that inference. He is pretty sure now that Margot's ex must have sent these photos, that this was his revenge. He too must have thought they were having an affair. But that was not why they went to hotels.

I cannot come to your office, William. I cannot go to the same place twice.

She would text him the hotel, and he would meet her there.

A different hotel each time. She would book a room, a different name each time. Sometimes they walked, using London's crowded streets for cover.

I cannot use my own name, William. You must never give yours.

She paid in cash. They would sit on the bed and talk. After their clumsy beginning, she told him her story in snippets; she could never stay more than half an hour, sometimes only twenty minutes. They never communicated other than by text. Together, by degrees, they made a plan. Will helped her organise taking the kids out of school, said he'd drive her to the airport himself. And yes, he fell for her, he did, even loved her, but not in that way. Even if he had, he would not have acted on it. He would never have acted on it.

But how can you explain something you don't even understand yourself? How can you explain something you should have explained long before when you've let it run away with you and now the evidence points in a different direction entirely, and your wife is crying and you are panicking and your life is falling to pieces in front of you and your kids are in the next room? How can you back-pedal when, in panic, you use the same phrase her father used to gaslight her when she was a child, traumatising her?

You can't. He couldn't. That is his failure. He can see now that when he met Margot, he'd got to a place where he believed Jessica didn't really need him. But from her reaction to those photographs and from everything else that has followed, he understands that this was never the case. Jessica is hurting just as deeply as he is. She did need him, just as he needed her. She loved him, just as he loved her. Loves him, as he loves her. What they have put each other through is proof. Those photographs gave her what she thought was incontrovertible evidence of his infidelity. His cowardice in the moment drove her into a locked box from which, too hurt, too devastated, she refused to come out. Hurt by her intransigence in his turn, Will climbed into a box of his own and pulled the lid closed. With a slow turn of a key, Ian Robbins locked those boxes shut.

Will has reached the top of the staircase, the wide landing with the large casement window at the end. Ignoring the kids' bedrooms and the bathroom, Will opens other doors – a double bedroom as perfect as a hotel, another just as pristine – until he finds a dark green room with wooden panelling, a desk facing the door. He flicks the switch. Three amber tulips on brass stems reach from an ornate ceiling. The desk is mahogany, a green leather top with gold trim. It is typical of Ian's taste: old-world, refined, antique, a taste Will sees differently now. Ian Robbins is a dock posing as a marina, a boozer posing as a gentleman's watering hole, a villain posing as a benefactor.

He closes the door behind him and immediately sees the cabinet to the left of it. Mahogany like the desk, it is as tall as a wardrobe, with glass doors, like a dresser or an armoire, and two wide drawers at the bottom, brass pull handles. He tries one but it is locked, as Dave said it would be. Will steals over to the desk. He can't remember what Dave said, which drawer, so he pulls them all open at random, rifling through each. Anxiety rises. But it is not yet nine o'clock and he has to find out what's in that cabinet.

At the back of the top right-hand drawer, his fingertips brush against two small keys stuck down with tape.

Look in his study. Trust me. He remembers the look of sly joy on Dave's face. What more secrets could there possibly be?

He unpeels the tape and retrieves the brass keys. He crosses over to the cabinet, crouches down to open the top drawer. Inside is what looks like a white tablecloth filigreed with silver, linen napkins of the same design. He digs beneath but finds nothing. It is possible Dave was playing with him of course, that he has sent him here on a fool's errand. Was he throwing him a ball, distracting him while he races off to find Ian? Are the two of them somehow in cahoots even now, one step ahead of Will, knowing that the scene in the lock-up would play out exactly as it did? Didn't he, Will, leave the unit first? He has no proof that Dave did leave his phone there, none whatsoever, only the word of a criminal, a person Ian Robbins claimed is a psychopath. Will trusted Dave because Dave told him the truth about Ian. Dave said that Ian was the psychopath.

But just because Ian Robbins is a psychopath, it does not follow that Dave is not.

He has to get to Jessica. He will drive there now, after he's looked in the second drawer – it won't take a second, and there is still the possibility that Dave was telling the truth.

He opens the second drawer. Inside are three photo albums, two dark brown and leather-bound, one white.

Trembling now, half weeping, he takes out the white album marked *Our Wedding* in silver cursive. He opens it, turns to the first page – and drops it. He falls to his knees, his fists hitting the floor. He is gulping air, unable to get it to his lungs.

'No,' he whimpers. 'No, no, no.'

After a long moment, he sits back and steels himself. He picks up the album once again. Pulls it onto his lap. Opens it with shaking hands.

On the first page is the photograph he has already seen: newly-weds, younger, much younger, smiling, holding hands.

Ian Robbins and Margot. Not the woman in the family photos downstairs, but Margot. Margot le Fevre was Ian's wife. The controlling husband, the man who terrified her, the monster from whom Will helped her escape was Ian Robbins.

Except she didn't escape. She and her kids never...

Struggling to breathe, tears breaking, he touches his finger-tips to her face. She is plumper here, quite beautiful without the fear that had lined her face and brow, sucked her cheeks back from their bones, blackened her eyes. But it is her, unmistakably.

Heart battering, Will turns the page. There is Dave, his hair longer, darker, thicker, his arm around a glamorous blonde. It is the woman in the photograph in Ian's sitting room, the woman Will presumed was Ian's wife. Not Ian's wife but Dave's; the kids presumably Dave's, not Ian's. He looks closer. There is a similarity between the blonde woman and Dave, the kids too. The woman's eyes and eyebrows are dark, like Dave's. Her hair is most probably dyed. Ian referred to a niece, the only person ever mentioned in association with Dave. Could this woman be Dave's sister, the kids his niece and nephew? They would be like family to Ian, wouldn't they?

With shaking hands, Will turns another page: Margot and Ian cutting a three-tier wedding cake, laughing, hands overlapping on the handle of the knife. Another: Margot and Ian dancing in an elegant ballroom; Margot and Ian staring lovingly into one another's eyes, champagne glasses raised.

Will is going to be sick. He bends forward, hand flat to his chest. He is heaving. He coughs, spits onto the floor. Still panting and in a daze, he picks up another album. A family album. Two kids, toddlers here, then maybe four or five, but he sees in their eyes that they are the children he dropped at the airport with Margot. They were young teenagers then, scared out of their wits, on the run. Margot never told him their names. For their safety, she said. There could be no names. He never pressured her to tell him anything she didn't want to.

So she never told him the name of her husband.

Still on the floor, he turns the pages, horror filling him, tears spotting the photographs: Margot as a young mum with the kids on a beach; Margot a little older, elegant in a gown at some formal function, still slim but not thin; school portraits of the kids, holiday snaps. Margot here in this house, sitting at the kitchen bar, smoking a cigarette and laughing; Margot in the sitting room, thinner here, something strained in her smile. Images of a woman in a life she was desperate to escape.

He almost got her there. Got her as far as the airport. He always believed she made it. The worst he has imagined is that perhaps she took him for a fool, stole his money and moved on to the next victim. But he remembers the terrified kids in the back, himself opening the passenger-side door. He thinks it was after their embrace that she reached to the footwell for her bag. In her panic, she pulled too hard; the bag upended, the passports spilt against the kerb. He told her to get the kids, that he would pick up the mess. He gathered up their passports, glimpsed her photograph, her name: Genevieve Margot le Fevre.

Ian Robbins had called her Jen. Not Jennifer, but Genevieve.

Nausea rises. Blood thrums in his ears.

She is dead. She and the kids are dead, shot in cold blood and lying in a nameless grave, possibly in the garden of this house. Will did not save her. He never saved her or anyone. He kissed her goodbye and told her to go, only for Ian Robbins to swoop in, force her and her petrified children into his car and drive them to their deaths.

'I'm so sorry,' he whispers, crying hard, mind racing. 'I'm so, so sorry.'

He stands up, loses his balance momentarily, steadies himself against the wall. Pushes his tears away, makes himself breathe.

Ian Robbins did not meet him by chance. That is what this means. Ian Robbins has had him in his sights since long before they met; he has watched him, followed him, photographed him. He knew where he worked, where he lived, knew his wife, his kids, but they did not know him. Ian Robbins sent the photographs. Of course he did.

All this, all of it, was some great master plan. Who would do that? Who the hell would do that?

A man who would sooner kill his family than let anyone else have them.

Ian Robbins was not content with stopping his family from escaping in the most brutal way; he needed more: to punish the man he saw as responsible, to take his family as this man had taken his.

Jessica. He has to get to her.

CHAPTER 37

JESSICA

Jessica reaches the end of Lena's shared front garden and bursts into tears. She is sobbing so hard she has to cling to the white fence.

What just happened? What the hell just happened?

The ache in her stomach is old, familiar. She is flooded with a memory of herself as a child, drinking a chocolate milkshake in an outdoor café in Sefton Park, waiting for her father to come back, knowing she shouldn't be there on her own, that she is too little. Her father has told to wait here and not move a muscle, but the milkshake is finished and when she sucks, she can hear the slurping sound at the bottom of the tall glass. Her stomach aches. She has nothing to do: no book, not even the scarf her mother is teaching her to knit. Her father said he'd be back soon. In a jiffy, he said. Wait there. She watched him walk away, a funny kind of half-run, as if he was desperate for the loo. He disappeared into the trees on the other side of the grass. She searches the people, the couples, the teenagers, scanning for his face. But he is not there.

Her fingers lock around Lena's fence. She cannot remember her father coming back, though he must have. It is the before she recognises, this exact feeling: abandonment. Rising panic. Loss. Her father abandoned her. Her husband abandoned her. Moments ago, her best friend abandoned her. She is alone. Utterly.

She turns back towards the flat. Wonders again about going back up. Lena is in the grip of something. She was not herself. She won't have meant it. She can't have. It wasn't her. Part of Jessica wants to pull Lena's hair out; another part wants to hold her friend's face in her hands, look into her eyes and say: *Hey. I'm Jessica and you're Lena. Remember? Without you, I would not be me. For God's sake, where has all this come from?*

The thought causes another violent wave of tears. She can feel the wood splintering in the palms of her hands, a griping pain in her chest. A heart attack, she thinks. All this pain. It will kill her. It will be with her for the rest of her life, a part of her, hard and black and wrinkled inside her like a pellet of slow-release poison.

There is only her mother left now. Just like before. The two of them against the world, trusting no one, no one ever again. Her mum and the kids. That's her family now.

But no. She will not think like that. She will not. She has friends. Women are brilliant. They are allies, soulmates, therapy. Lena was one of them. Lena was her blueprint, the most friendship could mean, a place where you're safe to shine and succeed or fall flat on your arse, knowing that both are OK. From the start, they agreed on rules Jessica had learnt from her mother: have each other's backs, don't trash-talk, don't let anyone else trash-talk. If in doubt, always think the best.

But Lena does not have Jessica's back. It seems she never did.

Does Lena even love her? Did she ever?

She cannot let go of the fence. She is stuck here, too stricken to move. Against her thigh, her bag vibrates. She rallies, pulls out her phone. There is a text from her mum: *I'm feeling a bit tired so can you come home now please? Love, Mum x*

Jessica wipes her face with the heel of her hand. That's a strange message. Her mother has never asked her to come home before. She never signs off on text. She never puts a kiss.

Jessica calls her. There is no reply. Perhaps she sent the message earlier and it's only just come through. She might be asleep. Jessica takes one last look at Lena's place. At the upstairs window, the curtain moves. Inside, the candlelight still flickers. Was Lena watching her?

She texts her mum back: *Everything OK?*

There are three missed calls from Will: *Call me when you get this.* Irritation fires in her but she calls him just in case. No answer. Whatever it was has presumably been sorted. He was probably just being his usual overdramatic self. If it's urgent, she's sure he'll call again.

But after the evening with Lena and the weird text from her mother, worry niggles at her. She texts him: *Call me back.*

She tries her mother again, but again, no reply. Nerves flutter through her. The universe feels like it's tilted, like nothing is where it was, where it should be. She opens Lena's gate and walks out. Her pace quickens, a fist of anxiety forming now in her belly. She calls her mother again, then Will. No reply from either.

It's nothing. Just weird phrasing. Texts are weird. They are a terrible way to communicate. But still, strange. If Will was so keen to talk to her, where is he now? Why didn't he keep trying?

A black Prius drifts by, but apart from that, there is no one on the street. Jessica walks on, calls her mother over and over. She stops for a second, tries the home phone, but there is only the answering machine. She tells herself to relax. Mum is probably on the loo, making herself a cup of tea, figuring out some cryptic clue from the crossword. She isn't glued to her phone like a young person. She'll be watching *Newsnight*.

Pocketing her phone, she continues walking. By the time she turns into Oxford Road, her breathing is shallow. Her crescent is less than a five-minute walk away now, four if she speeds up. The need to run comes to her, some feeling of urgency she can't quite name. She jogs a few paces, walks, jogs. She's being irrational. Lena has left her in pieces.

Halfway up Oxford Road, there is a dark bit of pavement where trees overhang the little archway that leads to the mini supermarket car park. This short stretch always freaks her out. Holding her bag close, she half runs. There is no one about. Once clear of the dark bit, she slows to a fast walk. Suburbs at this time on a weeknight really are completely deserted. Anything could happen and no one would know. She'd be safer in town, where the streets will still be full of people.

From somewhere behind her, she hears a cough, a man's cough. She freezes. Listens. When she turns, there is no one. Her nerves are shot. Everything is so unstable. These last weeks have left her all but shredded to ribbons.

'Hello?' she calls out. 'Hello?'

She speed-walks past the flats. The sound must have come from inside one of them, or from a car maybe. She is spooked, that's all. Lena, that text from Mum, the whole thing with Will, the sense of this shaky version of herself that she recognises all too well: alone, uneasy, waiting for a father who is never coming back.

A black Prius passes her. Is that the same one? It could be, though they all look the same. She is almost at the mouth of the crescent. No more than a minute away now. About twenty yards in front of her, the Prius pulls in. An Uber, she thinks, dropping a fare. A moment later, a man gets out – not out of the back, out of the front, the driver's side. He grins at her. Does he think she's his fare? She smiles back, to be polite. He takes a few steps towards her. From somewhere comes the revving of a car engine.

'Jessica?' he asks, smiling.

Her stomach folds with the fear of all women out at night alone. 'I'm sorry, do I know you?'

'I'm Ian Robbins.'

She has no idea who he is.

CHAPTER 38

WILL

Will reaches Lena's flat a little after nine. He has come here in the Nissan – it was the quickest way. He has to hope it doesn't have a tracking device on it. It is freezing out, prematurely wintery, the windscreen beginning to frost. Lena's flat is the upper half of a converted eighties semi. On her street, there are fewer trees to hide behind. The cars are bumper to bumper.

He parks at what he hopes is a safe distance behind a white van. The feeling that Ian Robbins is watching him, that he is everywhere, crawls over his skin. From here, he can just about see the window of what he knows is Lena's living room. At the gap in the curtains, pinkish light wavers. He can't see her front door, which is on the far side of the building. The front lawn is long, bumpy, overgrown. The shabby white picket fence looks like it's about to fall down.

He blows into his hands. This is ridiculous. He can't sit here and wait for Ian Robbins to attack his wife. Surely he could call the police now that the crime is imminent? Surely they could send someone by way of prevention, someone who could catch Ian in the act? As Dave said, Will can tell them the whole story

– well, perhaps not the whole story – afterwards. If he has to go to prison, it will be worth it if Jessica and the kids are safe.

But Dave was right. The police won't do anything. Ian Robbins hasn't committed any crime – at least not one they know about. Will has no proof he killed his family. And the police can't arrest him for walking down a street at nine o'clock in the evening.

Oh, but if Will doesn't call the police, Ian could kill his entire family and walk away, cover it all up the same way he covered up murdering his own. He has the means. He has the network. Favours he can call in. The man is invincible.

Will bangs his head against the steering wheel. This is a nightmare, a living nightmare. What to do what to do what to do?

A movement catches his eye. Jessica is emerging from the far side of Lena's place. She is crying hard, her hand over her mouth, her eyes almost closed, walking fast. This is all because of him. She is still so cut up about everything, as cut up as he is. She will have been crying on Lena's shoulder, making herself upset. Will feels his eyes fill.

'Jess,' he whispers, her name a frozen cloud in the cold interior of the car.

She reaches the fence, grips on as if for support. It is almost unbearable. There's no way she would be crying like that if she was happy. She is not happy then, with David Silverman, for all his good looks and soft-spoken charm. She still thinks his name is Ian Robbins, and all the while the real Ian Robbins is on his way to kill her.

It's too much. He can't do this. He pulls out the burner phone and dials 999.

'Hello, emergency service operator,' a female voice says. 'Which service do you require: fire, police, or—'

'Police.' Will's teeth chatter.

'Connecting you now. Please hold.'

Will thinks about ringing off, tries to think what he can say that doesn't make him sound like he's lost his mind.

'Hello,' another voice says, male this time. 'Where're you calling from please?'

Will gives Lena's flat number, street. The first three digits of the postcode is all he knows.

'And what's the nature of your emergency?'

'Someone's going to kill my wife.'

He hears the intake of breath. Not shock, but surprise. The pause that follows reeks of doubt. 'Is this person with you now?'

'Well, no. No, but he's on his way.'

'And is your wife with you?'

'No, but I can see her. She doesn't know I'm here. I'm... I'm in a car. The address I gave you is her friend's. He's going to kill her on her way home.'

'Do you have his name?'

'Ian Robbins. I can't prove anything. I just know he's going to do it. You're going to have to trust me. I'm not a time-waster, honestly. And I'm not mad. Please, can you come? I can't stop him by myself.'

'If you can just answer my questions, that'll be the most helpful thing. Can you tell me if you've got this person in your sights?'

'Her, yes, but him, no. But he's coming. I know he's coming. You have to trust me.'

'Can I have your name?'

'William. William Draper.'

'And are you injured, William?'

'I'm fine. Please, can you send someone? It could be any—'

'William? William? Are you safe where you are?'

'What? Yes. I'm in my... I'm in a car. I told you. I'm hiding. But I'm going to have to get out. She's in grave danger.'

'William, I want you to stay where you are, OK? Stay there. I'll send someone as soon as I can.'

Will closes the call, half crying now with stress. He chafes his hands, turns on the engine, puts the fan on hot. He pulls the gun from the glove compartment, checks it is loaded. He is desperate to shoot one bullet, just to check he's put them back in the right way round, but the noise would wake the whole neighbourhood. It's so quiet he can hear the achingly familiar high, stifled noise of his wife sobbing, the sound she makes when she is trying to hide the fact she is crying.

She turns towards Lena's flat and looks up at the window. He follows her gaze, thinks he sees movement behind the curtain. She's calling someone. Is she calling him? Has she seen his message? But his iPhone is in the pub; he doubts he'll ever see it again. Shit. Phone at her ear, she opens the gate and walks towards home.

Will turns off the engine. Slowly, silently, he opens the car door, puts the gun in his coat pocket and pulls his woolly hat down low. He follows, at a distance. The urge to run over and fold her into his arms is almost overwhelming. If the police don't get here in the next few seconds, he will have given them the wrong address. No matter, he will save his wife himself. He will put a bullet through Ian's leg, immobilise him, or wrestle him to the ground and hold him at gunpoint and call the police again. He will put a bullet through Ian's head if he has to. Hell hath no fury like a man who wants his wife back, and fury will make him a match for that evil bastard.

A black Prius drifts silently past Jessica. Instinctively, Will ducks behind a car, but the Prius continues towards Lena's flat. It is eerie, the lack of noise it makes, the sleek stealth of the electric engine. But it is only an Uber taking someone home.

Keeping Jessica in his sights, he sneaks out of his hiding place and silently trails her. Her head is bowed. She is still trying to get through to him, perhaps to Pat, to tell her she's on the way home. He keeps to the shadows, running when she does, slowing when she does. He is near enough that if he called her name, she would hear. She stops a moment, appears to listen without speaking – an answering machine perhaps – before sliding her phone into her pocket and walking on.

She turns into Oxford Road. Will stays as close as he dares. A few more minutes and she will be safe at home – but then what? A tickle comes to his throat. He stifles a cough. Jessica stops dead, looks about her. He ducks behind a black Audi SUV, crouches low, still keeping her in sight. Her shoulders are high and rigid. She looks afraid. *It's OK*, he wants to say. *It's only me.* And then she is walking once again, head up now, alert. He steals from behind the car, keeping to the shadows. As they near the crescent, the same black Prius drives past again – the only car on the road. There is no sign of the police, no sirens, nothing. Where the hell are they?

They don't believe him. They are not coming. Dave was right: *This is one battle you're going to have to fight on your own.*

That's OK. He can do this. He will go to prison, even die for his family if it means keeping them safe.

The Prius pulls in a little ahead of Jessica. Will's heart is in his throat. Because he knows, with a sudden and terrifying clarity. He knows who is in that car.

Everything happens at once. Ian Robbins gets out of the car and walks towards Jessica. An engine revs hard somewhere behind Will. A black Ford Focus rounds the corner on two wheels. Ian appears to say something. The Ford speeds past Will.

'Jess,' he cries, breaking into a run. 'Jessica! Jess!'

Jessica turns towards him, confusion on her face. Sirens sound in the distance. The Focus screeches to a halt. A shot is fired. Jessica drops. The Focus roars away.

Will cries out again: 'Jess! Jessica!'

The sirens are louder now. Ian is nowhere to be seen. A patrol car speeds onto Oxford Road, wailing, flashing blue. It roars after the Focus: sirens, blue whirls of light.

Will is running, running to his wife. Please, God. Please, God, let her be alive.

Jessica is kneeling on the ground, arms outstretched on the pavement slabs as if in prayer. Beyond her, Ian Robbins is lying flat on his front, his neck twisted at an odd angle, his face still, pale eyes staring blankly. He has not run away. He is down, possibly dead. In the pool of light from the street lamp, a dark stain blackens the back of his beautiful herringbone coat.

'Jess.' Almost choking on her name, Will crouches beside his wife. Reaches out, lays his hand on her shoulder. 'Jess. My love. My darling. Please be OK.'

Jessica stirs, pushes her hands to the pavement and raises herself to a sitting position. She screws up her face at him, her hand rising to her head. Overcome with relief, Will takes her in his arms.

'Jess. Oh my God. Oh my God.' He is weeping. Cannot stop himself.

'Will? What are you...?' Her gaze falls on Ian. 'Who's that? What the hell's happening?'

Will cannot speak. He cannot let go of her. He will not let go of her.

'You're not dead,' is all he can say into her soft, warm hair. 'You're not dead. You're not dead you're not dead you're not dead, oh, thank God. I love you I love you I love you.'

A phone is ringing. He and Jessica startle, look about.

'It's coming from him,' Jessica says, pointing to Ian Robbins.

Will makes himself let go of Jessica and steps carefully over to where Ian is lying. His heart quickens. Ian might still be alive. Tentatively he lowers himself, digs into Ian's coat pocket. His fingers close over what he knows is a burner phone. He draws it out. It is still ringing. Ian does not move. He really might be dead, Will thinks, returning to Jessica. For a moment, he and Jessica stare at the ringing phone before Jessica plucks it out of his hand. With a glance towards Ian, she presses the green button and holds the phone out so that Will too can hear.

'John?' It is Lena's voice. 'John? I heard sirens. John? Please tell me it's not all gone wrong. I can't do this. I can't do this! I've changed my mind. John? John? Are you there?'

Jessica's eyes widen. Silently she closes the call.

'Oh my God,' she whispers, her eyes meeting Will's. 'Lena.'

'Who's John?'

'I think he must be this guy.' She nods towards Ian, towards what might now be only his body, empty of all life.

CHAPTER 39

JESSICA

Another siren wails. A second police car pulls up, flashing blue in the amber-hazed suburban night. It stops in the middle of the road. A last *wow* from the siren and the lights die.

The Prius is still there. There was another car too. Another black car. A gunshot. Jessica feels like she's in some sort of dream. Ian Robbins is the man she was dating. But this Ian Robbins' name is John. John is an accountant. He is Lena's new boyfriend. So who is Supermarket Guy? Who the hell has she let into her life? Lena has had some sort of breakdown. What did John or Ian Robbins or whatever his name is want before he was shot right in front of her? And what is it Lena can't do?

Voices buzz through a police radio.

'Are you OK?' A policewoman is standing above them, high-vis jacket acid yellow. Behind her, another officer has two fingers to Ian Robbins' throat. Jessica stands up, her legs shaky. Will stands up too. Another siren is wailing somewhere – towards the river, she thinks, though she can't be sure.

'We're OK,' Will says.

Will has two black eyes, a swollen nose. One of the lenses in his glasses is cracked. She stares at him.

'That was the man,' he says. But he is not talking to her. He is looking at the cop and pointing at the man on the ground. The man looks like he might be dead. The gunshot. That really was a gunshot.

'He was going to kill my wife,' Will says. 'This is my wife. Jessica Jackson. She's my wife. She's my wife.'

Shock lands like a rock in Jessica's chest. She finds Will's green eyes with her own. He looks wretched, like he's been crying for hours. 'He was going to kill me? Lena's boyfriend? What the hell for? What have you done to your face?' The drug dealer, she thinks. David Silverman. Is that who this is? What the hell has Will got himself tangled up in?

'I'll get blankets,' the policewoman says. 'Don't move.' She strides back towards the car, talking into her radio.

'Will? What's going on? What's happening?'

'That man is called Ian Robbins. That's his real name. I think. He was going to kill you. I thought he was your boyfriend. Cassie said...'

'I was seeing someone called Ian Robbins,' she says, her eyes filling. It hurts to tell him. All of it hurts. 'But it wasn't him.'

'I know.' He holds out his hand. She takes it, feels its familiar touch, its warmth. Somewhere in her, she knows she should be furious. But she is too bewildered. And too glad that Will is here. 'I never slept with the woman in the photos,' he says. 'You have to believe me on that. We only met in hotels because she was scared of her husband. Her name was Margot. And she's dead.' Struggling to compose himself, he points at the man on the pavement. 'This man was her husband. His name is Ian Robbins. She was trying to escape from him. I helped her. He sent the photos. For revenge.'

Jessica closes her eyes, tries to process what he is telling her. So much information, all at once. Margot was never Will's lover. Will never had a lover. And Supermarket Guy was not

Ian Robbins. The real Ian Robbins, this dead man, was going to kill her.

'But who were you living with?'

'I wasn't living with anyone. I was staying in Ian's flat. He let me borrow his car. I thought he was my friend.'

'Oh,' is all she can manage. 'Oh my God.'

Will squeezes her hand. His eyes are soft, full of apology. 'I should've told you straight away, but I panicked. Margot made me swear never to tell anyone. She was so terrified. I was too. I thought if anything leaked out, this guy would come after me, maybe even my family. I would never have put us in this position. I didn't realise how dangerous he really was until it was too late, I just thought he was an abusive husband. You were so upset and I was so in the wrong. And then you... and then I... Sorry. I'm not making sense. I was confused. The photographs... the lovers in the hotel window... they weren't us, I swear. I don't know who they were, but I never slept with her, I never—'

'Hey,' she says, meeting his eye. If only he'd told her. If only she'd given him space to tell her. 'I believe you.'

'She's dead, Jess. I didn't know he was her husband. I had no idea.' He breaks her gaze. She follows it down to their hands. Softly he rubs his thumb over her knuckles. She can see that he's trying to be strong but that it's killing him. 'I should never have... I'd made a promise. I was scared. At the airport, it was very intense. I thought I'd saved her, but... I got caught up. I don't know why I—'

'I do.' She lifts his hand to her lips and kisses it. 'Because you're you. Because that's what you do.'

He closes his eyes, nods, sniffs. A moment of silence falls. In it, she feels all that they are to one another, to their children, her mother – their little family. How did they let themselves get this far apart?

Will has lost the battle to stop himself from crying. She knows she will have to hear all of this again, and again, and that there is more, much more. But a pain is hardening in her chest. Something bad is creeping towards her, something she knows and doesn't know, the sum of everything somewhere just out of reach.

'Will?'

'I didn't save her,' he says in a near whisper. 'He killed her and his kids. His kids, Jess. He killed his kids.'

'His kids.' Jessica's insides fold. Her hand slides from Will's, closes over her mouth. A heavy warm weight lands on her shoulders.

'Blankets.' The policewoman steps over to Will and places a grey blanket over him.

Everything is swimming. Threads and loops and loose ends. Ian Robbins. John. Lena. Lena's rage, her ugly mouth, the meanness in her eyes, the proud veins on her skinny neck. That was not Lena. John. Ian Robbins. The same person. John was going to give Lena a family. John was Ian. Ian killed his kids. *I can't do this.*

Will opens his mouth, but she holds up her hand. 'Let me think,' she says softly. 'Mum texted...'

I'm feeling a bit tired so can you come home now please? Love, Mum x

Mum never complains about being tired. She never signs off on text. She never puts a kiss.

Whoever sent that text was not her mother.

'The kids!' She throws off the blanket. 'Oh my God, the kids!'

'Take it easy,' the police officer says.

But Jessica is already running.

'Help,' she calls but doesn't stop. 'The kids!'

Her legs ache. Her breath burns in her chest. She can hear Will and the cop shouting after her. Will passes her then, running faster than she ever could. Her legs pump fast, faster than ever in her life. Her kids. Her darling Cass and Charlie. Her darling mum.

Lamplight glows from the living room window.

'Will,' she cries, digging in her pocket for her keys, but he is already opening the front door, staggering inside.

'Pat!' she hears him call as the hall swallows him. 'Pat? Are you here?'

Jessica runs inside. A moment later, she is in the living room. Will is bent over her mother, who is sitting on the sofa.

'Pat,' he says. 'Hey. Hey, hey, it's OK. It's OK. I've got you.'

Will is peeling tape from her mother's mouth, carefully, so as not to hurt her. Her mother's eyes are wide with terror. Her hands are bound behind her. She shakes her head violently and fixes Jessica with terrified eyes.

'The children,' she says. 'He took the children.'

CHAPTER 40

WILL

Jessica lets out a howl. Will's vision blurs, blackens.

The cop is talking into her radio.

'... children missing,' is all he catches before he's upstairs, pulling back duvets, staring at empty beds. He lets out a roar, runs across the landing, back down, feet battering on the stairs. In the living room, the cop is kneeling at Pat's feet.

'Can you give me a description of the man, Mrs Jackson?'

'He was tall,' Pat says, her voice trembling. 'Very well turned out. Herringbone coat.'

'It's the guy who was shot,' Will says. 'Ian Robbins.' The Prius. Ian Robbins got out of a Prius, but the Prius had already come past them, on its way to... 'I know where they—'

'Lena's got them.' Jessica is standing at the door of the living room, one hand on the frame. And then she's gone.

Will runs after her, catches her up. He can hear her wheezing, feel the searing heat in his own chest. His muscles burn. He passes her, glances over his shoulder.

'Go,' she calls after him, breathless, shooing him with her hand.

At the corner, the street has been cordoned off with police

tape. Two more patrol vehicles have parked up, silent and flashing. An ambulance. Paramedics are kneeling over the body of Ian Robbins. A cop ducks beneath the tape, striding towards him.

'She's got my kids,' he says. 'My wife's friend's got our kids. I know where they are.'

The cop gives a brief nod. Together they run towards a patrol vehicle. 'Do you know the address?'

'It's the one I called in. I'll direct you.'

He throws himself into the car. As he buckles up, the cop pulls out, sirens on, blue lights. The engine roars. Will feels himself being pulled back into the seat.

'Address,' the cop says.

'It's quicker just to direct you. There's no time for a satnav. Left at the end.'

'OK.'

'She's Jessica's best friend,' he says, making sense of it himself as the words leave him. 'Right at the next junction after the crossing. Before you got here, Ian's phone rang.'

'Ian?'

'The guy who was shot. We answered it. It was Lena, this friend, asking him where he was. Except she was calling him John. Whatever his name is, this is about me and my family. It's too long to explain now. Second left.' They pass Jessica, who is running flat out, but there is no time to stop. 'He must have dropped them with Lena before going after Jessica.'

'I need the address. Now.'

Will gives her Lena's address, which she radios in, calling for backup, repeating the address a further two times. Closing the call, she glances at him, tells him her name is Mary Langford, to call her Mary. Will closes his eyes, opens them to familiar streets now surreal, dream-like – a film set, a mock-up, a reconstruction. Not his streets, not his life.

'Up there on the left,' he says. 'Second semi in, left-hand side.'

The cop slows the car, parks in the road. 'How many doors to the property?'

'Just one. On the left side wall.'

'Stay in the car.'

'But—'

'Stay in the car.'

Mary opens the door and gets out. Will waits but after twenty seconds can wait no longer. He gets out, follows Mary, who is hunched low, jogging around to the side of the house.

'Sorry,' he says, joining her at the door.

'Stay quiet,' she whispers tersely. 'Do what I say.'

'OK. Sorry.'

She rings the doorbell then hammers on the door.

'Lena,' she shouts into the letter box. 'It's the police, love. I need you to let us in. Lena? Can you open the door for me? Let's get this door open so we can talk.'

Jessica is with them now, gulping air, hands on her hips, sweat wet at her hairline. Neither of them speaks. He reaches for her hand, holds it.

'It'll be OK,' he whispers. 'She wouldn't hurt them.'

Without breath enough to speak, Jessica merely shakes her head.

The door rattles. The cop – Mary – braces. Will feels for the gun in his pocket. He closes his fingers over it.

Lena's face appears, gaunt and red and smeared with black eye make-up. She is biting her thumbnail, crying in a kind of soft, dogged way. She looks so different from the last time he saw her: haunted, beaten, as if all the air has been sucked out of her.

'He made me,' she whimpers. 'I didn't want to. He made me.' She lets the cop pat her down, checking for weapons. The

sight is beyond all Will's imaginings. He has known this woman
for decades. She's just... Lena.

'Lena?' Mary says. 'I need you to come up the stairs with
me. Let's take it slow, all right?'

On the road, another patrol car pulls up. Two male officers
get out and run towards the flat. The air flashes blue. Outside
one of the flats opposite, a woman is standing in a pink dressing
gown, her arms folded, watching.

Mary pushes Lena gently by the shoulders, tells Will and
Jessica to wait outside.

The next few moments feel interminable. Will takes Jessica
into his arms and she leans her head on his chest.

'It's OK,' he whispers. 'She wouldn't hurt them.'

But after a moment, Jessica pushes against him and breaks
free.

'Cassie,' she cries out. 'Charlie.' And runs up the stairs.

Will follows. As he reaches the top, he can hear Mary's
voice coming from the living room.

'... will be taken down and may be given in evidence.'

Inside, Lena is in handcuffs, staring resolutely at the floor,
while Mary holds her by the arm and talks into her police radio.
Beyond Mary, Jessica is sinking into the living room floor, where
the kids are sitting cross-legged, watching television. In front of
them is a large plastic bowl filled with crisps.

'Mummy!' they call out, confusion falling into relief on their
faces as they take in the sight of their mum and then Will.
'Daddy!'

And then the four of them are on the floor, holding one
another tightly in a huddle. He fights to keep it light, doesn't
want to frighten them, but Jessica is crying, her breathing
ragged, and he is crying too and so are the kids.

'Where were you, Mummy?' Cassie says, her voice small.
'The man said you'd be here. Why did he make us go with him?
What's happening?'

'It's OK, darling,' Jessica says. 'A bit of a misunderstanding, that's all.' Her eyes meet Will's: *Help.*

'Auntie Lena told her boyfriend to come and fetch you because she thought Mummy couldn't get home in time for Granny, that's all,' Will improvises. 'She forgot you didn't know her boyfriend.'

'I didn't like that man,' Cassie says. 'I told him I couldn't go in the car with a stranger but he said you and Mummy said I had to.' She bursts into fresh tears. 'I'm sorry.'

'Oh, darling.' Jessica cradles Cassie's head, kisses her hair over and over. 'You did nothing wrong, darling. Mummy is very cross with Auntie Lena. Very cross. But everything's OK now.' She looks up; they exchange a watery smile.

Will presses his forehead to Jessica's. 'It's over,' he says. 'I love you. I love you so much.'

'I love you too.'

CHAPTER 41

JESSICA

A family liaison officer has taken the children home. Jessica is sitting on Lena's sofa next to Will, listening while he relays the whole story to Mary and another police officer, DCI something, she can't remember. Except Will is not telling the whole story. She's known him a long time and she can tell.

'I think the man who shot Ian Robbins might be a guy called David Silverman,' he is saying now. Jessica's ears prick. The drug dealer. She knew it. 'I don't actually know him, but I know he and Ian had a bit of history.'

'David Silverman?' she says, helping him out. 'Who is he?'

Will turns to her. 'I met him once in the pub while we were... apart. He was there with Ian. I don't know Ian that well either, to be honest. He was just a guy in the pub, you know? He let me stay in his flat for a few weeks while it was empty, that's all.' He turns back to the cop. 'As I said, Jess and I were... working things out. Ian told me once that Dave had a problem with him. I think I saw him at the wheel of that Focus. I don't know, I only glimpsed him.'

This is most certainly a lie. There was far too much going on. Jessica dares not look at her husband. A thought is closing in. A piece of the puzzle she is not sure she wants. David Silverman is Ian Robbins' accomplice and friend. Will is up to his neck in something bad and is claiming he doesn't know either man well.

'And why do you think Mr Silverman wanted to kill Mr Robbins?'

'I don't know. But I know Ian Robbins was after me because this evening I found out that a woman who came to me for life coaching was his wife. Margot, her name was. I helped her, you see. She was terrified of him, and I helped her leave the country. Ian Robbins took photos of us and sent them to my wife to make her think I was involved with Margot. Which I wasn't. I know from the photographs that he must have followed us to the Departures drop-off at Heathrow. Only I think something bad might have happened to her because I lent her money and she never paid it back, and also because Ian Robbins never told me she was his wife. I had no idea. I thought he was helping me out. But he wasn't.' He exhales, closes his eyes momentarily. 'Earlier this evening, I was at Ian's place and I saw a wedding album. That's when I realised he was married to Margot, and that's when I knew Jessica was in danger. Cassie had said Jess was seeing a guy called Ian and I put two and two together. That's why I called the police.'

'You thought he was going to kill your wife?'

'I was scared he might. Only because when I saw those photos, I understood he was out to get me, how far he'd gone. He blamed me for taking his wife. The thing is, I never heard from her again. Margot. I don't know if she even made it to France.'

The police officer scribbles madly. It is all too much. The facts are slipping and sliding even as Jessica hears them. For some reason, Will isn't telling the police everything.

Will scratches his head, a sign that he's nervous. 'I should've called the police sooner. But the problem was, Ian hadn't done anything. It was just a feeling.' He runs both hands over his head in a way she knows oh so well and knows that he's feeling like a fool.

More facts slip and slide. The dead guy, Ian Robbins, seduced both her husband and her best friend by the sounds of it. But someone else seduced her.

'David Silverman,' she says. 'How does he fit into all of this?'

Will gives her a look that tells her he will explain all of it later, when the police are no longer around. There is, she thinks, more to it, much more. But still, he opens his mouth, seems to hold it open for a second before his features crumple. 'I think you might know *him* as Ian Robbins.'

This is the something. This is the missing piece of the puzzle. Jessica feels the hairs on her head rise, a roll of nausea.

'Right.' It is all she can find to say. David Silverman was Supermarket Guy. The man she got so carried away with was also the man she was furious with Will for getting involved with, a drug dealer, a criminal, possibly a murderer. Dear God.

No more, she thinks. Enough.

'Can I please go home?' she asks the police officer, whose name she thinks is Mary. 'I really need to go home.'

CHAPTER 42

WILL

Will and Jessica are back home, propped up on opposite ends of their dilapidated sofa. They have been talking for hours. It is after five o'clock in the morning. At around two, Pat insisted on going home but did not manage to shake off the family liaison officer, who will be staying with her overnight. Once Will had checked on the kids, asleep and safe in bed, he found Jessica curled up in the dark in front of the gas fire.

He has told Jessica the fullest and most detailed version he can of the real story. His throat is raw. His eyes sting. His body feels like it's been in a car accident. But he is in his own home with his wife, his children are upstairs, and there is something scarily like hope in, well, wherever hope is located.

In her turn, Jessica has told him everything that has happened since he left. Together, piece by piece, they have constructed their destruction: how Ian Robbins must have begun his campaign to destroy Will and his family a long time ago with the slow seduction of Jessica's best friend. How he built it from there, used his charms to seduce first Lena and then Will, turning Lena against Jessica, using Lena to turn

Jessica against Will, his own charms to turn Will against Jessica, all the while moving with deathly prowess towards his goal: namely, to rob Will of everything he holds dear, everything Ian Robbins once had. Ian Robbins had laid the blame for losing his family squarely at the feet of William Draper, house husband and part-time life coach, man of no particular note.

'He must have realised Margot was sneaking out,' Jessica says now.

'Genevieve,' Will says. 'Jen.'

'Jen. He must have followed her.'

'I suspect that was David Silverman. Ian doesn't like to get his hands dirty.'

'Could have been anyone.'

'Maybe. He had a lot of irons in a lot of fires, I think. He gave the impression he enjoyed being a benefactor. He liked to hand out these extravagant kindnesses he persuaded you were almost nothing and given without expectation of any return. But he had a nose for weakness. He pulled you in and tied you up until you couldn't escape. Who knows who took those photos? Might not even have been Dave. Might have been someone else he'd backed into a corner and demanded his pound of flesh from without ever admitting that was what he was doing.' He pushes his hands through his hair, which feels sticky with dried sweat. 'I need a shower,' he adds.

'And he thought you were having an affair with his wife?' Jessica asks. She has already asked and he has already told her, but he understands. It is a lot to get your head around.

'I think my being a life coach would have been enough,' he says. 'He would've blamed me for encouraging her to leave. Empowering her. We only met half a dozen times. If we met in hotels, she could tell him she'd been shopping, which she was allowed to do. He liked her to dress well.' He gives a dry laugh. 'He liked *me* to dress well. He said she went back to Ireland to live with her mother, but she was French, Frankly, I have no idea what was the truth and what wasn't. She told me she was heading to France but she always said she was estranged from her family. She was hoping to start again under a new name. I don't know. Some bits were true, some lies. It was all a big confidence trick and, I think, a game. He didn't love her. I don't think he knows what love is.'

Jessica is silent for a moment before she asks, 'You told the police you didn't think she'd made it to France. Why didn't you tell them he'd killed her?'

Will meets her gaze. She knows all about the deadly quid pro quo he thought he'd found the only way out of. This last bit will terrify her, traumatise her, possibly, but he cannot, *will* not hold anything back from her, not any more. From now on, he will share everything with her, as they always used to.

'In the lock-up,' he says, 'Dave told me...' His breath staggers.

'Will?'

Tears prick. But he makes himself go on. 'Dave told me Ian forced his wife and kids back from the airport, took them home and shot them one by one. In that room I told you about. In the basement.'

Jessica nods, tears welling in her eyes. 'Oh God. In the house you stayed in with our kids?'

Will nods. 'I'm so sorry.'

Jessica shakes her head slowly. 'But that means two of them must've seen... must've known what he was about to do. My God.' She covers her mouth with her hand, tears running down her face.

'I didn't realise it was Margot,' he says. 'Not then, because Dave didn't tell me that bit. I didn't know Ian was her husband until I saw their wedding album. Dave told me where to look. He was toying with me. That's when I realised Ian had been coming for us from the start.'

'But to kill his wife and children,' Jessica says, her voice little more than a whisper. 'Why?'

'So that no one else could have them. That's what Dave said.'

The air fills with Jessica's shocked silence.

'Why didn't you call the police there and then?' she asks after a moment.

Will feels himself fill with shame, shame and regret. 'I was in a total panic. Dave said not to call the police. Said they wouldn't be able to do anything until Ian had gone down. He gave me the gun, said to shoot Ian in the leg and claim self-defence. He said it was the only way. Then he said he was going to play dead, to make Ian think I'd killed him, but obviously, that was another lie. I'm only just realising now that he was making sure I was too scared to call the cops. I'd given him Ian's location, hadn't I? He was making sure the coast was clear so he could assassinate him.'

'Why do that if he thought you were going to bring him down?'

'Rage? And I guess he knew I'd be hopeless. He'd seen how pathetic I was with a gun, probably couldn't trust me to do the job. I couldn't keep the gun in my hand even when I wasn't trying to shoot anyone.'

'You're not hopeless,' Jessica says. 'You're brave. And we've both been taken in. We've both been blind.'

'I thought if I pretended to agree, I could save you. I couldn't think of any other way. It's not my world, Jess. It's not my world at all. I didn't know what to do.' His voice breaks. 'I didn't know what to do.'

'I know.' Jessica shifts. They move towards each other, hold each other tight. 'It's OK,' she says. 'It will be OK.'

'Poor Margot,' he says when they break apart. 'Those poor kids.'

'I guess not having a relationship with her parents is the

only thing that makes sense of them not trying to find out where she'd gone after he—' Jessica stops, unable to say it.

'She'd informed the local authorities she was relocating to France. I helped her with that.' Will sighs, rubs his face with the flat of his hands. He feels gritty all over, inside, every part of him, cannot separate what he did for Margot and her kids from helping them to their deaths. 'What he was going to do with Lena and our kids, I don't know.'

His phone rings. An unknown number. His stomach flips with dread. He shows the phone to Jessica, whose eyes were closing but are now wide, round, a little bloodshot.

'Should I answer it?'

She nods.

'Hello?'

'Mr Draper?' It is a man's voice – familiar. 'DCI Turner. We met earlier... well, yesterday evening now.'

'Hello.'

'Sorry to disturb. I know it's late. Or early, but I thought you'd want to know—'

'Hold on,' Will interrupts. 'I'm here with my wife. Do you mind if I put you on speaker?'

'Sure.'

He adjusts the phone and lays it on the coffee table. The two of them lean over it.

'OK,' he says.

'OK. So yes, I thought you'd want to know that we apprehended David Silverman last night. We pursued him onto the M3 and managed to stop him at Junction 11, the turn-off for Winchester. He tried to fool us into thinking he was going straight on but took the turn at the last moment and fortunately – or unfortunately for him – came off the road. We arrested him at the scene and have charged him with the murder of Ian Robbins.'

'Wow.' Will glances at Jessica. 'And Lena?'

'Your friend has also been charged. She's being held in Kingston overnight. I'll have more information for you tomorrow, but we found a set of passports with false identities for Lena, Mr Robbins and your children, along with one-way plane tickets for Malaysia and packed suitcases. And a handgun hidden in the toilet cistern.'

'Oh my God.' Jessica covers her mouth with her hand.

Will feels sick. Hopes he wiped every last print. When he looks up, Jessica is staring at him, understanding passing between them. He'd been sitting in a freezing cold car for hours, he'd said last night back at Lena's. All right if he popped to the loo?

'I need you both to come in later,' DCI Turner adds. 'We need formal statements.'

'Yes. Yes, we'll be in.'

'And Mrs Jackson. Your mother-in-law, is it?'

'Yes. She'll come in with us.'

After the call, they sit for a moment in silence. Jessica closes her eyes.

'They'll assume the gun is Ian's,' she says.

'I hope so. And Dave owes me his silence. It's not as if grassing me up can help him.'

'Grassing you up?' Jessica makes a face. 'Listen to you.'

He feels himself blush. 'Splitting on me then. However you say it.'

'We almost lost our kids.'

So busy fighting one another, jumping to the worst conclusions. Will doesn't say it; he never will. He knows Jessica will be thinking the same thing.

'You're exhausted,' he says instead. 'We both are. Shall we go up to bed? To sleep, I mean.' Even to himself he sounds like a boy asking for a second scoop of ice cream. 'Not if you don't want to. I can sleep on the sofa.'

'Just to sleep,' she says, taking his hand. 'I don't want to be on my own. Let's leave everything else to the morning.'

'Jessica?'

'Hm?' She turns to him, her eyes finding his.

'I love you so much.'

CHAPTER 43

JESSICA

On the table between them in the visitors' room of HMP Bronzefield, Lena's chapped fingers are a raw pink knot around a flaking white tissue. So far she has not been able to look up, let alone meet Jessica's eyes.

Jessica waits. It's been four months since she has seen her best friend. She has not been able to face this conversation, is not sure she can face it now. But she must.

Eventually, seeing that the second hand has made another slow lap of the clock on the wall, she asks, 'Are you going to say anything?'

Lena nods, many times over. With a huge sniff, she pushes the scrappy tissue to her nose.

'Yes,' she whispers.

'I'm all ears.'

'Just...' More manic nodding, more fumbling with the tissue.

Jessica breathes in through her nose, feels her chest slowly rise, focuses on the out breath, the sinking of her breastbone. At her friend's parting, a fat grey centipede crawls across dull brown hair. This woman, her best friend, was planning to kidnap her children. She was going to take them to a distant country with her lover and pass them off as her own. It is a miracle Jessica is here at all; the memory is so fresh it feels like it happened last week.

Twenty-four hours after Ian Robbins was murdered, Mary Langford came to see Jessica and Will at home. It was dark outside, the kids in bed. The two of them were talking, as they had been, constantly, since the previous night. They had, as Jessica had remarked flippantly to her mother earlier in the day, quite a lot to talk about.

Over a cup of tea – so normal as to be surreal under the circumstances – Mary told them what the police had uncovered since the arrests of David Silverman and Lena.

'It appears that your friend Lena was planning to leave the country with Ian Robbins and your children.'

It wasn't any easier to hear the second time. Jessica reached for Will's hand and gripped it. 'We know about the passports and the plane tickets.'

'You said she had a gun?' Will asked, subtle as a brick. Jessica tried not to dig him in the ribs. He was right; he really was a terrible criminal.

'We believe that was Ian's handgun and that he had hidden it there without her knowledge. She had no idea it was there. She admitted to everything else; there's no reason why she would've lied.'

'Right,' Will said, the relief in that one word obvious perhaps only to Jessica. She pressed her knee against his – their code: *Shut up.*

Mary placed her mug carefully on the coaster. 'We believe Mr Robbins groomed Lena over months.' She glanced at Jessica. 'You said she'd lost weight and wasn't herself.'

Jessica nodded. 'She was disappearing in front of my eyes. The odd strange comment. Bitter remarks that weren't like her. But I was so wrapped up in my own stuff. I mean, I asked but she wouldn't tell me.'

'Gotcha,' Mary says. 'It fits. We found an iPhone matching the number from your WhatsApp thread. The photographs of Mr Draper and Genevieve le Fevre were still—'

'In Lena's flat?' Jessica interrupted. 'Lena sent the photos?'

'It appears that way. Her prints are all over it. She says Mr Robbins gave her the phone with the photographs already on it and told her to send them and then turn the phone off and get rid of it. But apparently she didn't get rid of it.'

'Oh my God. Did Ian take the photographs?'

'According to your friend, David Silverman took all the photographs apart from the final image of Mr Draper and Ms le Fevre at the airport, but we'll get that checked obviously.'

'It all makes such horrible sense,' Will said, his voice small. 'You'd have to pay someone a lot of money to trail around London taking photographs, wouldn't you?'

'Not necessarily,' Mary said. 'But yes, there will have been a lot of money involved in the larger operation. They say money talks, but a lot of the time it pays for silence.'

'Has David Silverman made a statement?'

'No comment,' Mary replied. 'As in, that's what he's saying, not me.' She gave a nervous little laugh. 'But we have police witnesses. Myself and the driver of the first response vehicle saw him drive away. We heard the shot. We haven't found the gun yet, but we will, and when we do, I'm willing to bet it will be a match. We don't live in a gun-crazy society, no matter what you read in the papers. You might not even have to testify.' She looked meaningfully at Will. 'We understand how dangerous these people are, how insidious they can be.'

'And Ian Robbins?' Jessica said. 'What did he do? Was he a criminal?'

'He's been on our radar for a long time, along with Silverman, but he was a very clever man. We have nothing on him, nothing at all. To all intents and purposes he was the epitome of respectability, was known to local fundraisers and charities, et cetera. But we're now actively investigating what happened to his wife and children, who never arrived in France on the date you gave us, Mr Draper.'

'They didn't?' Will shifted, coughed into his hand.

'If we don't find them, we'll issue a warrant to search his home.'

A silence fell. It was as if, Jessica thought, they all knew that Margot and the children were dead, knew that they were all thinking it but that some tacit understanding had been reached. It felt too like they were taking that moment to pay their respects, perhaps to reflect on the enormity of it all, the overwhelming sense of having escaped something beyond terrible, a fate that Margot and her children had not avoided.

A few days later, Mary called to tell them they had found the handgun they believed to have been used by David Silverman to shoot Ian Robbins. The weapon was with ballistics, but they were confident of a match.

A few weeks after that, she called once again to inform them that the remains of three people had been found in the garden of Ian Robbins' Kew home. They were believed to be those of Mrs Robbins and her children, a belief that was confirmed a few days later.

Now, in the bleak visiting room, sitting at a table bolted to the floor, Jessica stares at the mess of her former friend. The grief she has felt, the times she has wanted to call her, to see her, only to remember she is no longer there, no longer the same Lena, has been more painful than she can say. She feels sorry for what happened to her friend but only at a distance. She is not here to offer comfort or sympathy. She just needs to hear Lena tell her to her face what she did, and to see if she understands what she almost did.

'I'm so sorry,' Lena whispers into her hands.

Jessica waits.

'He just had this... power. Over me.'

Jessica's fingers bend and straighten, bend and straighten on the hard prison tabletop.

'He seemed so nice,' Lena goes on. 'He was kind without being flashy, like you always said I should go for. And he was so cut up about his wife dying. It was the first thing he told me, pretty much. We used to go for coffee after a workout, you know? It was ages before he asked if I fancied grabbing something to eat sometime. How was I to know it was all a lie? He made me feel like I was the first woman he'd been able to love since her. Like I'd saved him. I didn't even know he wasn't an accountant, let alone that he had kids... kids he'd...' Another huge sniff, and Lena rubs the end of her red nose with the tissue. Tiny spots of paper fall, like dandruff.

Jessica waits for compassion to come. It does not.

'I stopped eating because of him, but he never said I was fat, not in words. I said I liked things I didn't like – for him. I don't know why. I said... things about you. Bad things. It was like he coaxed things out of me and then he said them back to me in a different way, but I found myself saying them his way and then I didn't know what he'd said and what I'd said. I didn't know what I thought. I don't know how he made me do that. I just said the things and then somehow I... I thought them. I meant them. And then I was angry with you and Will for stuff that happened years ago. I was so angry and now I don't even know why. I can't remember.' She is crying as she speaks, as if she is so used to crying she no longer notices whether she is or not.

'You're in love with Will,' Jessica states.

'I'm not. You have to believe me. When you started going out with him, I was. I was pissed off for a bit, but he didn't love me so I let it go. I promise I did let it go. But then John... he... I don't know. He wound me up.'

'You never had a good word to say about Will. I always had to defend him to you.'

'I know. I criticised him because I didn't want you to guess that I'd ever been in love with him.'

'You hate me,' Jessica says. 'You've hated me all this time.'

'No, honestly. I don't. I really don't, I—'

'Yes. You do. Trust me, it's better just to own it. We're not going to be friends any more, so you may as well admit it – to yourself as much as anyone. You think you love me but you actually hate me. Give yourself a break.'

'I don't hate you. I don't! I loved you. I love you. You and the kids. And Will. And Pat.' Lena bursts into loud sobs. 'You were the best things in my life, but he... he made everything seem... I would never have gone through with it. I promise. I would never...'

Compassion edges in. Jessica has read up on how certain forms of manipulation can be tantamount to brainwashing. Lena always was vulnerable to the charms of men. And wasn't she, Jessica, vulnerable too, not so long ago? She rolls her shoulders, a physical attempt, perhaps, to splinter the ice she can feel reaching down through the length of her. She doesn't want to feel sorry for Lena, but she doesn't want to freeze over either. It is so lonely in the cold, believing the worst of those you love; she knows that all too well.

'You must hate me,' Lena says.

'I hate how you've made me feel. I hate how you...' It is Jessica now who struggles to compose herself. Her jaw clenches. She breathes deeply. 'You've taken away my best friend. I loved her. And now she's gone forever. I miss her. I think about her all the time, and I know I'll miss her for the rest of my life. And that makes me so sad.' Tears brimming, she rises from the table. She has to get out of here before she lets herself cry; before she lets Lena see her cry.

But Lena is already weeping into the palms of her hands. Her ears and neck have flushed dark pink. Above the sharp points of her elbows, her bony shoulders shake.

Finally compassion comes. It floods her. Lena is as much a victim as Will, as herself, in this horrible episode. She has known this almost from that night, when all was chaos and unreal as a dream. They have all been victims of toxic seduction. That their friendship is broken beyond repair does not mean she doesn't still love her friend, any more than betrayal could stop her loving Will. She does love Lena, always will. But she cannot have her anywhere near her or the kids. The pain of losing Lena is the price she will have to pay for the simple life she is determined to lead with Will, Cassie, Charlie and her mother.

'Goodbye, Lena,' she says, signalling to the guard that she needs to leave. 'Take care of yourself. I mean that.' She wants to say she forgives her but cannot. Maybe she will one day, but not today.

She walks away, her own tears streaming now, Lena's quiet wailing fading behind her. It is a sound she knows she will never forget. She doesn't turn around. She continues through the doors, the foyer and out of the prison, immediately spotting the rusted old people carrier in the car park, the familiar silhouette of her husband at the wheel. As she walks, the car reverses. Jessica waits at the kerb while Will drives around to meet her. A moment later, he pulls up and she opens the passenger-side door. Will's smile is still full of doubt. But they both made mistakes, and the greatest, perhaps, was in stopping communicating with one another – long before twenty-seven photographs landed on Jessica's phone.

At least that is what is coming up in their sessions. It was Will who suggested relationship counselling. They have worked hard these last months. They are still working hard. Through honest supervised conversation – and a lot of tears – they are discovering things they have hidden from each other and from themselves over the years, how those things caused them to move away from one another, caused resentments to form and harden. Existing on the different planets of work and home, gradually they lost the sense of each other, reaching conclusions that were not necessarily true, forming judgements based upon those conclusions, using them as steps to climb away from one another. It is time to stop guessing, stop assuming and lay every-thing out on the table. To ask and to tell and to listen, to be curious and open instead of defensive and closed. God, it's hard work! But they owe it to the kids to do it, to be the best, most loving family they can be. They owe it to themselves.

'Where to?' Will asks.

She meets his gaze and smiles. 'Take me home.'

A LETTER FROM S.E. LYNES

Dear Reader,

Firstly, thanks so much for reading this book. If it's your first by me, I hope you liked it enough to want to read some of my others! If it's your thirteenth by me, congratulations, you deserve some sort of long-service award. If you'd like to be the first to hear about my new releases, you can sign up to my newsletter using the link below. Your email address will never be shared, and you can unsubscribe at any time.

www.bookouture.com/se-lynes

I always try and share some of what went into a book. In this case, I really wanted to write what I would call a closing-net narrative, in which the protagonist finds themselves increasingly hemmed in as a result both of their own actions and of external factors working against them. Poor Will was that protagonist. Sorry, Will. But I wanted something more too. I wanted to explore how a loving relationship can be blown apart by a failure to communicate – a universal theme, I think.

Three seasons of *Couples Therapy* on BBC iPlayer formed the vast bulk of research for this study of how a couple can turn away from one another in moments of pain, how individual positions can become entrenched, both parties becoming ever more deeply aware of the complexities of their own hurt whilst becoming increasingly blind to the nuances of the other's, both ending up unable to find their way back.

Taking Jessica and Will's points of view alternately to create a satisfying and, I hope, enjoyably tense narrative proved incredibly tricky. I have to admit, about a third of the way in, I was struggling. Then a friend asked if I'd heard of the ladder of inference, a tool most often used in the workplace to understand how past experience colours one's response to evidence and how that can play out in less than helpful ways if not understood and managed. The ladder of inference demonstrates how we select 'data' from what we observe based on our past experience, how we add cultural and personal meanings to that data, how we then make assumptions based on the meanings we added, how we draw conclusions from those assumptions, create beliefs about the world from those conclusions and ultimately take actions based on those beliefs... all in a reflexive loop. Phew.

This ladder proved to be the key to unlocking the structure of the story. First of all, Jessica is traumatised as a child by the sight of her father cheating on her mother. When she is presented many years later with 'evidence' of Will with another woman, she selects 'data' from that evidence based on her past trauma and adds her own personal meanings... and so it begins – don't worry, I'm not going to do the whole ladder thing again. Meanwhile, Will, son of a scathing father and a domineering mother, selects his own 'data' from his wife's violently intransigent reaction, then from her attempts to maintain some self-respect, and so on, both of them climbing their ladders away from one another until the only way back is a dramatic event that will finally force them to communicate. I think, ultimately, this is what lies at the heart of this novel: the importance of communication.

Meanwhile, because this is a psychological thriller after all, darker forces were at work. Lena made me so sad to write. I think she was actually a good egg, but she was lonely, had been unlucky in love, and Ian managed to turn her inside out and back to front with his devious brainwashing powers. I really enjoyed writing Ian Robbins, the Renaissance geezer who makes a mean chicken jalfrezi and watches his cholesterol, and I hope you enjoyed reading him. I now know how a Glock automatic pistol works, though I'm not sure what to do with this information other than leave it where it belongs, in the fictional realm.

The Split is set in a fictionalised version of Brentford. The riverside development is real – you only have to drive over Kew Bridge to see the glass facades, the penthouses. The Express Tavern, where Will first meets Ian, is real. The Brewery Tap, where Ian hits Will with his devastating plan, is also real. At the time of writing, my son was working hard there to fund his dreams, so I gave him a cameo as the barman. Ian's house and flat are fictional, as are Will, Jessica and Lena's dwellings.

I hope you enjoyed – if that's the right word – watching Jessica and Will exist at cross-purposes while in the background devious agents were conniving to push them both towards disaster. I for one hope they work it out and that they never stop communicating ever again! I also hope that Pat continues to smash the crossword for many years to come.

That's it for now from me. If you have any questions about this or any of my other books, I would love to hear from you, so don't hesitate to get in touch! I always try to reply.

Until next time, take care for now.

Best wishes,

Susie

KEEP IN TOUCH WITH S.E. LYNES

facebook.com/Lynesauthor

x.com/selynesauthor

instagram.com/selynesauthor

ACKNOWLEDGEMENTS

First thanks go, as ever, to my publisher, Ruth Tross, the firm pair of hands to my shopping trolley with a dodgy wheel, who curbs my excesses and always finds a way for me to say what I want to say within the crazy universe of the psychological thriller.

Big thanks too to my agent, Veronique Baxter at David Higham Associates, for cheering me on from the sidelines, for sound advice and a shared obsession with *Couples Therapy*, much of which informed this book.

Thank you to the dynamic SWAT team that is Bookouture, particularly Noelle Holten and Kim Nash, Sarah Hardy and Jess Readett, my eagle-eyed copy-editor and proofreader, Jane Selley and Laura Kincaid, plus all my fellow Bookouture authors, who are the best virtual colleagues a girl could wish for.

Thanks to my mum and first reader, Catherine Ball, whose whizz cryptic crossword skills make an appearance in this book.

Huge thanks to fellow author Helen Fields for generous legal advice on the matter of divorce. Thanks to my friend, Alison Gaskins, for telling me about the ladder of inference, the key that unlocked the structure of this tricky novel.

As always and forever, huge thanks go to all the book groups, bloggers and readers who read and shout about my work from the virtual rooftops. I am blessed to have such a loyal readership, especially when there are so many incredible books out there.

Book groups to mention are, in no particular order: Tracy

Fenton and all the team at Facebook's The Book Club, Teresa Nikolic and the gang at Facebook's Socially Distanced Book Club, Anne Cater and all at Book Connectors, Wendy Clarke and the virtual coffee drinkers at Facebook's The Fiction Café, and the lovely Mark Fearn at Bookmark! Thank you to all the online book clubs and the people who gather there to share their love of reading. Do give me a shout if I've missed you!

Bloggers to thank, again in no particular order, are: Chapter in my Life, Random Things Through my Letterbox, Bookworm86, Once Upon a Time Book Reviews, Coffee Break Book Reviews, Pages and Pups, Little Miss Book Lover 87, B for BookReview, Blue Moon Blogger, Robin Loves Reading, Jan's Book Buzz, Melanie's Reads, TippyTupps, MyCosyBooknook, Spooky's Maze of Books, MeWriter, Curling Up with a Coffee and a Kindle, LianaReads, Cal Turner Reviews, The Staffy-Mum's Book Nook, StaceyWH17, Leona Omahoney, BooksReadByPrairieGirl, Read, Write & Drink Coffee, By The Letter Book Reviews, Ginger Book Geek, Shalini's Books and Reviews, Fictionophile, Book Mark!, Bibliophile Book Club, B for Book Review, Nicki's Book Blog, Fireflies and Free Kicks, Bookinggoodread, My Chestnut Reading Tree, Donna's Book Blog, Emma's Biblio Treasures, Suidi's Book Reviews, Books from Dusk till Dawn, Audio Killed the Bookmark, Compulsive Readers, LoopyLouLaura, Once Upon a Time Book Blog, Literature Chick and Giascribes... I have used their blogging names should you wish to check out their reviews, and again, if I have missed anyone, please let me know.

And thanks to my wonderful, generous, lovely readers, to name but a few: Mary Langford (a policewoman in this story), Jackie West, Claire Mawdesley, Helen Boyce, Lorraine Tippene, Gail Shaw, Gail Atkins, Sharon Bairden, Teresa Nikolic, Karen Ross, Eduarda Abreu, Nicky Dyer, Fi Kelly, Laura Budd, Tara Munday, Philippa McKenna, Karen Royle-Cross, Ellen Devonport, Frances Pearson, Maddy Cordell, Jodi

Rilot, CeeCee, Bridget McCann, Karen Aristocleus, Audrey Cowie, Donna Young, Mary Petit, Donna Moran, Ophelia Sings, Lizzie Patience, Fiona McCormick, Alison Lysons, Dee Groocock, Sam Johnson, my student crew from Richmond Adult Community College, and many more readers not named here. Thank you. I read every single review, good or bad. If you don't see your name here, please give me a shout and I'll include you next time.

Thank you to the tremendously supportive and precious writing community. You know who you are and are now too many to count. Special thanks to my eighties throwback #lucky-bitches writing retreat buddies Emma Robinson, Kim Nash and Sue Watson; and my spooky haunts writing retreat buddies Callie Langridge, Claire McGlasson, Bev Thomas, Kate Riordan, Emilie Olsson, Lisa Timoney and Clarissa Angus. To my little bun and tea side hustle, Emma Curtis and Nicola Rayner. You ridiculously talented and generous women are responsible for many of my happiest moments, not to mention the silliest and rudest jokes.

Thanks to my dad, Stephen Ball. Dad, you can read this new one with your new eyes!

Finally, as absolutely always, thank you to my other half, Paul Lynes. Thank you for building me a new desk while I was away on a writing retreat – that was proper top.

PUBLISHING TEAM

Turning a manuscript into a book requires the efforts of many people. The publishing team at Bookouture would like to acknowledge everyone who contributed to this publication.

Audio
Alba Proko
Sinead O'Connor
Melissa Tran

Commercial
Lauren Morrissette
Jil Thielen
Imogen Allport

Contracts
Peta Nightingale

Cover design
Aaron Munday

Data and analysis
Mark Alder
Mohamed Bussuri

Printed in Great Britain
by Amazon

43372935R00199